PRIVATE PASSION

Alysa shifted in the large tub to allow room for Gavin to join her. She sighed contentedly as he began to bathe her slowly and sensuously. The scent of countless wildflowers filled her nostrils as she floated dreamily in the milky water and her trembling body responded eagerly to his tantalizing caresses.

Gavin bent forward and touched his lips to hers, and they shared a blazing moment of feverish passion. He lifted her from the tub and lay her on a bed of fragrant leaves. Sunlight filtered through the trees overhead and danced off the beads of water on their naked bodies as he joined her and his hands and lips began to work lovingly, urgently . . .

JANELLE TAYLOR

WILD IS MY LOVE

PINNACLE BOOKS
WINDSOR PUBLISHING CORP.

For my good friends,
MADELENE *and* RALPH LEONE,
in appreciation for all you've done for me.

For my agent and close friend,
ADELE LEONE MONACO,
for your untiring support and assistance.

For my daughter,
ANGELA TAYLOR,
who was such a big part of this book.

For my good friend with many talents,
KATE BARR,
thanks for your help with the historical map.

Britain 430 A.D.

One

Princess Alysa Malvern walked half the distance to where her horse, a muscular dun with black tail and mane, was tethered in a deep gully, far enough from the dirt road to go unseen. Well-trained and loyal, Calliope would remain there until his mistress's return, alert yet quiet while he leisurely devoured the bunches of grass growing in his familiar hiding place.

The troubled girl followed a shallow stream which snaked its way into the ravine where Calliope awaited her, until the ground began to slope rapidly. The narrow stream abruptly widened and deepened, then gurgled over an entangled pile of rocks, vines, and twigs, tumbling into an oblong pool where minnows swam and lush greenery lined its banks.

Alysa sat near the lip of the pool and trailed her fingers in the clear, cool liquid. She laughed softly as the startled minnows darted into hiding beneath the greenery which teased the water's edge. Her gaze swept over the ferns, mosses, and wildflowers which thrived in abundance on the other bank. As a breeze fluttered leaves overhead, and shafts of sunlight sparkled almost painfully off the water's surface, Alysa closed her eyes and inhaled, the deep woodsy odors teasing her nostrils. The tranquil setting always seemed to calm her, and she needed to relax before returning home to face the coldness and hostilities there, so she lingered for a long time by the verdant pool, feeling the gentle breeze and listening to the sounds of insects, wildlife, and gurgling water.

Alysa did not care if it was a crime to leave the dirt road while traveling through the royal forest; she was the daughter of Prince Alric, this land's ruler, and no one would dare halt her, unless she was mistaken for someone else because of her peasant dress. She knew she could not do without this sylvan setting, considering it her private domain. It offered escape from the demands and torments of her daily life, especially since her father's marriage to Isobail four years ago, and his inexplicable changes in mind and body over the past year. Something was terribly wrong in the castle, in Damnonia, and with her father, but she could not unravel the mystery.

Alysa's dark blue eyes narrowed in dismay; she did not want to spoil her stolen reprieve with thoughts of her stepmother, but she could not prevent it. She was concerned over the brigands who were raiding her land, and worried about her father's health and strange behavior: he did not seem to care what was happening around him. Isobail was taking over more and more of his role as ruler. If her father did not vanquish his dazed state and soon take control again, Alysa angrily concluded, Isobail would rule everything and everyone!

At home she felt as if she were being watched constantly. Her stepsister Kyra, usually so cold, was acting friendly. But the servants—including her favorites, Piaras and Leitis—were wary and tense. . . .

Alysa cast a cautious glance in all directions, but saw only nature's lovely surroundings. She was not afraid of the woods, day or night, but it was always best to be wary. Since age eight she had sneaked into the forest with sons of knights or servants to play games and ex-

8

plore. But she had never ventured this deeply into the royal forest until the day, seven years ago, when she had found Giselde's hut.

The abode of her dear friend was constructed of timber and cruck, with a tightly thatched roof, and was larger and nicer than most peasant dwellings. The old woman's presence in the woods was a secret, and Alysa knew Giselde had not been granted permission to cut wood or to live in the forest. She often wondered who helped Giselde commit those crimes, offenses which carried a stiff penalty, sometimes punishable by death.

The hut was snuggled in a grove of trees, and nearly hidden by overgrown vines and bushes. Alysa fondly remembered how the walls seemed to glitter in the dappled sunlight, before the entangling greenery had overrun it, and recalled wondering if the hut was the magical dwelling of a witch.

Near the dwelling Giselde cultivated a garden which thrived with colorful plants also used in the practice of the Black Arts: another crime against the old woman. She raised mandrake, vervain, monkshood, nightshade, hensbane, roses, and more. Hemlock, yew, thorn apple, and oak grew nearby like sentinels for this forbidden plot of ground. Exquisite water lilies filled a stagnant pond not far away, with marsh primrose and other potent plants growing within sight of it.

Alysa had been told that gardens that contained such plants and trees belonged to witches; most people believed as much. Yet she knew that Giselde was not crazy or evil. The plants were used in the healing and magical arts which Giselde possessed and shared freely with those ill or injured or bewitched, for her friend had told her so, and she would never lie to her. Hold silent about certain things, yes; but never lie.

Alysa also knew that Giselde still believed in the old ways of the Celtic Druids, as well as those of the new religion, Christianity. There were so many mysteries

9

and powers in life, forces and secrets that Giselde understood and used to help others.

Giselde had come with Alysa's mother from the kingdom of Albany to serve as the princess's waiting woman. Dearly loved and trusted by Princess Catriona, Alysa's mother, Giselde had been privy to all that happened in the castle long ago, as she was now informed by friends who were still servants in or around the castle. Thus, it never surprised Alysa that Giselde knew so much about her parents and past events. In fact, she could not imagine her life without "Granmannie's" love and friendship. She adored the gray haired woman who had been her guardian and teacher at the castle, and had vanished mysteriously following the death of her mother.

Grieving for his lost love, for three years Alysa's father had traveled the length and breadth of his domain to flee the remembrance of Catriona's "presence" in the castle. Prince Alric had left his daughter in the care of servants until he could endure living there without his "heart," and could bear looking into the small face that resembled his dead wife's.

Those bleak months had been terrible for Alysa, until she had found Giselde secretly living in the prohibited forest only a few miles from the castle. Since that day she had sneaked countless visits with her cherished friend.

Alysa did not know why Giselde lived hidden in the forest, for the old woman refused to reveal such things to her. She had made Alysa promise never to tell anyone—even her father—about their friendship. Loving Giselde and fearing to lose her best friend once more, Alysa had never broken that vow of silence. She was very careful to hide her trail to Giselde's hut, and to make certain that no one followed her or suspected her actions.

When Alysa arrived at the hut earlier that morning,

she was surprised to find the front door closed, but unlocked. Once in the one-room dwelling, she removed the hooded cape of coarse green linen which cleverly helped her to blend into the dense forest, as did her peasant garments of matching yarn. She tossed the cape aside and shook her thick hair loose, then glanced about. The floor was firmly packed earth, and the hut was walled snugly with clay clump which had hardened over the years until it was as sturdy as stone. A small fire burned on an open hearth in the center of the left wall, its lacy smoke escaping through a chimney of mingled rocks and mud. The hut was clean, and a feeling of warmth and safety pervaded it.

Alysa glanced at the hearth, where a kettle was suspended over a low fire and from which delightful smells were rising. Her keen gaze drifted past a wooden table and two stools in the back corner before slipping over a large and colorful tapestry of a Druid ritual which concealed a small back door. Giselde had told her it was there for a quick escape in case of fire or other peril. She noticed the home-woven blankets, folded neatly and lain across the foot of a bed that had been constructed like a raised, oblong, wooden box, and filled with a straw mattress. A locked chest at the end of the bed held Giselde's clothes and personal possessions, which no one was allowed to view, and frequently captured Alysa's curiosity.

Yet it was the front right corner of the hut that most fascinated Alysa, for she had watched Giselde at work there many times. Above, below, and to both sides of a rough work bench were shelves holding numerous clay jars, straw baskets, cloth bags, and wooden boxes of varying sizes, in which all kinds of dried plants and curious items were stored. There were many copper and wooden bowls, knives, spoons, sticks, leather pouches, as well as pots for mixing and containing Giselde's potions, mortar and pestles, candles and crucible holders.

Alysa sat down on the stool before the wooden bench to await Giselde's return. A smile lit her eyes when the door creaked open and the older woman slowly entered carrying a basket of plants for her work. She bounded forward to embrace and assist Giselde. "Granmannie, I feared you would not return before I had to leave. Must you work so hard?" she entreated worriedly.

The older woman looked very tired and pale today, and moved as if every part of her body protested each exertion. Alysa watched the self-imposed change sweep over Giselde as she tried to mask her discomfort. The older woman's dark blue eyes took on a sparkle as she placed one arm around Alysa's waist and playfully scolded, "You should not have come to see me again so soon, little one. Others will pour questions on your head if they find you missing so often. Is there new trouble at your father's castle?"

Alysa shrugged, not wanting to burden Giselde with her problems until her friend rested. Instead she asked, "Why do you not return to the castle, where it is warm and safe? You can become my teacher and waiting woman again. I would not work you hard, and I could take care of you. I worry about you living here alone, Granmannie. Why must you do so?"

Giselde placed her basket on the work bench and turned to look at the young woman. Her aging eyes admired Alysa's beauty, and her heart surged with pride. Alysa's brown hair was wavy and thick, tumbling over her shoulders almost to her waist. Her eyes were large and expressive, the color of deep, tranquil blue water and capable of displaying a wide range of emotions. The perfection and softly defined angles of Alysa's features exposed her royal lineage, even though she did not wear the golden circlet around her head during these visits. How Giselde missed being with this girl each day, as she had been years ago. But things had changed. . . .

Giselde's voice was low as she replied, "It cannot be, my child, and I cannot tell you why. One day it will be different. Fret not; no harm can reach me here; the forest gods hide me and protect me. What troubles you, little one? I see pain in your eyes, and you fear to speak what is in your heart."

Alysa retucked straying locks of the old woman's gray hair into a carelessly rolled knot near her nape. Giselde was several inches shorter than Alysa's five-foot, five-inch frame, and Alysa could easily wrap her arm around her aged and work-bowed shoulders, which she now did. "First, sit and let me prepare you something hot to eat and drink."

"Later," Giselde murmured, her mind on other matters. "You are so like your mother, little one; you have her courage and curiosity, her eagerness for life and adventure. But, alas, you are as innocent and trusting as she was. Things have changed much since my Catriona died and that wicked Isobail took her place."

Both sat on the bed as they began to talk, all else forgotten for a time. Alysa said quietly "I am glad I was old enough to remember Mother before she was taken from me; yet, I was so young that I have forgotten much about her and those days. Tell me about them again," she coaxed, clasping Giselde's wrinkled hand between her smooth ones, ignoring the dirt stains upon its weathered surface.

Giselde laughed again—a clear and rich sound this time—and teased, "I have told you those stories many times, little one."

Alysa knew that Giselde enjoyed retelling those tales as much as she enjoyed rehearing them. "But you must repeat them, lest I forget the past. You know Father and Isobail removed all signs of Mother from the castle and our lands. Your stories and my scattered memories are all I have left."

Giselde's eyes clouded briefly. "Yea, it is bad to forget

the past, and it is bad to destroy the memory of one so precious as Catriona. I will speak of days long past and of people far away."

Her eyes glowed and her voice grew soft, almost caressing, as she began, "Connal, your great-grandfather, was a powerful chieftain whose village was attacked by fierce Vikings. They did not kill him, because he was a great warrior. Instead, they took him far away to their lands, where he cunningly earned their trust. There, he fell in love with a Viking woman, Astrid, and married her."

Giselde continued as if she could see the story she was relating, "The lovers bravely escaped back to this island, and Astrid gave birth to a son and two daughters. When the Vikings finally found them, they attacked, and Connal's son and oldest daughter were slain. One powerful Viking warrior named Rurik could not endure the sights and sounds of such brutal slayings and wanton destruction, so he left his people's camp to join Connal. With his knowledge and help, your great-grandparents won that terrible battle. Rurik fell in love with Connal's surviving daughter and married her. . . ."

Giselde's smile was warm with the memory, then her expression saddened. "Many of our tribe hated and mistrusted Rurik, and many despised your grandmother for choosing a Viking, but she loved Rurik with all her heart. The day he was slain was a dark and bitter one, as was the day when his daughter, Catriona—your mother—was lost to us. I wish such hatred and cruelty did not exist."

When Giselde paused and stared into nothingness, Alysa read enormous anguish in the old woman's expression. To distract her, Alysa quickly injected, "My grandmother's name was Giselde, like yours."

The old woman replied as if from far away, "Yea, like mine. Giselde and her barbarian lover Rurik had a daughter and they named her Catriona, which means

14

princess of the fair heart. Catriona grew into a beautiful young woman, and warriors pursued her. But her destiny was not with our people of Albany; it was with your father.

"Prince Alric met Catriona and desired her greatly. He was young and handsome and full of life, and he stole your mother's heart though he came from another tribe. He lingered with us for months just to spend time with her. The day came when Alric left Albany to seek his father's permission to wed Catriona. King Bardwyn, of Cambria and Damnonia, refused; he ordered his son to forget her, the daughter of a barbarian.

"But Alric was stubborn, and enchanted. Against the wishes of his people and the command of his father, Alric took Catriona as his wife under our laws. Astrid and Giselde begged Catriona not to leave our tribe and land, but she was in love and could not hear them. Alric promised Catriona and our tribe that his father and people would love her and accept her after they saw her. It was not to be."

Giselde inhaled deeply. Tears misted her eyes. "I wish Alric had obeyed his father, or Rurik had refused his plea. Then Catriona would still be alive. She was a terrible loss to our people and her family. No one has forgotten her. King Bardwyn was angry, and believed he had been betrayed by his son, but because Catriona was carrying Alric's son King Bardwyn was forced to allow them to marry under his law.

"Cruel tales flowed freely about Catriona's Viking ancestors, and it did not matter that she was an innocent. To give their people time to forget Alric's impulsiveness, King Bardwyn sent Prince Alric here to rule Damnonia for him. The King hoped that while exiled in Damnonia, the Cambrians would only hear of Alric's good and prosperous deeds, and not view the foreign princess at his side. But the journey and hostilities were so rough on Catriona that she lost their son. She was so unhappy that she returned home to Albany for a long visit.

"You cannot guess the torments that your mother, and your grandparents, and your great-grandparents, endured because of whom they chose to love. I warn you now, little one, take care with your choosing."

Giselde's cheeks were flushed with intense emotion, but she continued. "The Norsemen attacked our land once more. It was a bloody day and nearly all were slain. Both Catriona and I and others were rescued by Prince Briac, now the King of Cumbria, whose land borders Albany. Briac was gentle with Catriona, and his kingdom was peaceful. We remained so long that Alric feared Catriona would never return to his side. It would have been best if she had not, but that day is past.

"When Catriona returned to Damnonia, she brought me with her. Many people were angry at her for bringing another barbarian into their land, for news of the Viking raids along the coast had traveled faster than we had; many feared and mistrusted us, and said dark winds followed us. They said her presence in Damnonia would bring the Vikings down on it too. But Catriona begged Alric to let me remain at her side, and so I did. For many years they doubted she could bear more children; then you were born, and everyone rejoiced. You and Catriona won the people's hearts, and the dark past vanished. How happy we were until your mother died."

Giselde warned gravely, "You must share these secrets with no one, Alysa, no one. Never mention such days to your father or others, or ask questions about that time. The past is often dark and painful, and dangerous. They think I am dead, or if alive, far away in Albany. Believe me, Alric and Isobail will become angry if they learn I am so close, and they will prevent us from seeing each other again. I am a reminder of things they wish buried forever; they would view me as a threat. Never betray me to them, little one, with good intentions or by carelessness. Or they will have me . . . returned to Albany."

"I have given you my word, Granmannie, so you know I will keep all things between us a secret," Alysa vowed. "But you must not fear and mistrust my father so deeply. He would never harm you. He is kind, and he is very ill these days. For the past year he has grown weaker each month. Today I came to beg you to come to the castle to heal him. Will you, Granmannie?"

Giselde patted her hand as she shook her gray head. "I cannot, Alysa. His illness is of his own making, and my skills are powerless to help him. I have known Alric a long time, and many bad things have passed between us. He would rather confront the Evil Beast himself than face me. There can be no peace between us again, so do not dream foolish dreams or make perilous gestures of truce. My healing arts are of no use to Prince Alric."

"Why do you refuse to tell me what happened between you long ago? Surely it is only a misunderstanding that can be resolved. Let me help," Alysa urged.

"There is nothing you or anyone can do; some words and deeds cannot be changed. If such was possible, you and Isobail would be as mother and daughter. Keep your word and let things remain as they are. The day will come when peace will rule our hearts and lands again."

Giselde had told her more this morning than ever before, so Alysa asked, "Did my father do something terrible to you or my mother? Do you blame him for her death?"

Giselde realized such knowledge could put Alysa in danger so she responded, "Despite the shadows over them, Alric and Catriona were very much in love and were happy for many years, until Evil crept into this land. Evil hungered to conquer Damnonia. Evil claimed your mother's life, and Evil is still at work in this land."

17

Giselde shuddered as if very cold, and her face waxed paler. "Stir the fire and add more wood, Alysa; the air grows chilly for old bones."

Alysa did as she was told and probed deeper, "Is that why you live here? To find a way to battle this Evil? Is that what you fear, Granmannie? Come to the castle; my father will protect you."

Giselde answered, "Your father cannot even protect himself, little one."

"Who is behind this, Granmannie? What do they want? And why can my father and his knights not defeat them? You possess great skills; can you not help us?"

Giselde gazed into the entreating expression of Princess Alysa and saw Catriona reflected there. Tears dampened her eyes, and breathing became difficult. She pressed twisted fingers to her chest where slicing pains knifed viciously, and she willed the pain to halt. She could not tell this cherished girl of her suspicions, her knowledge, her plans. Alysa was too young, naive, and brave; and there was no guessing what the young woman would do with such information.

Giselde's response was guarded, "I cared for Catriona from her birth to her death, and I did the same for you until that black day when I was compelled to desert you. You are the most important thing in my life, little one. I could not protect your mother from Evil, but I will find a way to protect you. That is why no one at the castle must know I am nearby."

"Many know you are here, Granmannie. You go to the villages to heal the sick. What if Isobail learns of you? She will force Father to punish you, for he is too weak to battle her. You must not remain here or grow such plants; it is forbidden by law."

"Isobail cannot harm me, little one. I am very careful, and the villagers need me. Yea, they tease about me, but they do not betray me, and few could ever guess who I truly am. My appearance has changed greatly since I lived in the castle nine years ago. My hair is no longer thick and shiny, and its brown has turned to gray. The sea blue of my eyes has faded and they are drab like old cloth. See how much fat lives on my once slender body. And my skin," she remarked, laughing sadly, pointing out each area as she disclosed her changes, "my skin has more wrinkles than a freshly crushed leaf, and its color is as yellow as the primrose, not the pretty pink and white of the May apple, as yours is and mine was. Even my clothes are rags, not silks or fine linens, and no jewels adorn my body. I doubt even your father and Isobail would recognize me today.

"If I could heal your father my little Alysa, I would go with you and do so. It is impossible. His fate is in the hands of the gods whom he has offended," Giselde said, though her gods remained nameless because her religion forbid her to call them by name in fear of omitting or insulting one, and incurring their wrath. She had not lied to Alysa; even if she knew what was wrong with Alric, she could not help him. Alric had chosen his allies, so he must depend on their dark powers and aid now. . . .

But Alysa was saying, ". . . if only you were at the castle with me."

"Your handmaiden Thisbe takes good care of you, little one. Besides, I am too old for heavy chores and steep castle steps. I have returned to the way my people lived before I came here with my Catriona. Do you wish me to live in the castle and be as miserable as you are?"

Alysa frowned and shook her head. "I wish I could live here with you. Malvern Castle has not been home since Mother died. Even my cherished servants Piaras and Leitis do not act like themselves anymore. And Isobail handles everything for Father; it is as though she were our queen rather than Father's second wife. If only Father had not brought Isobail into our castle as Mother's waiting woman. Mother did not need her;

19

Mother had you to take care of her. I am sure she did not like Isobail or want her around. Neither did I, Giselde. Perhaps I was overly jealous, but sometimes Father played with her son Moran more than he did with me. I was glad when Moran left Malvern Castle to live at Sir Kelton's far away."

Alysa sighed. "I must pay for such wicked feelings, for my mind has begun to play tricks on me. I feel cold eyes on me each day, eyes I cannot see. I sense peril where I can find none. I feel lost, and alone, and afraid, Granmannie. I do not know what I shall do when Moran returns home. His training period is nearly over; soon he will become a knight. Is it always so hard to have stepbrothers and stepsisters?"

A cloudy expression filled Giselde's eyes, but she lowered her head to conceal the curious look from Alysa's gaze. "If Isobail can gather enough money and land for her son before his squire's days end, perhaps he will not return to Alric's castle."

"I am certain she will," Alysa said, "for he cannot become a knight without them, and Moran would never remain a squire past twenty-one." Alysa was glad that Isobail's son, who frequently had battled her with words and fists, had left the castle at age seven to become a page at Sir Kelton's: a knight and vassal for Lord Orin, who was a feudal lord for her father. A page's training began at seven or eight, squire training at fourteen, then knighthood at twenty-one, if a man had land and money to support himself and his duty.

Giselde observed Alysa as she was lost in thought for a time. Giselde suspected what Moran truly desired: to become Prince Alric's heir, making him the next ruler of this territory and possibly the next king after Alric's father, King Bardwyn of Cambria, the kingdom that owned the land of Damnonia. Too, from reports by Piaras—the castle's trainer of squires and knights—Moran had made it apparent during his occasional visits that he desired Alysa. That event could never take place, never. . . .

"You must return home, little one. I have herbs to prepare before they wither and become useless. I must warn you to beware of Isobail and her evil, for it grows darker each day. Days of great peril are ahead. A fierce conqueror is hungry for our lands and will do all manner of evil to obtain them. A wicked alliance has been formed by those you know, and it will cause great havoc in your life and lands. There have been other warnings in my dreams, little one, warnings that frighten me. Speak to no strangers, Alysa, for you are the child of two royal bloodlines from Cambria and Albany. To conquer, you will bring an end to the peace. Beware of a man with sunny hair and leafy eyes who wishes to make you and this principality his. He, like all his family, is greedy. His words will drip with tainted honey. His sweet smiles will conceal bitter feelings and rank secrets. He will pretend to be your only hope, and he will make you many false promises. He will ask for your love and trust; do not grant them. His evil bloodline must never mingle with yours, or you will be doomed forever." When Giselde gave Alysa this warning about Moran, she had not even seen the green-eyed man in many years and did not know that his once blond hair had darkened steadily to light brown. . . .

"I do not understand, Granmannie. Who is this wicked man? When will I meet him? Where? How will I know he is the one you speak of?" Alysa's lips over-flowed with frantic questions. She knew Giselde had knowledge that she did not fully understand. "You must not allow such evil to threaten us, Granmannie."

Giselde sighed. "My powers are meager next to those who desire these lands and revenge."

"Revenge?"

"Long ago many wicked things happened in this land and in others, little one. Each day more wickedness is

21

born. For such deeds, many yearn for just vengeance; others crave blind revenge. If Evil is not conquered and forced back into its dark cave, more will suffer and more will die. Go; there is nothing you can do but watch and wait. If you remain here, others will come to seek you. If I am slain, there will be one less to battle Evil."

"Isobail is part of this Evil, is she not?" Alysa asked. "I will keep my eyes and ears on her and those around her. I will tell you all—"

"Nay!" Giselde shouted. "Her advisor Earnon is a cunning wizard. No doubt it is his potent eyes that you sense upon you each day. You must do nothing to arouse their suspicions. Isobail has little use for the heir of Alric and of Bardwyn, so she ignores you for now. Do not make yourself a threat to her plans. Hear me well, my child: my powers are meager when compared to Earnon's; do not challenge him to destroy both of us. He is totally loyal to your stepmother and will do anything she asks of him—anything, Alysa," she said.

"Are Isobail and Earnon the ones to fear? Are they the reason you live in hiding? Did she frighten you away from the castle long ago, or do you also fear my father?"

"I can say no more, my child. Please, Alysa, obey me in this," the old woman pleaded. "I know of things you do not, and cannot be told. Help will arrive soon and free all from this Evil."

"What help, Granmannie? What evil threatens us?" Alysa rubbed the old woman's suddenly cold hands with her warm ones. She felt Giselde tremble, causing her apprehensions to mount. "Is my father in danger too? He is so weak these days. He hardly knows me. How can we defeat this danger?"

Pulling her hands free and rising, Giselde said, "You are in no danger my child. The spirits of Good protect you."

"Then why can I not help you and the others?" she asked.

Giselde walked to the doorway and halted there, gazing out as she replied, "Because Evil can cause danger to others if you interfere."

Alysa stared at the old woman's back and puzzled over her words. "If Evil has cast a spell over my father, I must free him. Tell me how, Granmannie. If you truly love me, help me; help him."

When the old woman spoke, her voice was weary. "Upon the heads of all I love," she said, "I am doing all I can to defeat Evil. If you interfere, all could be lost."

"Then I am helpless?"

"For a time all are helpless, little one, even me."

Long, silent minutes passed. Alysa realized that Giselde would tell her nothing more today. "Why not send word to my grandfather? King Bardwyn and Cambria are powerful, surely he will send warriors to help us."

Giselde was glad Alysa could not see her face as she responded, "If your father desired help from King Bardwyn, he would send word. He does not wish him to know of the trouble here. If Alric cannot defend Damnonia and make her prosper, then he can never become king after his father. He was sent here to prove himself, and he is failing. Do not be sad, Alysa. That is good, for his wife Isobail would rule beside him as Queen of Cambria and Damnonia; she would take King Alric's place as she has taken Prince Alric's place."

Alysa had not considered one vital point, for she had been too worried about her ailing father. What of Damnonia and what was best for it? she wondered. Where did her loyalty lie? In order to protect her father's honor could she stand aside while her land was destroyed? There was so much at stake, and she had to learn all she could before acting unwisely.

"I will obey you, Granmannie," she promised. *For now*, she added to herself. The blood of female fighters,

23

Viking and Celtic warriors, ran swiftly in her veins. Surely there was something she could do to help her father and their lands. . . .

Giselde turned and hugged her tightly. "Do not worry, little one. You will find a friend and ally where you least expect one." She watched Alysa cover her bountiful hair with the hunter's green cape and hood, then fade into the trees.

Now sitting quietly in the forest at the water's edge, Giselde's words kept running through her head, and she did not know what to think about them. Squinting, she gazed at the mesmeric glitters on the surface of the pool until she became drowsy, which came easily since she had slept little the last few nights. Slowly her green-clad body sank to the grassy earth, and she began to doze and dream.

Alysa witnessed a terrible battle being waged in a colorful meadow where grass and flowers were stained forever with bright red blood. She saw her people, dressed in glowing white garments, clash desperately with barbaric foes dressed as the darkest night. She was amazed to see female warriors, whose faces were shadowed, fighting skillfully beside their mates. She quickly joined them, for dear old Sir Piaras had allowed her to practice with the squires, until Isobail had put a stop to it.

Alysa moved agilely as she used her lightweight sword to defeat several foes, before grabbing her lance to pierce the bodies of two more. The reality of their deaths never entered her mind, for she was exhilarated by the fact that she was defending her land. Then she saw her mother wounded. Abruptly, Alysa tossed aside her bow and arrows, but before she could reach Catriona, her mother sank into the earth and vanished. Stunned, Alysa heard a female voice shrieking warnings of doom, and she turned to find Giselde standing on

24

a cliff which overlooked the meadow, a strong wind whipping her flowing white garments about her body. Before she could react, Giselde was slain by a giant black bird. Alysa knew she should stay and fight, but she wanted to run from the tragic scene.

As with all dreams, Alysa was tossed here and there at the whims of its images. Suddenly she was swept into a stranger's arms and they galloped away on his golden charger, her dazed mind dismissing the previous scene as if it had never happened. Her silky gown and long hair whipped about wildly in the wind. She could not make out the man's face, but she perceived blurs of gold and green, and a curious patch of blue. She felt strong arms banding her body, and thrilled to his sensuous touch and magical allure. Heady masculine smells—musky sweat, well-worn leather—filled her nostrils and caused tingles to race through her.

Alysa struggled to see him clearly, but his image evaded her. She perceived that he was a tall, muscular man, a fierce warrior with matchless skills, fearing nothing and no one; a man seeking many things in her land, a man with dangerous secrets, a conqueror of lands and enemies and women.

Alysa tried to pull free of the persistent and powerful stranger but something irresistible drew her to him, even though she sensed peril surrounding him, even though she knew she could not trust him. A terrifying feeling of entrapment invaded her entire body, and she struggled harder for freedom. Refusing to release her, he galloped through the castle gates, claiming both her land and her as his victory prize. He dismounted from the horse, smiled, and she felt as if the blazing sun was beating down on her. He called her name and beckoned her, exuding enormous magnetism, and she found herself wanting to yield to him. Her body warmed, her pulse raced, and she could not disobey.

She heard him murmur in her ear, "Come, m'love,

and soar the heavens with me, for no harm can reach you under my wing. Come, m'love, and we will drink passion's nectar from the same cup, until our thirst i sated. Come, m'love, for you are bound to me forever."

Alysa could not stop herself from walking toward him and reaching out to him. Suddenly they were outside the castle gates once more. She knew her father was in peril, but dark forces would not allow her to reach him. She pleaded with the tawny warrior for help, but he shook his head and told her, "He is doomed, and you are my captive."

Then Moran, her stepbrother, appeared and challenged the unknown warrior to do battle for her, the castle, and the Crown. The men fought brutally, until Isobail magically appeared and bound the stranger to a quintain, the post squires and knights used for tilting. As Moran galloped at full speed toward the helpless stranger about to pierce his golden body with a lance Alysa cried out and struggled to free him, but discovered she could not move, even though someone was shaking her.

Giselde, now very much alive, suddenly appeared and freed the warrior. Alysa flung herself into his arms and covered his face with kisses, until his lips fused with hers and caused her senses to spin wildly. She clung to his body, admiring its contradictory feel of hard stonelike muscles beneath soft flesh. She savored the taste of him and the feel of his mouth on hers. She knew so little about love and sex, for she had only experienced a few inquisitive kisses stolen by squires at her father's castle, and they were nothing like these These sensations were unique, frighteningly different yet they were as compelling as he was. She enjoyed his embrace, and feared it would end too soon, for never was too soon, and she was enchanted by him.

Alysa snuggled against his firm chest, greedily offering her lips to his again and again. She loved the way he gently caressed her flushed face and trailed his hands up and down her bare arm, then over her back. She liked the feel of his tawny hair surrounding her fingers, and liked how she boldly drew his mouth more snugly against hers. Alysa instinctively recognized the flames that licked at her fiery body and the fierce hunger gnawing at her womanhood: raging desire. But the intense yearning that filled her heart and bound her to him could be nothing less than love.

She began to writhe because the biting pains in her legs could not be ignored and they threatened to awaken her from this beautiful dream. Seeking a comfortable position, she squirmed against the warrior's rough clothing, which increased her discomfort and caused her to cry aloud, which woke her. Immediately Alysa was confused, for she found herself a willing captive in a stranger's arms!

Two

Before seeing the man clearly, Alysa pushed away from the muscular body which was clad in a curious warrior's garb. She was breathing erratically, and struggling to master her senses. The stranger made no attempt to seize her; instead he instantly rose to his feet and extended his hand to her to help her rise. But she did not accept it. Sitting on the ground, she straightened her garments, then her dark blue eyes began their appraisal at his feet and slowly traveled up his body.

Brown leather strips which had been studded with black metal circles—obviously the source of the discomfort that had woken her—were sewn to a large belt and dangled in a variety of lengths near his knees. This unusual warrior's apron was strapped over loose fitting black breeches which were tucked into mid-calf brown boots, his legs spread wide in a self-assured stance.

Brown leather studded with the same black metal pieces banded his neck, covered his heart, and became two strips that joined the belt; the back of the leather garment, she knew, formed a large X from collar to belt. From his size and stance, this was a man of great prowess and strength, a man with a body which—

Alysa hastily cut off that line of thought as she noticed the brown leather bands with black metal stubs that encased his hard, smooth arms from elbows to wrists. Suppressing tremors, she almost feared to lift her eyes.

When she finally looked at his face, she inhaled sharply and could not speak: he was the unknown warrior in her dream! If not for a ruggedly strong chin, his face would have appeared almost square. She found it breathtakingly handsome. His wind-tossed blond hair with sunny streaks curled slightly just above his powerful shoulders. His brows were wide and long, their color was dark blond; his nose a perfect size for its shape; his upper lip thinner than the full lower one, which seemed to roll downward, making it appear as if there was a slight indentation beneath it.

She continued her bold study, and he silently submitted to it. His face was as tanned as his body—a shade of dark honey—and his cheekbones set at a prominent angle above a stubbled jawline. She noticed how quick and alert he was, his more than six-foot frame moving easily and gracefully. But his green eyes most captured her attention—they spoke of mystery and self-assurance. Noticeably, his long and thick lashes were darker than his hair or brows, and edged his expressive eyes most temptingly. She could not stop her gaze from slipping over his entire frame once more, very leisurely and thoroughly. This time she realized that under his leather garment, his firm chest lacked any hair on its splendid surface, and that he was weaponless.

As Alysa continued to stare at him, the warrior knelt and lightly pushed aside her mussed hair, revealing how surprisingly gentle his large hands were. He smiled, and she felt as if the bright sun were beaming down upon her, just like in—She backed away from him.

"M'lady, forgive me, I did not mean to frighten you," he murmured in a mellow voice which teased pleasantly over her sensitive nerves. "But I heard your cries and rushed to your side. I fear the demons I sought to rescue you from are those of your own making. Come, I will see you home safely." He offered her his left hand once more.

Alysa gaped at the extended hand, then at his grinning face. "You speak falsely, sir. Not a moment past, you—" She halted as she wondered how much of what happened was only in her wild dream.

The warrior grasped her confusion. His fingers brushed over her mouth as he gazed deeply into her eyes and said, "I fear I did steal kisses from these sweet lips, m'lady, but I am not to blame. When I sought to free you from the dark spirits of your dreams, you reached out to me and blinded me with your beauty and desire. Never in all my travels have I seen one as beautiful and irresistible as you. If you are not a vision or a nymph, then speak your name and tell me you are not bound to another in life or in heart." He felt the powerful pull of her sea-blue eyes, and wondered if he could drown in those bewitching pools. Her shiny brown hair appeared as a wave around her face, shoulders, and torso, and caused him to think of little else but his entranced senses. Clad in green like a mysterious and alluring wood nymph, she reeked of potent magic and innocence, of seductive enticement.

Astonished by his words and manner, and baffled by her stirring reaction to him, the young princess said, "What man of honor and strength sneaks about preying upon defenseless maidens? I was asleep and did not know you were real. Who are you and why are you in the royal forest? It is forbidden to enter here."

"Do those same laws not apply to an errant maiden who sneaks from home to dally with a forbidden lover? Or are you the nymph who protects the forest?" he countered. "Surely it is more dangerous for a maiden as radiant as the sun and as lovely as the rarest flower to be caught alone here, than for a man who can defend himself or wickedly take what he desires. Or, if you are

30

flesh and blood, is it an enfeebled father or a blind husband who guards you so pitifully against such mischief?"

"Neither," she retorted haughtily. "I can protect myself."

"With what?" he inquired, grinning broadly as he watched anger flicker in her eyes and pinken her cheeks.

Princess Alysa Malvern frowned at the handsome man, but she knew he was right. She had no weapon, and although she carried one on Calliope, it was useless because the horse was tied far away. She had been careless to place herself in such danger. What if this man was one of Isobail's raiders, who could abuse her or abduct her, or a castle knight who could tattle on her? What if he was a desperate poacher who might do anything to prevent arrest? No, she concluded, he did not look like an evil brigand. "Who are you?" she demanded. "Prince Alric gives no one permission to invade his forest."

The man relaxed his stance. "My name is Gavin Hawk," he said. "I was returning home to Strathclyde from a long adventure. My friends and I joined others seeking the lost kingdom of Carthage, but we could not find it. Many say there are lost treasures hidden there, but the Romans left no stone standing or prizes to be found. Life is dull in my land, for King Cailean seeks to battle no foe. I am a warrior who needs a place to use his skills, so I seek adventures and pleasures in other lands. Many told us this land is overrun with Jutes and raiders. We came to join the fighting and to earn great rewards for helping those in peril."

"You fight for money and glory?" she asked. "How can you when peace is more valuable than war? Have you no home or family? Have you nothing to do but spill blood?"

He shrugged nonchalantly. "Each man must find his

31

own place in life, and that is mine. Peace is often purchased with the blood of men like myself. Who is better to have in your land, hired warriors or greedy conquerors?"

"Neither," Alysa stated firmly. She could not explain why she was not terrified of this man and why she did not flee quickly. She was intrigued by him, and enchanted. She wanted to know all about him and to remain here a while longer; yet, a curious panic was building within her.

"All people and travelers in your land face great dangers. Why does your ruler allow such Evil to go unhindered? Where is the castle of Prince Alric? How many knights and warriors does he have? Many strong warriors would come and fight for your princedom of Damnonia if he rewarded them. Tell me all there is to hear about your land, and perhaps I will stay and help defeat your enemies." But when she remained silent, he sought a question that would entice a reaction. "Are the tales of your princess true? Is she truly wicked? Surely some evil has befallen your ruler for him to endure such peril."

He waited for a response or a denial, but none was forthcoming. He could use a beautiful and daring female like her, he thought. "Can it be a brigand has stolen your tongue from beneath my eyes while you dazed me with your matchless beauty?" he teased when the silence continued.

Alysa was reluctant to reply because she did not want to discuss her stepmother with a stranger or spoil the heady magic of this unexpected meeting, which teased her senses like a wild ride on Calliope's back. Even if what he said were true, he was touching on dangerous areas. Indeed, he had insulted her father. But she had to acknowledge that he did not know to whom he was speaking so frankly. Still, it distressed her that he knew so much about Isobail. Had news of her stepmother's malicious ways truly reached far and wide, she wondered, even into other lands? If so, why had her grandfather, King Bardwyn, not sent inquiries?

No matter, she could not confide in a stranger, a man who hired out as a fighter, perhaps to anyone who could meet his price. Besides, he was a commoner—a foreign warrior—and she was royalty, although dressed as and obviously taken for a peasant. He seemed intent on obtaining information, especially on her land's strengths, and she was wary of this curiosity. She could not help but wonder what he would do if he knew her identity, which she dared not reveal. She decided it was rash to linger here any longer.

As she observed him, Giselde's words came to mind. Here was a man "with sunny hair and leafy eyes," whose words dripped "with honey," and whose smiles were "sweet." Could he be the "fierce conqueror" who had a "hunger for our lands and throne" whom Giselde had warned her about? she wondered fearfully. Without a doubt, he fit Giselde's description. Why was he in the royal forest, questioning her so intently?

A troubled look clouded his green eyes. "You fear me, m'lady, and I do not know why. I see many questions in your lovely eyes, and your body trembles. Surely a few stolen kisses do not frighten you so. I have come a long way and my body is weary, else my control would not be so lax. Forgive me and calm your worries. I only seek to rest here until I see your ruler and learn if he wishes to hire me and my friends to help him save his land from those who plunder it. If not, we must find ways to earn money for food and lodging along our way home. Surely your people would pay eagerly to be freed of raiders. Speak, for you are in no danger from me."

Alysa became more and more confused by the stimulating man and the hold he seemed to have over her. She could not dismiss the sense of mystery and danger exuding from him, nor the aura of great strength and tenderness which seemed to seep from him as honey escaping a ruptured comb. Little did he know that it was not fear of him that caused her tremors, but that she had the wildest urge to throw herself into his arms and to cover his mouth with greedy kisses; and far worse, to make passionate love to him here by the stream! Never had such unbridled, wanton emotions challenged her to such precarious self-control! If they were not strangers, she would yield to him and claim him as her own, commoner or not!

Alysa inhaled deeply to slow her thudding heart and to cool her passion. She told herself not to think such things or behave so ruttishly. A man like this could never become Prince of Damnonia and the future King of Cambria. She had duties to her father, to her land, to her kingdom. One day she would rule Cambria and Damnonia, and a man of equal rank or blood must become her mate and joint ruler. How wise Giselde had been to warn her to be careful of whom she chose to love. So many of her bloodline had endured anguish because of unwise choices; she must not allow herself to do the same over a mere physical attraction. She must be strong and loyal to her land. Whatever was drawing her to him, it must end today.

He was speaking again, repeating his promise, "Have no fear, m'lady; I will protect you from all harm, even from your rulers."

Alysa finally spoke. "I have no love for Princess Isobail, that is true. It is to Prince Alric I am loyal, and will be till I die. I do not know you, therefore, I cannot tell you about our land and rulers. But I will warn you, sir, it is certain death to threaten these lands and to remain in this forbidden forest. If it is Prince Alric and work you seek, his castle lies in that direction." She pointed westward. "Follow the road, and it will take you there. If your heart is black, leave these lands before nightfall, or you will surely die."

"By whose hand, m'lady?" he asked gravely. "For if powerful knights or brave warriors lived here, your land would not be in danger. Dusk approaches; I will see you home safely, then seek my fate. Come, Trojan," he called out, and a Flemish-bred stallion with a tawny hide and white tail and mane trotted forward.

Alysa's eyes widened as she saw the golden charger. "You are my enemy, sir, for I have seen you in my dream. If you remain in my land, I will make certain you are slain," she vowed, then pushed him aside to race into the engulfing forest.

"Wait, m'lady!" he called out, but she did not look back at him. "Stay, Trojan," he commanded, then pursued her.

Gavin could not believe how swift and cunning she was, for she seemed to vanish from sight instantly. Never had he been so smitten by a woman; this maiden thrilled him from head to toe. He wished he had not frightened her into running away, for he wanted to know everything about her. He had not even learned her name or where she lived! Or why she feared him so deeply. Had she been a castle servant, perhaps he could have enticed her into spying for him. She was one of the people he had come to help, yet he could not even tell her so, or who he was. Gavin's father, King Briac, close friend and ally to King Bardwyn of the neighboring kingdom of Cambria, had sent him here to help Bardwyn's son, Prince Alric, and the Damnonians. It was his duty to discover who was behind the debilitating raids on this land, and why. Survival of this principality and its people depended upon him and his men, sons of feudal lords and knights of Cumbria, all men who were unknown in this territory. He could reveal his identity and motives to no one except Giselde, the old woman who lived in the forest, who had sent messengers pleading for help from King Bardwyn and King Briac. If only the fetching girl had answered his questions she might have helped him in his mission. For a time he had thought she was as attracted to him as he was to her, but then decided he must have been mistaken.

Prince Gavin Crisdean, whose name meant "hawk," never imagined who the girl in green peasant garments was or why she had fled from him. He could almost taste the sweetness of her lips, and could easily recall the unbridled passion she had innocently revealed to him. He knew she had been drowsy and had not realized what she was doing; still, he'd been unable to stop himself from taking advantage of the tantalizing situation. He had known many maidens, in many lands, but none had tempted him as that blue-eyed peasant with her thick brown hair and fair complexion. No matter that he was royalty and she a commoner, and that no permanent union should come of such a match—he had to see her again, had to unravel the mystery in her parting words—*I have seen you in my dream.* Indeed, as dreamlike as she had seemed, he almost doubted her existence. But no matter how rare and exquisite she had appeared, clothed in forest green, he knew she was not a mythical wood nymph. She was real, and somehow he would locate her and vanquish her mystery and resistance. Even now his loins, and strangely his heart, ached for her. He vowed that when time allowed, he would seek her again and study her magical tug on him.

Alysa knew the forest well, and hid easily from the stranger. Experiencing an odd mixture of relief and disappointment when he was no longer in sight, she hurried to where Calliope was waiting patiently. Mounting agilely, she rode swiftly for Malvern Castle.

Fortunately when she reached home, everyone who might dare question her was busy, and others paid little attention to her late arrival. Alysa rushed up the side steps from the stable and made it to her chamber safely. The young princess flung off the peasant garb and freshened up with the water left by her servant, Thisbe, daughter of Piaras.

Nervously pacing the stone-walled room, Alysa reflected on all that had happened today. When Thisbe came to help her prepare for the evening meal, Alysa guiltily pleaded an aching head and asked the girl with mousy brown hair and large cow-brown eyes to make an excuse to her family. Her absence should not matter to them, for her father rarely left his chambers to eat with them anymore. Perhaps she could sneak a visit with him later, she thought, since he no longer shared a sleeping chamber with Isobail, and according to castle gossip, the woman rarely spent days or nights with the prince anymore.

Alysa lay across the bed and tried to reason out a plan to solve her troubles. It was frustrating, for there seemed no way she could get Isobail out of Alric's life, or contest the enemies of her land. She had no proof of Isobail's wickedness, and could do little anyway, since she was not yet Damnonia's ruler. But Alysa knew something had to be done before matters worsened. The brigands had grown bolder and were now raiding everywhere. She had to at least gather facts about her stepmother then convey what she discovered to her grandfather, King Bardwyn, and demand his help.

Help! her mind echoed, then filled itself with images of the enchanting warrior in the forest. No, she decided, she could not ask help of a man she did not know and could not trust. Not unless he proved himself to her.

Tears dampened her thick lashes. Even if the unknown warrior agreed to help, what could he do alone or with a few followers? Get himself slain by Isobail, or drawn into her evil clutches! No, information and facts were what she needed, and soon!

Thisbe realized her mistress was upset and wanted to be alone, so she left quietly, worrying about Alysa. She could remember when Isobail moved from a hut inside the castle's outer wall and into the east tower with Prince Alric, years before they wed, and she could recall how things had changed steadily since that dark day, and especially since their marriage. At least she could be grateful for one thing—she was servant to neither Isobail nor Kyra. Still, it distressed her to see how Alysa was mistreated by them.

The youthful servant knew that Isobail spent large sums on the garments for herself and her daughter and denied Alysa such lovely clothes. As a consequence Thisbe was always repairing old garments or seeking ways to make them look fresh. She and Leitis, her friend and the head servant, had actually stolen money to buy possessions they might trade for Alysa's garments. If they were caught . . . Thisbe refused to imagine what the wicked wife of their ruler would do to them if such crimes were exposed.

Many times she had wished and prayed for Isobail's death, for it frightened Thisbe to witness how much power and control Isobail was gaining. She could not understand why Alric allowed it to occur, or why he permitted such abuse of his only child; but these days the prince seemed so wrapped up in himself that he noticed little. One day things would change, Thisbe decided in annoyance, for the people would tire of Isobail's cruelty.

Surely the impoverishment of whole families to support Isobail's various henchmen and schemes could not be tolerated much longer. But then, the taxation and punishments were more well known than whatever policies they might be financing. Something, someone, had to help, before the princedom ceased forever to be as it had once been.

Gavin reached the hut that had been marked on his map and knocked on the door. He saw a woman leaning over a kettle at the hearth. Turning, she smiled warmly and beckoned him inside. The young prince entered, spoke the agreed upon code words in a clear tone, "I seek the maker of a Druid map," then stood quietly while she circled and studied him.

"Yea," she murmured, eagerly clasping her gnarled hands. "I am Giselde, the map maker, and you are the Hawk of Cumbria. At last you are here. Take heed, Evil Beast," she shouted as she shook her hand above her head, "your slayer has arrived. Welcome, Prince Gavin of Cumbria, son of Briac; I have been waiting for you many days. We will speak after we eat and you are rested."

Gavin watched Giselde dish up the Bubble-n-Squeak—a stew of meat, cabbage, and potatoes which had simmered for hours—and place the food on a table in the far corner of her cozy hut. Without further talk, the old woman motioned him forward to one chair. Then, as if she were alone and the best meal in the known world was spread before her, she took the other seat and began to eat heartily.

Gavin pushed thoughts of the intriguing peasant girl into the back of his mind for now, as the matter confronting them was urgent. He furtively eyed the old woman as they ate silently. Strands of hair had escaped a hastily braided plait that hung down her back like a heavy rope, and they fluttered wildly about her head with each movement. Her weathered skin had a yellowy, unhealthy tint which deceptively made her look older and weaker than she was.

Gavin could tell from her exertions that she was stiff

and sore, and in some pain, an observation that invited compassion. Her short body—clad in a drab but clean kirtle of cilice—edged on being plump. Her eyes, though faded by advanced years, were full of life and courage; yet now and then a slight hint of mystery—and long endured anguish—clouded them, as she slipped into deep thought and seemingly forgot his presence. Scrutinizing her while her attention was elsewhere, he could not determine her age or country, a skill he normally possessed.

Gavin wondered if the urgent messages to King Bardwyn and to his father could have been written by this almost pitiful creature. And he wondered if her charges against Isobail and Alric were true? or would they prove to be just an old woman's crazy ramblings.

But then, Gavin realized that some of Giselde's accusations were probably true, since he had heard more and more tales against Isobail with each mile he rode. Strangely, few people had seen their ruler, Prince Alric, in a long time, and many were growing restless over his absence and Isobail's apparent control over the principedom.

Another strange matter teased at Gavin's mind. No loyalty, trust, or friendship had ever existed between Alric's father and Giselde; so why had King Bardwyn believed Giselde and acted on her warnings?

When they finished eating and were drinking herb tea, Giselde asked, "Are you sure no one knows you in Damnonia?"

Gavin smiled and replied, "This is my first visit, and I have fought with no warrior from here. I am sure my face is unknown. Why did you seek King Bardwyn's help and intrusion in his son's principality? And why have you insisted that this help be given secretly?"

"You have changed much since I saw you long ago. You were five when my daughter Catriona and I stayed

40

in your father's castle. If he had not rescued us, we would have been slain."

Gavin was stunned. He could hardly believe this was Princess Catriona's mother, since Giselde looked nothing like the dim image of the woman he had spent time with as a small boy. Her appearance and surroundings told him that many grave things had happened over the years. Gavin said, "So, you are Giselde. Your father Connal was a brave and fierce chieftain. My people still speak of him, and of your valiant husband, Rurik. But tell me, Giselde, why is your identity kept secret from the Damnonians? And why do you live alone, hidden in a forbidden forest?"

Although she had appeared completely immersed in her meal, Giselde had intently studied the young man. Deciding she could trust him, she began to explain the troubled past. Listening, Gavin grasped her intelligence, courage, and sufferings, and nodded in sympathy. His father, Briac, had told him of his past love for Catriona, the woman of mixed Celtic and Viking blood, the woman he could not marry long ago because his duty toward his country outweighed his feelings for the half-Viking princess. As Giselde fetched more tea from the hearth, Gavin recalled that bittersweet tale.

Briac Crisdean, Prince of Cumbria, had met the daughter of Giselde and Rurik twenty-nine years ago. He had desired her greatly and had wooed her secretly for two years, until forbidden to see her again by his father. Briac had not yielded to his father's demand out of weakness; he had yielded because it was his duty to become king, a position which would have been lost by marrying the mixed-blooded Catriona. He had given up his love for Catriona and wed Brenna, Gavin's mother, and Briac had come to love Brenna as much as he had loved Catriona. But years later fate had thrown his father and Catriona together again when Briac had rescued her and her mother from a Viking attack, a raid that had devastated their camp and tribe For months Giselde and Catriona had lived in his father's castle, until weather permitted them to return to Alric's princedom. His father had suffered at the news of Catriona's untimely death, and was eager to save Alysa, the daughter of his past love. Along his journey to Damnonia, Gavin had pondered Princess Alysa Malvern many times, and was eager to meet the daughter of the woman who could have prevented his birth.

Giselde's remark invaded his reverie, "It is hard for everyone when an enemy is chosen for a lover. I know this only too well. Most of my people viewed both my mother and my husband as savages." Drawn to him, she confessed, "In Celtic eyes and hearts it was bad for Catriona to be a half-blooded child, but it was worse for me because I had both a Viking mother and a Viking husband. The men of my tribe felt betrayed by my choice of husband, and the women were angered by it. They had accepted my mother because they needed my father's prowess and wisdom, even though secretly most never forgave him for marrying a Viking princess. When the Vikings attacked that last time, my people savagely turned on Mother and my beloved Rurik, and killed them both. My brave father died trying to defend them, not battling Vikings, as legend tells; thus he became more disgraceful in the eyes of our embittered people."

Giselde looked into Gavin's eyes as she said, "If your father, Prince Briac, had not arrived, our Albanian clan would have surely slain Catriona and myself. You see, Prince Gavin, few people know that the Vikings actually came after us because we were the only living descendants of royal blood. They attacked because they wished us returned to them. Only through my lineage can the royal Viking line be restored. Thus is my granddaughter Alysa in danger graver than the Evil pervading this land, danger she does not even know about."

Giselde paused, then continued solemnly, "It is too late to dream of changing the past. It is time to save the future. I did not summon help because of my love for Damnonia. I summoned help to save my granddaughter Alysa from capture by Vikings—who are beginning to ride more freely—and from losing this land that belongs to her by right of birth. I know Isobail hired bandits from Logris to steal this land, and those Jute raiders have Viking ancestry. There are dark and perilous days ahead, Prince Gavin. Are you strong enough to face all dangers?" she challenged.

"I fear nothing and no one, save God and the loss of my honor."

Giselde eyed the handsome young man and knew his confidence was justified. She smiled warmly, and her face seemed to glow with gentleness. "That is good, for you will need both to win this battle. I long feared that Alric was part of a plot to make Damnonia a separate kingdom and to conquer other kingdoms, but I have learned the threat comes from Isobail and her allies alone. Those who aid me say Alric is very ill. They say he is so weak he is confined to his bed many days and to his castle every day. Isobail is the one who rules this land and who hungers to rule all of Britain. Yet Alric gave birth to the Evil which thrives here by his wicked lust for Isobail long ago, and he does nothing to stop her now. Know this, Gavin of Cumbria, Alric will never speak or move against her, because it will uncover his weakness—his loss of honor—in the past and in the present. To defeat Isobail we must also defeat Alric. Tell me this: to save this land, his people, Alysa, and all of Britain—will King Bardwyn allow the destruction of Alric, his only son?"

Gavin was not ready to answer that troubling question. He knew that first he had to examine the situation himself. Only then could he decide how to handle this difficult matter. King Bardwyn had granted him full authority to take whatever action was necessary to protect the peace, and he would do so when the time came

"What is this Evil you speak of?" Gavin asked. "King Bardwyn said the survival of Damnonia could be at stake. How so?" he asked.

"The survival of Damnonia and all other kingdoms is in jeopardy," Giselde replied, aware that Gavin had sidestepped her question. "Good men, loyal to Alric and to his father, are dying mysteriously, and Isobail's allies are gaining possession of their lands and knights. Raiders attack villages and castles and try to frighten people away from them. I believe Isobail has hired brigands and uses them to provoke war. She wants everyone to think that Logris is behind the raids. She wants to create an excuse to invade Logris and conquer it. Then she will turn her greedy eyes on other kingdoms. You must find the proof to end this madness. She must be destroyed, and Alric must be replaced. He is weak and unworthy to wear the crown. In his place Isobail schemes to gobble up land after land and put her heartless allies in control. She intends to be High Queen of all Britain. We must stop her."

"Does Princess Isobail know you are plotting against her?"

"Soon she will know. Her powerful sorcerer Earnon will perceive the forces of Good set against them."

"The only real magic lies in a strong sword and self-control, Giselde. Spells and enchantments are for peasants," he chided.

Her tone serious, Giselde refuted, "There are powers and secrets of which you know nothing, Gavin. But soon you will confront them and be compelled to accept them. If you believe in Good, then you must also believe in Evil. If there are gods, there must be devils. I have met and battled such dark forces many times, as you will. When they clash, which they will, forces such as you have never seen or fought before will be revealed."

Gavin realized the woman firmly believed in such things, so he dropped the subject. "You hate Isobail, do you not?" he asked.

"Yea, she is aligned with Evil. She murdered Catriona and took her place. She must die. I know of her evil, past and present, that is why I am a threat to her."

Gavin's brows lifted. "How do you know this? Why would Prince Alric marry her? Surely you are wrong."

Giselde shook her head vigorously, dislodging more gray hair and causing the loosened strands to shudder as if they had cold bodies of their own. Her voice shrill with emotion, she said, "I know many things about plants and spells, and her death was not a natural one. That is why I left the castle to live in hiding. If she knew I was nearby, Isobail would kill me. She has blinded Alric, perhaps enchanted him. Before Alysa was born, he brought Lord Caedmon's widow into his castle and dallied with her secretly. And after Catriona's death, Isobail traveled with him for years, then became his harlot until they wed. A man who selfishly betrays his wife, his child, his duty, and his honor, is unworthy of a crown or of life. Only Alysa, this land, and Britain concern us. He is doomed forever, as he should be."

"Does your granddaughter know who you are? Does she know all this?"

"Nay, for the truth could endanger her. And I would have your word that you will not divulge this truth to her."

"You have it," Gavin replied.

"When all is right again," Giselde continued, "I will tell her everything. Do you not hear my words with your mind and heart, son of Briac, and know they are true?"

Gavin reflected on the five kingdoms of Britain which Giselde claimed were in peril: Strathclyde, to the north, was ruled by King Cailean; Albany, to the northeast, was ruled by numerous chieftains, without a High

King over them, and had been tormented by fierce Vikings for many years; Logris, to the southeast and largest of all kingdoms, was ruled by Vortigern, and was a land with two chunks cut from its vulnerable belly on the southern coast and inhabited by savage Jutes; Cumbria, the kingdom ruled by his father, bordered all kingdoms and the sea; and Cambria, ruled by Bardwyn, was the owner of the territory of Damnonia, the southern peninsula of their large island.

The twenty-seven-year-old prince briefly mused on King Vortigern, one of the few warlords who had changed his rule and territory drastically after the Romans departed, but had kept his troubles and greed within his borders. Vortigern had used a Roman ploy by hiring foreign warriors to defend his land's borders; he had allowed many shiploads of Jutes—aggressive and powerful warriors from Jutland—to settle in his kingdom and keep his lands safe from other marauding Vikings and the possible return of the Romans—a terrible mistake which he could not correct, for the Jutes had demanded land as their payment instead of money or jewels, more and more land, and Vortigern dared not refuse.

The Jute chieftain was a barbaric but clever Viking named Hengist, and he owned and ruled the southeastern tip of land between the Thames River and the Oceanus Britannicus.* His brother Horsa had been placed in control of another large portion of land on the southern coast of Logris, halfway between Hengist's stronghold and the principality of Damnonia, an area that provided many openings to the sea for Hengist to bring in more warriors without Vortigern's knowledge. All Britons had been shoved from Hengist's domains, and according to rumors, the Jute chieftain's greed was increasing rapidly. If he were allowed the opportunity

---

*Later to be named the English Channel

to stretch his boundaries by accepting a challenge from Isobail or by joining forces with her to take over Damnonia and Logris, there was no guessing what horrors lay ahead for Damnonia and the other four peaceful kingdoms. It was up to Gavin to uncover such a sinister plot and to prevent it.

As if reading Gavin's mind, Giselde cautioned, "We must be careful with our moves until we know who we can trust. You must tell no one, no one, Hawk of Cumbria, who you are or why you are here. How will you mask your perilous search for the truth?"

Gavin repeated the tale he had told the girl by the stream, his explanation refreshing her enchanting vision in his mind. He was tempted to inquire about her, but realized he should not be concerned with personal matters at this time. "It is common for knights errant to ride about in other lands seeking adventures or glory or the chance to right wrongs, or for restless warriors to seek a little mischief and fun and money," he said. "Hopefully such actions will throw us into contact with those who terrorize this land.

"But I must be careful," Gavin added. "Only six men ride with me, though they are strong and full of valor and would follow me to the death. We will join a band of raiders and convince them there is no money or glory to be found in our old way of living, that we have joined them because we are weary of being poor and unknown. They will never suspect that we are not from Strathclyde, as we will claim. My men will call me Gavin Hawk, as I will call them by their first names. This way we will not expose ourselves with name slips. Thus will we gain the raiders' trust, learn who has hired them and their real purpose. Whether it be plundering or treachery, we will defeat them."

Laughter spilled from Giselde's lips. "Yea, it is a clever plan. It will close their eyes to your mission.

There is no surer way to unmask them but to join them."

Giselde was pleased with Gavin's cunning. If he succeeded, his deed would become legend. Exhilaration flooded her body at the thought of being part of victorious history. Not since leaving Albany years ago had the flames of warriors' fires burned so fiercely within her, or caused her heart to ache with longing for the old days and lost loves. Her Celtic father Connal and her Viking husband Rurik had taught her much about fighting strategy, knowledge she had tried to teach Alysa over the years, cleverly under the guise of games, as dear Piaras had done at the castle until Isobail halted him.

"Walk slowly and carefully, Gavin," Giselde warned, "or our enemies will guess your plans. Remember that Trahern—the Sheriff of Damnonia—is fiercely loyal to Isobail, and only Sir Piaras and Sir Beag can be trusted at Malvern Castle. Soon we will see where the lords stand. But Alric is little more than a vanishing mist. He cannot hurt you or help you. Never trust him, Gavin."

"What of Alysa, your granddaughter?"

"If you can, stay clear of her. Alysa must not be endangered by our plans. To draw her into them would provoke Isobail's fury against her."

"That is wise, Giselde. Since we cannot allow her to aid us, she would not understand our actions. If possible, I will make certain our paths do not cross." Gavin arose and stretched his tired body. "I must return to my camp and speak with my men. I will come to you every six days, unless I ride far away to carry out our plan. If I do so, I will try to get word to you before I leave. When I find the safest place to camp, I will return and tell you its location. But we must be careful when we meet, or we will expose our alliance." Gavin moved toward the door.

"Wait," Giselde called after him. She went to her work area and withdrew a small stone that had been polished and attached to a leather thong. Handing it to Gavin, she cautioned, "Wear this at all times. Never remove it, even to bathe. If you lose it or it is torn from your neck during a fight, as swiftly as you can, return to me to obtain another one."

Gavin stared at the necklace in his hand and asked, "What is it?"

Giselde's gnarled fingers reverently reached out to stroke the talisman which had come from a crushed Druid Stone, a megalith sarsen used by Celtic Druids during sacrosanct rituals. She explained, "It is a sacred amulet which will guard you. Long ago it was blessed by Good forces. It cannot protect you from injury or death, but it will keep your head clear of spells."

Gavin smiled indulgently.

"I beg you to wear it always," the old woman urged. "Even though you do not believe in the Old Ways, do this for me."

Gavin saw how distressed the woman was, and deciding it could do no harm to appease her, slipped it over his head and rested it against the leather shield that covered a symbol of death: a royal tattoo in blue. Royal and military tattooing was a custom started in his lands by the Romans, its dye coming from the woad of wild cabbage. When he was fighting or far from his homeland, he always wore garments over his heart so it could not be seen, unless he wished it so.

Giselde smiled happily when the young prince complied, then bid him farewell and good luck. As with Alysa, she watched his departure until the green forest swallowed him. Then the old woman went to her work bench and began mixing potions to enchant Gavin. During Alysa's visit earlier that morning, Giselde had sneaked strands of brown hair from Alysa's clothing which she had used for her granddaughter's spell, a binding spell to become effective the first time Alysa slept after it was cast. During Gavin's visit, Giselde had furtively taken honey-colored hairs from his head for the same purpose.

As she labored skillfully with the intricate arts of enchantment, she murmured, "When next you sleep, Prince Gavin of Cumbria, you will seek your heart's desire and she will come to you with the face and form of Alysa Malvern. Until you meet, Alysa will fill your dreams each night and your heart each day. Once you have gazed upon her, you will be captivated by her. When next you sleep, you will be ensnared by love and desire for only her."

Giselde dropped three rose petals into the liquid heating in her cruse. When delicate smoke began to rise, she added the tawny strands of Gavin's hair. She closed her eyes and murmured, "By all of the powers within and without me, I command you to bind Gavin Crisdean's heart and life with Alysa Malvern's." She mixed this potion with the one from Alysa's and stirred them together gently. "Let no woman claim Gavin's heart and eye save Princess Alysa Malvern. Let no man claim Alysa's heart and eye save the Hawk of Cumbria."

"It is dangerous to intervene in the fates of others, Giselde. She will be unable to resist this man to whom you have bound her heart and soul. I did not reveal my secrets to you so you could play games with others' lives."

Giselde turned on her stool as a tall, bearded man lowered the tapestry that concealed the hidden back door. She gazed at Trosdan, who had been her teacher long ago, and her teacher here in Damnonia since she had summoned him from Albany two years ago. At sixty-nine, Trosdan's hair was a blend of black and gray, yet his full beard was snowy white. His tall slim body possessed an air of dignity and grace, and Giselde could feel the power that flowed from him. His sky-blue eyes seemed to pierce flesh and bone, as if they could see into a person's mind and heart, or into one's very soul. Few men knew the secrets that Trosdan had mastered, yet he used them wisely and sparingly, for he recognized their hidden dangers. Trosdan was one of a dying breed of mystical and magical Druids, who had been outlawed by the Romans long ago but still practiced their beliefs secretly.

"You heard all?" she asked.

He nodded as he took a seat at the table. The Druid master pulled a cloth bag from his long tunic and shook it gently before spilling small, square rocks upon her table, runes from the same sandstone as Gavin's amulet. "Did you selfishly bind Alysa's heart to the Hawk of Cumbria and his to hers to save her from Moran until your victory?" Trosdan asked softly.

Giselde nodded and explained, "With Prince Gavin's protection added to yours, Alysa will be safe from all harm."

Trosdan warned, "Be wary of revenge, Giselde, it is a dangerous weapon. Once the forces of your magic begin to fill the air, Earnon will sense them and seek to stop you. He is totally loyal to Isobail. She will order your death and Alysa's torment, and her followers will seek to obey her."

Giselde argued, "Long ago many deadly secrets invaded our lives, Trosdan, but now I have you to help me. Until victory is won, your *fith-fath* spell will protect Alysa from all harm, for your powers are great and no Evil can pierce a *fith-fath* cloak. You taught me that a powerful spell can be used only once, so I know the peril I face. I know you cannot cast a protective aura around both of us, but it is more important for Alysa to survive than me. But if I fail . . ."

Trosdan shook his head. "I can do only that which is good and right. Expect no more of me, Giselde. If we are exposed, we will both die. Have you forgotten

51

that my cloaking spell protects her only from death, not from all harm?"

"That is why I needed Gavin's help and bound him to Alysa."

"What if the Hawk of Cumbria is pledged to another in his land? And what happens to them when their binding spell is broken at your death? I urge you to remove it now, before they sleep and it works its magic on them."

"I had to do it, Trosdan; I had no choice. It is too late to take another path. Alysa needs Gavin Crisdean."

The master Druid stared intently at the mystical symbols carved upon the smooth surfaces of the runes. "Yea, I know," he murmured, but did not reveal what he saw to Giselde. He would remain silent about the lovers' first meeting, which occurred before Gavin's visit to this hut, for it was too late to free Alysa from bewitchment, and it would soon be too late to free Gavin.

Trosdan, a Viking by birth and an Albanian Briton by choice, said, "As a young man, when I came to this isle with Rurik, my life was changed by a Druid master and your family. I still believe many of the things I was taught in my old land, but I have learned so much more in yours about the secrets of nature, as did your mother Astrid. You have learned much, too, Giselde, but you must use such knowledge and skills carefully.

"For years I feared Rurik's Viking tribe would learn about your survival and Alysa's birth, but I see no imminent threat to either of you from them. Alysa is the last Viking queen, my queen, so I owe her my fealty and love. I wish she did not have to suffer so deeply before all is set right once more."

Giselde did not have to ask Trosdan if he would keep Alysa's existence secret from the Vikings, for she knew his feelings about their barbaric ways. "The survival of this land and people is more important than Alric's miserable life," she said. "If Isobail is allowed to continue, all is lost. Between the prowess of the Hawk and our magic, we will save Alysa and Damnonia."

The old woman glanced at the simmering potion in the cruse and called Briac Crisdean to mind. A man's family was responsible for a member's deeds, so it was Gavin's duty to set right the wrongs of the past which had been partially from his father's weakness for Catriona. Besides, Giselde mused, no harm should come of her spell. Love was meant to be wild and wonderful and mysterious, as hers had been for and with her Viking husband Rurik.

The wise man cautioned, "Concentrate on the Evil that surrounds us and how we must fight it. A war has begun in which powerful forces will battle, and the losses will be great. Not even a powerful wizard or the gods can control a war between Good and Evil. Your valiant warrior does not know about the forces confronting him. Let us see what the runes say about our hero and this forthcoming battle. . . ."

Three

Alysa stood at her chamber window, gazing out at the inner ward of Malvern Castle, her home since birth over eighteen years ago. Malvern Castle was large and picturesque, one of the most well laid-out castles in all of Britain. The inner ward, or bailey, where most castle dwellers lived and worked, was constructed nearly in a square, with thick walls lined with defensive parapets stretching from tower to tower at each corner. The outer ward, large enough to hold the two closest villages, was surrounded by an imposing battlement which totally encircled the magnificent compound. Beyond the battlement the entire setting was protected by a wide and deep moat on three sides with a river on the fourth. Each entrance in the outer wall was guarded by two gates and a drawbridge.

The castle sat high on the riverbank, with its southwestern side sloping abruptly to the river wall, too steeply pitched for a direct assault, even if enemies were lucky enough to conquer the battlement. Alysa could see the river from a side window in her sleeping chamber, and she often enjoyed the lovely sight.

From her viewpoint, she could see little of the outer ward, but she knew the location and purpose of each area. Stables and barns for the knights' and soldiers' horses were built against the northwest wall of the inner bailey, with tiny rooms for stable lads. Beyond, animal pens and fowl cages lined the base of the battlement. The northeast area was lined with fruit trees and small herb and vegetable gardens, to sustain life if the castle fell under a lengthy siege. The southeast section, which Alysa could see from her sitting chamber window, served as the training yard for knights and squires.

The site, construction, and garrisoning of a castle were vital to a ruler because it provided a defense against enemies, discontented peasants, and rival lords. It also provided the ruler's subjects with stability and protection against foreign conquest which would throw their lives into chaos. A ruler controlled all of the land and people in his kingdom, and he could reclaim land grants or have people arrested and slain if he saw fit: crucial reasons to have a wise and just and valiant ruler.

Alysa thought about the duties that her father was allowing others, particularly Isobail, to carry out in his name. A responsible and honorable ruler traveled his lands most of the time, holding court in the castles of feudal lords or stopping in villages and hamlets to show himself to his people and to hand down judgments. A wise ruler visited lords to bestow knighthood and favors on those worthy of them. A smart ruler met with his retainers to discuss defense and problems in each area. And he hunted with his high-ranking subjects to study their loyalties, to show courtesy toward them, to retain their homage.

A just ruler was supposed to tell peasants when they could sell or trade animals or abodes, and to inspect their farms and workshops. He was to make judgments where crimes or misdeeds were involved, and settle boundary disputes. He was to approve, deny, or command betrothals and marriages, and collect fair taxes and special fees. Yet Prince Alric saw to none of these duties anymore, and many noticed this failure.

Giselde had told Alysa about the dissension growing among the powerful feudal lords, and the grumblings in many villages. The people no longer felt safe in this land, for they were burdened by Isobail's demands. Her taxes had nearly impoverished them, and her harsh punishments were resented. Too, the countryside had been terrorized by wandering bands in recent months, and no one in authority appeared capable of putting an end to it. At first they had feared for Prince Alric's health and prayed for his recovery. Then they had grown rebellious at the troubles his absence created in their lives. Many spoke out for a new ruler, and many of those rebels vanished or were slain by the marauding raiders.

One lord, Friseal, who had tried to incite the others to speak out against Alric and Isobail, had been arrested and executed for treason at Isobail's command, and his holdings confiscated and granted to Sheriff Trahern. The other three lords had been unable to help their unfortunate friend, for the man had spoken out publicly against their rulers, and many retainers had borne witness against him in the royal court. Alysa's father had presided over that court but had been unable to grant his vassal mercy, as the crime of treason had been proven against him. Yet Giselde had told Alysa that the matter had been instigated by Isobail's men, and the witnesses against the vassal had lied.

Worse, Giselde had told her that Isobail was plotting to take over every feudal estate in Damnonia and place her royal retainers in control of them. Alysa thought about the three remaining lords—Orin, Daran, and Fergus—and she fretted over their safety. She could not help but wonder if Isobail would also try to take Sir Kelton's castle at Land's End—property that once belonged to Isobail and her first husband, Lord Caedmon Ahern—and give it to her son, Moran. Long ago Isobail had struggled to retain Caedmon Castle for Moran, but

Alric had refused to allow a woman with small children to keep such a vital stronghold. Alric had taken Isobail and her children into his protection by bringing them to Malvern Castle and making Isobail his wife's waiting woman. How could a woman love and wed a man who had taken her home and son's heritage from her? Alysa wondered. But such conjecture presupposed that Isobail was capable of feeling love for another person—an unlikely supposition.

If Isobail was plotting against Sir Kelton and the other lords, she would know soon, as Moran's knighthood was approaching, a rank that required money and land before it could be bestowed. And if Giselde was right about the raids on the villages, then Isobail was trying to frighten the peasants into obeying her every whim. This land would run red with innocent blood if Isobail was allowed to carry out her intent. Alysa knew she needed proof of her wicked plots, and had to figure out how to obtain such proof and get it to King Bardwyn, her grandfather.

Alysa's chambers were in the south tower on the second floor, the smallest tower of the compound, the one built for nurseries and children, their guardians and teachers. The space and privacy had not been necessary, as Alric and Catriona had had only one child. Her handmaiden Thisbe's room was nearby, along with Alysa's privy and wardrobe. Beneath her on the first floor were the chambers of Princess Isobail's son and daughter by the deceased Lord Caedmon—Kyra and Moran Ahern—when Prince Moran was home.

To her right was a lengthy section housing knights and their squires, the prince's guard, the armory, and the men's eating hall. Then came linked twin towers on the western corner, which served as a massive gatehouse with its imposing turrets and portcullis, structures that were fortresses in themselves and served as the only entrance to the inner ward. The buttress-connected towers

57

contained the royal stables and farriers on the lower floors, and military retainers—castle watchmen, men-at-arms, and archers—on the second floors. Here was where her beloved friend Sir Piaras, the knight trainer, lived and worked.

Another lengthy section with numerous rooms and workshops was located between the gatehouse and the north tower. This was where the skivvies, armorers, smiths, carpenters, and other craftsmen labored in service for their ruler. Some slept in their workshops, while others lived in the nearby village or had huts along the inner wall of the southeast battlement.

The second floor of the north tower held the chapel and guest quarters for the traveling priest. Also Leitis, another of Alysa's favorite and most trusted servants, a woman in charge of the other female servants at the castle, had her quarters in the north tower. The butcher lived on the first floor, and did his tasks there, along with the candle and soap makers. Below ground was a dungeon which, fortunately, was rarely used.

The span between the north tower and the Great Tower housed servants, who often slept along the hallways on straw palliasses. It also contained rooms for food and grain storage, and areas were the wash was done, especially when the weather was cold or rainy.

The Great Tower, where Damnonia's rulers lived and governed, was a large, rectangular keep comprised of two interlocked towers. The buttery—for wines, cheeses, and butter—and the bakery were located in a section of the lowest level of the keep, as was the pantry for current food use, with the kitchen and cooks' quarters taking up the entire area of the first floor.

Alric's chambers were situated on the second floor of one of the two towers, an area that provided the most protection in case of an attack. The other tower of the keep housed Princess Isobail and her personal servant Ceit on the second floor and the Great Hall on the first floor. The span between the keep and Alysa's tower was living and working quarters for Guinn, the castle bard; Earnon, Isobail's advisor and friend; Baltair, Alric's personal advisor, friend, and Malvern Castle's seneschal; the stewards; and quarters for high-ranking guests.

Malvern Castle was a large and busy place which ran efficiently, but the joy of many of its workers had lessened under Isobail's control. Many knew her to be harsh and demanding, as was Kyra.

Alysa was glad she had avoided both women today, since she hated to spend energy and time battling words with them. Surely by now everyone had left the Great Hall and was going about his or her business. It was nearly dark, so she hoped she could sneak across the inner courtyard and up the spiral steps to visit her father. It was obvious that Isobail was trying to keep them separated as much as possible. The question was: Why?

Alysa wished she had the courage to use the secret passage that encircled the entire castle on the lowest level, which had concealed spiral staircases and openings only in Alric's and Alysa's towers and in the dungeon. Those stairways were very steep and narrow, and the passageway was only wide and tall enough for one person to travel at a time. An underground escape tunnel ran from the gatehouse to the river wall, where an entrance was hidden by rocks, water, and overgrown brush. Only Alric and Alysa knew of its existence; for as was common, such builders were slain the moment it was completed, to prevent its exposure. Since it had never been used, Alysa could imagine the numerous spiderwebs and rats that must infest it by now, not to mention the utter darkness of the passageway. She shuddered at the thought of entering it alone and walking the great distance to her father's chambers. No doubt, with the height of the river, the escape hole was underwater. Only the steep slope of the riverbank kept water from flooding the tunnel and steps, if its use was ever required.

Cautiously Alysa slipped from her tower and edged her way along the inner wall to the Great Tower. Sighting no one who would stop her, she raced up the steps past the kitchen and quietly approached her father's chamber door. She was relieved, yet worried, to find no guard or servant on duty there. She knew Baltair, his seneschal and advisor, was handling business for him at Lord Orin's.

She eased the door open slightly and listened for company. Hearing nothing, she sneaked into the dim sitting room and gazed about. The room seemed smelly and damp, and sad, almost as if it were trying to discourage life and visitors. Only two candlesticks—one near the entrance to the hall and one near the entrance to Alric's sleeping chamber—were lit, and their glow was hardly visible in the large area. Massive wood furniture appeared oppressive without warm light to reveal the wood grains and workmanship. Even thick drapes were closed over unopened windows, preventing fresh air and fragrant scents from entering the room. Not even a small fire smoldered on the oversized hearth in a dark corner. No papers, books, or quills cluttered his huge writing table. It was as if this chamber was never used or aired. No wonder her father's mood was persistently gloomy!

Alysa crossed the floor and stood before her father's inner door. How strange to feel nervous about visiting him. She wondered if she should knock or simply push the door aside and enter; she did the latter. This was the first time she had been in her father's chambers in several weeks, and she was shocked and angered to discover the way her father was existing, or being abused. At least a servant should be present to tend him!

The curtains were secured to the posts at each corner of the huge bed, which seemed to swallow the form lying on it. The room was damp and malodorous, like a dank, unused cellar, and she wondered how he could endure such unpleasant and unhealthy surroundings. Why had Baltair done nothing to correct this unforgivable condition? Why had she not been informed of it? When morning came, she would demand to speak to Isobail about this matter.

She flung aside the heavy coverings and opened several windows, inhaling the sweet odors of the evening air. The muffled sounds of animals, night birds, and people's voices ended the deathly silence in the room. She lit every candle she could find to dispel the dispiriting darkness. "Father?" Alysa called to him as she sat down on the edge of his bed.

Alric's face was sweaty and pale. Though fifty years old, he looked much older tonight, older and weaker than when she had been allowed to see him last: two weeks ago. The sandy brown shade of his hair was losing its battle with lifeless gray, and its curls had vanished. Only years ago his body had been as taut as an archer's bowstring and as golden as ripe wheat, but now it was flaccid and white. His profile had been that of a man of royalty; now it was marred like a chipped blade. Where was the handsome, strong, and valiant man he had once been? Alysa wondered sadly as tears glimmered in her blue eyes.

"Father?" she called to him again, stroking his clammy brow. "Are you ill? Shall I fetch you something?"

Alric stirred slightly. It seemed as if he were sinking into a bottomless pit at a very slow pace. He felt weak and lifeless, as if it were easier to yield to the forces pulling him ever downward rather than battling to escape his trap. He heard his child calling to him, and he knew he had to find the strength to answer her. Soon, he feared, all of his strength would be gone forever. Soon he would pay for his foul misdeeds. If only the gods could show mercy, could call back the sands of time, could allow him to live his life of the past twenty-one years over again. . . .

Alysa took a cloth and wet it in the tepid water from a pitcher. She gently wiped his face and spoke soothingly to him, as if he were a sick child. "I will make you well again, Father. You must have fresh air, and sunshine, and hot food. You cannot lie abed each day and night if you wish to regain strength. Until Baltair returns, I will ask Leitis and Piaras to help us. You must not give up hope."

Alric's bleary green eyes tried to focus on his daughter, and he attempted to smile at her; both were difficult actions. As with a newborn pup, his flesh and muscles refused to obey him, and sometimes his bodily functions did the same. He knew he must look a terrible sight. He did not want his daughter or his subjects to witness such humiliating disabilities, which was why he remained confined to his room and bed so much these days. He wanted no one's pity or jests, and he did not want any enemies to learn that Damnonia's ruler was on the verge of total incapacitation or death.

The prince thought that if people believed he was very ill, or simply too busy to visit or receive them, they would leave him alone to endure his mental and physical anguish as best he could. From reports by the stewards—Sheriff Trahern and Baltair—Princess Isobail was running the land smoothly and prosperously. When he had to make an appearance, Isobail spent several days personally tending him to help him gain enough strength to carry it off without shaming himself, and he was very grateful to her. Too, he had Captain of the Guard Phelan, and Piaras, to see to his knights and soldiers. His feudal lords and seneschal Baltair were trustworthy and intelligent, so he could depend on his vassals to handle everything until he was well again.

"You should not be here, my child. I am too ill for

visitors. Go and do not worry; my servant will take care of me," he chided weakly. Alric's pride was bruised deeply at appearing so vulnerable, so helpless, so forgotten by the gods whom he had offended and wronged. He did not want Alysa to see him like this, and he had agreed with Isobail to keep her away from him. "It is nothing more than the spring gripans. You forget I am no longer a young man, and it takes me longer than you to conquer such a persistent foe. You can tend me no better than my faithful servants. Worry not, I will be riding with you again soon."

It hurt Alysa to suspect that her father did not want her with him, just as his last remark pained her deeply—as they had not gone riding or hunting together for two years, and she doubted if they ever would again. "You are hardly old, Father, and it is no longer spring. I will punish the servant who sneaked from his post to play sticks with the knights or to dally in some dark corner with a serving wench."

Alric tried to dismiss her vexation with laughter, but the sound of it was unnatural. "I sent my servant to rest while I napped. He checks on me every hour. I am in no danger, need nothing while I sleep. You should visit Lord Orin's or Lord Daron's, loyal vassals who have sons soon to be knighted. Perhaps, my child, you are in need of diversion, or of a worthy suitor or two," he hinted.

Enforced wedlock, her mind shrieked in panic. Once married, she would be compelled to leave her home and father to live with her husband until she became ruler. What if Isobail had contrived that path to get rid of her? she thought. Her blue eyes sparked with protest, and she replied, "I desire only for my father to be well again and in control of his land and people. How can this ever be when you do nothing to strengthen yourself?"

"Has my child learned the arts of healing since I

became ill? Speak only of those things which you know. If all I needed was a good healer, I would be riding with the hound and hawk this day. Pour me some wine to wet my throat," he ordered.

Alysa obeyed, then placed the container on his bed stand once more. "Our kingdom needs you, Father; I need you. Please let me help you." Realizing the need to break through his dazed state, Alysa spoke sternly. "Has no one told you of the fierce brigands who raid your villages? Who terrify and slay your people? Your lords grow impatient and angry at your continued absences. There are troubles and perils all across our land. You are our ruler; you must get well and solve them."

Alric sighed wearily as his stomach began to cramp anew. In his distress, he spoke sharply. "Why does my child tell me such foolish tales and speak so harshly? You are mistaken. My wife and loyal retainers give me reports each week. Not three weeks past, we met with the lords and they greeted me with open hearts and arms. They spoke of no troubles."

"But what of the raiders, Father? Why do your knights not stop them?" she demanded, then reminded herself he was ill and her father.

Beneath the covers Alric's body seemed to burn and sting. Spasms ripped at his insides and he felt himself becoming nauseous. Beads of sweat began to soak his sleeping gown. His throat was dry and fiery, and he asked for more wine before replying, "My wife sees to royal matters for me. Princess Isobail is alert; she will warn me of problems."

"Are you sure you can trust her, Father?" Alysa spoke before she could stop herself. "She is in control of everything, and many do not like her. A woman should not take the place of a great ruler. You must defeat this illness and return to your duties."

Alric knew he was going to soil himself and his bed any moment now. He was too weak to get out of bed, and he could not allow his daughter to assist him. He had to get her out of his chambers swiftly. Summoning the strongest voice and angriest expression he could manage, he shrieked, "Do not make me ashamed of my illness! I am not immortal. Leave me in peace to bear it and to conquer it as best I can. Is my child not a woman who will rule this land after me? Speak no more evil of my wife. She does only as I command her. I trust no one more than she. Go to the chapel and pray for forgiveness for your harsh words. Do not return to my chamber unless I summon you."

"But, Father," she protested frantically. "There is much you—"

"Go! Or I will be forced to summon the guard to remove you," he threatened wildly, knowing he could not endure this agony any longer.

Alysa stared at her father in disbelief. His green eyes were narrowed and chilled; no, they blazed with a fire she did not recognize. She noticed the beads of sweat that glistened on his face, and decided it was sickness causing him to behave this way. But what kind of sickness? It seemed most unnatural. . . . It occurred to her that perhaps someone or something was keeping him so ill and confined to his chamber. Perhaps he was being poisoned? She was shocked at the idea, and spoke urgently. "Please, Father, let me help you, or find someone who can."

"The only way you can help me is to depart my chamber and leave me in peace to heal or to suffer as the gods decide. You are like your mother: disobedient and selfish. She wished things her way, and caused me to suffer. Perhaps it is her barbarian blood within you which stains your heart and honor. Cleanse yourself of such wickedness, child."

Alric's face was twisted with agony, which appeared to Alysa as fury and hostility. He did not know how he

65

was cutting his child's heart viciously with his wil[d] rantings.

She turned and raced from her father's chamber. I[f] the castle gates were not closed and barred for th[e] night, she would go to Giselde's hut and perhaps neve[r] return to Malvern Castle! She had never seen her fathe[r] in such a state, and never wanted to do so again. Sh[e] could not imagine why he had been so hateful to he[r.] It had been rash to speak against Isobail without proof[,] for clearly the woman had befooled him. Yet it was hi[s] insults about her mother that troubled her most. Whe[n] next she visited Giselde, she thought, she must ask he[r] old guardian why her father would say such things. Bu[t] who could help her prove her suspicion of Prince Alric'[s] poisoning?

In her chambers Alysa quickly removed her overtuni[c] and kirtle, then brushed her long hair without waitin[g] for her handmaiden's assistance. To let Thisbe kno[w] she had turned in for the night, the young princes[s] doused all candles but the one near her door. The roo[m] was nearly dark, giving Alysa a feeling of being trapped[.] As if in defiance, or in search for any type of freedom[,] she eased between her covers naked.

How she yearned to have someone hold her and com[-] fort her as the unknown warrior in the forest had. No[,] she quickly realized, not someone, but him. Her finger[s] moved back and forth over her lips as she remembere[d] the feel of his mouth on hers, and she hungered t[o] experience those sensations once more. Her han[d] slipped to a breast as she gently caressed it, recallin[g] how wonderful it had felt when he had done this i[n] her dream, and perhaps in reality. Was it wicked t[o] crave that same behavior again? she mused. Was i[t] wicked to desire more from him, with him? Her hear[t] and body seemed to ache for him, and she tossed upo[n] her bed as she tried to vanquish such emotions.

She could not rid herself of those longings, and ad[-]

mitted it to herself. But how could she find him again, unless he came to the castle to seek her father? And if she were gone at that time, he could be sent away without her knowing. Yet if she remained here and he failed to appear . . .

Alysa tossed the covers aside and walked to the narrow window overlooking the river. There was a village nearby, to the west of the castle, and one ten miles away, north of the castle. But he had been in the forbidden forest, which was southeast. Would he come here seeking to hire out as a paid warrior? Or would he try his luck earning money from the villagers or other lords? Or would he ride from her land to seek his fortune elsewhere?

A breeze came off the river, playfully teased her face and body, and gently ruffled her hair. She watched moonlight dance upon the water's surface, and wished she could go for a relaxing swim. She suddenly realized why she was gazing almost mesmerically at the moon's reflection—it reminded her of the shiny streaks in the stranger's blond hair. His eyes were as green and lively as the forest not far away. She sighed dreamily as she recalled how they had brightened when he smiled. She adored his mysterious, self-assured, romantic gaze, and wanted to feel it caressing her again. She wanted to kiss him, to touch him, to talk with him, and to make love to him. Never had a man created such wild feelings within her.

After a time Alysa returned to bed, closed her eyes, and helplessly summoned the enchanting stranger to visit her dreams. . . .

She walked toward the tall man who was chopping wood near a small hut in a lovely glen. His exertions and the heat of the sun caused moisture to form and glisten on his bare torso. His sleek muscles rippled as he labored easily. Her gaze traveled up firm legs, over slim hips clad in a leather warrior's apron, past a taut

waist, and over a strong torso, then settled on a we
tawny head. The closer she got to him, the more her
tension and warmth increased. She did not hear the ax
striking against the wood; only the pounding of her
heart and the muffled sounds of tranquil nature
reached her ears. As a stirring breeze came from no
where, she closed her eyes to inhale its captive fra
grances and enjoy its cooling freshness.

When Alysa opened her eyes, the handsome male was
smiling down into her upturned face. Her trembling
fingers teased over his lips, then her hand encircled his
head to bring his mouth to hers. She shuddered with
desire at his taste. When his arms tightly banded her
body, she did not mind the way his sweaty body damp
ened her garments. Then suddenly her clothes were
missing and their bodies were pressed together, sealing
tightly and hotly like candle wax to tender flesh.

They kissed and embraced until rampant fires leapt
within and between them. Their tongues danced and
mated wildly and joyfully. Their hands boldly caressed
and explored the other's sleek flesh. Words of love were
exchanged, and hearts were bound for all time.

The daring and possessive stranger swept her into his
arms and carried her into their hut, and Alysa drifted
off to peaceful sleep.

But in the forest not far way, the same dream was
filling Gavin's mind, and knowing more about men
and women than Alysa did, his dream continued for
a time. . . .

He lay the beautiful and irresistible girl on a bed of
straw which was covered by several blankets. He reclined
on his side near her, his green eyes and deft hands
roaming her shapely body at will, causing his body to
respond eagerly to her sensuous allure. His lips played
over her mouth and slowly moved down her throat.
There was a nectar upon her skin which drugged him
with fervid desire, and he could not have enough of

her. She was the most ravishing creature he had ever seen, but she was afraid of him. Why, he did not know. He entreated her to trust him, to love him, to yield to him. He saw her smile into his imploring gaze and heard her whisper, "Not yet, my love."

As Gavin reached for her, she rolled away and teased, "Not yet, my heart's desire, but soon, very soon . . ." And he was asleep.

Alric snuggled weakly into the clean gown and covers that had been changed by his servant. He had finished the hot soup and bread, as ordered by his wife after each attack, and he did feel a little better. As always, after an hour or two from their onset, the gripes and nausea passed. Yet each bout left him weaker and more depressed than the last one, and he wondered how long he could live in such misery. His punishment for the dark and bitter past, he thought again.

He realized he had been harsh with his daughter, but it had been necessary to protect his privacy. When he was better, he would earn her forgiveness. For now, all of his energy and attention must focus on getting well. If there was real trouble in his land, Baltair would tell him. True, Isobail was greedy and aggressive at times, but she would never dare to betray him and her rank. He was a prince, one day to become a king; he was confident that his vassals would remain loyal while he was ill. All knew that to oppose him was the same as opposing King Bardwyn of Cambria. No one would dare such a fatal offense! Alysa was young and did not understand certain matters, he decided; wicked bandits always preyed on villages. In the morning he would discuss his daughter's worries with his wife.

* * *

Earnon, the advisor to Princess Isobail, paced his chambers apprehensively. He could not dismiss the feeling that something was gravely wrong this night. His black eyes stared into the candlelight as he tried to visualize what was troubling him, but no image would take shape. He inhaled deeply, then shuddered. The air around him flowed with eerie forces, intimidating forces, powerful forces. He went to a cabinet and withdrew a silver bowl with strange symbols carved upon it. After filling it with a golden liquid, he mumbled an incantation, then blew upon its surface and watched the ripples carefully. Someone was becoming a threat to his mistress, and he had to discover who it was; too, he had to know why that threat included and alarmed him. Yet some unknown and perilous power seemed stronger than he tonight, and it prevented his answers.

Four

Princess Isobail closed her eyes and sighed peacefully as her servant Ceit began to brush her long hair for one hour, as was their nightly custom. Isobail was glad her hair was white blond, so that not a single silver strand could be spotted on her head. Of course, she was only forty-three, and hopefully it would be many years before age began to show itself on her. Thanks to special herbal creams, her body was soft and silky, as supple as a newborn leaf and as ivory as an airy summer cloud. Early in life she had learned to use her light blue eyes with beguiling skill to make herself appear innocent or bewitching; yes, she had used her enchanting beauty and provocative allure to get her way, while laughing at men who fell prey to her charms.

Isobail's thoughts floated dreamily. Her need to be a powerful ruler was inherent, an insatiable desire, the driving force of her existence. Why not? she mused, since her mind worked and her body flowed with the hungry blood of warrior queens. Her ancestor, Queen Boadicea of the kingdom of Iceni, which was now called Logris, was famed for her fierce battles with their Roman conquerors. If other rulers had been as loyal to their people and lands as Boadicea had been to hers, the Roman army would never have gained a foothold in Britain!

Her body tensed and her jaw grew taut as she reflected on her golden heritage, her lost heritage. How could brave and honorable kings, chieftains, and warriors allow children to be slain, lands to be stolen, villages to be plundered and burned, women to be raped or captured? Only Boadicea had resisted them, and had died for her valiant struggles and immense courage. If Iceni had not been stolen forcefully from Boadicea's bloodline, she, Isobail, would be its queen this very day. Soon, she vowed, she would have Iceni back, Iceni and all of Britain!

What did it matter if she had to sacrifice many lives to regain her rightful place? Isobail mused. Boadicea had slain over seventy thousand Romans, and had lost many of her faithful warriors in those legendary battles. How strange that her own life nearly matched Queen Boadicea's.

Isobail frowned as she recalled that when her first husband died, Caedmon Castle and her status had been taken from her by Prince Alric, just as all status had been stripped from Boadicea at the death of her husband, as if the King of Iceni had been the one ruling that kingdom instead of the clever and brave Boadicea. Fortunately, one of Boadicea's daughters had survived and escaped into Damnonia. Since that black defeat, from mother to daughter their fate had been retold from generation to generation, lest their royal blood and true heritage be forgotten.

The Romans had changed the name of Iceni to Logris, and all signs of Boadicea had been removed. Today, Logris was ruled by Vortigern—a foolish and unworthy king, Isobail thought with scorn. But not much longer, she vowed. The moment Vortigern was dead and Logris was in her control, she would return its rightful name: Iceni.

Long ago she had begun her plot to reclaim her heritage. At seventeen she had married the powerful overlord of Damnonia, only to have King Bardwyn send his son Prince Alric to rule it. Her husband became nothing more than a feudal lord who never accepted having another man rule his lands. Caedmon Ahern had been a fool, she decided, for he had provoked Alric continually, particularly by subtly insulting Princess Catriona. In private Caedmon had raged against the twist of fate that had taken his rank, and he had vowed never to "bend a knee to that Viking wench." Caedmon had done everything he could to make Alric appear the fool to himself and to others, but his ploys had failed miserably. Soon it had become clear to her that Caedmon was walking on slippery ground and would destroy her with himself if she allowed it.

At first Isobail had despised Alric Malvern for stealing the means she needed to set in motion her plan for Logris's conquest. Then she realized that Alric was the perfect answer to her problem. After meeting and spending time with the handsome and virile prince, she contrived a better scheme for victory: get rid of Lord Caedmon and Princess Catriona, then marry Damnonia's ruler, the future king of Cambria. With the power and possessions of Queen Isobail, she could then take over all of Britain.

Filled with revulsion for the aging and groping lord for whom she had no further use, Isobail disguised herself and purchased a potion that would render Caedmon impotent. Afterwards she had taken a secret lover to appease her carnal desires until she could rid herself of Caedmon and entrap Alric, for she wisely realized how odd the deaths of her husband and Alric's wife would appear if they occurred too closely together. But something unexpected interfered. . . .

Isobail found herself carrying a child and pluming swiftly! On discovering that incredible state, she had been terrified and confused, for there was no denying her condition. Yet it would have been impossible to convince anyone, certainly Lord Caedmon, of her nescience. She could only trust her loyal servant Ceit to help her. Since it had been too late to rid herself safely of the unborn child, her path had been clear: the death of Lord Caedmon, her husband, became vital to ensure the safety of herself and the child.

While time passed and she sought the right moment to end her peril by Caedmon's death, she recalled dreamy bouts of passionate lovemaking, but not the face or name of the man who had visited her for so many nights. The harder she tried to call forth his image, the hazier it became. She came to realize that a magical force must have been at work on her. One night a startling answer occurred to her: Baltair had been visiting their castle with Prince Alric during those mindless nights, and must have enchanted her to do his bidding! She had been ensnared.

Later, when she and Caedmon were together in the nearby forest, he had guessed she was with child. She had killed him then, plunging a knife into his heart, actually enjoying the rush of power that raced through her entire body as she witnessed his shock and pain. She placed the blame on a desperate poacher, whom she also murdered, after he stumbled onto the bloody scene at the perfect moment. Never did she forget the heady sensations that came with those first two slayings.

For a long time it appeared as if her plans would never come to pass. Alric had confiscated the Caedmon land grant and given it to Lord Orin, who placed the strategic stronghold in the care of his vassal, Sir Kelton. She had been taken to Malvern Castle to become a lady-in-waiting to Princess Catriona. She scoffed, nothing more than a lowly servant to conquerors, as with her ancestors the noble Icenians! But she bided her time until the right moment to strike down her second obstacle. When it came, she poisoned Catriona. Then she gradually took the dead princess's place in Alric's castle, life, and bed. One day, as with Caedmon, she would have no further use for Alric.

Ceit interrupted Isobail's reverie by massaging her mistress's forehead and warning, "My sweet princess, calm yourself or these lines will deepen to tiny rivulets. What troubles you?" she inquired gravely as she returned to the brushing of Isobail's hair.

Isobail forcefully relaxed the frown on her face. "My hatred of Baltair has simmered for twenty long years, dear Ceit. Soon I must be rid of him. If ever he confessed his shame of the past to Alric, all would be lost for me."

"He has kept his dark secret for all of these years; he would not reveal it now. Surely he convinced Prince Alric to bring you and his child here so he could be near his son and give him all he can. No doubt Baltair is the one who entreated Alric to make a knight of Moran. Baltair is kind and gentle; he would never blacken his only child's birth by claiming him."

"Men do horrible things in the name of honor, Ceit, especially when death nears their life's door," Isobail said coldly. "I must make certain he never exposes himself as Moran's father and my seducer. To do so would cast dangerous suspicion on me about Caedmon's death. Besides, Baltair interferes with my plans. He is a threat to me and my victory. His lips must be silenced forever. When morning comes, I will speak to Earnon on the matter."

Earnon, Isobail mused dreamily. How fortunate she had been to meet him years ago and to form a bond with him. While visiting Lord Daron's after her marriage to Alric, Earnon had spoken of Iceni to her. She had been astonished to learn Earnon was one of her countrymen, and a powerful sorcerer. She had brought

75

Earnon to the castle as her guest, and he had never left her side.

"If too many die too quickly or curiously, sweet mistress, the other lords will seek answers to such a riddle. Are your vassals totally trustworthy?" Ceit asked worriedly.

Isobail nodded. "Soon all lords will owe homage and fealty to me alone. Any who oppose me shall die. Boadicea's blood runs swiftly in my body, dear Ceit. I can be no less brave than she. I cannot rest until Iceni is mine, and I need Damnonia and Cambria to accomplish such a victory. All who get in my path will perish. Fret not, dear Ceit, my bands will obey me without question, for I chose them wisely and carefully."

"Moran will be coming home soon," Ceit said. "It is approaching time for his knighthood. Do you still plan to take Kelton Castle for him?"

"He loves the place where he was sired, and has served his years as a page and squire. That castle and land grant are his by right of birth. Alric was a fool to take them from me, and a bigger fool to trust me. Before Moran's return to my side, I will push Sir Kelton off the cliffs and into the sea."

Isobail ran her fingers through her straight hair, which rested near her firm buttocks. When her serving woman asked if she wished it braided, Isobail shook her head, loving the sensual feel of her silky mane against her bare arms. "I have planned slowly to prevent suspicion; now it is time to increase my pace."

Ceit helped Isobail out of her kirtle, and Isobail walked to her bed and lay down on her stomach for Ceit to massage her body with fragrant oils. "Alric is a weakling; that is why it was so easy to entrap him," she mused. "The gods blessed him only in looks and virility, and both are nearly gone. He dared to think me too stupid to run Caedmon Castle and lands, and dared to take them from me and give them to another, then to make me live as a handmaiden to his barbarian wife! Never did she allow me to travel with the court and enjoy the good times. I was left behind as some foul secret she was ashamed of. For eleven years I endured such shame, until I rid myself of that barbarian princess. I had to chase Alric and make him ill before he yielded to me. Even then I had to pretend I was carrying his child before he would wed me! His sins against me are large and numerous, dear Ceit, as you have witnessed over the years."

Ceit spread Isobail's hair on the bed beside the princess's head as she began to rub a musk-scented oil on the woman's back. Relaxing under the ministering hands of her adoring servant, Isobail murmured, "I could not survive without you, dear Ceit. You know all. I will let Alric suffer for his many deeds against us before I slay him, slowly and painfully. His only use to me is in obtaining Damnonia and Cambria, so I will keep him under my control until I no longer have need of him. Do not forget to add more herbs to his wine while he sleeps tonight."

"Is that wise, my sweet mistress? We have given him much lately. His life runs swiftly from his body, and he grows weaker each day. Perhaps a milder dose is best for a while," the servant suggested.

"I have much work to do in the next few days, and I need Alric out of my way. Soon I will lessen the herbs and allow him to regain a little strength. I will tend him myself and watch him grovel in gratitude." She laughed wickedly as she pictured her husband, her vengeful tool, lying in his bed in agony. "When I am Queen of all Britain, I shall give you servants of your own, dear Ceit. They will pamper you as you have done for me. We have worked a long time for our victory, and soon it shall be ours." Isobail began to stretch like a contented feline.

Guessing the princess's mood from Isobail's sighs and

squirms, Ceit asked, "Do you wish me to fetch Guinn for you tonight?"

Isobail uninhibitedly rolled to her back and flexed her nude body. As her hands teased over her bare flesh, she smiled and said wantonly, "Yes, dear Ceit, send him to me; I have a great need for Guinn tonight. And send Phelan to Trahern's to announce my imminent arrival."

Kyra, the daughter of Princess Isobail and Lord Caedmon, observed her mother's servant as Ceit knocked on Guinn's chamber door and whispered a message. As with each night for the last two weeks, Kyra studied the intriguing situation and decided her suspicion was correct: her mother was having an affair with the court bard. Seizing a dark cloak, she flung it over her head and shoulders to cover her white-blond hair and followed the two at a safe distance.

Concealing herself just around the corner from her mother's room, she watched the handsome man enter Isobail's chambers. She leaned against the wall to see how long the green-eyed man remained there. The door reopened and Ceit walked to her room across the hallway.

Kyra cautiously slipped to an indention in the stone wall nearby and hid behind a tapestry suspended over it. Hours passed, and Kyra's light blue eyes and slender body grew weary at her vigilance. She knew the bard was not relaxing her mother with soft music and sweet words, and tried to envision the scene in Isobail's bed. Surely the virile body of Guinn was giving her mother great pleasure for Isobail to take such a risk beneath Alric's nose!

Ever since the twenty-six-year-old entertainer had been hired, Kyra had desired him. How like her greedy mother to take him, as she did everything. Kyra often confessed to herself that she disliked Princess Isobail,

78

who had hardly been a mother to her over the years. Yet she begrudgingly admitted that her mother was dauntless when it came to winning her desires. Kyra had been spying on Isobail for years to learn the woman's secrets, her strengths and weaknesses. . . .

For twenty-one years Isobail had made her feel unwanted, lavishing her affection only on Moran. Sometimes Kyra hated her younger brother, too, hated him for taking more than his portion of Isobail. Maybe, Kyra speculated, Isobail was jealous of her, for she was nearly her mother's image, a younger and prettier image. No matter, it was wrong for a mother to treat a child as Isobail treated her. She vowed to one day find a way to hurt Isobail for those numerous wrongs.

The same was true for Princess Alysa, who treated her just as badly, as if she were of a lower class. That was no longer true, thanks to her mother's clever marriage to Prince Alric. She was a royal princess, even though Alysa was the heir to the Crown and Throne. Kyra wondered maliciously what would happen to the Crown and Throne if Alysa met with an untimely end. As long as Alric lived, Isobail would rule in his stead, no doubt the reason why her mother took such pains to keep the sickly ruler alive. Craving the power her mother wielded, Kyra often dreamed of snatching them from Isobail's grasp. If only Isobail did not have Earnon on her side. . . .

Ever since his arrival, everything had been going Isobail's way, including Prince Alric's curious illness. Soon, with Earnon at her side, Isobail would control all of Damnonia. Kyra realized her decision to spy on that intimidating man had been a smart one. With persistence, she could uncover all she needed to know, and then would make things go her way for a change.

Her mother's door opened and Guinn peeked in both directions before sneaking back to his own chamber.

Kyra smiled devilishly, as it would be dawn soon and the bard had lingered too long for innocent reasons.

Shortly after dawn Alysa mounted Calliope and took an invigorating ride, planning to return to the castle before the unknown warrior could arrive to speak with her father. Although Prince Alric saw few visitors these days, Alysa did not doubt that the stranger would be granted entry to her father's chamber. Many times last night she had awakened after dreaming of the young man, knowing she had to see him again. If only he could help save her father's land. She pushed aside memories of last night's painful scene with her father and her unsettling suspicions and gave her steed his head. As if physically joined, they raced joyfully toward the village ten miles northeast of the castle.

Her land was greatly diverse: sheltered valleys and rolling hills where cattle and sheep roamed; stone-walled or hedged areas which enclosed fields; towering cliffs and intimate coves where gray granite and dark serpentine rock yielded wild beauty; misty moors which called softly and fragrantly to lovers; fields of golden gorse which implied that the glorious sun was imprisoned within; castles where ivy-covered walls cloaked stone with lush green; jagged coasts which often lured boats into peril; peaceful streams and woods which beckoned to wildlife, moss, and lichen; and assorted estuaries where a river's current battled the ocean's tide. Her land was also one of numerous scents: delicate primrose, sweet narcissus, laughing daffodils, gay fuchsia, and many more.

Today the sky foretold a beautiful day, and her surroundings were peaceful. Enjoying his mistress's exhilaration, Calliope increased his stirring pace, galloping blithely through the flower-filled meadow. Alysa savored the feel of the fresh air rushing through her hair and over her skin as the fragrances of a new morn delighted her nose. Nearing the treeline between the castle and village, she tugged gently on Calliope's reins to halt him, quickly dismounted, then allowed him to walk to cool his warm body.

Noises suddenly filled her ears, which caused her blood to run cold: a dawn attack on the village, a brazen one so close to Malvern Castle. She tied Calliope's reins to a bush and commanded him to stay quiet while she slipped from tree to tree to get a view of the daring raid. She hoped to espy the raiders and expose their identities to the castle knights.

Gingerly she made her way forward, but remained hidden from view. Clad in her green garments, she knew she could blend into the forest and go unseen unless one of the raiders came in her direction. She lay on the damp earth and carefully pushed aside the underbrush. The sight that greeted her repulsed her: dead peasants lay here and there, thatched roofs were aflame on several huts, children were crying and screaming, animals were racing about wildly in terror, women were being raped or captured, and raiders were laughing as they delighted in their destruction. Quickly she covered her mouth to suppress a scream. Her eyes enlarged as they helplessly witnessed the cruelty before them, and she realized she had to ride for help.

Without warning she was flipped to her back and imprisoned beneath a strong masculine body. Her mouth was covered by a large hand, preventing a shriek of surprise or a scream for help. She struggled frantically until a familiar voice whispered in her ear, "Lie still and quiet, m'lady, or we will be seen."

Alysa's eyes gaped into the face of the man who had filled her dreams all night, Gavin Hawk. His dark blond hair was tousled and damp, and forest trash peeked from its locks in several places. His green eyes were gentle, and her fear vanished.

Gavin leaned forward and whispered, "There is nothing we can do to help them, m'lady. If we try, we will join their fates. When the raiders leave, I will enter your village to tend those injured while you ride to the castle for help."

The girl's unexpected appearance had changed Gavin's plans, which had been to follow the raiders to their camp. He assumed this was her village and that she had been spared its brutal fate because she had been walking in the forest, perhaps to gather wood or herbs. He could not leave her alone, fearing she would endanger herself by racing to her people's aid. But he wanted not just to protect her, but hold her, kiss her, make love to her, savor her. Never had he been obsessed by a woman, but he had been unable to get her out of his mind since meeting her. She had filled his dreams all night, and they had been wonderful dreams which he craved in reality. She was so consuming that he had trouble keeping his mind on the danger nearby, and found his distraction upsetting.

Alysa grimaced in anguish as more screams reached them. Gavin's embrace tightened comfortingly around her and he hid her face against his chest. "I am sorry, m'lady, but I am helpless alone," he murmured against her fragrant hair. When she looked up at him with misty sea-blue eyes, he bent forward to kiss away her tears.

Witnessing the bloody raid so soon after her tormenting confrontation with her father, Alysa began to weep softly from the pent-up distress. The warrior hugged her more tightly against his strong body, and she welcomed his compassion. Her arms slipped around his waist and she pressed herself against him. His lips pressed light and comforting kisses over her face, until their lips touched and fused as if by chance, and by design. Hungrily and almost desperately their mouths locked, demanding, seeking, taking, and yielding.

The damp coolness of the ground did nothing to steal the heat building rapidly within Alysa's body and spreading excessive warmth to Gavin's. She tingled and trembled, and Gavin did the same. Greedily they feasted on each other's mouths and clung to each other, as if fearing to halt this wild madness. Lost in the splendor of unleashed passion, their kisses became more urgent and demanding, their caresses bolder. Neither thought about the consequences of their behavior nor recalled they were strangers. Just as neither knew nor cared why the other had this stimulating effect, each merely accepted it and savored it as the perils beyond them lessened.

Surprisingly, it was as if both heads cleared at once, and they ceased their wanton actions. Even so, neither seemed embarrassed by their loss of restraint. They stared into each other's smoldering gazes, gazes that said, "I want you and I need you, and it is sheer torment not to have you." They were breathless and flushed, and their arms refused to release each other. Parted lips silently begged to be reunited. With desire blazing dangerously between them, their inflamed bodies yearned to complete the wild journey they had begun. Longing filled both, as did the knowledge that this was not the time or place to continue exploring such irresistible feelings. Yet neither spoke nor moved again, until the loud shouting of merciless raiders and the pounding of retreating hooves filled their ears and broke the magical spell that had enthralled them.

"Go, m'lady, and return with help quickly," he ordered in a husky voice. "I will see to your people," he promised.

Gavin stood, then pulled Alysa to her feet. For the first time she noticed how differently he was dressed this morning. He was wearing a dark green tunic which ended just above his knees, under which were green trousers which were tucked inside ankle-high boots. A multicolored band edged the neckline, short sleeves, waist, and hem of his garment. Resting over his hips was a wide leather belt which held two weapons: a large knife, and a sword in artistically carved sheaths. A matching cloak had been tossed aside when he had found her.

Absently she straightened her own simple garment and studied him. "You may have saved my life, Gavin, and I will be grateful forever. Do what you can for them. I will hurry." Alysa turned and ran into the forest. She knew he was a brave man, not a foolish one. It would have been certain death for him to ride into the village and challenge so many raiders. How strange to be so close to death and destruction yet feel so safe. But now, she told herself, she must concentrate on seeking help.

Gavin rubbed his rough jawline in thoughtful silence. He had missed his chance to follow the band and discover its location and size, unless he could track them later; which he doubted, if they were smart. He gathered his cloak, threw it around his shoulders, and fastened it. Glancing toward the ravaged village, his green gaze narrowed and his forehead wrinkled in fury as it observed the wanton slaughter. There was only one reason to be happy this morning: he had found that bewitching girl again. Suddenly he realized he still did not know her name!

Alysa hurriedly mounted Calliope and spurred him into a swift gallop toward the castle. She was amazed to see knights rapidly heading in her direction, and before them were riding Isobail and Phelan, Captain of the Guard. She kneed Calliope to speed to join them, yet instinctively sensed they were heading for the village. Evidently one of the peasants had reached the castle and summoned help.

Isobail halted the knights when they reached Alysa. She eyed the breathless young princess oddly. "What are you doing out this early, Alysa?" she demanded angrily "Dangers abound everywhere."

Alysa promptly explained her morning ride and the trouble in the village. "I was coming for help," she finished, annoyed with herself for feeling cowed by the haughty regent.

"We know there is an attack on the village. You delay our help. Return to the castle."

Alysa flushed, and bristled at the woman's behavior toward her in front of the knights. Isobail had no right to speak to her or to treat her so badly! "I will return with you," Alysa replied. "Many are wounded and will need help."

"What help can a young girl be to them?" Isobail scoffed. "Do as I command. I am the ruler, not you. Teague," she called, "escort Princess Alysa home safely. A bloody village is no place for a child."

Alysa watched in astonishment as Isobail rode off with her band of knights, leaving her with Teague, Lord Orin's son. Alysa twisted in her saddle and watched the riders until they vanished, her teeth clenched as her mind filled with outrage. She wanted to defy Isobail's orders, but if she disobeyed, it would give Isobail the authority to punish her. And after last night, she knew her father would not object. To him, Isobail was perfect; she was his eyes, ears, and hands while he was ill.

She was furious because she knew she could be of help to those unfortunate people, people whom she would rule one day; and because she would not get to see the warrior again. She sighed heavily and turned to meet Teague's sympathetic gaze. "Sometimes—" she began, then stopped. It was not proper to malign her stepparent before others, even a friend.

The red-haired twenty-year-old squire smiled and remarked, "I understand, Princess Alysa. Do not distress yourself. She is right, perhaps there is still danger in the village. You must be protected; you will be our ruler one day."

"If such is true, Teague, then why is it safe for our present ruler to confront such peril?" she reasoned. "I am no weakling, and I know how to fight. Piaras taught me. How did she know about the attack?"

Teague's blue eyes exposed his skepticism as he said, "Earnon had a dream. He awoke the princess and warned her. She summoned the guard, and we were on our way to learn if Earnon's premonition was right. Was the raid a bad one?"

"It was terrible. They killed and burned as if it were fun, Teague. They laughed and joked while cutting the life from innocent, unarmed men. I could not believe such horror. They must be punished. Surely someone can learn where they hide and why they are doing such wicked things."

"They are black-hearted brigands, Your Highness; they need no other reason but their greed and wickedness."

"But they raid so boldly, Teague, as if it were a game. Something terrible is amiss in our land. These raids are clever and well-planned, then they vanish like mist until the next one. I fear a sinister mind is behind them."

Teague eyed the young princess and mused on her words. His father had voiced that same opinion the last time he went home. "Even if such is true, Your Highness, we will find a way to defeat them."

"How so, Teague, when Earnon sees only what and when he wishes to see?" she asked pointedly. "I do not trust him," she added bluntly. "The same is true of Sheriff Trahern. How can it be that no raider has been captured and no stolen possession recovered? It seems as if our side is being misled intentionally. Someone must be helping the raiders and hiding them."

"You must not say such things aloud, Your Highness," he warned. "Many claim Earnon has ears in the wind and eyes in the sky. If his powers are true, he could harm you for such insults and charges."

"I am not afraid of Earnon, or Isobail," she said, her anger simmering. "But I will be careful. Come, we will ride for home. Perhaps you can sneak a visit with Thisbe before Isobail returns. No doubt Isobail would delight in marrying the two of you off to others if she learned of your love."

Teague's cheeks grew rosy at the mention of Sir Piaras's daughter. He had loved Thisbe for a long time and eagerly awaited the day he was knighted so he could ask for her hand in marriage from Prince Alric. He grinned and nodded approval.

Together they returned to the castle, and Alysa tried to see her father again, to learn if he was better this morning. Today a guard and a servant were positioned near Alric's chambers, and she was refused admittance by Isobail's orders. Alysa implored them to allow her to see him, then demanded a visit: all were denied. She fumed at this added outrage by her stepmother, but returned to her chamber to plan another course of action.

In the village Princess Isobail took all of the credit for riding to the aid of "her subjects," even by placing her life in peril by doing so personally. She ordered her men to do whatever they could to assist the wounded and distraught peasants, and she vowed to capture and slay those responsible. She tended the injured and soothed the anxious. She sent part of her band in pursuit of the raiders who had carried off several of the women, told the people she would send them food and supplies from the castle's stores, promised that castle workers would come to the village to help build new huts or repair those damaged.

The simple folk were filled with gratitude for the devious woman who remained in the village until her band returned with the weeping captives, who said they had been cast aside as the raiders fled Isobail's knights. Over and over she was thanked and praised, and her hands kissed by her subjects who were duped by her pretense. Not once was Prince Alric mentioned, as if he did not exist. . . .

Isobail sat upon her prized mare and shouted to the peasants who surrounded her, "Do not worry, my people; I will not allow my knights to rest until the guilty hang from the gates of my castle. I will allow you to judge their black deeds and to place the ropes around their necks. Then I will give you their bodies to burn."

The villagers were fooled completely by the clever woman. The air was filled with praises for Princess Isobail as she smiled and waved to the peasants before riding off with a few of her men. The others were left behind to carry out Isobail's promises. Soon, she vowed, she would own the people's fealty and obedience; they would consider her their ruler, and be glad she was!

Returning to the castle, Isobail closeted herself with Earnon before Alysa could speak to her about the guard against her at Alric's door. Alysa walked to the gatehouse to see what she could learn about the attack, and was surprised that Gavin had not returned to the castle with Princess Isobail and the knights.

Beag, a dark-skinned knight with brown eyes and hair, was relating the episode to Piaras. He did not halt when Alysa appeared. She was stunned by Isobail's glory-snatching ways, and suspicious of how the woman took advantage of the incident. When Beag finished, Alysa asked, "Who was the stranger who helped?"

Sir Beag looked confused, then shrugged his shoulders. "I saw no stranger there, Your Highness, only peasants." When Alysa said she saw one earlier, the fabled knight said, "Perhaps he was one of the raiders.

He was not there when we arrived, and no one mentioned a strange warrior. Shall I ask about him?"

Alysa was mystified. Numerous questions tumbled over and over within her mind. Where had Gavin gone? If he had entered the village as promised, no one could have missed a stranger with his exceptional looks and build. Why would he vanish as mysteriously as he appeared? Who was he? Why was he here? How odd . . .

"Your Highness, do you wish me to return to the village and search for him?" Beag asked. "If he is one of the raiders, he can lead us to the others if we can capture him and force the information from him. Once bound to the rack, he could not hold silent."

"Surely I was mistaken, Sir Beag. I was distraught by what I witnessed. He was not dressed as a warrior or raider; he must have been a peasant."

Alysa did not know why she lied to them, especially to Piaras, but something kept her from betraying Gavin. She needed to know why he had not come to the castle to see her father, and why he had not been in the village when the others arrived. If he had friends with him, as he had told her, why was he always alone? Alysa called his image to mind. He looked and behaved so gently, too gently to be evil. His eyes pulled her to him, and his manner tempted her as the flower did to the bee. She could not envision him robbing, beating, or raping anyone. But when they met again, she would demand answers.

Five

Alysa completed her bath and dressed in a soft kirtle of blue, then drew on a knee-length tunic of white with blue borders. She sat patiently while Thisbe brushed and braided her hair and used the brown plait to encircle her head. She wore no jewelry and omitted her circlet of gold, which sometimes antagonized Isobail with its meaning. Sitting in a wooden chair, she gazed off dreamily as her handmaiden slipped on her sandals and laced them snugly over slender ankles.

"Your mind drifts as far away as the clouds, mistress. What land and dream do you seek?" Thisbe teased merrily.

"One such as you have found with Teague, little Thisbe," Alysa retorted playfully to the petite girl of her own age. She wanted to speak of anything except the nightmarish scene she had witnessed earlier. Too, Gavin was very much on her mind.

"Why must you seek what can be yours for the taking? Any nobleman of the land would give his life to capture your eye and heart."

"What if my eye and heart are set on a warrior whose land and ways I do not know?" Alysa replied unthinkingly. She laughed as if she were joking, unaware of the gleam that brightened her blue eyes.

Thisbe was delighted and intrigued by her mistress's mood, a rare one for the beautiful princess. She knew that Alysa was aware of her beauty, for men frequently pointed it out to her with their looks, remarks, and pursuits. Yet the gentle princess had never been known to use it unfairly. "Where did you meet this irresistible stranger?" Thisbe inquired.

"What stranger?" Alysa asked. She was almost afraid to talk about Gavin, as if doing so would make him become a dream instead of a reality.

Thisbe was not fooled. "The lucky man who causes your cheeks to burn and your eyes to glow," she pressed. "I have not seen such a look upon you before. Who is he?"

Alysa sighed deeply. She had never been able to conceal anything from her astute servant, and in fact, she wanted to share her thoughts about Gavin. "I do not know, dear Thisbe. I met him while riding one day, but no one has seen him save me. Perhaps he is only in my dreams, for he fills them each hour. He stirs me so strangely, Thisbe, yet I know little about him."

"When you met, did he not speak his name and land?"

"His name is Gavin and he said his home was in the kingdom of Strathclyde in the north. He is a man such as I have never known before, a warrior who hires out as a paid fighter to any ruler who needs him. He only seeks adventures and glory and money in our land. He told me that word of our troubles had lured him here to help us, if Father will hire him and his band."

"You do not sound as if you believe his claims."

"I am unsure, Thisbe. There is a mystery around him. He comes and goes like the mist, and never leaves a trace. If the words he shared with me were true, why has he not visited the castle to speak with Father, or even Isobail?" Then Alysa unexpectedly asked, "What is it like to love and desire a man?" When Thisbe recovered from her surprise, Alysa laughed softly. "Do not tease me, little Thisbe, or I shall punish you."

The handmaiden laughed at the playful threat. "Love is when thoughts of but one man fill your heart, when he means more than life to you, when you know you would do anything for him and shall die if he is taken from you. Desire is when you ache to see him and touch him, when he causes your body to burn and tremble. Desire does not demand love before it can ensnare you, but desire with love creates a powerful bond."

As Alysa mused on those words, Thisbe asked, "Do you love him and desire him? Do you wish him at your side and in your bed forever?"

Alysa swallowed the lump in her throat. "Even though he is a stranger, the bond you speak of exists for me. Each hour it grows stronger and tighter, and that troubles me. When he is near, I feel as a snared rabbit, yet I have no wish or the strength to escape him. Gavin has stolen my heart and wits. I hunger to learn all about him. When I think of him, I yearn to be in his arms. When I am with him, my mind flees and he controls my will. Pain fills me to know it cannot be. I am not as you, dear Thisbe. I am a princess, a future ruler; I cannot marry whom I choose, unless his rank and ways match mine. Nothing can change who and what I am and must be."

"Does the Crown mean more to you than he does?" Thisbe asked gravely. "More than love and happiness? Can a circle of gold warm your heart and soul? Can it stir your body to blazing life? Do not choose the Crown over love until you are certain you can live without him. If it is so hard to say 'it cannot be,' think how much harder it will be to endure his loss forever."

Alysa winced at her words. "You are wise and clever, Thisbe, but how can I learn such things? Life has been different for you. I have not been free to explore these matters."

"Test your feelings for this Gavin as men test their mettle in the games and upon the battlefield. Be brave and cunning. Find your path to victory. Do you wish to marry a man not of your choosing? What if you cannot love him or desire him? Can you lie in his bed and allow his will with your body, as is his right? Can you bear his children?"

"How do I test my feelings for Gavin? What if his are not the same?"

"Spend time with him. Your heart and head will give you the answers you need."

"But I know nothing of him. Is it not wrong for me to chase a man like him?"

"Why must a man always be the hunter and a woman the prey? I desired Teague, so I made certain he knew of my feelings and I worked hard to make his match mine. You must seek him out and cease this battle within you. He cannot read what is inside your heart; you must reveal your feelings to him. Only then can you discover if his feelings match yours."

Alysa trusted Thisbe, as they had been close friends since childhood and had shared many secrets over the years. She believed nothing and no one could persuade Thisbe to betray her, no matter the price involved, just as Alysa knew she would do the same for Thisbe. Now, she related how she had met the stranger and what had taken place between them.

"From your words, he is also drawn to you," Thisbe said afterwards. "Even if you choose the Crown over him, he will live in your heart forever, and his loss will cause you misery. Your father did not love and marry a woman of his lands and rank. Why must it be different for you?"

"You know how terribly my father and mother suffered for their choice, for I have told you of such unhappy times," Alysa replied. "I do not wish such pain to fill my life. Besides, there is so much evil threatening my land that I have no right to think of myself first. My father is gravely ill. If he died, my duty should come before my wishes."

"Does that not tell you that you need a strong arm and love at your side? Perhaps he will prove himself more than worthy to have you."

"We talk and I worry over a day that might never come. What if he is one of the raiders? What if he is deceiving me? What if he only desires me but does not love me? Or seeks the Crown through me? How can I trust a stranger?"

"You are a good judge of people, mistress. He would not stir you so if he were wicked. Perhaps he fears a princess cannot be won by a common warrior. Will you reject him when he comes to visit you?"

Alysa's eyes widened as she recalled Gavin's words near the village, and she realized he knew nothing about her. "He cannot. He does not know where to find me. I have not told him my name or rank. Each time we met, I was dressed as a peasant."

Thisbe smiled victoriously. "Then he desires you for yourself and does not know he reaches for one far above him. Do not reveal yourself until his testing is done."

"But that is dishonest. What is your meaning?"

"In your position, dear mistress, it is the only way to learn the truth. If he is wicked, he will reveal secrets to a peasant girl before doing so to the Princess of Damnonia. Be as mysterious as he is. You say he is a warrior who craves adventures. Intrigue him, and entice him to desire you beyond reason. Seek to know him fully. Afterwards, perhaps he will lose his great appeal. A man often dons a pretty face and charming manner to snare a tempting woman. But if his words are false, his allure fades with time, and you are left wiser about men and life than before. What harm and danger can there be in such learning?"

"I will think on your words. For now, I must speak

94

with Isobail and demand to see my father. I must make him hear me. Father does not realize how grave matters are. I think Isobail keeps the truth from him, just as she keeps us apart."

It did not take Alysa long to discover that during her bath Isobail had taken her retinue and left the castle for ten days. Ecstatic, she rushed to see her father, but the guard still refused to allow her to enter. This time he told her it was under both Alric's and Isobail's orders, and nothing convinced the man to obey her instead.

To avoid everyone until her temper cooled, Alysa went to the Great Hall, which was empty this time of day, and paced its length. Her soft leather steps were muted on the stone floors, and the immense room appeared to swallow her. She trembled from a damp chill which was unusual for this time of year. Without a cheery fire in the oversized hearths, and servants busying themselves with their tasks, the Great Hall was gloomy and forbidding.

Only two windows had been opened to allow sunshine and fresh air to enter, while all others remained covered by heavy tapestries which could be pulled up by cords to bare them. No candle was lit, and no hound was there to follow her or to beg a morsel from her hand. She glanced at the minstrel's gallery around three sides of the hall, and realized how much lovely music enlivened the huge room which was deathly silent at this moment.

At one end of the Great Hall, on a raised dais, were located two ornately carved throne chairs for Prince Alric and Princess Isobail. They were situated well above floor level to emphasize the rulers' rank over their subjects. The construction was Isobail's idea after her marriage to Prince Alric. No items of beauty decorated the dark tables and chests surrounding the royal chairs, as if Isobail thought barrenness would intimidate nervous guests, as it did.

Alysa could imagine Isobail binding her enemies to the towering pillars that supported the roof and torturing them, for she had witnessed the woman punishing unlucky servants in such a manner. Alysa wondered why they did not all hate her, but knew they could not try to run away, which would have been their most pronounced expression of hatred. Servants and peasants were not free to leave any place without permission, and could not find work in other territories. Even if a servant or peasant did not worry about punishment falling on the heads of his family—as a man's kin was as liable for his deeds as he was, each servant knew that his lot in life would be worse if he left home without his ruler's approval. The few who had tried in recent years were captured and flogged, and sometimes lost an ear or a tongue or a hand, which put an end to the attempts to escape. Alysa recalled that her mother had always been kind to the servants, and that they had loved Catriona. She suspected, from the not entirely hidden expressions in the castle, that it was not so with Isobail. When her father got well, she thought, surely he would not permit Isobail's ill treatment of his servants to continue.

Alysa's gaze drifted around the hall, and she was repulsed by the numerous heads of animals mounted all around her, more and more of them each year. What was Isobail's obvious fascination and love for death? she wondered. Yes, the Great Hall was no longer warm and inviting and lovely as it had been long ago.

Alysa leaned against one of the pillars and nibbled on her lower lip. She had to figure out a way to get to her father and to reason with him. Somehow, life in Malvern Castle and in Damnonia had—

"Do not fret so, Alysa, the raiders cannot attack

here," Kyra teased as she entered the enormous hall. "No doubt they are reckless Jutes who are ruled by a blood lust. Soon Mother's forces will have them fleeing to safety in Logris. You look so unhappy. Did the attack on the village frighten you?" Kyra wished she had been here. Surely it was exciting to see a bloody life-and-death struggle. She could imagine how blood-stirring such actions must have been.

Alysa's gaze slipped over the blue-eyed blonde who was grinning mischievously at her. At twenty-one Kyra Ahern was an exceptional beauty, something the vain girl knew too well. Alysa looked forward to her stepsister's marriage and departure from the castle, when and if the girl ever decided to marry. So far the older girl had eluded marriage.

The two girls had never gotten along, so Alysa had stopped trying to make peace a long time ago. She felt that Kyra was too much like her mother: untrustworthy, mean, greedy, and selfish. "Your mother refuses to allow me to visit my father. Why does she do such a vicious thing?" Alysa demanded of her stepsister, wishing it was the offensive Isobail who stood before her.

"You are a stupid girl, Alysa," Kyra scoffed, provoked by Alysa's tone.

"When I am your ruler, Kyra, perhaps you will not speak so boldly to me," Alysa stated in warning, weary of Kyra's antagonism. Today in particular she was in no mood to verbally battle her.

Tired and edgy from her long vigil last night, Kyra had not meant to remind Alysa of their hostility by speaking so hatefully to her. Presently it was Kyra's intent to mislead Alysa with friendship, something she kept forgetting these days since it was annoying to play this part. How else could she protect herself if, or when, her mother's black deeds were unmasked? Someone as reckless as her mother always made a slip and was exposed, she thought, as with Isobail's careless love affair with Guinn. Besides, the sickly prince could die, and Alysa could become her ruler any day now. If she wanted to remain in the castle and retain her current rank, she had better be careful of her attitude toward Alysa. "I beg your pardon, dear sister. I fear I did not sleep well last night, and I am moody this morning. I meant to say, you are foolish for not guessing the truth."

"What do you mean?"

"Do you know nothing of a man's pride? Your father ordered my mother to keep you and everyone from him. He does not wish anyone to see how ill he is. Perhaps he will be well soon, for he has agreed to follow the advice of the healers. Do not worry."

"I cannot help but worry when he is so ill and our land is so overrun with trouble. It distresses me to do nothing to help."

"Mother is taking care of everything for Prince Alric until he is well. Has she done something to displease you?"

"What could possibly displease me about her actions?" Alysa asked slyly.

"Sometimes Mother can be too stern and demanding. She forgets others have feelings, and she tramples them. She feels that if she does not gain the people's loyalty, all could be lost while your father ails. Each day she carries out your father's commands until the Prince is strong enough to give them himself. Even now, at his request, she rides to study the people's problems for him. Surely you do not wish to take her place and rule for your father? It is a great responsibility. Why do you not spend time at her side to learn all you can before your day comes to rule? How could she object? You are Alric's daughter, heir to the Crown. I admit that she does have strange ways at times, but you can learn much from her. Surely you can see how very smart she is."

"Why do you speak such words this morning?" Alysa

asked. Her senses were on full alert to uncover Kyra's motive.

"We have fought too long because I was jealous of your rank. I feared you would never accept me as your sister. When we were children, Alysa, it was natural for us to quarrel. I was angry when you played with Thisbe instead of me. You two were always together, laughing and having fun, always leaving me alone. You made it appear as if a vassal's daughter was more important and better than Lord Caedmon's daughter. None of the other children would play with me if they could play with you. You do not realize how difficult it has been for me to live in the shadow of one as beautiful and highly prized as you are. Many times I vexed you just for spite or to make you notice me and include me. I realize how badly I behaved over the years because of my hurt feelings and injured pride. Now we are women, and it is wrong to continue our childish rivalry, which makes us appear foolish to others. I have recognized and confessed my guilt and meanness; surely that is enough to earn your forgiveness. Even if we cannot become friends, must we remain enemies? Please do not say yes," Kyra urged.

Alysa did not believe Kyra was being sincere, but she was intrigued by her words. "I have never wished to be your enemy, Kyra. A woman as beautiful and highborn as you has no reason to be jealous of another. I wanted us to live and behave as sisters, but you refused to allow us to get close. I have always believed you resented me and did not wish to be my sister or friend. Ever since Father called Sir Piaras here to be his trainer of knights after Mother's death, Thisbe has been my closest friend. You were away with Father and Isobail, and I was all alone. But even though Thisbe and I got along so well, I never thought she was better than you, or you better than her. Rank should never choose one's friends or sway one's feelings toward others. I did not know such things troubled and confused you." Alysa hoped she did not look as insincere as she felt by speaking such words. "There is much I did not understand, Kyra," she continued. "If I did things to hurt you, I did not mean to do so, and I ask your forgiveness. I desire peace as much as you do. Can it be that way for us?"

"If we work hard, it can," Kyra vowed.

Not taken in by her stepsister's obvious deceit, Alysa smiled and said, "Yes, we will both work hard on our friendship. I am sure peace between us will make our parents happy." An idea came to mind, one that might lure Gavin to the castle. "Perhaps when Isobail returns, she will allow us to have a large feast and invite all of our friends. We will show them we are good sisters, and all will be happy for us."

"It is a wonderful plan, Alysa. I will speak to her the moment she returns. Sir Calum is escorting me for a ride. Do you wish to join me? Mother asked me to check on the villagers once more."

Another of Isobail's tricks to ingratiate herself with my people, Alysa thought. There was no guessing what that woman was up to with her unexpected journey, but she would seek the reason. "I will go tomorrow if I am feeling better. I pray I am not coming down with the same gripans as Father, but my stomach rebels against me today."

"Go to bed and let Thisbe tend you closely, little sister. If you are better by morning, we will ride together then." Oddly, Kyra smiled brilliantly, embraced her, and left the castle.

Alysa dismissed the two crafty women from mind and headed for the kitchen to locate Leitis, to implore the head servant's secret help with her father. If there was a devious reason why her father was ill, she must discover it, and she realized that the trusted servant might be the one to help her.

She found Leitis giving orders to the other maids and

servants. As she waited for the woman to finish so they could speak privately, Alysa noticed how the head servant's auburn hair was changing gradually to gray. At forty-eight, Leitis was tall and stout, and possessed hazel eyes that sparkled with life. Sparkled more and more each day, Alysa mused, since Leitis and Piaras were drawing closer and closer. She could not help but wonder if those two subjects would marry soon. Both had been widowed for too many years, and both deserved love and happiness.

When the kind-hearted and efficient Leitis completed her task, she smiled at Alysa and approached her. The young princess asked if they could find a place away from others' ears to speak. Leitis guided Alysa to one of the storage rooms, then waited for the girl to explain what was troubling her.

Alysa paced the dim room before turning to meet Leitis's eyes. "I do not know where or how to begin, Leitis."

The older woman placed an arm around Alysa's shoulder and coaxed, "Tell me what is in your heart, my sweet child. Whatever you reveal, I will hold your words secret, and I will try to help you. Surely you are guilty of no terrible offense."

"This is no girlish matter. What I need to ask of you is dangerous. Perhaps you will think me daft."

Bubbly laughter spilled forth as Leitis affectionately embraced the princess. "Never could madness or deceit take root in this lovely head," she teased. Turning serious at Alysa's worried expression, Leitis said, "You can trust me with your life, my child. Do not fear to speak of things which torment you. It cannot be as bad as you think."

"It concerns my father, Leitis," Alysa hinted.

"What of Prince Alric, my child? Does he grow worse?"

Alysa spoke slowly. "I believe he may be ill because

101

. . . someone desires it to be so. I do not think hi[s] sickness is natural. Perhaps someone wishes Father con[-]fined to his bed and chambers."

Leitis looked aghast. "Who would—" Her mouth dropped open and her hazel eyes widened as she grasped Alysa's implication. "Why would she do such a wicked thing?" the woman asked, as if fearing to speak Isobail's name aloud. "Would she dare? It is certain death."

"Not unless she is caught."

Even though she had promised Giselde not to inter[-]fere with the evil plaguing Damnonia, Alysa knew it was her responsibility to set things right in her land once more. Alysa explained her suspicions that harmful herbs were being added to her father's food and drink, no doubt with the aid of Earnon and Ceit. If, during the ten days while Isobail was away from the castle, they could insure that only wholesome food passed his lips, he might begin to recover. Leitis agreed to oversee all food served to the prince. The two women hugged then parted, Leitis returning to the kitchen and her chores while Alysa headed for the stable.

Guinn, the handsome green-eyed blond, studied one retreating back then the other until both women van[-]ished. He suspected that something was afoot, and the guileful bard wished he had been close enough to hear their words; his fetching mistress would still be in[-]trigued by such a curious meeting.

Since meeting her, Guinn lived only to make Isobail happy. The regent was a demanding lover with many tastes and desires. Some people would call her wanton; to him, she was the most exciting and enslaving woman he had known. She was like a fever that caused him to burn with obsession for her, to burn fiercely and con[-]tinuously without being consumed. He would die if she ever cast him aside for another lover, or returned to Prince Alric's bed.

When she was away, he wrote passionate poems and songs for her, then whispered or sung them into her ear during lovemaking. He wanted and needed her desperately; yet he could never have her openly, for he was a simple bard and she was a princess. Perhaps he should go and sing to his gullible ruler, he mused. Who could tell what he might learn from a groggy-headed victim, an unsuspecting fool. . . .

Alysa mounted Calliope and rode toward the forest to see Giselde. Keeping her eyes and ears alert to any danger, she left the animal in his hiding place and hurried to the hut. Once inside, she argued with the old woman, who protested her dangerous return so soon after her last visit.

"Please, hear me first, Granmannie; then I will leave. I know how dangerous our area is these days. I was more than cautious today."

Quickly Alysa explained her suspicions about the village raid and her father's condition. She told Giselde what she and Leitis were doing to thwart Isobail and to help her father. "You must give me medicinal herbs, Granmannie," she concluded, "a potion to make Father strong and well again."

Giselde considered their predicament, then agreed. "I cannot promise my herbs will heal your father, since we are not certain he is being poisoned. And even so, there are many poisons. Without knowing which one is being used, it is hard to guess the right herb to defeat it. Surely Earnon must have many poisons. But if Leitis keeps the poison food from Alric, and you give him these herbs, perhaps he will get better before Isobail's return."

Alysa hugged the woman tightly and laughed with joy Giselde warned, "Do not smile yet, little one. I will give you the herbs only if you promise to do nothing more than help your father. Swear you will not provoke Isobail by spying on her."

"How can I spy on her when she will be gone from the castle? No doubt she is away duping the peasants and charming the lords. I swear, Leitis and I will be careful."

Giselde glared sternly at the young girl, then snorted. She went to her work bench and fetched herbs, tying them inside a clean cloth. Alysa knew she should tell Giselde about Gavin, but she did not want to upset the old woman further, and surely it would distress Granmannie to hear that she was chasing a strange man, and that she had been at the plundered village. To her, Giselde looked older and weaker each time she visited.

Giselde did not meet Alysa's gaze as she handed the neatly bound cloth to her and explained how to use the herbs. "One more promise, little one," Giselde pleaded. "No matter how much I love you and shall miss you, promise you will not risk coming here again soon."

"But, Granmannie, how can I tell you what I hear at—"

"There is no need, for others will watch and reveal all things to me. If Isobail and her men are not watching you now, they will be soon. By coming here, you will lead them to me. Need I tell you what Isobail would do to me, child?" she asked, using the only excuse she felt Alysa would accept.

"I would never do anything to hurt or endanger you, Granmannie," Alysa declared.

Giselde caressed the young woman's warm cheek. "If I need you or there is danger, I will send someone to you with this object." She opened her fist and revealed a ring with a dazzling light purple stone. "Whoever places this ring in your palm, come swiftly and without question with that person, be it woman or man. If anything happens to me, my precious child, the person who gives you this ring can be trusted as you would trust your mother or Granmannie, or the gods."

Alysa took the ring to study it closely and memorize its lines and features. "See the letters inside," the old woman pointed out to her. "Even if someone tries to fool you with a matching ring, no one knows of the message inside the band."

"What do the letters say, Granmannie? I do not recognize them."

"It says, 'I command Thor to protect my love forever.' They are Viking words. The ring was given to your grandmother by Rurik. It is to become yours on the day you marry."

Alysa held the precious ring tightly as she struggled not to weep from the intense emotions tugging fiercely at her heart and mind. The ring was very old and exquisite, and priceless to her. It was a tangible link to her past, a bond to her deceased grandparents. In a strained voice, she said, "I am glad you took this treasure with you when you left the castle. No doubt Isobail would have found it and taken it. When all is settled, you must come to live with me again at the castle, and you must tell me all there is to know about my grandmother and grandfather."

"Yea, when all is settled, I will live with you again, and I will leave nothing untold about your family and its history. We shall find such happiness and victory one day," Giselde murmured, then wiped at her damp eyes as if annoyed by the moisture that had gathered there unbidden. "Go now, little one, and keep your promises. Do not lose hope if the herbs fail to heal Alric. Perhaps his illness is true, or it requires more time for the poisons to leave his body."

Alysa handed the old woman the amethyst ring and embraced her. After kissing Giselde's cheek and hugging her once more, Alysa left.

Giselde slipped the ring on her finger and pressed

it to her dry lips. Tears rolled down her cheeks and dropped to her soil-stained kirtle. "Oh, Rurik, my Rurik, my only love, I would give my soul to the Evil One if he could steal you from Valhalla and return you to me. Hear me, my love, and speak to my heart. Tell me what I must do to win this battle. I can no longer decide what is right and what is wrong, for my love for Alysa and my need for vengeance sway me."

After watching the girl until her eyes could follow her no farther, Giselde went to her work area and covered the clay jar from which she had taken the herbal mixture. "Forgive me, my precious granddaughter, but I cannot allow Prince Alric to heal. I know my deceit will cause you to doubt Isobail's guilt, but it must be so. My herbs will thwart the poison that eats slowly at his body, but they will not rejuvenate him. As much as I hate Alric, I am sorry he must die at Isobail's hand, for his blood runs within you, and my daughter loved him. But if I helped him to get well during her absence, Isobail might be provoked to worse evil. I must protect Alysa and Prince Gavin. I cannot allow our discovery. Revenge must be mine for my murdered child." She removed the ring and locked it in the chest with her other possessions, knowing no thief would risk being cursed for robbing a witch.

To prevent leaving a trail to Giselde's hut, Alysa headed in the opposite direction from where Calliope awaited her. After a lengthy distance, she slowly began to make a wide half circle back toward the ravine. Coming to a stream, she removed her leather boots, lifted her skirttail, and stepped into the rushing water, thus concealing her tracks. It was not long before she ducked to pass under a broken limb, and nearly fell into Gavin's arms when her bare foot snagged between two rocks and caused her to stumble.

The handsome warrior chuckled as he eyed her with delight. His voice was mellow as he murmured, "So, we meet again, m'lady."

Alysa stared at him in surprise, and warmed with pleasure. His white teeth were revealed slightly by a playful smile, and his green eyes danced with mischief. His hair and body were wet, as if he had just finished a bath and donned his pants hurriedly. As if shyly concealing his naked flesh, she noticed that he was clutching a dark tunic to his golden chest. He seemed to read her mind, for he grinned, turned his back, and pulled it over his head, amusing her with his action.

When he faced her once more, his hands grasped her wrists and he murmured huskily, "I shall not release you this time until I learn your name and where you live. You are far too swift and cunning for even a trained warrior such as myself to catch you in this dense forest."

Alysa laughed and her eyes glowed. "I am called Thisbe and I live at Malvern Castle," she replied dreamily, pretending her words were true.

Their eyes locked, and tingles shot through them at their contact. Their surroundings and wits seemed to vanish as their bodies irresistibly moved closer.

Six

Within a few feet of them, a buck and three does bounded loudly across the stream and dashed into the trees on the other bank. At the startling intrusion, Alysa struggled to clear her head. Whatever was she doing? she asked herself, rolling about in the grass like a loose-thighed wanton. This was only the third time she had seen Gavin, and all three times she had fallen uncontrollably into his arms! Whether on love's or passion's wings, he had carried her to the heavens and soared wildly with her there. She seemed to crave him desperately. What was his mesmerizing effect, which overshadowed her upbringing and morals, stole her wits and willpower? Whatever power or charms he possessed, they were dangerously enticing!

Alysa scolded herself, *I am Princess Alysa Malvern, future ruler of this land; I cannot behave this way. I must restrain myself before it is too late and I have lost what should belong to my husband alone.*

If only Gavin's lips and hands were not so enticing, so insistent, so stimulating as they teased over her mouth and flesh. Knowing she must stop this behavior, she could not help but enjoy it for a few moments longer, until she realized her wits were spinning away from her again. Even as she pushed Gavin aside and breathlessly commanded, "No, we must not do this," she trembled at the flames of desire which raged within her body.

Gavin was intoxicated by desire for her too, but he read panic in her dark blue eyes. She looked as if she were imploring him to save her purity because she lacked the will to do so. Her eyes pleaded, "Help me! Be strong for me. Not today, not this soon . . ." His body ached to possess hers, and his ragged respiration was almost painful. He could not even imagine from where his control came, but it gradually strengthened, and cleared his head. If he had been a conquering warrior, or less of a man, he would have the brute strength and hunger to take what he wanted. But Prince Gavin Crisdean could never rape any woman, particularly this one.

The son of King Briac sensed how much she wanted him, but was afraid to yield to desire's calling. It was too soon; they were near strangers, and she was pure of heart and body. That realization thrilled him, as he wanted to be the man to teach her about lovemaking. She was a special prize, and it had been a long time since he had sated his desires within a woman, but he could wait to woo her and claim her gently "Have no fear, Thisbe; I will not harm you, even though my body burns with a curious fire only you kindle. Never has a woman so dazed my head and so easily stolen my control. I must watch you closely or you will be leading me by a yoke," he teased her.

Alysa's body rebelled at being denied its cravings, and her respiration seemed to refuse to slow to normal as her chest rose and fell rapidly. Her cheeks burned hotter at his suggestive words, and she timidly pulled her gaze from his. How could she not want him even more when he was being so gentle, so understanding, so patient and caring? If he were a wicked rogue, or she meant nothing to him, he would be angry and insistent on having her. Surely he realized how vulnerable she was to him and how easily he could entice her into submission. She was naive, but not ignorant; she had heard of the discomfort and vexation a man suffered after being highly aroused then denied appeasement. Obviously Gavin was a rare and wonderful man, and her heart throbbed with love and gratitude. Hoarsely she murmured, "I am sorry, Gavin; I did not mean to . . . I do not know what possessed me to behave so wickedly."

"Perhaps it is because I am as irresistible and enchanting to you as you are to me," he replied, then chuckled when her gaze flew up to his.

Alysa felt heat spread from her cheeks, down her neck, and onto her chest. Yet she did not look away from him this time. Boldly she replied, "It seems your words are true, my wandering warrior, else we would not be lying upon the ground together in the forest. Your strength lies not only in your body, but also in your mind and honor. It pleases me greatly to meet a man such as you; I feared they were as extinct as dragons, or as rare as truth these days."

Gavin stroked her fiery cheeks and silky skin as his leafy green eyes roamed her exquisite features. "You praise me highly, and I must do nothing to destroy such trust. I never wish to hurt you. I see desire in your eyes, and caresses which match mine; for now, that is enough for me. When you are ready to conquer the unknown, you will come to me. Only then will it be right for us to surrender to this potent force that draws us together. It is our fate to share such a unique passion, sweet Thisbe, else the gods would not keep throwing us together in such private and romantic spots as this one."

Gavin's wet hair caused its color to appear a darker blond, and she noticed how its drying edges curled mischievously in all directions. His damp tunic clung to his body. For an instant she wanted to rip it off to feel his bare skin against hers. She knew, if he pressed her . . .

"How did you learn and master such self-control during moments like this?" she asked seriously, lifting her hand to trace her fingers over his full lips.

Gavin laughed heartily. "I cannot answer, for it is a new trait of mine, one which you inspire, my fetching maiden. Since we met, I have been obsessed with having you for my own. Yet I know I cannot take you until . . ." He hesitated as he searched his mind for the answer. "It is strange, but I do not know the reason or words. I do know if we do not end our contact and speak of other things, I swear it will vanish. Why are you in the forest again today, and what is your rank at Malvern Castle?" he inquired as he pushed himself to a sitting position and helped her do the same.

As she straightened her clothes and finger combed her tangled hair, Alysa turned away, preventing Gavin from sighting her dismay at having to deceive him. Playing Thisbe gave her the freedom and ease to behave as she wished. If he discovered she was Prince Alric's daughter and heir, there was no guessing how that news would affect him and their budding relationship. She had to allow them time to get acquainted before she intimidated him with her rank. She had to make certain it was she that Gavin wanted, for the price of his love and acceptance would be enormous for her to pay.

"I am the handmaiden of Princess Alysa, and I live in the south tower near her. When I am not needed to attend her, she allows me to come and go as I wish. Here in the forest I find peace. I am free to say or do or be whatever pleases me. Since no one is allowed in the royal forest without permission, I have always been safe. Besides, my father and his friends taught me how to hunt and trap, and how to escape enemies. You see, my wandering warrior, I am an adventurer at heart, as you are in life. You are fortunate to be a man, and a powerful one at that, because you can choose your path and follow it. Even if I were not a servant bound to others, it would be dangerous for a vulnerable woman to seek out her dreams."

Gavin lifted a handful of brown hair and teased it beneath his nose as he inhaled its fragrance. Being the princess's servant explained what he had noticed only moments ago: her speech and manner. No doubt she had learned them from the ranking members of the royal court. "I have no doubt you can obtain any dream you desire. You are very brave and wise for one so young and beautiful. Are all of the castle knights so blind that not one has demanded you for his wife? I am astounded that Prince Alric has allowed you to remain unwed, as surely many men must battle amongst themselves over you. I beg you, sweet Thisbe, say no man woos you earnestly."

What would his father and people say if he brought this common servant to his castle and took her as his wife? he wondered. Could he make a servant the Queen of Cumbria? Being a servant in a castle was far different from ruling one. Whatever he decided later, this was not the time to consider such a wild idea. And if there could be no entwined future for them, he should not be enticing her falsely. Yet he wanted her desperately, as if he would be cursed if he could not have her.

Alysa observed the shadows clouding his eyes and creating a frown upon his face. For some reason he had drifted away from her and this place. To bring him back, she nudged his arm and replied, "Fret not, no man tempts me as you do, and no man has approached my father for my hand in betrothal. What of you, Gavin? Does no woman of any land await your return?"

Gavin realized he had spoken foolishly and too intimately. He had made it sound as if he were courting her or claiming her, and she was most agreeable. But he was in no position to make a commitment to her, or to any woman. For now, at least, he had to back away. The befuddled prince carelessly answered, "I have made no woman promises I cannot keep. My blood lusts for adventures and glory which cannot be sought by a wedded man. Until I have seen and done all I desire, I cannot think of settling down to a wife. If any woman awaits my return, she waits in vain. I can belong to no one until I have conquered my fate." Gavin hoped she would not be dismayed by his words, but it was necessary not to raise her expectations, not unless he claimed her as his own. He wondered and worried about being doomed to repeat his father's tragic mistake of falling in love with the wrong woman, and of being forced to sacrifice her for his duty.

Alysa reflected on his words and actions during their three meetings. There was contradiction within them, she thought. She hoped Thisbe was right about her being a good judge of people, for she intended to enlighten Gavin to his confusion. "You are wise and generous to be so truthful with your numerous conquests." She smiled radiantly and stroked his rough jawline as she added almost playfully, "But perhaps it would be kinder to them if you gave your warnings before they were enchanted by you. I am sure there are many maidens who await your return, even if they know it is futile. Is that why you halted our reckless behavior, to give me my warning? It was unnecessary, as I understand what a devilish rogue you are; that is why I find you so fascinating," she teased. Her blue eyes danced with coquetry as she grinned at him.

Gavin was baffled by her light-hearted manner. He did not like to be led around in feminine circles. He had assumed that she knew little about using girlish wiles on him, but now feared he had been mistaken about her. "I halted," he said, "because you had lost the will to reject me, even though you did not wish to surrender to me so soon. I am experienced in . . . such

113

areas, and I could tell you are unskilled and unlearned about such matters." He hoped she would concur with his implication. "It would be unfair to misguide you while your mind was dazed with unfamiliar emotions."

Was she so green that she did not enthrall him as he utterly enthralled her? Alysa wondered. Yes, she admitted, she was ignorant in some areas about sex and lovemaking, but she was not stupid. She knew how to kiss and embrace, and the other parts should come to her instinctively. Shouldn't they? she mused worriedly.

His words had stung, and she forgot she had provoked them. "You are most kind to protect my endangered honor," Alysa said tartly. "How shall I reward you? I have no coin with me. Perhaps if we meet again, I shall be prepared to repay your good deed." Her blue eyes glittered like colored ice, for he was denying her something she wanted fiercely: himself. He had made it seem as if he were available and enchanted; now he was telling her that he was not, that he only wanted to amuse himself with her until he moved on to his next adventure! How could he change so quickly? she fumed. As Thisbe had warned, she needed to see him in different situations before she could be sure of him.

Gavin stared at her, and she glared back. Their frosty looks fused and battled, but passion began to melt their icy resolves. Suddenly they both smiled then burst into merry laughter as they comprehended the ridiculous misunderstanding.

Gavin declared, "I desire you and you desire me, but this is unfamiliar ground for both of us and it must be traveled carefully. We are near strangers who must get to know each other. Yet we can make no promises to each other, as our lives do not match. Is it settled, my bewitching maiden, no more silly battles of words? For now, we do nothing more than learn about each other and this attraction. Agreed?"

Alysa watched him lift her hand and kiss the back of

it before turning it to kiss the palm. His eyes never left hers; thankfully, or he would have noticed she did not have the hands of a working servant. "Agreed," she murmured. "The sun moves swiftly and I must return to the castle; but first, why have you not come to see Prince Alric about being hired as a fighter for him? And why did you vanish from the village?"

He had already prepared an answer for her, one which should sound reasonable and smart, and held bits of honesty. "I am a warrior for hire, sweet Thisbe, but I am a careful one. I cannot walk blindly into a situation that reeks of mysteries. Battlelines, enemies, and rewards must be explored. Before I approach your ruler, I must travel your land and study it closely. No amount of treasure or glory is worth risking my life rashly. I must learn who needs help and how much, and why. No matter how good and brave I can fight, if Prince Alric's men cannot or will not do the same, I could be slain by their lack of skills. As for leaving the village, I thought it best. I am a stranger here, and in the confusion of the moment, I might have been mistaken for one of the raiders. Before I could reach Trojan and ride into the village, I heard the castle knights approaching. When I saw they could handle everything, I slipped away before I could be seen. By traveling around your land, your people will get to know me as a friend, and then it will be safe for me to ride openly. I am sure your prince would trust me more if I have already proven myself before we meet."

"As you journey through my land, beware of Princess Isobail's reach," Alysa said. "She is known to be greedy, even though she pretends otherwise." To test him, she casually added, "Some say she is the leader of the brigands and uses their raids for her own purposes."

"Can such things be true? What could be her motive? Tell me all you suspect of her," Gavin coaxed. This girl

115

was brave and smart, but would she spy on Isobail and Alric for him? Would it be too dangerous for her?

Alysa shifted nervously at his questions, and was anxious to leave before she revealed something. Even if he was not one of Isobail's men, later he might be tempted by the woman's beauty. To protect herself and others, she replied, "I know little, for Princess Isobail keeps to her tower or to herself at the castle. I hear wild talk, but I cannot say what is or is not true. I should not spread rumors which could be false. Besides, it is dangerous to speak against our land's regent. Perhaps you do not know: Prince Alric is very ill and remains confined to his chambers. It is Isobail who rules our land and people, and I fear for both under her control. I can say no more. If someone heard me, I would be whipped brutally. She has done this to others."

Gavin clenched his teeth as he vowed, "If she dared to harm you, I would crush her with my bare hands. Do and say nothing where she is concerned. I will discover the truth for myself during my travels."

Alysa smiled at his reply and concern for her safety. "Isobail left the castle this morning, and she is not to return for nearly two weeks. Be careful if you cross her path."

Plans filled Gavin's head; he had to follow and observe Isobail, but he hated to be so far away from this girl. "I must leave this area for a while. Each time you come to the forest, check this place for a message from me," he told her, pointing to a hole near the base of the tree nearby. "You will meet me again when I return, will you not?" he entreated.

"Yes, Gavin, I will await your message and meet you here again. And I will expect no promises from you. Nor must you expect or ask any from me. Is it agreed?" she demanded.

Gavin was intrigued and mystified, but he nodded. "If you have a message for me, I will look for it when

I return. Stay safe and well, my sweet Thisbe." His hand reached forward, clasped her neck, and pulled her head forward to seal their lips a final time.

At Giselde's hut Gavin related his plan to follow Isobail to observe her actions. He let the gray-haired woman know where he was camped, and where he would camp whenever he was in this area. Giselde told him about Earnon's alleged dream about the village attack, and both decided it was too strange to be true.

"I will return soon, Giselde," Gavin said. "Listen and watch well, but take no risks. We must be careful while we gather our proof. If something should happen to either of us, or I cannot get near your hut, where can we leave a secret message for the other?"

Giselde thought for a moment, then said, "I know a spot. I will walk a distance with you and show you."

Near the stagnant pond where she gathered certain plants, Giselde halted and knelt. Turning over a large rock near its edge, she said, "We can leave messages here in case of trouble."

Gavin agreed, and they talked a while longer. He mentioned he had met a girl named Thisbe near the village, who worked at the castle, and he wondered if the old woman knew her. Gavin had decided that perhaps it was the mystery surrounding Thisbe that intrigued him and kept the irresistible creature on his mind so much. Once he knew more about her, surely he could conquer this curious obsession for her.

Gavin's words surprised the old woman. If her binding spell had worked, the young prince should not be inflamed by any other woman, so Gavin's obvious interest in Alysa's servant caused Giselde to question her skills. Perhaps she had made a mistake during the incantation, or carelessly added the wrong item to her mixture. After Gavin left, she decided she would repeat the binding spell, sear the images of Gavin and Alysa into each other's mind until neither could think of nor desire another.

Giselde warned, "You must stay away from Thisbe. She is my granddaughter's handmaiden. Alysa is with her at most times, for they are close friends. If you are exposed, it could be dangerous for my granddaughter to be seen near you. Thisbe is sweet and lovely, but it would be foolish to have her gather information at the castle, if that is what you had in mind. We have no need of her help; I have spies at the castle, trusted knights named Piaras and Beag."

Giselde explained who the men were and how they were helping her. "Thisbe is Sir Piaras's daughter, but she does not know her father works secretly with me against our rulers. Besides, Thisbe's heart has been captured by Squire Teague, son of Lord Orin."

Gavin said, "I think not, Giselde, for her eyes lingered upon me too long for a woman in love with another."

Giselde frowned. "You are wrong about her, Prince Gavin. She is smitten with Squire Teague, and he with her. My granddaughter has spoken of their love many times, for Thisbe confides in her. They wait for Squire Teague to be knighted soon, then they will request to marry. Until Prince Alric gets well, they closely guard their feelings for fear Isobail will bind them in marriage to others. Trust me, Prince Gavin, for I know my words are true."

Gavin did not like what he was hearing, thinking, or feeling. He could not help but suspect that if Giselde was right, Thisbe was not whom she had appeared to be. He recalled the strange words she had spoken to him at their first parting: "You are my enemy, sir, for I have seen you in my dream. . . . I will make certain you are slain." He had not asked her about her meaning. Perhaps she saw her attraction to him as a threat

118

to her wedding a knight who would one day become a lord, quite a catch for a servant.

Giselde felt there were certain things she should keep secret from Gavin, and so she said nothing about Alysa's suspicions of Alric's poisoning and what Alysa was planning to do about it. Too, she did not want Gavin to know she had tricked Alysa to keep Alric disabled. She tugged his arm and coaxed, "Do not worry over such matters when there is so much work to do. Forget Thisbe; I tell you she is intent on another, and not suitable for a prince. You must choose your woman wisely, for you will be king one day."

Gavin shielded his warring emotions from Giselde. He smiled and nodded. "You are right. There are countless women from which to choose, with more rank and beauty than a common servant. I will return to your hut in two weeks or such." He made sure that his tone was convincing, but as he walked away, he plotted how he would gather the truth about Thisbe, the beautiful, seductive woman from the forest.

Soon after Gavin left her, Giselde gathered items for the binding spell, but added additional ingredients to make the potion stronger. "When next you sleep, you will each other's mind and inflame each other's passions; you will be entwined forever," she murmured, then smiled.

On her return to the castle, Alysa met with Leitis in the storeroom and gave her the herbs from Giselde. "Make certain Father gets only the food and drink you have prepared with these healing herbs. I will allow him to get better before I try to see him again. At present, his head is too woolly to hear me and understand his danger."

Leitis said, "Isobail's man, the servant who usually feeds Prince Alric, was called to his wife's side after she

119

gave birth to a son, so I was able to prepare and serve your father his noon meal myself. Tonight I will add these herbs to his soup and wine."

The women talked and planned while Leitis concealed the pouch, then went their separate ways.

Guinn watched the ailing Prince Alric intently as he sang for him. The ruler appeared better this evening. While Guinn sang, he inwardly fumed. Were he not afraid of discovery, he would take the pillow and smother his sickly rival.

Guinn did not think he could bear the loss of his lover which was sure to happen if Prince Alric were to recover and demand his wife's return to his sleeping chamber. But if he were to kill the prince, he knew he would be under immediate suspicion. Guinn forced himself to quiet his envy and dreamed about making love to Isobail while he played his lyre for the cuckolded prince. When he knew Alric was dozing peacefully, the bard slipped from the oppressive room. He rubbed his protesting stomach, and realized he had skipped the noon meal while composing a new lovesong for Isobail. He decided, as soon as he put away his lyre and bathed, to go to the kitchen to eat.

Leitis was frightened as she exchanged the dishes on Alric's tray while the servant fetched fresh bread from the bakery below the kitchen. With shaking hands she placed the ones the man had prepared on a corner table. After the servant left with the tray, she would discard them. The servant returned with the delicious smelling bread and took the tray to Prince Alric. To make certain the man could not add anything to the food, Leitis followed the servant and observed his actions closely. Since the guard was not on duty outside

120

the prince's chambers, she followed him into the outer room and watched the servant's movements until Alric was eating the food she herself had prepared. Quietly the stout woman returned to the kitchen, pleased with her cunning and delighted that Prince Alric had the strength to feed himself tonight.

"What are you doing?" Leitis asked the bard who was eagerly devouring the possibly tainted food. "Those are mine."

In a nasty mood, Guinn scowled, and snapped, "Fetch yourself others, old woman; I was starving."

There was nothing the servant could do except allow the sullen poet to eat his fill. Leitis realized one good thing about the accident: if Guinn took ill, that would tell her that Alysa's suspicions were right.

Alysa stripped off her garments and eagerly stepped into the tub of fragrant water prepared by Thisbe. She laughed softly as she recalled how Thisbe always teased her about taking too many baths for good health and propriety, but she loved taking a short one to awaken her body each morning, and she loved relaxing in a long one after a sweaty ride or a hard day. Alysa closed her eyes and bathed leisurely. How she wished Gavin did not have to travel now.

She bolted upright in the tub and wondered how she could slip away from the castle for a few days to follow him, to discover along with him what was happening in her land. But she would have to do so without exposing her identity. She thought of a few plans, and immediately dismissed them as implausible. Feeling frustrated, Alysa dried herself and slipped into a worn but soft gown. She eased between covers upon which she had placed fragrant drops of scent. With great effort she relaxed and succumbed to sleep. . . .

Alysa shifted in the large tub to allow room for Gavin

to join her. She sighed contentedly as he began to bathe her slowly and sensuously. She was lost in his green eyes and the tingly sensations that warmed her body at his touch. The scent of countless wildflowers filled her nostrils as she floated dreamily in the silky water and her trembling body responded eagerly to his tantalizing caresses.

Gavin bent forward and touched his lips to hers, and they shared a blazing moment of feverish passion. He pulled her across his lap while his mouth lavished attention on her face and neck and his hands roved her inviting flesh. His body ached for hers, yet he continued his leisurely love play.

Alysa stroked Gavin's sleek frame with gentle hands. Her fingers played in his bronze locks and she pressed her naked body to his. As if starving for him, she drew his head toward hers and feasted ravenously on his mouth.

Gavin lifted her from the tub and lay her on a bed of fragrant leaves. Sunlight filtered through the trees overhead and danced off the beads of water on their naked bodies. His smoldering gaze warmed and dried her flesh, and hers did the same for him. He joined her, and their hands and lips began to work lovingly and urgently on each other.

Gavin moved atop her, and her welcoming thighs invited him to possess her. Their eyes met and they smiled, then the dream faded in Alysa's mind in her castle bed . . . and in Gavin's mind on his sleeping mat in the forest not far away. . . .

Seven

On hearing the bard had taken violently ill during the night, Earnon, Isobail's sorcerer, went to Guinn's room to check on him. He asked the bard questions and examined him, and was alarmed by his findings. "What did you eat and drink, Guinn? When and where?" he asked. "And leave no morsel or drop untold," the sorcerer demanded sternly.

"Soup and wine in the kitchen last evening," the poet replied in writhing agony. "Leitis was angry with me for taking those she had prepared for herself and left on the table, but I told her to fetch herself others. I missed the noon meal, so I was ravenous and could not wait." Guinn cradled his raging belly and groaned in pain. His fair complexion waxed ashen and beads of sweat glistened on his face. "An hour or so after I ate, I was feeling terrible and wanted to go to bed, but his Highness commanded me to sing him to sleep. I obeyed, but my throat became dry and then felt encased in flames. The prince was feeling strong and he wanted more music and singing, even though I told him I was ill. When he was not looking, I sneaked a drink of the wine near his bed. Before the night was half gone, I was hot and cold, and my innards were screaming for release. Perhaps I went too near Prince Alric and he shared his illness with me. Help me, Earnon, do not let me waste away as he is," the bard pleaded.

Earnon handed Guinn the drink he had prepared in case his suspicions proved correct, which they had. Somehow Guinn had ingested the drugged food meant for Prince Alric. Alric had been given small amounts for months and his body was accustomed to the mild poison, but Guinn's was not. Earnon resolved to discover how this mistake had been made and to be assured it would never be repeated, as it could expose them all. "Drink this healing potion, Guinn. Remain in bed, and take this second potion before your next meal. Drink no wine for several weeks. It is only a bout of gripans, but wine intensified the pain, and it can make it return even after you heal. Drink ale instead." Earnon hoped that his warning would keep the bard away from Alric's wine in the future.

Earnon then questioned the servant who was supposed to be utterly loyal to Isobail. The apprehensive man swore he had prepared the food and drink himself and taken it to Prince Alric, but in the evening instead of at noon. The servant explained that due to the birth of his son he had been called away from the castle during the morning and had not returned until late afternoon. Guinn had confessed to sneaking Alric's wine, but neither man could surmise how the bard had gotten the soup meant for Alric.

The servant swore he had added Earnon's herbs to the bowl of soup. He said he had retrieved the empty containers later, so Alric must have consumed them. Yet the prince did look much improved. . . .

Earnon accepted the man's explanation but cautioned him against another lapse. The sorcerer knew why Alric was feeling better; for almost two days the prince had escaped his doses of poison. Earnon grinned satanically, and thought, *Weakling of a ruler, you will be in torment again before dusk.*

Earnon went to the kitchen to speak with Leitis. He was satisfied no trickery was involved when Leitis told him that the server who was distracted by his first son's birth, took so long fetching the bread that she assumed the soup was chilled. She had prepared another bowl and set aside the other one to warm for herself later. While she was finishing her chores, she explained, Guinn ate it. Leitis asked Earnon if she had done something wrong, since she *had* fetched the soup from the same kettle. . . .

"No, Leitis," Earnon said, "but we must be careful with all things that go to our sick ruler. When Guinn took ill and told me he had eaten soup here in the kitchen, I had to investigate any curious matter pertaining to Alric's food. But Guinn has nothing more than gripans, and it will soon pass. One important matter we must follow in order to protect our ruler, Leitis. If the server misses his task again, make certain no one touches Prince Alric's food and drink except you."

After Earnon left the kitchen, Leitis sighed heavily in relief. She had not anticipated the threat of discovery so soon, and lying to the sharp-eyed man had been difficult. Only by feigning surprise had she concealed her terror of discovery. She had realized instantly that Guinn's reaction to the meal intended for Alric corroborated Alysa's suspicion that her father was being poisoned. She would have to watch the servant to see where he concealed the deadly herbs, and exchange them for the healing ones Alysa had given to her. Then she would not have to worry about finding clever ways to insure that her beloved ruler did not ingest any tainted food. She would take any risk necessary to prevent his untimely death.

Leitis felt sorry for the bard, even if he was sullen at times. She prepared a goblet of warm milk and added some of the healing herbs to it. Guinn was so miserable that he was delighted with her compassion, and as he drank the soothing liquid, he related the same information to Leitis that he had told Earnon.

Alysa was sewing in her sitting chambers when Leitis came to see her. "What is wrong, dear Leitis?" she asked. "Do you hesitate with bad news?"

Leitis explained in minute detail what had taken place, including Earnon's visit to her kitchen and her conversation with the bard. On hearing she was right, but wishing she were wrong, a bittersweet feeling filled Alysa. "How could anyone be so wicked as to plot to slay her own husband and ruler? It will become harder to guard his food, but we shall defeat them. And when Father recovers, we will tell him everything. Now that Earnon is on guard, we cannot make mistakes that might alert him to our actions. If only we knew when and how they are poisoning Father. . . ."

In a castle the first meal of day was a light fare which was served early: bread and ale for most, plus a slice of meat or cheese for the rulers and high-ranking retainers. The main meal of the day was served from about eleven o'clock to noon; it consisted of a variety of meats, among them mutton, pork, beef, bacon, wild game, fish, and fowl, as well as fruits, berries, vegetables, and freshly baked bread, butter, and cheese. There was also ample drink—wine, ale, and milk. At dusk a small meal was eaten, unless there were guests to be entertained.

As Prince Alric's illness had worsened, most of his meals were small and light, and usually served in his chambers. When he was at his weakest, he was compelled to remain in bed and accept his server's assistance, which usually occurred after the noon meal. . . .

Now Alysa's eyes widened in comprehension. "When Father first took ill, Isobail was always with him at the midday meal. Even now that her trusted servant has

126

taken over his care, Father is always sickest during the afternoon. By dusk he is so weak that he nearly passes out until noon the next day. No doubt the dose is given to him at noon. You must concentrate on swapping the main meal. Once—" Alysa halted and frowned. "My reasoning cannot be right; Guinn received the poison at the evening repast. Oh, Leitis, I thought I had solved our mystery."

"You have," Leitis said excitedly. After she explained how she had served Alric his noon meal yesterday because the servant had been called away, it made perfect sense to them, especially when Leitis revealed how nervous the man had been about missing the midday meal but not the dawn or dusk meals. "I know you are right, Alysa. When I asked him moments ago if he wanted me to serve the prince at noon while he tended his wife and child, he immediately refused. Do not worry; I will find a way to thwart him again today, and I will watch him to discover where he hides the poison."

"I shall be grateful forever, dear Leitis," Alysa exclaimed, and hugged the woman. "But you must take no unnecessary risks. I could not bear it if you were harmed for helping me."

"If I am exposed, pretend you know nothing of my deeds," Leitis commanded. "If you come to my defense, it will put them on guard against you, then you could not save our ruler after I am gone."

Tears blurred Alysa's eyes as she realized that Leitis was willing to sacrifice her life to save her father. She embraced her once more before the servant left.

Alysa paced her chamber anxiously, for she had grasped another fact that she knew she must handle herself. She recalled how her father had reacted violently after drinking wine that night she had visited him, and recalled what Leitis had said about Guinn sneaking sips of her father's wine last night. While the midday meal had to be the main source of poison, the

127

ever-present goblet of wine also had to be laced with it. Somehow she would summon the courage to use the secret passage to exchange the wine in her father's room.

There was another whose intrigue had been seized by Guinn's illness: Kyra. While boldly visiting the handsome bard in his chamber, Guinn again related all that had happened to him. Kyra was pleased with her cleverness when she enticed the guard to reveal that Prince Alric seemed slightly improved today. She needed to ask questions about such things, and knew Earnon was not the one to approach. The woods witch would know such things, she decided. Yes, she must visit that old woman and buy some information, and perhaps a potion or two.

"Are you sure you want to go riding with Kyra?" Thisbe asked her mistress as she helped Alysa change her clothes.

Alysa frowned and shook her head. "No, but yesterday I promised I would go with her. She is dangling friendship before me, and I must discover why. I know she is up to some mischief, and this is the only way to seek answers. A truce with her might provide them."

Alysa was surprised but relieved to learn Kyra had just ridden off by herself. Obviously her stepsister was not afraid of the fierce bandits who roamed the countryside and had attacked nearby only the day before. She decided to follow and observe her stepsister.

Alysa was shocked to discover that Kyra had gone to Giselde's hut. She remained hidden, watching for her stepsister to leave so she could discover what she was doing there.

Meanwhile, inside the hut, Giselde disguised her

voice and manner, as she usually did with Kyra, asking in a shrill tone, "Why came ye 'ere, girl? Who tol' ye where tae fin' me?"

Kyra eyed the hunched figure with wild hair and the scowling face which could terrify a child. She stared at her gnarled and dirtied hands and her torn dress. The old woman's skin was wrinkled, and her distorted expression implied her sight was bad. "I have been here before," Kyra replied. "Have you forgotten me? Has your mind faded like your dress?"

Giselde dramatically shrugged and snorted. "Tae many come 'n' go tae bother with names er faces. What be yere needs?"

Kyra asked, "Tell me how I would know if someone is trying to poison another slowly and secretly. I will pay you well for such facts."

Giselde squinted and looked the girl over intently, "Ye be tae pretty an' colorful tae be gittin' pazzin."

"Not me, old woman . . . a friend of mine. How would I know?"

Giselde decided to be honest about the effects of poison to see how Kyra would react. She watched the astonishment, then pleasure wash over her face, and realized that Kyra had guessed the truth and was trying to decide how to use her newly found secret. "If it be pazzin, all ye kin do is git it away from 'im. I got nae potion tae kill pazzin. I kin sell ye ae curse on ye foe, or ae amulet tae protect yeself," she suggested.

"Yes," Kyra replied, "make me an amulet of protection."

Giselde took a dried rose from a basket on her work bench. She held it between her cupped hands and chanted, "Keep safe from 'arm tha one who 'olds this charm; if ae soul sends 'er pain, make 'im melt in tha rain." She handed the flower to Kyra and warned, "Keep it in ye pocket dae an' nite. Tae save ye friend, ye must do as I sae, zackly as I sae. Magic is dangerous, girl, but mistakes er worse; stray not from my words er ye kin be harmed. Steal ae possession of ye foe, wrap it in henbane, burn it tae ashes, an' bury them near ae well. If nae one disturbs tha magic grave, ye friend will not die. If tha grave be disturbed, ye friend will enter 'is."

"You said I had to remove the poison to save him," Kyra reminded her.

"Tha spell cannae heal 'im, only keep 'im alive. Tae heal 'im, ye must allow nae pazzin tae cross 'is lips. Listen closely, girl," Giselde chided harshly. "If Black Magic comes back on ye, ye kin die."

"How can I destroy this enemy?" Kyra asked unexpectedly. She held out several coins and an expensive jewel. "Give me a spell or potion to kill h—him, and these are yours, old witch."

Giselde was glad she was able to conceal her shock at Kyra's real intention for coming. Joy flooded her entire body and soul. What sweet revenge to have Isobail slain by the hand of her own child! Yet she read indecision in the girl's eyes.

Giselde fetched several items and turned to Kyra. "If ye be brave an' sure, girl, I kin teach ye tha killin' spell." She waited for Kyra to respond eagerly before she continued, "Pull ae piece of yarn from ae garment still warm after ye foe's wearin'. Prick tha ring finger of ye left hand an' catch ae tipple of blood. Pour ye blood into this liquid an' shake it good before ye soak tha yarn in it. As ye chant, tie ae knot in tha yarn for each dae ye foe tae have left. On tha last dae, wash tha bloody yarn in ae goblet of wine an' let yere foe drink it. Afore tha new morn comes, ye enemy will die, an' nae one will guess tha truth. I cannae tell ye what will happen if ye speak tha chant wrong er dinna carry out tha castin' spell just as I teach ye."

"Teach me the casting chant, old woman," Kyra ordered. Giselde swayed and murmured:

"Acumla me Ra, when this curse is begun,
Acumla me Ra, grant me power till it is done.
Acumla me Ra, knots of weakness and of hate.
Acumla me Ra, let death be their fate.
Acumla me Ra, let no one change my spell.
Acumla me Ra, Acumla me Ra."

Kyra asked, "What if I change my mind after I speak the chant?"

"Ya can change your mind till tha last dae," Giselde replied, slipping back into dialect without Kyra noticing. "Oncest ye mix tha wine, blood, an' potion an' give it tae yere foe, ye cannae halt tha spell. After it is done, all that was yere foe's will belong tae ye," Giselde said temptingly, knowing it would be the poison, not the spell, which would slay Isobail, if Kyra possessed the hatred and courage to use it. "Ye best do it quickly, girl. When ye hates deep, it gives off forces which ye foe kin feel. If ye wait long, ye foe will defeat ye first."

Kyra took the items from Giselde's hand and repeated the chant twice to make certain she knew it word for word. She asked the woman a few more questions, paid her generously, then left. With the rose amulet in her possession, Earnon and her mother could not dupe her to do their bidding. As to saving Alric, she would have to consider that good deed a while longer. Her next task was to convince Earnon to teach her all he could about his skills, no matter what she had to do for the sorcerer in payment. Whatever happened, she had the means to rid herself of one enemy. . . .

Alysa waited for ten minutes after Kyra's departure before approaching Giselde's hut. When she entered, Giselde looked at her and sighed heavily in displeasure. "Do not scold me, Granmannie. I was following Kyra and she led me here. What did she want? Does she know who you are?"

Giselde warned, "It is dangerous to trail her or her

mother, Alysa. If you are seen, they will know you suspect them of evil. I fear you are going to defeat us with your blind intrusions." Despite the hurt look on Alysa's face, Giselde did not apologize or soften her words. "Kyra came to see the witch, not Giselde," she disclosed, then related the girl's visit, except for her teaching of the "Acumla me Ra" chant.

"Why would you help her, Granmannie? You know Kyra was speaking about my father. Do you think she will try to help him?"

"The burying spell and rose amulet are harmless tricks to fool her. I would never help Isobail's daughter hurt those we love. She suspects her mother's black deed, but I do not think she would thwart it. Why did you not listen at the back door?"

"I feared it would creak and warn her of my presence. You were right to warn me not to come here at this dangerous time. I shall obey you now."

"Is your father better today?" Giselde inquired.

"I do not know, but others say he is. I thought it best to wait a few days before I try to see him again." Alysa told Giselde what had happened to the court bard and what plans she and Leitis had made.

Giselde worried over Alric's returning health. If Leitis was swapping the drugs, Alric should remain abed. How, she fretted, could he be getting better? "I know you wish to help your father, Alysa, but is it right to endanger your life and those of your loyal servants to do so? Do you realize what Isobail could do to you and to them?"

Alysa's expression revealed that Giselde's words had struck home. "Do not worry, Granmannie. After Leitis exchanges the poison for your healing herbs, she will take no more risks. I did not tell her I also suspect Father's wine is being drugged. I will use the secret passage to swap the wine jugs each day. As soon as he is stronger and realizes what has been happening, he

132

will put a stop to it. We only need a few days and it will be over."

Giselde knew about the secret passage from her daughter Catriona, but she had not given it thought since leaving Malvern Castle. Later she would think about the secret passage and its possible use. "What if you carry out your plans and Alric does not get well?"

"If they are poisoning him and we stop it, he must recover."

"Yea, *if* they are poisoning him," Giselde said.

"What about Guinn? He ate Father's food and became ill."

"What if the food was bad? What if he has the real gripans? Be careful until you possess the truth, Alysa, even if it is not the truth you expect. Be cautious of Kyra, my naive princess, she is wicked. Do not trust her despite her overtures of friendship."

"I know she has not changed," Alysa said. "One day she will be sorry for her wickedness. And I promise I will not chance coming here again unless it is urgent. Stay safe and well, Granmannie." They embraced fondly and Alysa departed for home.

As Alysa walked Calliope from the hidden ravine, the sound of pounding hooves reached her, then Squire Teague rounded a bend in the dusty road and sighted her. Teague had lived at Malvern Castle since age seven, when he'd been sent there by his family to become a page, as was the custom. Often Alysa had played and talked with him as if he were her brother. She was delighted that her two closest friends—Thisbe and Teague—had discovered each other and hoped to marry. Now she joked with Teague and parried his questions about why she was in the forest by explaining her desire to seek a few hours of solitude. She felt guilty at not explaining her real reason for being in the area, but knew that by doing so she could endanger the lives of others.

As she mounted, Teague glanced at Alysa's garments and frowned. He said, "Many would not deem it proper for our future ruler to be riding around the countryside dressed as a peasant girl, especially without an escort."

Alysa laughed merrily and challenged him, saying, "Prove I need an escort by keeping up with me." She kneed Calliope and raced down the dirt road until she almost reached the edge of the forest.

When Teague pulled up beside her, she laughed and joked, "See, dear Teague, I can outrun any man. I do not require an escort, not even a handsome one like you."

Gavin's heart sank at the obvious affection in his love's voice. So, this is "dear Teague," he thought from his concealed position. He wondered what she would do if confronted by both men simultaneously. Whom would she pick, her knight-to-be or her "wandering warrior"?

Just then, Alysa glanced over Teague's shoulder and sighted Gavin, grinning devilishly. Her eyes widened and she inhaled sharply. Teague missed her reaction to Gavin's surprise appearance because he was striking at a bee.

Alysa felt her heart quicken as Gavin motioned for her to join him before he stepped out of sight. She hurriedly dismounted, calling over her shoulder to Teague as she hurried into the trees, "Meet me at the edge of the forest. I need a few moments of privacy."

Gavin guided her a short distance from the road to speak privately. "What are you doing here?" she asked breathlessly. "I thought you left this area yesterday."

"I had to gather supplies for my men and me before we begin our journey. I shall be leaving immediately. I was returning to our spot to leave this for you," he said, pulling a small bouquet from behind his back. The colorful flowers were bound with a strip of green yarn that matched his eyes.

Alysa's hands trembled as she accepted the gift. She inhaled the sweet fragrance of the wildflowers and lifted her eyes to meet his compelling gaze. There was a curious sparkle in his expression which she could not comprehend, but it intrigued her. If only she could yield to him as she did in her dreams, wildly, passionately, and shamelessly. She dreamed of him every night, which caused her desires to mount, her resistance to lower. Everything was so natural, so romantic, so uninhibited in her dreams. Why was it not like that in reality?

Gavin reached for her and drew her into his arms, and she eagerly sealed her lips to his in a knee-weakening kiss. He was pleased that she so willingly accepted his attentions, but not anticipating her unbridled desire, he was caught unprepared to control this assault on his senses. His arms tightened around her and his kisses intensified with longing. He was disappointed when she pushed him away, until she said, "I must go now. Please return soon, my wandering warrior; we must talk, for you haunt me day and night."

As Gavin watched Alysa's retreating back, he thought victoriously, *Giselde must be wrong, for you came when I beckoned. Next time we shall not part before we settle this matter between us, for you, too, haunt me day and night.*

Guinn did not get well that day, and Earnon was baffled by the lingering illness. But the bard failed to mention his visit from Leitis and the drink she brought him, milk laced with the herbs from Giselde. Earnon concluded that part of Guinn's problem must be the gripans, and he dismissed the minstrel from mind.

Earnon remained in his chambers most of the day while devising a plan to get rid of Baltair, Alric's advisor and seneschal who was away from the castle on royal business. Baltair was too loyal to his prince, and a threat to Isobail. He had to be dealt with soon because he'd begun to question Alric's lingering illness. Therefore, it was the next day before Earnon learned that Alric had continued to improve, and he did not suspect it was because Leitis had again provided a healthy meal.

Responding to the knock on his chamber door, Earnon was surprised to find the beautiful daughter of Princess Isobail standing there. "It nears bedtime, Princess Kyra. Did you wish something from me?"

Kyra smiled as she boldly walked past him into his outer room. She turned provocatively and answered, "Yes, dear Earnon; I wish to talk with someone whose words are worth hearing and whose company is worth sharing. I have been restless for months, and now I know what troubles me: my life and energies are being wasted. You are a master wizard, and I hunger to learn the mysteries of nature. I wish to learn about the forces and powers in and around us. I wish to learn how they are controlled. Teach me all you know, Earnon. Let me study with you. It would be a great honor to serve you as your assistant. You have no child, Wise One; let me become heir to your vast knowledge."

As Earnon stared at her as if dumbfounded, Kyra realized he was caught unprepared for her requests. Her glance slipped over his almost ebony eyes, matching hair, and dark complexion: colors reflected in the same dark blue sheen of his tunic. Although not handsome, there was something compelling in his strong, dark features. Perhaps, she mused, it was an aura of power and mystery which drew her to him. Such an attraction would make her task easier, if he asked in payment what other men might demand. She stepped close to him, rested her hands on his chest, and coaxed, "Please, Earnon. Let me work with you. Share all you have with me, and I will do the same with you. Ask anything of me to test my honesty. Anything, Earnon, anything . . ."

Earnon gazed into Kyra's upturned face and was ensnared by her soft eyes and flesh. His hands longed to wander into her silky hair, hair as bright as the full moon, hair that reached below her tiny waist. Kyra was not cold, unreachable, greedy like the mother she favored. The thought of Princess Isobail and everything he stood to gain or lose flooded his mind. "I do not think your mother would wish me to instruct you in such mysteries as I know."

Kyra noticed the heat in his expression, the trembling of his body, and the change in his breathing. She knew what she wanted from this man, and she was willing to do anything to get her way. She pressed her full body against his and murmured, "These matters are between us, Earnon, and no one, not even my mother, should interfere. Can you not sense the strong bond between us? Or feel the fires that burn within us? They have been growing stronger every day since your arrival. I have waited three years for you to seek me out as your student and lover, but you have avoided me. Your lips have not called to me, but I can resist your mind's summons no longer. Tell me I am mistaken, that you grasp no bond between us, and I will leave your chambers and never enter them again." She caressed his tense jawline and rubbed her loins against his. "I am of age, Earnon, but no man has appealed to me or taken me, for I dream only of you. Either it is fate drawing me to you, or you have bewitched me. If you are concerned because of your position with Mother, we will hold all things that happen between us a secret."

Earnon's desire was so large and his heart was thudding so forcefully that he had difficulty breathing. The only time he took a woman was when his body demanded appeasement and he forced a pleasing wench to do his bidding. This girl was ravishing; she was ripe and tempting, and she was offering herself to him. Maybe the liaison was perilous, but her offer was too stimulating to resist. "You must not reveal our closeness to your mother," he said. "She has many things on her mind, and she would be angry with us for distracting her. I am certain she would not agree to giving her daughter to a lowly wizard."

Kyra's arms encircled his body and she snuggled against his chest, hiding her victorious smile. "I swear she will suspect nothing between us. I wish to learn all things from you. But tonight, there is only one thing you must teach me," she said, then pressed her lips to his.

Kyra grasped the height of Earnon's lust when his arms banded her body and his mouth claimed hers almost painfully. As if he could not master his craving for her, Earnon's hands hurriedly undressed Kyra and guided her into his sleeping chamber. Casting aside his flowing garment, Kyra saw he was eager for her possession. Tasting a victory over her mother by proving her power over Earnon was stronger than Isobail's, Kyra greedily feasted on Earnon's mouth as the man took pleasure from her body.

Eight

In his chambers at Malvern Castle, Prince Alric was trying to walk, testing his gradually returning strength. His mild recovery delighted him, as he had eaten and drunk little for days.

For two days he had not suffered from vomiting, or soiled himself like an infant. As he did yesterday and the day before, Alric did not eat the thick soup. He nibbled on the hot, crusty bread and a delicious fruit treat he had been served. Neither had he touched his wine yet. He moved from bed to table to chair to window to door to bed again. He quivered from weakness and his body was damp from his exertions, but he felt good. His head was clearer than it had been in weeks; no, in months. Even his color was better today.

The prince returned to his bed and leaned on the pillows lining the headboard. The slow walk had been tiring, but refreshing. Hope returned to him. He sipped the insidious wine as he sent his thoughts to wandering. For years he had been consumed by guilt over his secret seduction of Isobail and over not claiming his only son, Moran, born of that folly. Those burdens had weighed heavily upon him, but he felt there was no way he could remove them. If he held silent, Moran would never know he was heir to the Damnonian Crown after Alysa, nor would Alysa know that Moran was her half brother, not her stepbrother, as she and all believed.

During these seemingly endless and miserable months in bed, Alric had time to reflect on his past and on his character. He had come to recognize his flaws. He realized how many mistakes he had made, most of them because he was selfish or a coward or a weakling. He realized he could have destroyed himself and all he loved if it had not been for Bardwyn, Catriona, and Alysa. If only he were more like them; but he was not, and never could be.

His life had been so lonely since Catriona died. How he wished he could find another love to replace her. Isobail was not that woman. If Isobail had not been carrying his child four years ago—or claimed she was—he would not have married her. The ravishing blonde was enormously pleasing and eager to sate his desires, but she did not know how to be a friend when a lover was not needed. Alric could not share his life with Isobail as he had with Catriona. He missed genial talk, smiles and laughter, romantic walks, leisurely rides, swims in the river, cozy evenings by a fire, and countless other things he had enjoyed with Alysa's mother.

With Isobail at his side, he was not free to seek another special love like Catriona had been. He hated to think of his life remaining until death as it was now. Yet he could not cast Isobail aside without a just reason.

Just reason, Alric mused as he sipped more wine. According to his spy Guinn, Isobail was not giving him cause to put her aside as she had done with Lord Caedmon Ahern.

Alric wondered if the warlord ever suspected about the other man, or men, in Isobail's bed. If her husband had lived a while longer, the unborn Moran would have become an undeniable truth to Lord Ahern about his wife's infidelity. There was no denying that Caedmon's death had been most convenient for his deceitful wife.

140

Yet, Alric begrudgingly admitted, Isobail did have some good skills; she seemed to be running his castle and land efficiently while he was sick. And before his illness she had been excellent in bed. There was no denying that Isobail possessed the knowledge to drive a man wild, then slake his carnal needs most pleasurably. He had never forgotten those obsessive nights with her at Lord Caedmon's, nor those following Catriona's death; body-pleasing nights that had entrapped him. He mused: if only Isobail were a wife in ways other than feverish lovemaking. . . . The only true wife and love he had ever known was Catriona. He still missed her, and feared this emptiness would never leave him, for how could any woman replace such a rare prize? Nothing had dulled Catriona in his heart, not removing all signs of her, nor taking another wife. He would give anything to have her back at his side once more, and the realization that her loss was permanent induced sheer agony. He prayed that she had died unaware of his lustful betrayal, as she would never have understood a man's weakness or forgiven him for joining his body to another woman's and siring another's child, especially a son, when his true love had been unable to bear him one.

When he had married Catriona and taken her from her home in Albany, he swore to protect her, and he had failed. As he had failed his father, King Bardwyn. The king had once opposed his marriage to a "pagan savage," a woman of mixed Viking and Celtic blood. But then his father had relented and given him the principality of Damnonia to rule. No doubt Bardwyn hoped he would become the son and worthy leader that he should be. But Alric felt he had failed himself, his land, his family.

It was the death of his and Catriona's first child, a son, that had caused him to err. As always, he had blamed his flaws on innocent events. His beloved wife had rushed into the arms of her people to heal her wounds, not into his, and he needed her desperately after that loss. He had been lonely, angry, and jealous during her year-long absence from his side, and had used those feelings to justify his wickedness and failures.

Now he could no longer hide from the dark truth tormenting him. He was a ruler who had appeared strong but was not; not without his love. When Catriona sought her comfort elsewhere, he had fallen into Isobail's arms.

It happened while he was visiting Lord Caedmon, a vassal who always seemed to compete with him in words and wits. Caedmon Castle was located nearly at the edge of his land, bordering on the sea. Its surroundings were on black slate headland, a bleak area with a nearly impregnable dwelling. The rock coast and gloomy setting added to his sullen mood. The cliffs outside the castle windows were steep, and waves slapped angrily against them. It was a stronghold few warriors dared to challenge. Yet there was a wild beauty about the place with its coves and cliffs of serpentine rock, its gray granite lands and mystic moors.

He had needed something to appease the fierce emotions warring within him, and Isobail had been there. After days of quarrels with Caedmon, he had been filled with the malicious urge to shame his rival. Stimulated by the malicious thoughts of cuckolding Caedmon and of mentally punishing Catriona for her continued absence, Alric had sought out Baltair, his advisor. He had forced Baltair to prepare a potion to be slipped into Isobail's wine.

Concealing himself in the woman's chambers, he had spied on Isobail as she prepared for bed that night. Isobail had been, as she still was, a ravishing creature with long white-blond hair and sky-blue eyes. Her skin was as soft as freshly milled flour and nearly as smooth

142

and white. Her sleek body had caused waves of desire to flood his loins. He watched Ceit, her servant, brush her hair until it glimmered in the candlelight, then massage her shapely body with fragrant oil. As the two women talked, he learned about her passionate nature, and her husband's impotency.

That night, and for six weeks of stolen nights, the potion that drugged Isobail enabled Alric to slip into her bed and have her without resistance. Baltair had warned him over and over of the consequences of his actions, but he had been too intoxicated by his sport and blinded by his pleasures to stop. Too, the secrecy and danger of the liaison had enlivened him.

Finally Baltair had persuaded him to cease his madness and to leave Caedmon Castle. Later, Alric learned of Caedmon's sudden death and of Isobail's pregnancy. Since the knight who had been her lover had died before he left Caedmon Castle, Alric assumed the baby she was carrying was his.

He brought Isobail and her small daughter Kyra to Malvern Castle and placed them in a comfortable hut located in the outer ward. When Isobail bore her second child, Alric had raged inwardly at the injustice of his firstborn son bearing another man's name. Moran should have been born a Malvern, not an Ahern. He had ached to claim him, but he could not.

Meanwhile, his beloved Catriona had returned, bringing her mother with her. The bloodthirsty Vikings had been raiding heavily again, and the people were afraid. Fearful of dissension in his land, he had resisted the old woman's presence and had despised Giselde for tainting his love's blood. He was trapped in a terrible dilemma, for even though he loved his wife above all else, he despised her for her heritage. Giselde had suspected his betrayal, and never forgiven him for it.

Wanting to keep his only child, his son, nearby, Alric made Lady Isobail Ahern his wife's waiting woman, a move Giselde had bitterly contested. He had no doubt that the canny woman had perceived his curious bond to Moran, and to Lady Isobail.

Over a year passed, and Catriona presented him with a beautiful daughter, Alysa, who was the heir apparent to the Crown of Damnonia and Cambria, since Alric could never claim Moran. For years he suppressed his secret, but could not forget that Moran was his firstborn, his only son, a royal bastard. When he feared he might cause suspicions by the way he treated the boy, he sent Moran to Sir Kelton's as a page, to train there to become a squire and knight. In return, Lord Orin sent his son Teague to Malvern Castle.

The Viking threat lessened and life was quiet. Alric's court traveled frequently, and Isobail was left behind at the castle. But tragedy struck when Alysa was nine—Catriona died. Alric raged at the gods who were punishing him for his black past, but nothing could bring his wife back to him.

Worse, Giselde had gone mad after her daughter's death. The old woman had accused him of slaying his wife in order to claim Isobail and Moran. She had threatened him with vengeance, but instead Giselde had vanished mysteriously. He had never learned how she discovered the dark truth about him, or what she might have told Catriona.

Tormented by shame, Alric had gathered his retinue and left Malvern Castle, managing to stay gone for three miserable years. Gradually he realized that the agony he was trying to flee had been carried around within him, so he had returned home.

Guilt added to guilt to plague him daily, until he became ill. Lady Isobail insisted on caring for him herself. For days he wallowed in his misery and remorse while she tempted and enticed him day and night. Yet he resisted her, fearing what Giselde might do if she returned and found them together. Then a night came when his sufferings were so intense that he recklessly allowed Isobail to soothe them with her gentle hands and passionate body; that erotic night led to others, and finally to marriage, when Isobail suspected she was carrying another child. He could not allow their second child, possibly another son, to be born unclaimed. In his crazed state he thought the gods were showing their forgiveness by giving him a chance to be happy again. He even imagined that they had chosen Isobail as his rightful wife, for he had been warned not to marry Catriona. It seemed as if he and Isobail were thrown together time and time again, so he had yielded, later discovering there was no child.

For three years he used Isobail's exquisite body to slake his desires, used her with an almost punishing frenzy, which she seemed to enjoy. Then he suddenly became ill and his manhood ceased to do its duty. He could not help but think of Caedmon and what the man had endured, knowing he could not take his wife or appease his cravings with any woman. Perhaps, he thought, that was the reason Caedmon had been so quarrelsome, and why their former rivalry had developed: so Caedmon could distract himself from his torment.

A curious resentment toward Isobail sparked with Alric. He tried to conquer it, for the bewitching Isobail had been seemingly blameless in their affair; and she had been nothing but kind and patient with him since his illness began. In fact, she had done everything she could to protect him from public shame and to keep his princedom running perfectly, and had always been loyal to him. serving him in any way he commanded.

His illness had come and gone for eight months. Princess Isobail had apologized and moved into the other tower, vowing she could not sleep while he groaned and thrashed in agony, or tolerate the odor of his chamber. Humiliated, he had not forced her to stay with him.

Yet in his wretchedness, his mind played cruel tricks on him and wild suspicions plagued him.

Alric knew he did not love Isobail and never had; but he would never allow his wife, the Princess of Damnonia, to cuckold him in his own castle, as she had done to Lord Caedmon when he could no longer sate her desires. He had hired a gifted bard to live and entertain in his castle, and to watch Isobail and make certain she took no lover; he believed that Guinn had done both jobs admirably for five months.

Five long and agonizing months. . . . That was how long it had been since this strange illness had worsened, often confining him to bed for weeks at a time. He was relieved that Isobail had taken over for him; she had protected him from total humiliation and had kept Damnonia from suffering as he was suffering.

Alric now realized with dismay that he was rubbing his rumbling stomach. "Ye Gods, no," he shrieked in anguish, then grabbed for the chamber pot to heave over it. Afterwards, weak and shaking, he drank the rest of his wine, plus another goblet, to remove the foul taste from his mouth. He dropped his head to his pillow and closed his eyes, forcing the tears that had gathered there to roll down his cheeks. It had been only a brief respite, perhaps a taunting one by the gods. Wanting to end his misery, Alric consumed a third goblet of wine.

By the blood of Brutus! his mind ranted angrily. *Will it never end? Will I never be the man I was long ago? Must I always suffer and pay for one black deed, one short period of madness? Ye gods, forgive me, or end it now,* he pleaded, then began to weep.

Alysa paced her chambers nervously. She had everything prepared to carry out her daring task: the torch, the wine jug, her locked door, and her courage. Now she had to wait for a later hour before she could safely approach her father's chambers.

Leitis had visited her earlier and told her she had seen the prince's server hide a pouch behind a keg in one of the storage rooms. As soon as everyone was busy in other areas, Leitis had exchanged the baneful herbs for Giselde's healing ones.

Alysa was relieved that it had been accomplished without Leitis being seen. That left only the need to replace the wine which might be tainted. A jug of wine lasted for two or three days, so at least it wouldn't have to be changed daily and endanger them as often. With luck and courage, Alric should be well soon.

Alysa went to the secret panel and pushed on it. Nothing happened. She tried once more, and still nothing. It felt as if the panel was sealed from the other side! She forced the panel with all of her strength, and it moved slightly, then continued to force it until it opened just enough to slip through. The odors that assailed her nostrils nearly caused her to retch. She peered into the darkness and shivered from a damp chill, then lit a torch, fetched the wine jug, and stepped into the secret passage.

Poised on a square stone landing, Alysa glanced to her right and left several times, allowing her eyes to adjust to the eerie shadows. Steps descended in both directions into enclosing darkness, and she hated to think of what she might find at the bottom. The ones to her right led to the gatehouse and the escape passage at the river. She needed to head left to the Great Tower, where her father's chambers were located. The secret panel in Alric's room hidden in the woodwork near a recessed window.

The torch flickered and crackled, air pulling at its leaping flame. Alysa recalled that narrow shafts had been constructed near each fireplace along the path of the passageway to provide air for the hidden route. Realizing that smoke from the burning torch could alert someone to her movements, she extinguished the torch and returned to her room to fetch a candle to light her path, which she knew would give off less light along her scary journey. Then pulling the panel closed behind her, she clutched the wine jug tightly and began to make her way down the steep steps.

She halted at the bottom to slow her racing heart and steady her hands. Even her legs were trembling! She wished this task was not necessary, but knew it was. Moving again, dreading each step, Alysa edged her way along the stone hall. She shifted the candle up and down to sight any obstacle in her path. Eventually she concluded with relief that it was too damp and barren of food in the eerie corridor for rats and spiders. Here and there foul water soaked her leather slippers and skirttail, and she cautioned herself to be careful of the damp stones which were slippery in places. If she fell and injured herself, no one would ever find her.

Musty, dank odors fouled the air from the mold and slime that seemingly surrounded her, and she crinkled her nose in displeasure. Alysa knew she was walking beneath the chambers of Earnon, Guinn, and Baltair; yet through the thick stone walls no one could hear her passing. It was like being inside an ancient tomb. Just as she reached the point where the passageway widened slightly near the Great Tower, she stopped short and gasped.

In a recessed area, two skeletons were chained to the wall. Alysa guessed that the builders had been entombed here so no one could know of the existence of a secret passage. It dismayed her to realize that her father was responsible for this cruel action, and she shivered while hurrying past.

Locating the steps to her father's chambers, she climbed to the landing then stopped to rest. She placed the candle and jug on the floor and looked for the catch to open the panel.

Her heart drummed wildly as it creaked open. She peered into the darkened room and saw no one, but spotted a form beneath the bed covers. She waited tensely to see if the noise had awakened her father, but it had not. Lifting the jug, she moved into his room and toward his bed.

Her long brown hair fell forward as Alysa leaned over her father to find him sleeping deeply. Even though the light was dim, his color was very pale tonight. She poured the wine in Alric's goblet into his jug and re-filled it with wine from the one she had brought with her. She placed the new jug on the table, remembering to mark the bottom of it so she could tell if it was swapped again before her next visit, then put the tainted jug in the passage.

Taking a rag from the table, Alysa wiped away tracks on the floor from her soiled shoes. From the smells in Alric's room, she knew he had been sick again tonight. Surely between hers and Leitis's actions, everything should be all right from now on, she concluded optimistically.

Again Alysa entered the passage, closing the panel securely. Retrieving her candle and the old jug, she gingerly began her return journey. Moving swiftly now, she noticed how the candlelight did ghostly dances upon the walls. Her body was tense and her ears on alert for any sound of an unwelcome creature.

Halfway back, the flame flickered erratically and the candle went out, the smoky odor of the extinguished candle permeating the imprisoning hall. Alysa halted in terror as blackness engulfed her. The foul odors seemed stronger to her nose in the dark, and it was almost deathly silent, except for her noisy respiration and the loud drumming of her heart. She strained to make certain she heard nothing and no one approaching her. Hating this cold black place and wanting out of it quickly, she commanded herself not to scream. *Be calm and think, Alysa.*

The dampness attacked her, causing goose pimples to cover her flesh. She shuddered and dropped the jug; it crashed loudly at her feet and splattered her kirtle. She smelled the wine and felt it rolling down her legs. She had no choice but to complete her journey in pitch-black darkness. Wiggling her toes carefully, she pushed the broken shards aside and shakily continued her walk. Her hands rebelled at moving over the slimy wall surface to guide her, but they obeyed.

After what seemed like ages she stumbled against the bottom step that led to her chamber and fell forward to the stairs. Before she could prevent it, she squealed with pain. Slowly, limping, she ascended the stairs until she reached the top one, freezing in her tracks when a frightening sound touched her ears. *Bats!* her mind shouted in panic; bats flying down the chimney. She did not know whether to remain rigid or to hurry.

When something darted past her head, she hurried onto the landing and fumbled for the release catch. A series of high-pitched noises sounded near her. She ducked her head and prayed none of the creatures would become entangled in her hair. She had seen that happen, and a servant had been forced to cut the bat from the petrified girl's hair. Alysa wished she had left the torch lit, and vowed to the next time. She would simply light a fire in her brazier to disguise the smoke from the torch.

At last she got the panel open and nearly fell inside her room. Quickly she closed it and leaned against it. Her chest was rising and falling furiously, and she closed her eyes and breathed deeply to calm herself. When a small measure of control returned, she glanced at her clothes and shoes; they were filthy.

Without delay, Alysa stripped them off and tossed

150

them inside the secret passageway. She would decide what to do with them later. She washed off in a basin and donned her nightgown. Her brown hair was a mess, and she wondered how she would explain it to Thisbe in the morning. The least she could do was brush it, which she did.

Afterwards she fell across the beckoning bed, exhausted from her daring episode, and was asleep within minutes; to dream of scary places and a handsome rescuer.

A few nights later, Alysa repeated her actions; she once more exchanged the wine jugs in her father's chamber, then made certain they were not switched again by checking for her mark on the jug's bottom. Yet her father remained violently ill and muddleheaded. She paced her floor and tried to accept Giselde's warning: poisoned food and wine might not be Alric's problem, or its entirety. Leitis had swapped Earnon's herbs for Giselde's, and had seen nothing unusual during her intense observation of Isobail's hirelings. Alysa felt helpless, and had to face the fact that she might have been mistaken about Isobail being responsible for Alric's condition.

Perhaps Isobail was up to some other unsavory action, Alysa thought. Since her time and energies appeared wasted here, perhaps it would be best if she tried to see what else Isobail was doing. *Gavin,* she mused, and a smile crossed Alysa's face. Where was he? What was he doing? Could he help her? Would he? The thought of sinking into his protective arms warmed her, and she trembled with longing. Whether she decided to seek Isobail out and spy on her, or wait here for Gavin's return, she must go to their meeting spot and leave a message for him.

When Alysa drifted off to sleep each night, her mind filled with constantly changing dreams of Gavin. At first she was in the dark passageway, running from a terrifying peril in the blackness behind her. All manner of scary sights and sounds tormented her. Suddenly Gavin was before her with a bright and warm torch. She raced into his beckoning arms and clung to him for protection and solace.

When she lifted her head to gaze into his handsome face, they were riding swiftly over a heather-covered moor on Trojan's strong back, riding toward freedom from all of their troubles, riding toward a blissful life together. He smiled at her before tenderly fusing their lips.

Then they were lying beside a waterfall, the sound of it roaring in their ears as loudly as the pounding of their rapid pulses. His mouth slashed hungrily across hers and compelled her to respond feverishly to him.

Once, they were clad in peasant garments, but craved to yank them off so their fiery bodies could touch.

She wanted him and needed him. Thoughts of him were driving her wild with irresistible desire. Surely she would perish if she did not share love's banquet table with him soon. Only by taking him could she end these haunting dreams of unrequited love and passion.

In her dreams Gavin yearned to make her his, and raged against the obstacles that prevented his possession. He vowed to challenge any man who tried to take her from him. As she walked away from him to return home, he pursued her and seized her within his demanding embrace. He could not release her until their lives and hearts were one.

Alysa watched the priest marry them, then saw Gavin gather her into his arms and run into a flower-strewn hut that glittered in the sun. He tantalized her with kisses and caresses until she was trembling and pleading for appeasement. As he pushed her top aside and fastened his mouth to a breast, she thought she would faint from bliss. His hand slipped beneath her skirt and rapturously up her thigh. . . .

Alysa moaned and thrashed upon her bed until peaceful slumber replaced her bittersweet dreams. And far away, Gavin's damp body was released from a matching bout with beautiful passion.

In her chamber Kyra stretched and grinned as she mused over the last few nights and days with Earnon. She had him duped completely. He was teaching her marvelous, even frightening, magic, and his skill in pleasuring a woman was surprisingly varied. But despite her confidence in her beauty and charms, Kyra had not expected to ensnare Earnon so easily. She doubted if he realized how many clues he had dropped about Isobail while he was making wild love to her or was training her. Soon she would control his soul, she thought, as she now ruled his heart and body.

Today she would increase her pace with Earnon, as only a few days remained before Isobail's return. Before then she must make certain Earnon was hers. She would drop more hints to her teacher about her mother's greed, cruelty, flaws. She would help Earnon realize that Isobail could not be trusted completely.

Kyra ate and dressed quickly before hurrying to Earnon's chamber. Once inside, she kissed him hungrily. After a passionate bout in his bed, Kyra looked into his dark eyes as she said, "I wish we did not have to worry about the eyes and ears of others, Earnon, so I could remain with you all day and night. I hate sneaking about as if we are mischievous children. I long to awaken in your arms and to see your face at first light on each new morning."

Kyra's hands wandered over his pliant body and her lips drifted over his tingling flesh. As she nibbled playfully at his ear, she murmured huskily "We are alike, you and I, Earnon. We belong together. When matters are settled in our land, we must convince Mother to allow us to marry. Once she is our ruler, she can take Lord Fergus's or Lord Daron's grant and give it to us. If she is to take over Damnonia, she needs loyal vassals at every castle. If we help her, she must reward us."

Kyra rolled atop the impassioned man and between greedy kisses said, "Think how wonderful it would be for us to marry and have our own castle. We could spend all day on our work and all night on our love-making. What a pair we will make some day, my sweet Earnon."

Earnon pressed Kyra to her back and stared into her eyes. "Would you truly marry me, my beautiful Kyra?" he asked. "Will you feel the same when your mother refuses to allow us to be together again?"

"She cannot, my love," Kyra protested. "I could not bear to lose my heart and soul. You are important to her. Force her to give me to you as payment for your skills. She is selfish, but she is fearful of your powers. She would never refuse your commands because she needs you. But I warn you, my love, never let her become stronger or smarter than you are. She sucks life and knowledge from people, then casts them aside. She has never loved me or wanted me, and she will be happy to be rid of me. She owes us our chance for happiness, Earnon; she owes us marriage and a castle. We should not have to fear her or obey her, yet we do."

"When Isobail returns, I will wait for the right moment to speak to her about us," Earnon replied. "Until then we must keep our love a secret. She often looks at me with desire in her eyes. If she craves me, she will be angry over my loss. You know Alric is no man in her bed, and she is a woman of great passion, as you are, my beautiful Kyra."

Kyra cleverly shared one of her secrets with him, saying, "She craves many men, my love, but I pray she has not set her eyes upon you. She is greedy, and I fear how she always gets her way. She tricked Alric into marriage by swearing she was carrying his baby. And even as a child, I remember the men who visited her bed when she thought Ceit had me busy elsewhere. Poor Guinn has been sneaking into her chambers since his arrival, and he loves her blindly. Has she not told you they are lovers?"

"I did not know about them," he replied in surprise. "Does she not realize how dangerous it is to keep a lover so near?"

"If she loved him as I love you, I would understand, but she does not. Mother loves no one except herself. Beware of her many lusts, my love. As you know, she will stop at nothing to obtain her desires. I am no fool. I know she killed my father, and I know she is destroying Alric to seize Damnonia. If you are helping her, please be careful, for I could not bear to see you harmed if she is caught. Promise you will take me with you if you are exposed and forced to flee."

"Would you hate me if your words about me are true?" he asked. A worried look filled his black eyes and lined his face.

"Never, my love," she vowed, and kissed him.

He smiled and stroked her flesh. To prove his love and trust, Earnon said, "Soon all will be finished and we will find a way to be together always. Even now she rides to delude the people and to defeat Lord Daron to gain control of the Logris border. She plans to place Sir Calum in charge there. When it is safe and wise, she will replace Lord Fergus with Phelan, and Sir Kelton with Moran. Then she will control the land and people. For my help, she has promised the castle of Lord Orin to me."

"Outside of Malvern Castle, that is the largest and best in Damnonia. Oh, dear Earnon, how happy we shall be there. Ask for me soon," she coaxed, then covered his face with kisses.

"The grant will change once Isobail is in power, my

beautiful Kyra. Most of the land and serfs will go with Sir Kelton's holdings. Isobail told me it was Moran's heritage. I will control little more than Orin's castle and a parcel of land around it; all else will be united to Moran's domain, and I will be his vassal, as Sir Kelton is Lord Orin's first and then Alric's. You have much here; will that be enough for you?"

"Nothing here is mine except you, my love. I would go anyplace and do anything to have you. What would riches be without my heart?"

"My beautiful Kyra, you make an old man's heart soar with joy."

"You are not old, my love. Have you not proven your youth and prowess in this very bed? But tell me, my love: What would you do if she betrayed you?"

"She would not dare. Isobail knows I have the power to slay her," he lied. How he wished he did control the matchless powers that he claimed and which others believed he possessed. True, he was highly skilled in alchemy, but his work always required physical help to obtain success. Simple folk could be fooled forever, but a smart woman like Princess Isobail . . . She paid him highly and gave him much honor. If he ever failed her, or she guessed the truth, she would have him killed instantly. If only he did possess real magic instead of tricks and illusions, instead of secrets about herbs and nature.

Earnon lifted Kyra's chin to look into her sky-blue eyes. "Isobail is giving me Lord Orin's domain for helping her defeat the lords, but I will demand you as my reward for keeping Alric abed with my powers."

Kyra warned, "Do not wait too long, my love. Sir Calum is chasing me swiftly; he said Mother would betroth us soon."

"I will never allow Sir Calum or any man to have you except me."

Later, Earnon said, "If we destroy a certain foe for Isobail, she will lean heavily in our direction."

"What foe, my love? And how shall we destroy him for Mother?"

"Baltair. If we get rid of him, Isobail will be forced to relent to our request. I have a plan. Will you help me win her favor?"

"I will do whatever you say, my love. How shall we kill him?" she asked eagerly.

"I will place a spell on him that will cause him to desire you beyond control. While he is trying to ravish you, trusted knights will rescue you and slay the madman. It will appear an innocent crime."

Kyra protested, "But I will be shamed. What if others think I enticed him? What if he harms me before your men—"

Earnon placed his finger to her lips. "I swear you will be safe and blameless. If I can persuade your mother to use this plan, all will be settled for us. She would not dare refuse us anything if we help her."

Kyra thought about his plan. Yes, she decided, It would be smart to pretend to help him and her mother, and to be rid of someone as dangerous to their cause as Baltair was. "I love you and trust you, dear Earnon, so I will do whatever you say."

Earnon retrieved something from his work area and returned to the bed. He placed the small bowl to her lips and told her to drink from it; afterwards, he did the same. Within minutes colorful lights danced before her eyes and her head began to whirl dreamily. She began to tingle as a strange heat and craving filled her. She smiled and reached for him, and they sank to the bed entwined.

Nine

Gavin had been trailing Isobail's retinue for several days. The Cumbrian prince wished he could get closer to Isobail's tent to eavesdrop, but it was far too dangerous. Obviously the woman was more cunning than he had realized: she always rested or made camp in the open, and had dogs tied at intervals around her tent to prevent anyone from sneaking up on her. Yet he was learning a great deal by following her at a distance.

It was clear what Isobail was attempting with this journey: she not only needed political and military control of Damnonia, she also needed the loyalty—or bridling fear—of the lords and peasants. She had halted her retinue at every village and hamlet to work her charms and deceits upon the peasantry. If necessary, she used intimidation or coercion to win allegiance. She appeared to grasp people's strengths and weaknesses, and was skilled at using them to get her way.

Among the ways Isobail ingratiated herself with the populace was to have her knights hunt down local bandits and turn them over to the populace to judge and punish. On one occasion she misled them by having petty thieves dress like the merciless raiders who had attacked that particular village recently. Isobail assumed an air of their champion as she talked about the attacks on that village and others, until she incited a blood lust in the people. After which Gavin witnessed horrible acts of vengeance perpetrated on the unfortunate bandits. Later the villagers surrounded the artful slaker to praise her courage, spirit, and defense.

Isobail's ability to gain influence and authority over so many people worried Gavin. He concurred with Giselde: Isobail was greedy, deceitful, and dangerous. Giselde was right, he concluded; the woman's pretense was alarmingly masterful and an imminent victory could be hers!

Gavin guessed that Isobail was heading to Lord Daron's, near the Logris border. At her current pace, she would reach his castle before dusk the next day. He settled back against the tree to think and rest for a while. The six men he had sent in separate directions, to see what each could learn, were to meet in about a week to compare their findings. While he followed Isobail to Sheriff Trahern's and other places, Tragan was to see what he could learn around Lord Orin's, Lann had been ordered to scout the Logris border, Keegan had been sent to spy at Lord Daron's, Dal was to observe Sir Kelton, Bevan to watch Lord Fergus's, and Weylin to remain near Malvern Castle.

Malvern Castle, his mind echoed, then traveled there. He could hardly wait to meet with the beautiful Thisbe again. Despite the possibility of her deceit, exquisite images of her filled his head. He could almost smell the fragrance that lingered on her flesh and hair. His lips hungered to taste hers and his arms ached to hold her. Yet his yearnings were not just physical; he wanted to be with her, to share all things. His jealous mind told him that he had no competition in Squire Teague, or so he hoped. Surely after meeting him, sweet Thisbe could not retain desires for another man, not after the way she behaved with him. After all, she had left Teague's side to race to his in the forest, and had seemed eager for his swift return. If she had her mind set on capturing Teague, she would just have to change it! He smiled, and sighed peacefully as he began to recall those heady meetings in the forest.

As Gavin eased into slumber, Alysa's words kept running through his mind: "Please return soon . . . for you haunt me day and night."

Gavin stealthily approached the tempting maiden who was leaning against a towering oak, her eyes closed. Before the enchanting nymph in woodland green could clear her wits, his strong arms imprisoned her between them. As she tried to duck beneath one arm and flee him again, his muscular body pressed her slender one snugly against the trunk. "Nay, my fetching damsel, you shall not escape me again. You must fill my life and passions as you fill my dreams. Surrender to me and share my life."

"It cannot be, my wandering warrior, for we are worlds apart," she said in an emotion-choked voice while her ocean blue eyes glistened with unshed tears. "A mortal cannot mate with one who is not human, not without a heavy price." Suddenly she was free, and his body refused to obey his command to chase and recapture her.

"Surely any price or sacrifice is worth a bond between us," he reasoned frantically as he struggled to move. Finally he could, but she eluded him. "Return to me," he implored.

As she darted here and there behind trees and bushes, she replied, "Nay, Gavin, my love. Do not torment us with a plan that cannot be ours. Here, only in our dreamworld, can we become one."

Gavin searched for her as he shouted, "Nay! I must have you in the real world or live as half a man."

He found himself beneath her on the grass and she was teasing her long brown hair over his face and bare torso. "I can never leave you or lose you," she murmured, then sealed their lips in an urgent kiss.

As he rolled her to her back and lay atop her, he vowed, "I shall make you mine or die trying." The stimulating dream slipped away as water between his fingers, and he slumbered contentedly. As did Alysa.

The next day Alysa realized how quiet the castle had been since Isobail's departure, and how quiet her life seemed without Gavin. There was little to do, and she was bored. She had tried to visit her father once more, but his head was too fuzzy to comprehend her presence. She discussed this distressing matter with Leitis, who was as stumped as she was. The only good thing to happen in the last few days, she thought, was Kyra's absence; her stepsister was rarely around to trouble her. Alysa decided it would be safe to visit Giselde. She told Thisbe to do as she pleased since she was going riding most of the day.

With Isobail gone, and Kyra and Earnon keeping to themselves, Thisbe could usually sneak romantic meetings with Squire Teague. But today, Sir Calum was restless and demanded that the red-haired son of Lord Orin scour the countryside for bandits with him. No one knew that Calum was in a sullen mood because Kyra was avoiding him.

Fortunately, Princess Alysa Malvern saw the two men leave the castle and watched which direction they took. Once they were out of sight, she headed her horse toward the forest and secluded ravine. First she went to the spot where she had last seen Gavin. She sat down where they had kissed and caressed, and daydreamed of him.

She thought of how his dark blond hair curled at his neck and around his handsome face. She smiled as she recalled that undeniable air of self-assurance in his manner. She remembered every feature on Gavin's face, and warmed as her mental eye roamed his body. She loved the sensual pout of his lower lip and the strong line of his jaw. She loved the feel of his skin and the way his stubbled face teased against her smooth flesh. He was very much a man, perhaps too much of a virile man for one woman to satisfy.

Alysa sighed in loneliness and yearning. How easy and wonderful it was to be held in his arms. How stimulating to touch him, to kiss him, to be captured by those compelling green eyes. If he were here this moment, she would give herself to him, even without promises. Nothing would make her happier than winning him.

Heading for Giselde's hut, she prayed the old woman could lift her spirits, as nothing seemed to be going right for her lately. Giselde, however, was not in. Alysa waited for her to return home as time passed and shadows lengthened. She wished she could get inside the locked chest to hold the precious ring, the one that had belonged to her grandmother. Perhaps Giselde would teach her about healing herbs, she thought, to pass the days until her life was righted once more. No, it was too dangerous to spend much time here. That thought warned her it was past time to return home.

Alysa walked through the forest slowly. She did not want to return to the dismal castle and her solitude, but there was nothing else she could do this late in the day. She could not go on like this, she told herself, and dreaded to think of Isobail's return while her father was still sick. Worse, she hated to think of Gavin never returning. She must have him, she simply must have him!

That evening Alysa stood over her father's bed and wept, for she could not arouse him at all. She feared he was dying, and anguish pricked her heart. If only Gavin were here to help her at this difficult time. It didn't matter to her what her father had done, she loved him and wanted him to survive. Perhaps he should no longer be the ruler of Damnonia, but Isobail was not the one to take his place. If it came to a battle for the Crown, she would defend her right to the throne! Yet the moment she placed it on her head, Gavin might be lost to her forever.

"Oh, Mother," she cried, "if only you were here to help us . . ."

Somewhere inside her head Alysa heard an urgent plea in Catriona's voice: *Save him, my child, save him from that evil woman. Soon he must join me, but not until his enemies are defeated. The blood of kings and chieftains flows within you; call upon your heritage to give you strength, wisdom, and courage.*

Alysa glanced around the room and found it empty. Had the voice come from the spirit world or her imagination? The girl of Celtic and Viking bloods smiled and shook her head. She caressed her father's cheek and murmured, "Do not worry, Father, I will save you from harm. First I must tell Leitis to eliminate all herbs in your food and drink. If they are not sneaking poison to you in another way, perhaps the healing ones do not lie well in your belly. We shall see. . . ."

Princess Isobail's caravan reached Lord Daron's castle at sunset the following day. Servants busied themselves unloading the numerous wagons and settling the royal party into proper chambers or clean quarters. Lord Daron, his wife Gweneth, their two daughters, and one of their two sons welcomed the royal visitor and her retinue into their home. Sheriff Trahern and Phelan, Captain of the Guard, stood on either side of the princess as she spoke politely with her host and greeted the other guests—Lord Orin and his wife Lavena, Sir Kelton and his wife Kadra, and Alric's seneschal Baltair—who were present for this weekend of hunting and feasting which was wrapped around a hurriedly prepared schedule of official functions, with Isobail holding temporary court in Alric's name.

The Great Hall at Lord Daron's castle fell silent when Isobail entered the room, and hesitated as a loud voice announced: "Her Highness, Princess Isobail Malvern, Regent of Damnonia and wife to our noble ruler, Prince Alric, future King of Cambria. In the name of Lord Daron, welcome."

Isobail gracefully headed for the recently constructed dais at the far end of the large hall, amused that the man had gone to such trouble to please her on the day before his death. . . . The men bowed and the women curtsied as the ravishing princess passed by, smiling and nodding to most, but pausing briefly to acknowledge a few by allowing them to kiss her extended hand or by addressing them personally.

Few rulers had appeared more regal, more poised, more radiant than Isobail did at that moment. She looked strong, yet gentle. She looked innocent, yet seductively earthy. As if she had the crowd mesmerized by an artful illusion, each saw in her what the observer desired.

Isobail's white-blond hair tumbled to her firm buttocks and was held in place by a gold crown which reflected the glimmering light of numerous candles. To match her eyes, she was wearing a flowing tunica in soft blue, a flattering style carried over from their Roman conquerors. The thin material that caressed her shapely figure was girded just below her waist with an artistically braided belt whose cords dangled near her knees and swayed sensuously with her movements. Suspended from a gold chain was a heavy, jewel-encrusted square which rested in the swell of her breasts and drew attention to their pleasing size and lift. It was obvious that her waist was slim and her hips softly rounded. Her feet were encased in leather slippers which fit them perfectly and matched the belt that encircled her body. Her fingers bore many rings, and her left arm was adorned with several bracelets. No one could deny how beautiful and royal she appeared. Many thought she looked and moved like a goddess.

Reaching the dais, Isobail was seated at her private table. She glanced around the room, then asked two men and their wives to join her: Lord Daron, Lady Gweneth, Lord Orin, and Lady Lavena. As soon as their places were set, as it would have been presumptuous to have placed more than Isobail's dishes at the head table, the two couples joined the smiling princess.

Strolling minstrels provided music while the food was being served and eaten. Isobail feasted happily on the delicacy of lark's tongue pie, along with a variety of meats and vegetables. While conversing with her table guests, she nibbled daintily on figs and raisins and sipped sparingly on the best wine from Daron's cellar.

Laughter filled the room, and joyful smiles could be seen on every face. For a time, she knew, problems in Damnonia were forgotten by those present. While an assortment of fruits and sweets were being served, a troupe of tumblers entertained them, followed by a talented magician. Soon everyone had eaten his or her fill and the noise increased in the hall.

Isobail signaled she was ready for music and dancing, which began immediately with her and the host Lord Daron taking the floor first. Afterwards she danced with Lord Orin and Sheriff Trahern, the only men of enough rank to be allowed such a privilege.

As she swept close to Trahern during a series of intricate steps, she whispered, "Come to my chamber as soon as it is safe. Make sure Phelan knows his orders."

"Everything is in readiness, Your Highness. End this night swiftly," Trahern replied, his voice low his eyes scanning those nearby to insure that no one eavesdropped on the exchange.

At the end of the dance Isobail spoke, and all lips went silent. "I have not enjoyed myself so much in many months, Lord Daron. I thank you. When my husband and our ruler is healed, I will beg him to plan a deer hunt in the royal forest near Malvern Castle. I shall repay my dear friends and loyal vassals with a great feast," she promised.

Isobail's laugh was deep and sultry and rose above the cheers that filled the hall. "When we hawk tomorrow, I shall claim the largest rabbit taken for my evening repast, and I shall give the best trainer this scarf in gratitude." She waved a sky blue one over her head, her gesture calculated to charm them. "After our hunt and meal, we shall sit together and decide how to resolve our problems. I wish to learn from each of you," she said, knowing there would be no court tomorrow night after the brutal slaying she had planned. Already she had prepared a splendid funeral oration.

Isobail glanced around the room and said, "I do not see my vassal Lord Fergus. Has he taken ill?"

Lord Daron's youngest son, a squire at Fergus's castle and a messenger for him tonight, stood and bowed before replying, "Lord Fergus sends his regrets, Your Highness. Many brigands have been raiding his lands lately. He thought it best to remain at home to defend against them."

"All areas of our lands are under attack. Lord Fergus would be better served to attend this meeting to decide how to end such matters. He cannot defeat the raiders alone. We must band together, as they have done. We need the cunning thoughts of all our lords. Only then can we defeat them, crush and slay them for all time. I am sad he has chosen to disappoint me. I will depend on Lord Daron to report on our decisions and plans to him."

"Ye best git someone else to depend on, Yer Highness." The accusation rose from the far comer of the great room. "Lord Daron is not to be trusted. I beg ye to rule on the way he has wronged me and others. I paid for two new assarts, but he kept my money and the land," the farmer shouted as he struggled to push forward. But strong arms prevented him from reaching Isobail.

An assart was a clearing or an enclosure near the woods or on heaths for which a peasant could buy permission to cultivate. When a peasant, or any subject, felt he had been wronged or abused by his local lord, he could seek justice from the traveling court—if he dared. The princess feigned shock at the man's charges. She glanced at Daron, who had risen to his feet, and held up her hand to silence the outraged feudal lord. "There is no need to defend yourself, Lord Daron. I know such words cannot be true. Perhaps there is a misunderstanding here and you shall settle the matter for me. I know you are a generous and kind lord, and I trust your judgment." To the peasant, she said, "Return home, sir, and ponder your wild charges against this fair man. If you still feel you have been wronged, return tomorrow to discuss it with him. This is my command."

The desperately poor peasant mumbled something, then nodded and left the hall, intending to meet with Sir Phelan for his payment. It was not until the next morning that his body was found outside the castle walls.

Isobail smiled and walked into Trahern's arms, delighted he would be the one to sate her desires tonight instead of the lovesick bard. Guinn was a pleasing lover, but she was only using him until it was safe to rid herself of Alric's "spy." It had been six nights since the poet had pleasured her, and her body was eager to surrender itself to Trahern's skills.

The sheriff had been her ally and lover for eight

years, even before her marriage to Prince Alric. He had been rewarded with land grants she bestowed after her rise to power, for it was he who passed messages between herself and the raiders. The devilishly good-looking Trahern was one of the few men whom she both liked and trusted.

Isobail eyed his sleek black hair and tanned features, then twirled his mustache around her fingers and stroked his heavy beard. The thirty-four-year-old man watched her tempting play through deep brown eyes. He grinned and stripped off his garments, revealing a strong and virile body. Slowly he removed Isobail's garments, noting how her body differed from Kordel's, his too-slender wife.

As his hands cupped and caressed her breasts, Isobail asked, "Did Phelan take care of our foolish peasant?"

"He served us well, my sweet. You have the lords fawning at your feet. No one will be the wiser when our guilt-riddled farmer is found dead by his own hand. It was a clever ruse which will win favor with the lords and prevent any suspicion from falling on us when Daron meets his fate tomorrow."

A wicked smile settled on Isobail's face. "I am eager to quicken our pace, Trahern. I have waited a long time for my final victory. Soon all the foolish peasants will doubt that Alric's lords are strong enough to defend them, and they will notice that it is my loyal vassals who fear no raiders and safely guard their domains. Make certain the raiders understand that no vassal of mine is to be attacked, or my protection will seem no stronger than Alric's."

"They will obey us, my sweet. You are right to allow them to attack the feudal lords and their retainers. The raiders make a nice profit from reselling horses and cattle, and women to the slave trade; as it is, they cannot steal enough from the poor peasants to keep them here. I have passed along your warnings to attack only when and where we tell them it is safe. We cannot risk having one of them captured and questioned. I told the leader it was certain death to be caught, and worse to be loose-tongued."

"Our plan will succeed within two days," Isobail said. "Sir Calum will control this area for me. Unfortunately, I thought it would be safe for my men to steal Fergus's cattle and leave a trail into Logris, but I misjudged the old fool. How dare he ignore a royal summons to join me at this meeting! He must die slowly and painfully."

"Perhaps we can arrange a surprise or two for him in my dungeon," the sheriff suggested.

"Trahern, my handsome devil, you think of such wonderful things. I can imagine what fun you will have with him. Grease your racks and chains," she advised amidst cold laughter. "Within a few days you must execute publicly a few petty criminals. We need a few scapegoats to keep the peasants' blood hot and flowing.

"Here is the plan: tomorrow Daron will be slain during a raider attack; Fergus will simply vanish, as if he had been abducted; Sir Kelton will perish by accident. That leaves only Lord Orin, whose life this courageous ruler will save—for now. But we must yet think of a plan to rid ourselves of Lord Orin. No two deaths can look the same, or we may come under suspicion."

"I can see it now," Trahern declared between chuckles. "Daron's body being sliced open like a ripe pear while a beautiful woman desperately battles a fierce enemy to save her friend and vassal from certain death. . . ." He bent forward to seal his mouth to her breast.

Isobail's fingers wandered through Trahern's hair, and she said, "As we agreed, it is wise to sacrifice one of our raiders. It would look suspicious if he killed both Daron and Orin, but left me behind. Besides, it will further our cause to bravely rescue Orin, for no doubt he will sing my praises across the land."

Trahern lifted Isobail and carried her to the bed. "Why is Earnon not traveling as part of your retinue on this trip? We might have use of his powers."

"He can serve me best at the castle by keeping watch on Alric. My husband must not be allowed to heal and intrude on our plans. Hush now, my handsome devil, and make love to me. It has been much too long since we have lain together, and my body aches for yours."

"We must find ways to meet more often, my sweet Isobail."

"Only when it is safe, Trahern, not before," she replied softly. "Obey me well or all is lost, including our lives."

"I shall obey you, queen of my heart. What is your command?" he asked playfully, then flamed at her tantalizing response.

The hunt began shortly after an early repast of hot bread and cold meat. The plans were to hunt until midday, halt for another small meal, hunt until early afternoon, then return to Daron's castle to rest and bathe before a large feast and serious discussion.

Hawking was the favorite sport of noblemen, involving boastful challenges, heavy gambling, and fierce quarrels. Lords had been known to lose a serf or strip of land or a pouch of gold over a bet. Losers were in foul moods for weeks. The "greatest huntsman of all" was the most highly skilled falconer, and few of his possessions were more valuable than his prized bird.

A man's education in falconry began during his days as a page, when it was his duty to follow the hunters, to wait upon them, and to observe the birds' training and assist the falconer. As these hunting birds were capable of shredding flesh with their razor-sharp talons, they were kept hooded, with bells secured to their feet signaling their presence at all times. During the night or when not hunting, the birds had to be tethered securely to blocks, or they would attack each other lethally. The prized birds were housed in the castle mews and tended carefully, and to allow one to suffer harm or to escape meant certain death for the attendant.

That morning, Isobail rode at the head of the party, leading the way to the clearing. The nobles and their retainers were on horseback, the numerous servants walking behind them or riding in carts with the hunting supplies and refreshments. The sporting birds were carried in wooden frames called cadgers, which prevented injury and escape before the hunt began. An assortment of leashed dogs, pointers and greyhounds, trailed their masters and eagerly awaited the action.

After the group halted, some of the birds were released. They flew high to their pitch and hovered as they awaited the action, which they seemed to anticipate as eagerly as their owners. Other birds remained hooded with rufters and tethered with jesses on their masters' gauntlet-covered arms, to be released after the quarry was flushed by the dogs. Once the sport began, the birds swooped down at awesome speeds to attack their prey with initial blows that killed or maimed. Trainers hurried about after each victory to retrieve the slain animals and birds before the trained birds of prey could tear into their kills.

Princess Isobail stood between lords Daron and Orin as the men laughed, talked, and wagered on the next episode. She merrily joined their conversation and encouraged the boyish behavior of both men. As each prize was brought to them, she examined it and remarked on the skill of the bird that had brought it down without mangling it, or commented on how swiftly the bird had completed its task. She glowed with excitement and pleasure as the event continued. Several times she even bravely rewarded the victorious bird by feeding him strips of raw meat.

At noon the trainers replaced leather hoods and leg straps, and either placed the bird in his cadge or tethered it to its wooden block. The guards gathered not far away to eat their meal and drink ale. Servants had prepared a delicious repast for their lord and his guests, and spread covers upon the ground for them.

Before Princess Isobail could take her place and eat, thundering hooves and alarming yells rent the air. Daron and Orin quickly drew their swords to defend their regent, but already were cut off from the others by circling brigands. Within minutes, bloody corpses of men-at-arms and castle servants dotted the clearing, while amidst screams and shrieks of pain, others raced toward the woods.

As Daron's men were kept busy defending themselves against an overwhelming number of savage raiders, one large and powerful attacker stalked the two lords and the beautiful princess. The man's fur and leather-clad body bulged with muscles, and his expression warned of death. His hair and beard had not been clipped recently, and he looked a horrid sight, one intended to petrify his victims. He chuckled cruelly as he playfully circled them on his horse, taunting them with his huge sword by striking it nonchalantly against the other men's blades.

"Move aside, old men. All I want is the woman, and your riches. Challenge me and you die," he threatened.

"Lay one hand on Her Highness and I shall chop it off!" Lord Daron shouted.

The raider's eyes widened at those words. "So this is the rarest jewel of Damnonia," he sneered. "What a fat price you shall bring from our great chieftain Hengist," he declared, licking his lips as if he wanted a taste of her before that sale.

Isobail drew her dagger and warned, "Touch us and die, slayer of innocents and destroyer of good lands. Be

172

gone from my domain or perish at the hands of my knights."

"How shall you conquer me, lovely creature," the brigand scoffed, "when the least of my warriors can defeat both of your protectors in the flick of an eye?" In a foreign tongue he called a bandit to his side and ordered, "Slay the men and bring the woman to me, without even a tiny scratch to mar her matchless beauty." He chuckled heartily as he rode away.

While the lords were stunned momentarily to inaction, the bandit pierced Daron's body, brutally twisting his sword as he withdrew it. With blood flowing swiftly between his fingers, the nobleman sank to the ground on weakened knees, clutching the fatal wound. The imposingly large bandit turned his attention to Orin, who desperately tried to defend himself. The two men battled fiercely, yet the raider made jesting comments with each parry, and made no attempt to kill the lord.

Isobail's knights and guards, who supposedly had been searching the area for danger, suddenly rode into sight. The brigand leader signaled his men to withdraw, which all did safely except the bandit playfully fighting with Orin. Sheriff Trahern and the knights charged forward to rescue noble and commoner alike.

During the melee, Isobail seized her victory right after the bandit had nicked Orin's arm, causing the nobleman to drop his sword and cringe in fear of death. She stealthily approached the raider from behind and stabbed him in the back. The warrior tumbled to the ground, and Isobail snatched up Orin's fallen sword and plunged it forcefully into the dying man's heart, shouting angrily, "Die, blackhearted villain, by the sword of an honorable man!"

Hurriedly she cut a strip from her kirtle and bound Orin's arm. "I will tend it properly when we reach the castle, Lord Orin. We must return there quickly, while our knights ride after them." She rapidly moved to

Daron's body and checked it for life. Finding none, she wailed, deceitfully. "They have slain our beloved Daron."

Isobail jumped to her feet and shouted to her approaching men, "Pursue them swiftly, and slay each one! Do not halt until Lord Daron has been avenged." She was aware that people had begun to gather around her for instructions, comfort, and protection.

Sheriff Trahern and Captain of the Guard Phelan simultaneously protested, "We cannot leave you unprotected, Your Highness."

"Lord Daron's men will remain here to guard us from harm and to escort us to the castle," she replied. "Never before have we been given the chance to overtake the brigands. You must go swiftly before they mask their trails and are lost from sight again."

"What of the wounded and dead, Your Highness?" Phelan asked, stalling to allow the bandits time to escape.

"These are our people, Sir Phelan, and we must help them. Worry not. The brigands cannot return if our valiant men are chasing them."

"What if there are others hiding nearby, Your Highness?" Trahern speculated. "This could be a trick to lure us away so others can pounce upon you after we are gone. Think of your people's sufferings if you are captured."

The princess lifted her chin and declared, "I must not think of my own life when those of my loyal subjects are in peril."

"If there are more brigands lurking nearby, all will be in danger."

Isobail glanced around as she pretended to weigh her dilemma. "Your words are wise, but painful to accept, Sheriff Trahern. Help us to load our wounded on the carts and escort us to the castle. Afterwards you must race after those merciless slayers and bring back their heads. Later I will send others to gather the precious bodies of our dead."

One of the guards asked frantically, "Are you wounded, Your Highness? Your hands and garments are covered with blood."

Isobail looked down at her clothes and hands, and wailed dramatically, "Nay, my faithful knight, it is the blood of our beloved Lord Daron. We must defeat these fierce killers, for I can bear no more blood of our loyal vassals and subjects upon my hands. If I were a warrior, I would ride after them myself. Surely I have failed my people. . . ."

Lord Orin clasped her hands in his and pressed them to his heart. "Nay, gentle lady," he refuted emotionally, then addressed the people. "These strong hands saved my life, dear friends. If not for the courage of our fearless ruler, I would be dead." Orin related the daring episode to the others, who looked on in awe. Pressing Isobail's bloodstained hands to his flushed cheek, he told them, "Our cherished ruler tried to save Lord Daron, but his wound was too great. This day must never be forgotten, as our land abounds in luck to have Princess Isobail stand in Alric's place while he is ill. No kingdom could have a better regent than this noble woman before us. May the gods grant you immortality, which you truly deserve," Orin concluded fervently, then bent his knee to pay homage to Isobail.

"Rise, Lord Orin. I do only as I must while my husband lies ill. I depend upon our loyal retainers to help me through this trying time. I have much to learn before I deserve your homage."

But the guards, knights, and servants bent their knees before her, and praises for her actions filled the air. False tears rolled down Isobail's cheeks, and she vowed, "My heart floods with joy and pride this unfortunate day. I shall never forget this moment, and I shall work hard to deserve your love and fealty.''

Unknown to each other, two men watched the events before them and worried over their meaning: Baltair and Gavin. When the attack began, Baltair had been gathering special herbs which grew in this forest, and Gavin had just returned from futilely trailing the raiders in the heavily wooded countryside. The events had happened so rapidly—the attack and the timely return of Isobail's troop—that neither man could have done much except lose his life or reveal himself rashly. Yet both astutely noticed how the brigand who had been struck down from behind had not feared to turn his back on the dagger-armed princess.

As the pitiful caravan departed, Baltair and Gavin approached the clearing to witness the action more closely. They sighted each other, and halted to assess the other's purpose. Neither made any intimidating moves, and each realized there was no reason for them to tangle. They glanced at the retreating party, then at each other again. As if each understood they were allies who had come to the same conclusions about this deceitful episode, they nodded slightly to each other before the blond turned to call his golden charger to his side.

Baltair watched him mount and leave, a curious sensation washing over him. Then he smiled, for he knew he was not fighting this dark battle alone. Yet fears and worries assailed him, and as quickly as he could, he hurried back to Malvern Castle to reveal everything to Alric, which would be possible for once with Isobail gone.

Ten

It was late when Sheriff Trahern and his men returned to Daron's gloomy castle to report that the raiders' trail had disappeared. "It suddenly vanished like the mist, Your Highness. We scoured the area until darkness halted us. I do not understand this mystery; it is as if some terrible god aids and conceals them. We beg your pardon and understanding, Your Highness, but there is no clue to follow."

"Fret not, Sheriff Trahern, I know you did your best, and I do not expect you to do the impossible. I have every confidence that the raiders will make a mistake soon and you will capture them. This very day your timely arrival saved many lives, including mine and Lord Orin's. This is a sad night for me, but a grave matter must be settled promptly. I have chosen Sir Calum to take charge of this castle and crucial location. I command him to defend it until Lord Daron's sons come of age and are knighted. Sir Calum must observe the Logris border, as I am certain the evil brigands use it to their advantage." To Lord Daron's family, vassals, and servants, she ordered, "Obey Sir Calum as you have obeyed your ruler. The brigands fear my knights; that is why they departed rapidly this afternoon, and why they do not attack when my forces are near. With Sir

Calum in charge, this area will be safe from another attack. Your home and grant will be protected until the sons of Daron take his place."

Isobail gazed around the room, then continued. "Our hearts are heavy and our blood is hot with hatred, so this is not the time for a merry feast or an urgent talk, my people. We must all return to our homes to mourn the loss of our dear Lord Daron. In ten days let us meet at Malvern Castle to knight more squires to help defend our land and people, and to make plans for our defense. If there are other problems or requests, bring them there. By then my husband should be well enough to advise us. Is there one among you who does not agree? Speak freely," she said.

Lord Orin stepped forward, saying, "Surely all agree with such wise words, Your Highness, all of them."

"You are most kind and generous, dear Orin," she responded. "These days are difficult for all of us, so I will not collect the geld which is owed. Loyal retainers can use this money to aid our poor subjects," she suggested, referring to the tax paid to the Crown by landholders. "My husband is a good man and will agree with this kindness. If he does not, I shall accept the blame and pay the tax with my jewels."

After a few more minutes of misleading talk and charming smiles, Isobail dismissed everyone from the Great Hall.

It was after midnight when Trahern slipped into Isobail's chamber to spend a few hours with her. Their naked bodies clung together, and he teased, "This is dangerous, my sweet, but I cannot resist you."

Throaty laughter filled his ears as she teased them with her teeth. Isobail replied, "Danger is what makes life appealing. Tonight we shall sleep very little, if any. First I must tell you about Phelan. He saw me slay that raider, and it frightens my Captain of the Guard. Phelan must not learn that their leader agreed to let

178

me kill his man. He believed the bandit was to slay Daron, fight with Orin, then flee at your arrival. Phelan is worried over my slaying one of my own hirelings. I finally convinced him the bandit panicked and was about to kill Lord Orin to make good his escape. He seemed to believe me, but I worry over such weakness. If the captain becomes a problem, you must get rid of him during a battle."

"As you wish, my sweet," Trahern concurred, as he owed loyalty to nothing and to no one except Isobail and himself.

She held him at bay and added, "Another thing. I ordered Sir Beag to return to the castle with us. I thought it unwise to leave him here with Sir Calum. We must allow no one to interfere with our plans. Soon we will cast our eyes on Lord Fergus and Sir Kelton. Before another winter, Trahern, all will be ours. I will be ruler, and you shall be my lover until it is safe to become my consort."

The news thrilled him. "Unless you desire otherwise, my sweet, I will keep my wife Kordel in my castle until our time is ripe. As Daron's sister, Kordel provides me with a protective cover."

"Keep her and use her as you wish until I can make you mine," Isobail said, then laughed wickedly. "When must you leave my side?"

"I meet with the raiders at dawn. Until that hour I serve only you." His eyes gleamed with the promise of ecstasy.

"Nay, beloved Trahern, tonight your ruler serves you. . . ."

At Malvern Castle a similar bout of passion was taking place between Isobail's traitorous daughter and sorcerer. To make certain Kyra did not become pregnant, Earnon was providing her with herbs that prevented such a perilous accident. In fact, Earnon was too smitten with the sensuous Kyra to discover that the server who saw to it that Alric's food was tainted had been killed that morning—in one of the few genuine accidents to have recently occurred at Malvern Castle: the unfortunate server had been trampled by a wild horse.

Alysa tossed and turned in her bed, unable to sleep. She had ordered Leitis to stop giving all herbs, good and bad, to her father. If they could keep Earnon from learning about his servant's death, the nasty man could not replace his hireling or interfere with Alric's recovery. All they needed were a few days with careful tending and without injurious drugs, then she could have a grave talk with her father. If she could not get through to him soon, she would bind him, abduct him, and carry him to his father. In Cambria she would make her grandfather, King Bardwyn, listen to her and believe her!

If that drastic action became necessary, she hoped Gavin returned before Isobail, so she could enlist his aid. If she could persuade him to do so after lying to him about her identity . . .

Alysa flung the covers aside and paced her room. The wildflowers Gavin had given to her had died, but she kept them drying in a bronze goblet. She fingered the buds dreamily now, as she reflected upon him. Surely she was in love, or falling in love, with him. If only she were not a princess, a future ruler whose life was not her own, and if he were not a traveling warrior . . .

An idea came to mind: Gavin was a warrior for hire, and she possessed enough jewels and coins to pay for his escort to Cambria to her grandfather for aid. In the morning she would leave a note for him, indicating that she was in trouble and needed his help, no matter his price. She would tell him to respond by note as soon as he returned, that she would check the tree hole each day for his answer.

"Can I trust you, my mysterious warrior?" she asked softly. "What if you learn my identity and realize how valuable my exposure to Isobail could be for you? Nay, you would not betray me," she protested to herself. "You burn within me as a roaring blaze, and oftentimes I fear such a wildfire will consume me. Yet your eyes and touches say you care deeply for me. You are my only hope, Gavin; please be the man I believe you are, even if I must pay you to help us."

Alysa pondered what could happen between them on such a long journey if they were alone; but they would not be alone. She wondered what her father would think about Gavin, about her love for a commoner who earned glory and money as a warrior. He was not even a knight-errant, she fretted, knowing that rank might be more favorably looked upon. Could she make a happy consort out of such a restless male? If it came to a choice between the Crown and Gavin, she wondered, which one would she choose? How wonderful life would be if she could have both.

"Where are you, Gavin?" she said aloud again. "What urges your heart to seek the life you do? Could you be happy in one place, with one woman?"

At dawn Gavin gingerly trailed the Sheriff of Damnonia to a large camp where most of the raiders were sleeping. He wished he could get close enough to hear the words spoken between the bandit leader and Trahern, but it was too dangerous. Guards on full alert were posted around the camp. Clearly the leader was not a foolish or careless man.

Within twenty minutes Trahern departed. The fierce leader of the raiders grinned satanically as he watched the sheriff leave. Gavin nodded to himself realizing that the foreign warrior was as deceitful as those who had hired him. The traitorous Isobail, Gavin decided, was as foolish and blind as Vortigern of Logris had been when he had hired Hengist.

Gavin studied the camp for a time. It was not a permanent one, and there were too many of them for him and his knights to challenge. Besides, he needed to bind Isobail to the treachery. More proof was needed, and the best way to obtain it was by joining the brigands and defeating them a few at a time. First he had to catch their attention. . . .

Nothing could convince him that Isobail had not carried out a death trap for Lord Daron. And he did not have to wonder why she had spared Lord Orin's life. Obviously she had realized it might be suspicious to kill both men simultaneously, just as she must have surmised that "saving" Orin's life would aid her plot. Gavin had not bothered to follow the knights in pursuit of the raiders, since it was clear that the sheriff would not lead his men in the right direction. Instead he found a hiding place and used the hours to get some much needed sleep.

After Trahern's return to the castle the night before, the Cumbrian prince had made contact with his friend Keegan. While Gavin had observed the castle and waited for Trahern to ride out the next day, which he concluded the sheriff would do as soon as it was safe, he had seen his man Keegan, dressed as a peasant, slip into a bailey of Daron's castle.

Inside the gates, each group had assumed Keegan was part of another group, allowing him to move around easily to do his spying. When the means was presented to him to slip safely into the castle itself, the brave knight had done so. Keegan had gathered many clues from the talkative servants and careless men-at-arms, which he reported to Gavin: Isobail's flowery speeches, the people's reactions, and the dismissal of the geld. Paying close attention to the princess, Keegan had seen Trahern slip into Isobail's chambers, and with an attitude that left little doubt that Isobail was betraying her husband.

Keegan later related how he could not follow the hunt without arousing curiosity, and so he had remained in the bailey to observe there. Gavin ordered his friend to continue his task until Isobail departed for Malvern Castle. Gavin himself would trail the woman's party, then meet with his men at the appointed place in the forest near Giselde's hut. Clearly they were gathering plenty of information, but they had to tie Isobail to the treachery afoot.

Despite the recent tragedy, as Isobail headed homeward she halted in every village and hamlet to ingratiate herself with the people, and so she would not arrive at Malvern Castle for three days.

Baltair entered Alric's chamber that next afternoon to find the prince sitting in a chair near his window. The seneschal smiled with pleasure to find his ruler much improved. He took the seat nearby and met Alric's inquisitive gaze. "Yes, my ruler, there is trouble in our land," he replied to the unasked question.

"Tell me everything, Baltair. You are my most trusted retainer and closest friend. Why have you kept such news from me?"

Baltair's eyes did not evade Alric's as he said, "I do not trust Princess Isobail, and I feared to speak openly before her. She has not allowed us a private visit for many months; even now we must speak hurriedly, before Earnon learns I am here with you. Times are bad."

"Why do you cast aspirations on my wife?" Alric asked.

"I feared she would slay you if you suspected her plot," Baltair replied bluntly. "Although I have no proof, I believe she is behind this strange illness of yours, and behind the blackness that plagues Damnonia. It is past time to relate all she is doing in your domain."

Prince Alric remained silent for a long while as he deliberated on this staggering, but not totally incredible, information. Except for one relapse, he had been getting better during his wife's absence, especially since Leitis had begun serving his meals three days past. He recalled his daughter's visit and her words on the night he had been so violently ill. Then he pondered his wife's first husband's timely death, reflecting on the way Isobail had entrapped him with marriage and how she had kept him in "protective" solitude. He remembered, too, many little things that told him Baltair could be right, things he had been too blind or foolish or muddleheaded to accept. "If such is true, Baltair," he finally replied, "I must arrest my treacherous wife and punish her. Send the Captain of the Guard to me."

Baltair shook his gray head and implored, "You must not make a move against her yet." His brown eyes were filled with panic as he warned, "She has duped the people and has won the favor of many knights and retainers. We know not whom we can trust, my friend. I suspect that Trahern and Phelan are working with her, as are others. I have told you of her clever doings which blind your subjects. Perhaps they would think your charges come from your illness. I must gather proof and deliver it to your father. We will need King Bardwyn's help to defeat her. You do not realize how powerful and evil she is, or the grave peril surrounding you. If she feels threatened by you, she will have you slain and make it appear an accident. We must use all caution and wisdom."

Alric arose weakly and leaned against the window. Peering out, he asked, "How can I allow such evil and betrayal to continue?"

"For your survival and that of your domain, sire."

Alric half turned toward Baltair, saying, "What of the safety of my child? Alysa is heir to the throne, not Isobail."

"Unless your wife feels threatened, I do not believe Alysa is in danger at this time. Isobail would not dare slay all loyal lords, the prince, and the heir in such a short time. For now, she is trying to place her men in control, then she will seek the throne. We can trust Piaras. I will ask him to gather information about the fealty of others. While I am gone, Piaras will guard you and be prepared to summon your loyal retainers if Isobail makes a strike at the throne."

"It is a good plan, Baltair, and we will follow it. Many times my pride has gotten me into trouble. This time I will use the knowledge you have gathered. You warned me long ago not to be enchanted with this woman. I did not listen, and I have paid dearly for my weakness and lust."

"What of your son?"

"Do you suspect him of working with his evil mother?"

Baltair read the anguish in Alric's face and voice. "If he is truly your son, he will not side with Isobail. But if her blood runs thicker than yours within him, he is unworthy of your protection. Do you not realize, my liege, that he might not be your son?"

"I wish he were not my bastard son," Alric confessed. "His existence has always tormented me. Each day he is a reminder of the Evil that should not have occurred. Yet he is innocent of my shameful deed, and has been denied his rightful name and heritage. The gods have punished me sorely."

"It was a mistake, sire, and it happened long ago, when you were consumed with grief and loneliness. Do not continue to whip yourself for it. You must never break your promise to hold Moran a secret. Isobail would require nothing more than such a confession to

185

destroy you. Forgive yourself for that rash span of time. It is gone forever."

"It will not end until all concerned in it are dead. When I betrayed my love and myself, I loosened Evil forces in my heart and land, Baltair, forces only death can cease."

"Do not speak so, my liege. You shall know victory and honor again."

"Only Alysa and Damnonia matter now, Baltair. If I cannot defeat this sickness and Evil, help them to survive." Before the seneschàl could reply, Alric advised, "Go quickly, my friend, before you are discovered here. I need you to obtain the truth. If you cannot get to me privately again, go to my father with your knowledge. And take my child with you."

"I will obey, my liege and friend, as always," Baltair vowed.

They exchanged smiles and clasped hands before Baltair left to seek out Piaras for assistance, and Alric covered his face to mourn for his friend Daron.

When Leitis told Alysa that Baltair had returned to the castle, the young princess rushed to the seneschal's chamber. "You must do something to save Father, Baltair, he is in grave danger," Alysa said, and quickly told him what she and Leitis had been doing during his absence. Then she commanded, "Tell me what you have learned during your travels."

Baltair pondered his response for a time, and eventually decided to confide all in Alysa, in case something happened to him. He had been trying to shake this overpowering sense of doom, but could not. If anything happened to him and to Alric, Alysa needed to know the truth so she could flee to King Bardwyn for help.

Alysa's blue eyes grew large in astonishment as she listened to the news of Isobail's travels around the land

186

and the events at Daron's castle. "What can we do, Baltair?" she asked. "Father is not well yet, and cannot escape her evil grasp."

"For now, Princess Alysa, you must do and say nothing to alert anyone to our discoveries." He told her how he planned to get Piaras to help him until the right moment came to approach King Bardwyn. "If we go to your grandfather without proof, the people might resist us. She is cunning, Alysa, and she has completely fooled too many people. You must keep your eyes and ears open. Tell me everything you see and hear, and I will do the same. Beware of Earnon, for I fear he is as dangerous as his mistress. Be careful whom you trust."

"Dear Baltair, can things get worse? If only we could find warriors of our own to hire, honest and brave warriors whose faces are unknown here," she said, eager to test his reaction to her plan.

"I saw a stranger near Daron's castle following the deadly attack," he said absently. "His garb was not of our land, and his aura was that of a powerful and mysterious warrior. He did nothing but observe the bloody battle from the cover of the forest. Perhaps he was one of the raiders, a lookout, perhaps even their leader. After the brigands left and our people returned to Daron's castle, he mounted his golden horse and rode away. It was very strange. . . ."

"He rode a golden charger? What was he doing there? Describe him to me, for I think I have seen him before."

After Baltair described a man who could be no one other than Gavin, he asked, "Where have you seen him, Your Highness?"

"I saw him near the village that was attacked a while ago, during your absence. He was doing the same thing, watching silently from the woods. Later I asked Sir Beag about the stranger, and he said no one who fit his description had been in the village when they arrived.

How curious that he is around at such times and remains hidden. . . . What does it mean?"

"I do not know, but we must watch for him. It was odd, but I did not feel threatened by him. There was something special about him, but I cannot explain my perception."

"Could he have helped those under attack if he wished to do so, Baltair?"

"Perhaps he could have slain a few raiders and saved a few peasants, but it would have cost him his life. He was wise not to intrude on such insurmountable odds. But be wary of him, too, Alysa."

Guilt touched her because she had not told Baltair the entire truth. "If I see him again, I will be careful," she said, "but I will try to learn more about him. If he is not a brigand, perhaps he will work for us."

"You must not approach him!" Baltair spoke sharply. "A man like that can be dangerous. Warriors who roam other lands seeking adventures cannot be trusted, and they cunningly mislead innocent young girls. Remember your rank, your highness."

"Do not worry about me, Baltair. Father did not birth a fool or a weakling as his heir."

Baltair embraced her and said, "Do not speak of our talk to your father. His mind is filled with worry for you. He is angry and frustrated because he is so weak. If he thinks you are endangering yourself, his panic will increase and might compel him to act rashly."

"We will work together, and tell no one. Father must think of nothing except getting well. Will you warn him about the food and wine?"

"I will tell him to accept nothing that does not come from Leitis's hands. I must keep your part a secret. I will go to him with this warning now, before Earnon learns I am here and places a guard at his door against all visitors."

As she was leaving, Alysa turned to entreat her trusted friend, "Guard your life well."

Returning to her chambers, Alysa curled into an over-large chair. At least she had help now, someone who would allow her to assist her father, and who thought she was smart enough and brave enough to help. Consternation filled her as she pondered the things Baltair had told her, and she realized they had no choice but to battle Princess Isobail. She must tell Granmannie nothing about her work with Baltair, or the old woman would be frantic. Her father should be safe for now, with Leitis and Baltair watching over him.

Kyra sneaked to Earnon's chamber to relate an alarming tale: Guinn had told her that Alric was out of bed today and doing nicely. Added to that news were the discovery of the server's death days ago, the arrival home of Baltair, and the impending return of Isobail. "We must do something quickly, my love, or all is lost," Kyra urged.

"Do not upset yourself, my beautiful lady, I will tend to Alric myself. A trusted servant cannot be replaced without time and study. You must watch Baltair with a hawk's eye and a mole's ear. I must know everything he does and everyone he sees. We shall delight your mother with our cunning and successes."

"After you take care of the prince, return to my side to spend the little time we have left together." Kyra had to make certain of her hold over the sorcerer before Isobail's return. She began to nibble on Earnon's neck as her hands brazenly roved his body, sparking it to fiery life. She felt his response and heard him moan.

"There is much to do, my beautiful lady, and danger of discovery," he protested weakly, closing his eyes as he savored her touch.

"Mother will arrive tomorrow, my love. Our time is

short and precious. She will keep you busy and close at hand. We will be lucky to find one hour a week to be together. Please do not deny us this last day of pleasure." Kyra sank to her knees, parted his blue-black robe, and soon removed any resistance he had.

Alysa went riding to place a note in the tree marked by Gavin. She could not endure this mystery surrounding him any longer. No matter what she learned about him, she had to learn something. She told him it was urgent that she see him immediately, and she would check the tree for his answer each day. She started to go to Giselde's, but changed her mind. She could tell the woman nothing at this time, and she feared Giselde would read deceit in her features.

Though Alysa did not visit Giselde, Piaras was heading in that direction. The aging knight, who trained others in the skills he could no longer carry out to his best, felt he had to inform Giselde of Baltair's return and clever plan.

Giselde was both pleased and worried over the man's words. If Alric was getting better, that meant he was not ingesting her herbs. She fretted that Alysa had uncovered her ruse, as her granddaughter had not visited her in a week. Then Giselde chided herself for her silly fears. After all, she had ordered Alysa to stay away from her.

Baltair's information also told her about Isobail's crafty and sinister behavior during her travels. Two lords had been slain and replaced with her loyal retainers, leaving only two who were known to be loyal to Alric. Piaras also revealed that Baltair had sighted a mysterious stranger near the site of the brutal attack at Lord Daron's. Giselde realized he spoke of Gavin, and that she could expect him to return with Isobail tomorrow. She decided to leave Gavin a note, urging him to meet with her the moment he was back.

It was mid-morning when Alysa made her way back to the secret tree to check for a message from Gavin. There she discovered that the hole was empty! Her hand searched it once more and found nothing. She wondered why if Gavin had found the note, he had not responded. If he had not taken it, then who had?

Alysa leaned against the dying tree to ask herself a distressing question: Had she been discovered, or betrayed?

As her face grew moist, Gavin stepped into her line of vision. Their eyes locked searchingly, hungrily, evocatively. For a long time all they did was look at each other, as if their expressions could reveal everything inside. The dreamy aura that surrounded them was laced contrastingly with serenity and tension, anguish and joy, doubts and confidence. They felt like strangers, yet had never seemed closer than they were this moment—as if they had always been together, as they had been in their enchanting dreams. Neither seemed able to move or speak for a time. At first sight hearts that had begun to throb slowly, almost painfully with thick emotion, steadily increased their pace until both Gavin and Alysa feared their hearts would burst. Their throats became as constricted as their chests were, and their labored breathing could have been heard if the lovers were not so enthralled with each other. At this close proximity the warm glows that teased over their flesh rapidly burned brighter and hotter, until they seemed to fuse into one roaring blaze. Without awareness, their dreamworlds fused with reality and took control of their senses.

Of their own volition, Gavin's hands captured her face between them, and he bent forward to kiss away her tears. His lips brushed her skin ever so lightly, causing both of them to tremble. His mouth drifted across her cheek to her ear and whispered, "Do not weep, m'love; I am here to protect you from all harm. Ask anything of me and it shall be yours."

His gentle touch was too much for Alysa, and she flung herself into his arms. "It seems as if you have been gone forever," she murmured against his tunic-covered chest.

Lifting her head and looking deeply into her blue eyes, he smiled and replied, "Yea, m'love, it feels that way to me. I returned as quickly as possible. I missed you and could not wait to see you again." He drew her close and tight. He inhaled the fragrance that came from her brown hair and soft flesh, and sighed peacefully.

Alysa cuddled into his strong and compelling embrace. She loved the feel of him, the manly smell of him. She ached to have more of him. "I missed you too. I missed you terribly."

Gavin's mouth roved her face with sheer delight as she snuggled to his pleading body. He did not need a woman as much as he needed this particular woman. Many emotions filled him, unknown ones, conflicting ones, powerful ones, frightening ones. . . .

Sinking to the grass, they caressed and kissed, pleading mutely for an unbridled union. At that moment it did not matter who they were or what was facing them. They pressed more tightly together, and their hands roamed wildly and freely. Their mouths locked and their tongues danced feverishly. They seemed to breathe, to work, to think as one, and their bodies urgently demanded to join as one.

Alysa was wearing a short over-tunic and kirtle, and both were moving upward steadily. Gavin had not removed his tunic, and her hands eased beneath it near the wide sleeves and caressed the hard muscles of his shoulders and arms. His body felt strong and sleek beneath her quivering fingers. It was intoxicating, enlivening, to touch him and stimulate him. His smooth flesh was a soft golden covering for an enticing physique which had been hardened and toned through years of training and fighting. She knew his naked body had to be splendid, and she longed to admire it with her hands and eyes as she had done in her fantasies.

Gavin's lips traveled down her throat, sampling her flesh as they wandered about aimlessly but directly. They passed over her rumpled garments to tantalize the hardened peaks that revealed her enormous desire. As his mouth labored lovingly there, his hands journeyed lower and lower, kindling her passions to an uncontrollable wildfire. Skillfully he untied her undergarment and eased it out of his way. His hand moved beneath it and sought another peak which was ablaze with desire. As his hand absorbed the heat of her womanly domain, one finger slipped carefully and gently within her to create almost mindlessly blissful sensations.

When Alysa inhaled sharply and arched her back, the warrior's mouth and hands strove to increase her rapture. Her right leg was trapped between his, and it could feel the height of his arousal. She could not stop herself from touching him there, causing him to groan as if simultaneously assailed with agony and ecstasy. The knowledge that she could provoke him to such painful pleasure sent her mind spinning. She did not want to halt this sensual episode, which she had craved since their first meeting. Yes, she admitted honestly, since that first look and touch.

Although she was tempting him and thrilling him beyond mercy or control, Gavin knew she was an innocent. He knew he had to move slowly and tenderly, at a pace that sorely tested his self-control. He could not believe how happy he was to be taking possession of her, and wondered how he could hesitate so long before slaking his carnal hungers with her. But then he realized again that this woman was unique; she was all he needed and wanted. Somehow he must find a way to keep her forever, even if marriage between them was impossible.

Gavin's lips claimed Alysa's and they kissed in every way imaginable. He loosened his loincloth and tossed it aside. He moved between her thighs, pausing briefly to make certain she was willing to carry their passion to its limit. His intense gaze fused with hers as he asked huskily, "Do you want me, m'love?"

The question was simple and direct, and the love-ensnared Alysa responded likewise, "Yea." She had to finish what her dreams did not.

Gavin sealed their mouths as he carefully pierced her maidenhead and slipped within her moist and receptive body. When he was fully inside her, he halted to allow his torrid manhood to adjust to such a blissfully devouring setting. He prayed he could master the urge to ride her wildly and freely, as she rode her energetic stallion. She had stiffened for a moment and had seemed to hold her breath, but then relaxed, and her passion had rekindled quickly. Surely that meant he had taken her without excessive discomfort.

Soon their bodies worked in unison as Gavin guided her along this first journey to ecstasy. He knew how to give a woman great pleasure, but he tried harder to please Alysa than he had ever done with another woman. He called on all of his control and knowledge to make this the most magical moment in their lives. He could tell, from what little she knew, that Alysa was doing the same, and learning quickly.

Alysa matched Gavin's loving pattern. She kissed him deeply, caressed him boldly, and followed his lead instinctively and willingly. She sensed an intense force building within her, a force that caused her heart to beat swiftly and her body to ache. She knew there was more to this union than the pleasures she was experiencing; she realized a blissful storm was about to break over and around and within her, and she beckoned it eagerly.

Both shuddered when the climax to their loving act began. Heat and tingles raced over their united flesh. They clung fiercely, devouring and savoring every drop of love's nectar. They continued to labor rhythmically until every spasm subsided, leaving them limp and sated.

Gavin's lips traced over her damp features as they leisurely returned to reality. His fingers drifted lightly over her skin as a cloud across a blue sky. He sighed peacefully, closing his eyes to press this moment into his memory. When she cuddled against him, he smiled. Their naked flesh seemed to cling together, as if reluctant to part.

Propping his elbows on either side of her head, he was careful not to pull on the wavy brown hair tumbled around her head. His eyes danced sluggishly over her serene face, where no hint of remorse or fear was visible. He warmed to the expression in her sea blue eyes, one of appeasement, trust, and . . . love?

Alysa's voice asked him two questions she had asked herself not long ago, "Who are you, Gavin? Will your restless heart ever allow you to be happy in one place, with one woman?"

Fearing an untimely confrontation coming on, Gavin shifted nervously and pulled his troubled gaze from her probing one. She held silent as he pondered many things. Then his eyes returned to hers and he replied, "I am the man who has rashly stolen your heart and wits before I can make promises to you that I can keep. Each day I am near you causes my heart to calm a little more and to ache for you alone. Give me time, m'love; that is all I can say for now."

Alysa's eyes softened and glowed as she smiled up at him. She caressed his jawline, then allowed her fingers to wander into his tawny hair. "For now, my heart's desire, that is all I need to hear."

Gavin was surprised and pleased by her reaction. Suddenly he recalled her note. "You said it was urgent to see me. What trouble could possibly entangle one as gentle as you, sweet Thisbe?"

Alysa ignored the name he called her. "You are a warrior for hire, and I need help."

"What kind of help, m'love?"

"Forgive me if I hesitate, for I no longer know whom I can trust," she replied candidly. "No matter what has happened between us today, we are nearly strangers. There are so many dangers tormenting me and my land that I hardly know where or how to begin."

Gavin remembered what Giselde had told him about Thisbe and Squire Teague, and he wondered if she was confused over which man to choose. From her point of view a future lord and knight had more to offer her than an adventurous warrior, if Princess Isobail would allow such a match. "Tell me what troubles you so, my sweet. You can trust me with your heart and life."

"Can I, Gavin? Baltair, Prince Alric's seneschal, saw you hiding near Lord Daron's during the raider attack. What were you doing there, sneaking about in the forest?"

"Have you forgotten our talk and why I have remained here?" he reminded her. "I told you I was going to travel your land, observing it. How else can I decide if it is safe or wise for me to find work here? Did Baltair tell you it would have been certain death if I had tried to help them, just as it was near the village with you?"

"Yes. Still, I cannot help but wonder why you are always around when the raiders are . . . Or where Isobail is," she added quietly. "You must realize how curious these episodes appear to me, and to others."

Gavin watched her intently. Considering the trouble in this land and the short time they had known each other, he could not blame her for her doubts. Yet those feelings did not run as deeply as she imagined, which he pointed out by saying, "If you truly believed I was one of the brigands or Isobail's hirelings, you would not be lying with me this moment, flushed with contentment. Nor would you say such things to me."

"You are right," she admitted, "but I must hear you deny both."

Gavin's fingers teased over her lips, and he smiled. For now, it was easy to speak the answers she longed to hear. "I am not a brigand or one of the princess's hirelings. I knew nothing of the attack on the village or at Lord Daron's until I witnessed them. Since there is trouble all over your land, it is not difficult to be around when peril strikes. You were at the village and Baltair was at Daron's, both in hiding. Should I question and doubt you too?" he teased.

Alysa's eyes studied him intently, then she smiled. "I knew you could not be evil. Forgive me for asking such questions."

"There is nothing to forgive, m'love. You would be unwise if you ignored possible clues that could help your people. Why did Baltair reveal such a thing to you?" he asked.

Although she loved this man and felt she could trust him, Alysa knew this was not the time to expose herself. After all, he was here with fellow warriors who might not be trustworthy or loyal to him. She had to be patient and wary. "Baltair spoke with Princess Alysa and related many terrible things to her," she said. "You witnessed the attack; surely you realize how suspicious it was. Isobail journeys around the land duping the peasants and nobles, trying to turn them against Prince Alric in her favor. Princess Alysa fears that Isobail is after the Crown itself, and she fears she will be forced to battle her stepmother for it."

This news alarmed Gavin. "I saw Isobail many times during my travels, and Princess Alysa speaks truthfully, but foolishly. Isobail is powerful and clever, and many cling to her. To challenge her would mean certain death. You must warn Alysa to be careful."

"There might be little time, Gavin. Alysa believes her father's illness comes from slow poisoning. She cannot prove it, but she has arranged to safeguard his food and drink every day. Alysa must be right, as Prince Alric grows stronger each day since Isobail's departure. Only a servant named Leitis, and now Baltair, know of her actions. Alysa must do something to rescue her father, but he is too weak to flee."

"Your note said you wanted to hire me. What did you mean?" he asked. Apprehension filled him as he recognized the direction she was taking. He and Giselde had not known that others were working against Isobail, which could place the two groups at cross-purposes. He had to learn all he could, then hopefully dissuade the untrained fighters before they endangered all of them. He had not wanted to involve his precious Thisbe, but it was too late.

Alysa licked her lips and tried to control her suddenly rapid breathing. "Princess Alysa wishes to hire you . . . to help her get her father safely to Cambria, by abducting him if necessary." She watched Gavin's astonishment mount by the minute. She hurriedly went on, "Until Baltair's return, Prince Alric did not know what was happening around him. He refused to heed Alysa's warnings, since he did not believe his wife would dare to commit such treachery. Isobail has duped him, yet Alric is too feeble to challenge her, even though her strikes are becoming bolder. Two feudal lords have been slain and replaced, and I fear for the lives of others.

When Prince Alric is well enough to travel, Alysa wants to escape with him to Cambria. There, she can persuade King Bardwyn to send loyal knights here to defeat Isobail. She will need the help of a clever guide and a strong guard to reach her grandfather. You said you have friends here with you. Can she not hire your men as her escort? Name your price."

"Money is nothing in this matter, sweet Thisbe. But survival is, survival for your ruler and my men. The moment Prince Alric was missed, Isobail would send warriors, perhaps the raiders, after us. Even if Prince Alric was strong enough to travel swiftly, which he is not, I have only six men, and she has many. If Princess Alysa's suspicions are right, we would be chased and captured . . . and perhaps slain. It is too dangerous and foolish to risk at this time. You said there is no proof against her; that is what you need to gain the people's support, and King Bardwyn's. Alysa could never bring charges like these against Damnonia's beloved regent without it, plenty of it," he emphasized.

"But how can I gather such proof?" she asked frantically.

"As I travel around, I will see what I can learn. It is not enough to suspect Isobail is behind the trouble; we must prove it. If I discover anything of value, I will tell you so you can pass it along to your mistress. Keep your eyes and ears alert, and I will do the same for you. But take no risks, m'love," he cautioned.

"If things grow worse at the castle, would you help . . . us flee?"

"The moment you feel you are in danger, come here and wait for me. I will protect you with my life," he vowed.

"My life does not matter, Gavin, only that of my . . . ruler."

"Nay, sweet Thisbe, your life does matter, to me. No woman has pleased me as you do. If you avoid trouble,

I will take you with me when I leave this land," he teased, hoping to lighten her heavy mood.

Dismayed, she scolded, "This matter is grave to me. I cannot avoid trouble as long as I must seek ways to help Prince Alric. If danger strikes and you cannot help us, I will find someone who can, or I will handle everything myself. Do not worry about me, for Piaras, the castle's knight trainer, taught me how to fight. I can use a sword, bow, lance, and knife. Have you forgotten how easily I escaped you when we first met?"

Gavin knew she was serious, and his deep concern caused him to miss unwitting clues to her identity in her words. "Promise you will do nothing until I can study this situation and choose a safe path to travel."

Alysa's face brightened with happiness and relief. "You will help us?"

"I will try, but you must tell no one about me. If news of my intrusion reached the wrong ears, we could all be cast into Isobail's dungeon. As you said, you do not know whom to trust. Sweet Thisbe, there is a heavy price for my work," he hinted roguishly.

"Name it, and Princess Alysa will pay it," she replied.

He shook his head. "Only you can pay it, sweet Thisbe. The price is you, here with me when I can endure your absence no longer."

A scarlet flush swept over Alysa's face. "I am to pay you by . . ."

He chuckled, hugged her tightly, and shook his head again. Dark gold waves shifted with his movement, and his green eyes gleamed with reborn desire. "Nay, not like that, m'love. It was a jest. When you come to me, it must be because your desires match mine. Without desire, our union would be bitter."

Alysa's eyes observed him for a time, then she remarked, "You are a strange man, Gavin. Will I ever know you?"

"One day you will know me perhaps too well. I wonder how you will feel about me then," he teased. Gavin was overjoyed that she had not mentioned Squire Teague, or summoned help from his rival.

"I cannot imagine feeling any differently than I do now," she said.

"And how is that, sweet Thisbe?"

Alysa gazed into his sparkling eyes and grinned. "One day you will know that answer perhaps too well," she playfully retorted.

Gavin nibbled on her ear, then murmured, "Perhaps I know it now, and that is why I feel your exquisite trap closing around me."

"You must not fear such an imprisoning snare, or you would be fleeing swiftly. Why do you linger here in such peril?"

He leaned his head backward to fuse their gazes. "For once in my life such a womanly snare does not frighten me. I wonder why."

Musical laughter filled the air. Alysa drew his mouth to hers and kissed him soundly. Before he could claim her lips again, she murmured dreamily, "Yea, I wonder why. . . ."

Within moments they were making love.

Eleven

Giselde lovingly stroked a drawn image of her deceased daughter, and murmured, "Soon I can reveal myself to Alysa. Rest well, Catriona, for I will guard our little one and avenge your murder. It has taken me years to hone my skills and to find the right allies. Now I have both, and it is time for revenge and justice. By the gods who serve and defend us, I swear the Evil seed of your traitorous husband and his wicked whore will never sit upon the throne of Damnonia or any land. If need be, I will die seeking Isobail's destruction."

Trosdan, the Druid High Priest and wizard, observed Giselde worriedly, for she was treading slippery ground. He wished he could reveal the truth about Alysa and Gavin to the woman, but the runes had forbidden it. Perhaps he should not be concerned about that matter, for Giselde would learn the truth herself very soon. "I thought your hatred for Alric had lessened, Giselde," he hinted.

The elderly woman confessed, "Yea, it is hard to despise a man who has grown so weak in mind and body. Alric is no longer the handsome man who stole Catriona's heart so long ago, and he is being punished terribly for his betrayal of her. Yet Damnonia's prince has only himself to blame for his troubles. Now he must pay for his foolish greed. Poor Alric is like a careless hunter who trapped himself in his own clever snare. Only he can free himself, if he desires escape. So far, he has made no attempt to do so. How can I forgive him for becoming entangled with Isobail for a second time? For giving her the chance to slay my only child? And for placing Catriona's murderer within striking distance of my granddaughter and the Crown? My only concern is protecting Alysa and her inheritance."

As painful memories invaded her mind, Giselde muttered, "Alric said everyone here would hate me for having two bonds to the Norsemen, a mother and a husband, and he claimed my identity might birth new hostility toward Catriona. He commanded us to remain silent about our relationship. It was hard to play Catriona's servant, but at least it kept me near her and my granddaughter. That secrecy was wrong, Trosdan, and it will knife Alysa's heart when she learns about it. After that lie was accepted as fact, the time never came to dispel it without risking dissension among Alric's subjects. Even so, if Alric had truly loved my Catriona, he would not have visited Isobail's bed so many times while my daughter was away healing from the death of their first child. Then, to bring that woman and their bastard into the same castle with my sweet and trusting Catriona . . ."

Trosdan reminded the agitated woman, "But Isobail did not know Alric forced his counselor to drug her so he could sneak into her bed each night while he was visiting Lord Caedmon during Catriona's absence. Isobail thought it was her lover coming to her. I have often wondered what she thought when she learned her lusty knight was dead and she was carrying a child."

"She thought it was best to murder Lord Caedmon so he could not expose her and have her slain! No doubt she believed a mischievous spirit or even a god had visited her and sired her son. If Isobail knew the father was Alric, she would use Moran to get everything she wants. It surprises me that, during a moment of passion or illness, Alric has not confessed his dark deed to her or Moran. No doubt he fears she will slay him for his lustful trickery, as she killed her first husband."

As Giselde continued, she revealed how she had discovered Alric's dark secret: "After I heard him discussing his shame with Baltair I hid in every corner to learn all I could. Alric pretended he loved only Catriona and Alysa, but I saw him sneak away many times to play with Moran or just to watch him. And the prince made certain his bastard was well placed in life, first sending him into knight's training, then making him a prince by marriage."

"If Alric craved Isobail so much, why would he wait for years after Catriona's death to marry Lady Isobail?" Trosdan reasoned.

"After those stolen nights at Lord Caedmon's, Alric continued to lust for Isobail. He only hesitated after Catriona's death until it was safe to marry that vicious witch. Besides, he feared me because I knew about them. I am no fool, Trosdan, I know why Alric took that whore everywhere with him while little Alysa was suffering alone at the castle. Now the gods are tormenting him for his sins. We must not allow Moran to claim Alysa or Isobail to steal the crown of Damnonia. Their Evil must be stopped and destroyed."

"Why do you not tell her more about her father, so she might better help him?"

"Alric is too ill to battle Isobail but he is responsible for her being here and for his weaknesses. I wish I could tell Alysa about his iniquities, but this is not the time. I cannot tell her how weak he was, and that he fathered a son while her mother still lived. He betrayed my daughter and caused her death, even if he did not help Isobail poison her. He has allowed that woman to enslave him and to torment my Alysa. He deserves pain and death."

"Are you certain you can trust King Bardwyn to help you?"

"Yea, Trosdan, for we have known each other for years. As does King Bardwyn, I know of his son's flaws. Many, including Bardwyn, have suffered greatly for Alric's weaknesses, disobedience, and impulsiveness. The King of Cambria is a strong and noble man, and he kept his vow to never lay eyes on his son's mistake, for that is how Catriona was viewed in the beginning. Even after my daughter's death, no warrior especially a king, could break his vow of honor. All knew that Alysa came to mirror her mother, Alric's so-called weakness, more and more each year. Many feared the prince's impulsive marriage could prevent him from becoming king after Bardwyn's death. How sad for everyone, as Bardwyn longs to see his only granddaughter."

Trosdan appeared puzzled, so Giselde explained, "We know how vital it is for a territory to have a powerful ruler and strong feudal lords. Since this part of the kingdom is separated from Cambria by water and another kingdom, Bardwyn needed a regent here who was powerful, one who was loved and respected and obeyed. He removed Lord Caedmon Ahern as his warlord and regent and placed Prince Alric in charge so his son could prove himself. How tragic for everyone that Bardwyn did not know about Caedmon's antagonism and his wife's evil."

Giselde sighed deeply. "Bardwyn sent for me after Catriona's return to Albany. He realized from Alric's messages how my daughter's absence was affecting his son. I hated to encourage Catriona to return to her husband, but Rurik and my parents persuaded me to meet with Bardwyn. When I spoke with the King, he begged me to help settle the tormenting matter between Alric and Catriona. He confided his guilt over their

205

unborn son's death and his unfair treatment of my daughter. He felt if he had behaved differently, the Cambrians might have accepted her as Alric's wife. Bardwyn said he knew the good changes in his son were due to Catriona's influence and Alric's love for her. Despite Alric's flaws, his father loves him; that is why Bardwyn banished him to his own domain rather than humiliate and disown him. He prayed, with time and Catriona's touch, Alric would become the man he should be.

"In the time we spent together, Bardwyn and I became friends. We came to trust and respect each other. We agreed to keep our meeting a secret from Alric and Catriona because we did not want them to feel as though we were interfering in their life. But we did not have to intrude. Evil forced Catriona back into Alric's arms when the Vikings attacked that last time. While we were staying in Cumbria after Prince Briac's rescue, I saw Bardwyn again in secret. He feared that this new trouble could cause more problems for our children, but he pleaded with me to take Catriona back to Damnonia to Alric, and I did, to my sorrow. If only Alric had been more like his father. . . ."

"This is why King Bardwyn trusts you," Trosdan remarked.

"Yea, he knows I have spoken truthfully about his son and the danger here. That is why he appealed to King Briac for help and why they sent Gavin to aid us. Even so, my word is not enough to bring about an attack on Princess Isobail or to dethrone Alric. To prevent dissension, Bardwyn needs undeniable evidence against her."

"Prince Gavin will gather it, if he is not exposed to the Evil forces before time also becomes our enemy. . . ."

* * *

Two hours later at Malvern Castle, Lord Fergus arrived and asked to meet with Prince Alric on an urgent matter. Alric surprised everyone by appearing in the Great Hall within minutes, dressed, but looking pale and emaciated from his lengthy illness. Apparently in high spirits, the ruler smiled at those gathered to visit him, his gaze softening and lingering briefly on his daughter. Not wanting to tower over Lord Fergus from the dais during this meeting, the prince—with Baltair's assistance—walked slowly to the eating area and sat down at a table. Alric's faded green eyes took in those present: Baltair, Earnon, Kyra, Alysa, Guinn, Fergus, a few of the lords' men, Piaras, castle guards, and three of Alric's servants. He summoned the feudal lord to sit nearby, then motioned for the others of enough rank to join them. Alric and Alysa exchanged loving smiles again, and she sat down within a few seats of him, as did Baltair and Kyra.

Alric ordered refreshments for everyone and waited until they were served before stating, "My friend and retainer Baltair tells me you wish to address me, Lord Fergus. Speak."

Fergus put aside his glass of wine and warm bread to reply, "My news is bad, Your Highness. Raiders from Logris have attacked my land, stolen cattle, and driven them into Vortigern's domain. My men followed them to the border, but dared go no farther without permission and help. I do not have enough knights and men-at-arms to battle them alone. I request the loan of yours to answer this challenge."

Before Alric could respond, two parties arrived at nearly the same time: Isobail's, and Lord Orin's and Sir Kelton's combined. They were shown into the Great Hall, and all eyes widened to see their ruler present and entertaining a small group at a table. During the commotion, no one saw Kyra's hand move toward Alric's goblet.

Baltair and Alysa noticed the astonished expression that crossed Isobail's face, then her quick glance at Earnon. Then Isobail hurried forward to greet her husband and inquire about his health.

"What are you doing out of bed, my husband?" she softly chided.

Alric did not look at her or smile as he replied, "I am listening to the words of my vassal, Lord Fergus. Why has the trouble that plagues my land been kept from me?" he asked sharply.

Isobail took a seat opposite the prince, compelling him to look at her. "You have been very ill, and I wanted to spare you worry. I have been watching matters closely and tending to them, as you requested. Ask the lords if I have done anything wrong, or have done less than you, my noble ruler could have in my place." Isobail glanced at the solemn Baltair and said, "Surely your trusted servant Baltair has learned of the attack from those who rode ahead of my party, and has told you of Lord Daron's death. I hurried here to tell my liege such things. I asked the lords to meet here to discuss these troubles with us.",

Lord Orin stepped forward and concurred with Isobail's explanation. "Be proud of your wife, my liege, for she saved my life at great risk to her own. While you have lain ill, she has comforted your people's sufferings and appeased their fears."

"My wife has done many good things which have reached my ears," Alric stated in an odd voice. "She can rest now, as I am well enough to rule my domain once more. The raiders' terror must end. I will call the knights and warriors together and set traps for them." Alric halted long enough to motion for Orin and Kelton to be seated. "Sheriff Trahern." He called the bearded man forward. "Why have these dangerous events been allowed to continue so long? I am vexed with you."

Trahern cleared his throat and responded, "The raiders are sly, my liege, and they plan their attacks cleverly. I send spies to watch many areas, but they strike elsewhere. By the time we learn of a new raid and reach the area, all signs of them have vanished. My men and I cannot follow a trail that does not exist. I need more men and arms, sire, to guard our lands."

Alric rested his head against his chair as he debated irritably, "Cattle tracks cannot vanish swiftly and completely, Trahern, as you claim the brigands' do. Lord Fergus's men followed them for days, but they were outnumbered and had to retreat. You should have been there to help them. Perhaps what we need is a new sheriff, one who is smarter and braver than our enemies." He watched Leitis serve the new arrivals as he sipped from his goblet.

Isobail declared boldly, "My husband, you speak unwisely and cruelly. If not for the courage of Sheriff Trahern at Lord Daron's, those of us in this very hall would be dead. Your loyal vassal has not failed you or your people. He has snared several brigands and executed them, but others take their places. Sheriff Trahern should be thanked and rewarded, not shamed." Orin, Fergus, and Kelton nodded in agreement with Isobail's words, as she had made certain those deceitful claims would appear true.

"Yet our land and subjects remain in peril," Alric replied.

Fergus related the dire events around his castle to the newcomers. "They fled into Logris, but we must pursue them, my liege."

"Nay, Lord Fergus," Alric protested. "We cannot enter Vortigern's kingdom to capture petty thieves. He would take offense to our invasion, then we would have two foes to battle. To prevent more trouble, we must capture and slay the brigands while they are in our land."

"They are not 'petty thieves,' my husband. They

plunder the lands, burning, robbing, and raping, and they must be halted, no matter where they flee and hide. Perhaps Vortigern of Logris allows these evil men to use his kingdom for their camp, or perhaps he is behind them. Since they were attacking at Lord Daron's and Lord Fergus's at nearly the same time, surely that means there are several large bands of them."

Isobail used this situation to her advantage, as she wanted to initiate her move against Logris. "The rustling of cattle and the raids on the villages are challenges. It has been this way since the birth of this land. Rivals test the strengths, skills, and weaknesses of others. Indeed, if we fail to retaliate, we risk losing the support and loyalty of our subjects. Vortigern will think us weak and afraid, or the brigands will. They will view our lack of action as an excuse to continue their attacks. We must strike back."

Today Alric was irritated by Isobail's enchanting beauty and appeal, traits that had ensnared him too many times. This woman had dared to imagine she could steal his crown and slay him! She had dared to delude his subjects! Presently she dared to seize control of this meeting! He had not realized how clever she was, but he did now. The lords and others were hanging on her every word, and agreeing with her. Baltair had warned him to walk slowly and gingerly, and it was good advice. It took every ounce of strength and wisdom Alric possessed not to expose her treachery. Not yet, he cautioned himself.

"My wife will hold silent! I am the ruler here." Alric spoke tersely. "It would be rash to challenge Vortigern in his own land. Logris is larger and more powerful than Damnonia. He could crush us. We have no proof Vortigern has become our enemy. We will send a message to him and request his aid in this grievous matter."

Alric halted a moment to catch his breath and sip the wine Leitis had served him earlier trusting that whatever she placed before him would be untainted. "If he refuses, or if I learn he commands the brigands, then I will decide how to defeat him. Peace has ruled our island for many years because no kingdom has invaded another. Hasty actions could destroy this balance of power and set us all on a path of bloody destruction."

He gazed around to see how his words were falling on his vassals. "Have you also forgotten we are a part of Cambria? For Damnonia to declare war on Logris is the same as Cambria doing so. We must challenge these mysterious brigands carefully. If we cannot defeat them in this territory, we will summon help and permission from the king, then pursue them wherever they ride."

The prince wiped moisture from his face and trembled slightly, but he was too distracted to notice the returning symptoms. He wet his throat again with a sip of wine. "Sheriff Trahern, place your spies near the Logris border to discover when and where the brigands cross it. After they enter my land, set your trap at their return point."

"It is a good plan, Your Highness, but it has failed to date," Trahern protested. "Each time we have lain in wait for them, they did not return by that road. I will try it again. They cannot evade us forever."

"I will send a warning to my father in Cambria so he can be prepared to aid us if necessary. Trahern, select two of your best men to deliver my message to King Bardwyn. Send them out immediately."

"As you command, my liege."

"Our prince is right, and we must obey him," Lord Orin said. "To invade Logris without proof of Vortigern's guilt would be dangerous. It would be wise to approach him peacefully before we make war against him. Perhaps he will join us to push the brigands and Jutes from both our lands."

Fury consumed Isobail, although she kept silent and appeared respectful. But before this day ended, she vowed to herself, Alric would be writhing in agony again, and soon he would be out of her way forever! First she must learn how and why he had gotten well? . . .

Alric began to fidget in his chair. He felt a distressing flush creep over his body and nausea steal into his throat. Those warning pains sliced through his insides again like a white-hot blade. He feared the damnable illness was storming his body anew. He glanced around at the others, to discover that the food and wine—from the same platter and jug—were not affecting anyone else in this tormenting way. No one had gotten near his food and drink, so neither could be to blame this time. It had to be the malicious return of his accursed illness. He squirmed in his chair as the spasms grew worse. Knowing the swift and embarrassing pattern of this sickness too well, Alric was desperate to flee the room.

Isobail comprehended Alric's problem. "Are you taking ill again, my husband?" she solicitously inquired. "I knew you should not be out of your bed so soon." She called servants to assist Alric to his chamber.

"Be gone!" he yelled at them in distress, startling everyone. "I am not a child or an old woman. I can walk to my chamber alone."

Isobail rushed to his side and whispered, "Come with me quickly, my husband, or you will humiliate yourself before them. Do, not fight me, Alric. I only wish to help you."

The prince was weak and shaking. He knew he had hesitated too long at the table. There was no time to argue, so he accepted her assistance. Yet he made it only halfway up the winding stairs before his stomach and bowels cut loose with a vengeance. They halted only long enough for the violent attack to cease.

Afterwards, Isobail urged Alric to his bed. She stroked his sweaty brow and entreated gently, "I know it has been difficult to remain abed so long, but you

212

must not push yourself before you are healed properly. Next time do not leave bed the moment you feel better. For once, allow your body to rule your head."

Her light blue gaze settled on the miserable prince as she vowed, "I have done nothing more than to love you and help you, to fill your place while you are ill, even if I made mistakes. I do not understand why you suddenly mistrust me. The way you treated me downstairs humiliated me. I beg you, Alric, do not do so again. I live only to serve you and your people."

Tiny points of guilt pricked Alric after Isobail departed his chamber. She had looked so hurt, so vulnerable, so misjudged, so innocent. When she was like this . . . No, he protested, it is simply a trick to deceive me. The acts against her are too great. *But, are they facts,* his groggy brain argued, *or only doubts and fears?* Baltair and Alysa had never liked Isobail, he concluded, and perhaps they were mistaken. If his wife wanted him killed, she had been given plenty of opportunities. At the mercy of the potent herb, Alric's befuddled mind ran this way and that, playing cruel tricks on him.

Baltair had prevented Alysa from rushing after Isobail and her father. He knew what was about to take place, and he wanted to spare Alric the shame and Alysa the dismay of it. As they spoke quietly, neither could place this relapse on Isobail or Earnon. Baltair said, "If it were in the food or drink, we would all be ill. To be certain, I have taken his goblet and will give the remaining wine to a servant and watch her closely. If she does not take ill—"

"You are so clever Baltair. I am glad you are helping me." Alysa realized that Alric's relapse prevented her from undermining Isobail's influence. She would do as her lover suggested, wait and watch. As arranged today, they would meet again in two days.

Isobail returned to the Great Hall and spoke with the feudal lords who were standing together. "My friends and retainers, to make certain my husband stays abed until he is well, we must not trouble him again with our problems. He is vanishing before our eyes, and we can do nothing to help him while he suffers from this *disease*." She used the last word deliberately, knowing it would intimidate the others into staying away from Alric. "He is too dazed to realize Vortigern's Jutes are challenging us. I fear if we do not strike back, they will invade us and destroy us. But we will obey our liege by gathering the proof he demands. When it is in our hands, then we will resolve on our course of action."

Anxiety filled the eyes of those present at the thought of catching a wasting-away disease. "We can be of no help here, Your Highness," Lord Orin stated, giving her the title of regent again. "We should return to our homes and await your commands there."

"You are most kind and loyal, dear Orin. I shall never forget your defense of me today. I shall send news within a few days, or come to visit you. Will that pleasure you or burden you at this time?"

Orin was heady from this royal attention. He smiled broadly and gushed, "It will be a pleasure and an honor to entertain you, Your Highness. I will rush home to prepare things and await your arrival."

"I will journey there after three nights." She watched the men leave quickly, and wanted to laugh aloud at their stupidity.

Isobail summoned Trahern and quietly ordered, "I need not tell you to keep those messengers from reaching Bardwyn or all is lost. Do not fret over Alric's nasty words; if he tries to replace you, the lords and peasants will side with you. This setback is annoying, Trahern, you must find more ways to implicate Logris and Vortigern in these troubles."

"I shall obey you, and miss you," her lover replied.

"As I shall miss you. Meet me at Orin's in four days." The princess turned to locate her sorcerer and said,

"I wish to see you in my chamber, Earnon." To Alysa, she remarked, "I will speak with you tomorrow, Alysa. Do not disturb my husband tonight. I hope you are not the one who encouraged Prince Alric to harm himself today by leaving his bed too soon. Even when I am not here, you must obey my orders."

Baltair placed his arm around Alysa's shoulder and squeezed a gentle warning to keep the princess from verbally battling her stepmother. Alysa hated it when Isobail spoke and behaved like a queen, The Queen! Alysa clenched her teeth and glared, but held silent.

Isobail grinned. "Baltair is wise, Alysa, heed him well. Until your father heals, I am regent of Damnonia; remember that."

Alysa watched Isobail's departure, Earnon trailing her like a mindless sheep. She glanced around the hall to find everyone gone. Looking into Baltair's warm brown gaze, she promised, "She will never be ruler of Damnonia, not while I live and breathe!"

Isobail whirled on Earnon and demanded, "What was that fool doing out of bed? I left you here to keep him there."

Earnon concealed his anger and tried not to appear defensive. "Your servant met with an accident four days past, and I have not replaced him yet. I must move cautiously to find someone we can trust. Each day I have tried to sneak the herbs into Alric's food and wine myself, but it has been difficult. His head was already clearing when I discovered the servant was dead. And there is another problem. . . . I think Alric suspects we are slowly poisoning him. He has been refusing all wine until today, and allowing only Leitis to serve his food. I did not have the power to change his orders to the guards and servants. But I have been observing Baltair closely since his return, and saw nothing odd there."

Isobail pondered his words, then commented skeptically, "You were not near him downstairs. How did the attack seize him when others drank from the same jug and ate of the same bread?"

"Your daughter slipped it into his goblet during the excitement of your return," he replied, having planned his strategy well.

"Kyra? Why would that little snip do such a thing?"

"Kyra is smart, like you. She even cleverly exchanged the goblets during Alric's frantic departure, in case someone checked it later. She thinks much like you, Isobail, and guessed your plot against Alric. She persuaded me to allow her to help us get rid of Baltair."

"You told her everything?" Isobail shrieked.

"Do you think me mad?" he shot back. "She asked me things and made remarks that told me she knew too much and should be taken into our confidence. Kyra can be a great help to us. She proved that downstairs when she laid your husband low, and did so without arousing a single suspicion. She can aid our plot against Baltair. Your daughter worships you, Isobail, and she craves your love. All she wants is to help you, to make you proud of her. She would do anything you asked of her."

"If that little snip can discover our plot, then we are being mindless, Earnon, and others can do the same. Perhaps she told Alric the truth."

"Isobail, Isobail, you are being silly," he scolded her. "She only guessed because she is so much like you. Why do you hate her? Do you not realize what a prize she is for you? She is not as beautiful, but she resembles you closely enough to play your part at a distance, if you ever have need of an alibi."

"I have told Sir Calum he can have her soon. I need him."

His heart pounding in trepidation, Earnon argued, "Presently you need Kyra more. Any loyal knight can fill Calum's place, but only Kyra can rid us safely of Baltair."

"What is your plan, my bewitched sorcerer?" she teased.

"We must be serious, Isobail. Times are getting perilous for us too. Your plot has taken root and now grows rapidly. Do not allow foolish spite against your own child to hinder its growth and bloom."

"Do not scold me like a child, Earnon. I am your ruler."

"Heed my words, Your Highness, and you will become everyone's ruler," he retorted frostily, as if fearless. "If not, my powers are of no use to either of us. Which shall it be?"

Isobail fumed and paced, then glared at him. Sighing loudly and deeply in annoyance, she yielded, "I will listen to you . . . and agree."

"While you were gone I studied my books and found the perfect potion to destroy Baltair. Since he knows much about herbs, it must be a clever one." He explained the wicked spell to her and watched her beam with delight.

"Do it quickly, dear Earnon, but do not allow the guards to rescue little Kyra too quickly. Let Baltair have his fun before he dies."

Earnon comprehended her implication and gaped in shock. "We cannot allow him to ravish her. It is only a trick to slay him. She will never agree to defilement. She will feel betrayed."

"It will be more convincing to everyone if Kyra is . . . injured slightly by the madman. If she truly wishes to help me, she will obey. You did say she would do 'anything' I asked of her."

"But she is your own flesh and blood."

"There are more important things at stake than little Kyra. If you wish to remain at my side throughout this victory and to earn Lord Orin's castle, you will convince her to obey me."

"I will try, Your Highness," he murmured, knowing he would not. He had known she was evil, but not like this. If she could betray her own child, his secret love . . .

"Do not try, Earnon, do it," she ordered sullenly. "Then I will hand her over to Sir Calum as his reward. Soon I will make him a feudal lord. She will be both a princess and a lady. What more could she want from me?"

"It will require a little time. The planets must be in perfect position for the maddening spell to work. I am charting them now."

"How long?"

"The sun and moon must shine a certain way on the wheat I use. I will know within a few days."

"Tell me when I return from Lord Orin's. What of Sir Kelton? Have you devised a plan to get rid of him too? This time I want a simple accident, one that cannot be questioned."

"I know how to do it, Your Highness, but not who to carry it off. What about your son? Will he join you and help you?"

"I do not wish to involve Moran yet. Find another."

"I have no excuse to visit Sir Kelton's, but you do. You are most convincing, my beautiful queen-to-be."

Isobail grinned. "It will be done before I visit Lord Orin." Isobail's gaze hardened when she added, "Find a way to frighten Leitis into taking our dead servant's place."

"I have already decided how to do so, but I will require your assistance." He related his "spell" to her and her laughter filled the room.

"I am tired now, Earnon. And I am most pleased with you. Forgive my hasty scolding and fatigue. I shall have Ceit relax me with a rubbing while Guinn soothes my mind with sweet music."

Earnon nodded and left, not fooled by Isobail's last words. To make certain Kyra was not mistaken, he would observe this matter himself. If Ceit left the two alone, he would know it was safe to spend a short time with his love.

Twelve

Giselde was disturbed by the information Gavin had shared with her since his arrival an hour ago. Alysa had promised her that she would not take this deadly matter into her hands, but she was doing just that, and coaxing others to do so. Gavin had related the events taking place at the castle between Alysa, Baltair, and Leitis. Giselde was concerned as to why Alysa was not giving the herb blend to Alric, and why her granddaughter had not come to see her lately. The old woman's head was spinning with questions which caused her to hesitate because she did not want to endanger the life of King Briac's son, and she was worried over how much Thisbe knew and why the girl had revealed so much to Gavin. Their relationship confused and alarmed her. She could not understand why her binding spells refused to work on him. Surely it had nothing to do with the amulet she had given to him.

Gavin continued, "I explained to Thisbe why your granddaughter should stop interfering in these deadly events and why I could not help them escape. Thisbe promised she would convince Princess Alysa to do nothing more while I nosed around and came up with a plan. I do not know about your granddaughter, but my Thisbe is a clever girl. She is braver and smarter than any woman I have met. She said her father taught her how to fight with many weapons, and I have witnessed some of her special skills. If I truly were an adventuring warrior, she would be the perfect mate to ride at my side." Gavin's expression softened noticeably as he spoke of the girl. "I did not want her involved in this work, but she is, so I asked her to keep her eyes and ears open at the castle and to tell me what goes on there. She agreed. I told her I would do the same."

Giselde observed the handsome prince and listened closely to his tone of voice. "It is dangerous to include Thisbe or anyone else in on our plans," she replied. "The more people involved, the greater our risk of discovery."

"I know you are right, Giselde, but Thisbe and Alysa appear stubborn, and determined. If I refused to help them, they would work on their own. By pretending to be working with them, I can keep an eye on them and hopefully keep them safe. Besides, they might pick up some valuable clues for us. We are to meet again Friday, after Isobail leaves the castle for Sir Kelton's."

"I wish you two would not see each other. I fear you are falling in love with her. This should not be so, Prince of Cumbria. Have you forgotten that such a match is impossible? Have you learned nothing of ill-fated love from my family's troubles? What about Squire Teague?"

At her warnings, Gavin winced as if in physical pain. "I did not mean to start anything with Thisbe, or with any woman here. It just happened, Giselde. I could not help myself, nor could she. Thisbe cannot be in love with Squire Teague, for she loves me. It must be fate, as we keep being thrown together and cannot resist each other. I must seek a way to have her. She is so beautiful and unique. When she looks at me with those entrancing blue eyes . . ."

Blue eyes? Giselde's keen mind echoed. Thisbe did

221

not have blue eyes, nor was she "beautiful and unique," "braver and smarter than any woman," or overly "clever." Thisbe's eyes were nearly the same color as her hair: dark brown. She was a sweet and gentle girl, not a trained fighter who would make the "perfect mate" for a man such as Gavin. Giselde asked, "Tell me more about Thisbe. I have not seen her for years. I suppose she has changed much. How did you meet? When?"

She observed Gavin as he modestly skimmed over his entanglement with the alleged Thisbe, for the woman he spoke of could not be Piaras's daughter. Giselde's heart beat erratically as she grasped the identity of the girl involved and the depth of the unspoken details, for she perceived an undeniable aura of intimacy. Clearly Gavin and Alysa were bewitched, as she had meant them to be irresistibly bonded; and Giselde remembered how wild and marvelous love could be.

Yet Giselde knew something was amiss, and she searched herself for answers. If she asked too many questions, Gavin could become suspicious of the girl, and she did not want to expose Alysa until she learned the meaning of this ruse. She worried over Alysa's reason for playing Thisbe to a handsome stranger, fearing her granddaughter's motive could be good or bad. If Alysa was trying to discover who Gavin was and why he was here, it could ruin everything. Too, it could place Alysa in grave peril. It had been rash and selfish, as Trosdan warned, for her to bind them together at this dangerous time! Perhaps she should confess the truth to Gavin and Alysa. Nay, it was too late to break the spell. "You are certain you can trust her?" she asked.

Gavin nodded. "Yet sometimes I feel as if she is holding something back. It probably has to do with Teague. She expected to marry him and have everything she desires, but she met me and I ensnared her. He will become a knight and lord, but supposedly I am only a traveling adventurer, a warrior for hire, a single man for life. I saw them riding together one day, but they appeared to be only friends."

"Thisbe was out riding?" Giselde asked as casually as she could.

"On a large dun with black tail and mane," he answered, recalling that sight, missing Giselde's reaction. "Your granddaughter must be a kind mistress, for she lets Thisbe come and go as she pleases. They must be good friends to confide in each other. When this matter ends, I will be eager to meet Princess Alysa."

Giselde knew that no one rode Calliope except Alysa, and so now had no doubt that Gavin's "Thisbe" was her granddaughter. What was Alysa up to with this pretense? she wondered.

A series of heavy knocks interrupted their conversation. Giselde had bolted the door to prevent anyone from walking in on them and exposing their connection. Still, she was alarmed at the intrusion. She asked who was there and was relieved to hear the response, "Piaras."

Giselde gestured to Gavin to go out the back door, as she did not want Gavin and Thisbe's father to meet and talk today. She straightened the concealing tapestry, but left the door ajar so Gavin could overhear Piaras's words.

The aging knight told her about Lord Fergus's visit to the castle, about Isobail's return and behavior, and about Alric's relapse. "I have never seen the prince act that way before. He tore into the sheriff like Trahern was food and he was starving. He was mean to Isobail before the others, and they did not like it because she has them charmed. Isobail has a tongue as smooth as a new blade, and she cuts things up as she wants them."

Piaras revealed what Sir Beag had told him about the episodes at Daron's castle. "Beag said he was ordered to remain at the castle during the hunt, then ordered back here after the trouble. He thinks she does not want him in that area for some reason. Sir Calum is in charge now, and he left his squire here. Very strange, Giselde; it's as though the princess was afraid he or Squire Teague might see or hear something. Isobail is talking about knighting most of the oldest squires, to give us more fighters, but I think she is up to no good. 'Course, Thisbe will be happy for Teague. Never seen two people more in love.''

Giselde quickly turned his attention away from Thisbe and Teague. ''Tell me about Alric's illness,'' she urged.

''Came on him all of a sudden while they were drinking and talking.''

''Perhaps it was bad food or wine. Did anyone else become ill?''

''Only His Highness. Everyone was eating and drinking from the same jug and platter. I watched everybody closely. Nobody was near enough to fool with his servings, if that is what you were thinking.''

Giselde knew that Piaras's conclusion could not be true, though she did not tell him so. He then spoke about Baltair and Alysa, but she learned nothing new. She cautioned Piaras not to confide in Baltair or Alysa, thinking to avoid a slip of the tongue that might somehow endanger either one. ''Be careful when you meet with Baltair,'' she said. ''Isobail has spies everywhere. No help will be coming, Piaras. By now Isobail and Trahern have had those messengers to the King slain. But do not worry; I will locate someone trustworthy to carry the message to King Bardwyn.''

''I should hurry back before I am missed. Isobail is leaving for Sir Kelton's in two days, then she is heading for Lord Orin's. If you have somebody who can trail her, it would be a good idea.''

''I have the perfect man,'' Giselde replied, ''and you shall meet him soon.''

Following Piaras's departure, Gavin entered the hut

once more. Looking grim, he remarked, "Thisbe does not favor her father at all, and he does not know her in the least. But just as you found a way to have Rurik, I will find a way to have Piaras's daughter."

"And will you suffer more or less than I have over the years?" she challenged. Giselde's mind was so engulfed by fears and clouded by plans that had been building for years, that she believed the safest path to walk at this time was a separate one. To slow the pace of Gavin's untimely romance, she reasoned, "What of Thisbe? Have you considered her feelings? Do you realize how difficult a marriage between a prince, a future king, and a simple servant can be, if it is allowed? Many will be against her, and will turn against you for straying from your duty and rank. Can you hide her away as your secret whore? Or give up your kingdom to marry her?

"Before it is too late, Hawk of Cumbria, remember your responsibilities. What if you two are seen together? What if Isobail suspects she is spying for us? What if they use her to lead them to us? Each of you is a threat to the other. Discourage your love affair at least for now, Prince Gavin, at least for now, I beg you."

It was after midnight, and Leitis was dazed by the potion Earnon had slipped into her goblet of warm milk at bedtime. The alchemist had no trouble getting past the flimsy lock on the head servant's door. He approached her bed and placed several more drops on her lips. The tingling sensation caused Leitis to lick them and slip deeper into a susceptible condition.

Earnon spoke compellingly to the woman in the hypnotic state. "Each day you will season Prince Alric's midday meal and his evening wine with a few grains from this pouch. You will tell no one of this task, and you will never fail to perform it. You will keep these herbs hidden, and you will not recall using them. If you try to remember my orders or try to disobey them, visions of the Evil One devouring you will torment you until you obey."

This was one power he was positive he possessed: the power to hypnotize certain people. Leitis's mind was vulnerable; he would be able to control her easily. "Now tell me what you know about Alric's illness and about Isobail's plans," he ordered.

Leitis revealed what little she knew about those matters. Earnon silently pondered the information and decided not to relate it to Isobail. He reasoned that Alysa was no real threat and could do little, if anything, to thwart their plans, especially with no one to help her or believe her. Once she was deluded by Leitis about Alric's food, she would cease her interfering actions. But Earnon also did not want to expose Alysa, because he knew that Isobail would deal harshly with her, which could endanger their plans. He had learned that spite was Isobail's worst flaw, one to be controlled. More importantly, he sensed a powerful force around Alysa, one he did not want to challenge.

As if this were actually a magical enchantment, Earnon stated softly, "Let no force break this spell unless you hear these words spoken: Non Rae."

Gavin finished his talk with his men. Everyone had returned to camp safely and given his report. The superficial evidence was mounting against Isobail, but he needed hard facts before taking action. One did not attack a ruler without it. Along his journey he had left two men camped halfway to King Bardwyn's castle, just inside the Cambrian border. He ordered Keegan to deliver their current findings to those men, one of whom would pass it on to Bardwyn.

"Return as quickly as possible, Keegan. I will need

226

you soon. As for the rest of us, it is time for us to make our presence known." Gavin glanced around the circle of close friends, all dressed alike to signal they were a unit and to prevent them from being mistaken for the bands raiding the countryside. He had been charting the brigands' attacks to see if there was any pattern, but did not have enough information to expose one yet. "All we can do is try to make contact by foiling their raids. We play carefree adventurers for a while, men seeking to earn a little money and glory, and to find a little fun. If we come across them, remember we can be bought for the right price. We must convince them we are restless, hungry, and greedy."

Weylin, Gavin's best friend, remarked, "This will be a hard task when we are accustomed to fighting for good and right. What if we are tested? How far do we go with this pretense?"

"We do whatever is necessary, except slaying innocents. If we have to steal, we shall return the goods later after dark. This land is not the only one at stake; our known world is in trouble. I have seen this woman at work; she is more dangerous than most enemies we have battled. Do not allow yourselves to be fooled by her. She is beautiful, but she is deadly and cruel and evil. She has spies and allies everywhere. Trust no one except the men in this circle and Giselde."

"Why would King Bardwyn heed the old woman's words?" Lann asked.

Giselde had confided the reasons to him, but he had promised not to repeat them to anyone. Gavin hated to think of any ruler being as flawed as Alric Malvern. Bardwyn must know his son well to have accepted the old woman's charges against him. It must have pained the king badly, he thought. "There are good reasons, Lann, but I was told them in confidence," he replied honestly, and his men trusted him and accepted that answer.

Gavin smiled at each one in turn: Keegan, Lann, Dal, Bevan, Weylin, and Tragan. He had ridden with these men countless times as they defended Cumbria's borders against foreign bandits. They had helped settle clan disputes in Albany. They had captured common thieves and Viking spies. They had laughed together, talked and joked, sang and danced, lived and almost died together. Each would give up his life for one or all of this group. No matter what confronted them, no one would turn against the others. And no man could be forced to betray the others, even if it cost him his life.

Before Keegan headed for Cambria and the others on their exploratory ride, a hand was lain atop hand until all hands were stacked in the midst of a tight circle which represented their unity. As always, they said together, "If you are slain, my friend, I will mourn you and avenge you. Until fate calls, we ride as one."

Alysa knew she was not to meet Gavin again until Friday, but she wanted to pass on certain information today, unaware that Piaras had given the same news to Giselde yesterday. She went to the appointed tree, sat down, wrote out the facts, and stuffed the note in the decaying hole. She had ended the note by telling him she missed him and would see him tomorrow.

Afterwards, she went to visit Giselde, but the old woman was not at home. To let her friend know she had been there, she left an innocently worded, unsigned note. Then, too tense to return to the castle, she let Calliope race off at the pace and in the direction that pleased him.

Alysa loved the way the wind whipped through her long hair and over her bare arms as she rode Calliope. It provided such an uplifting feeling, one she sorely needed today. When Calliope was at last winded, Alysa tugged gently on his reins to slow him. He instantly obeyed, altering his pace to a slow walk. Alysa pulled the green hood over her mussed hair and straightened her cape, as it would look improper if she were seen in this disheveled state, if anyone recognized her as Princess Alysa Malvern.

She glanced before her, noticing a coppice on either side of the wide road, but thinking nothing of it. But just before reaching the end of the wooded section, three men on horseback appeared from behind the trees to her left and blocked her path. Coming to full alert, she quickly reined in her mount and stared at them briefly. Their garments were made of fur and leather and they looked unkempt. Warnings thundered through her head, and she pulled sideways on Calliope's bridle to turn him and flee.

Immediately she saw three more riders come from the trees behind her on the other side, cutting off any retreat. The two groups began to move closer to her leering grins upon their dirty faces and mischief in their gazes. Alysa realized she had encountered six brigands before time and space were left for escape. She looked from one direction to the other knowing she had to think and act swiftly.

Calliope sensed danger. The loyal steed pranced and snorted in warning, but had no effect on the brigands closing in on his beloved mistress. His head yanked back and forth on the loose reins.

Understanding the animal's instincts, Alysa did nothing to quiet him. She wanted to keep his blood flowing wildly so he could react swiftly to her command. By now two men had separated themselves from the others and had taken places on either side of her, several feet away leaving two men before and behind her. She was encircled, but cautioned herself to keep a clear head.

As her eyes studied each one quickly, Alysa recognized them as men of Viking birth from Juteland.

There was no doubt that these men were part of the outlaw band terrorizing Damnonia. Never, she decided, would she surrender easily.

"A fine beast ye have there, little maiden," one said.

"Hand him over and ye will meet no harm," another added.

Alysa did not trust the bandits, and her expression said so. "Out of my way!" she yelled arrogantly, hoping to startle them into opening a gap for escape. It did not; they merely laughed at her bravado.

The circle tightened slightly. Calliope anxiously neighed and stamped the ground, whipping up dust around his hooves. Alysa's eyes darted about and she guided her mount round and round, trying to watch all of them. Suddenly one of the brigands reached forward and yanked off her hood, causing her brown locks to tumble free. She yelped in pain, for he had seized hair, too, and snapped her head backwards. Her shriek caused Calliope to whinny and to paw the air frantically with his forelegs, but the well-trained rider kept her seat. The hasty movements sent her tresses flying about her, to settle around her shoulders in wild disarray.

The sight of her enormous beauty brought forth crude remarks, and more boldness. Another man grabbed at her cape, jerking it from her body and dropping it to the earth, where Calliope nervously trampled it. That action almost unseated her, and she was glad the fibula broke loose. By now Alysa was as apprehensive as her horse was, but she tried to conceal it.

The bandits began to taunt her, making lewd suggestions. One edged close enough to trail his soiled fingers over one bare arm. As she whirled to avoid his grasp, another reached for her from the other side. Clearly these men intended not only to rob her, but to ravish her. Her courage was giving way to panic, panic that denied clear thinking.

"Ye will fetch a high price, even used," one man jested.

"What are we waiting for?" another asked.

"Lay one hand on me and you shall lose it," Alysa warned in a tremulous voice. She snatched her dagger from its sheath and waved it in the man's face. "Touch me if you dare."

"She is a proud and snarling wench, but we can tame her."

"Should we take her to Skane?" a bandit asked.

"Our leader has his hands full. She be ours first, then we sell her."

"Ye know our orders," the first bandit shouted. "No raids without his permission. We were to scout only. Skane will burst with rage."

The other laughed sardonically and said, "If Valhalla appears before us, are we to refuse to enter her? This wench offers heaven itself. My body swells and aches with need. I must have her."

The frightened man glanced at her blue eyes and tousled hair. "Look at her. She cannot be of earth and man. She is more like a Valkyrie who will send us into the arms of Odin."

"Is that what ye are, pretty maiden?"

"I am more than that, foul human! I am Freyja," she snapped, claiming to be the goddess of love, beauty, and fertility: leader of the Valkyrie, warrior women who served the Viking god Odin and who were said to be unconquerable.

"Riders are coming," one of the brigands yelled.

The man in charge of the band glanced down the road, then back at Alysa. She could tell he was deliberating his next move. Both knew he could not escape with a fighting woman, and she would fight.

"Next time, my bold wench," he sneered, then ordered the men to depart, and led a hasty retreat.

Alysa turned in her saddle to see an astonishing but

delightful sight. It was not castle knights bearing down on them, but Gavin, with five men trailing him, all with swords drawn in readiness. She could hardly believe the brigands had fled without a battle, actually run like cowards.

Her rescuers halted to see if she was all right. Staring at the men who were dressed alike, except for Gavin, she merely nodded. Her lover's eyes roamed her from head to foot to make certain she was not injured. Satisfied she was unharmed and only shaken by the incident, he ordered his men to pursue the raiders.

"Capture at least one if you can, then meet me back in camp. I will see this maiden home safely. If they join up with others, take no risks."

Gavin studied her before asking, "What are you doing out here alone, Thisbe? You know the raiders are everywhere these days."

"I have always ridden when and where I desired, but I see that is no longer possible, or wise. I am glad you arrived in time to save me, and I will not be so foolish again. I was pleased to see your men. Did they agree to work for Princess Alysa?"

A new scowl lined Gavin's handsome face. "We have not decided yet. But your rescue will catch the bandits' attention, and that of Isobail."

Panic nibbled at Alysa. "If anyone learns of this attack on me, I will not be allowed to leave the castle. To meet with you again," she added. If this news became public, she thought, her true identity would be exposed to Gavin. Besides, she needed him and his men to work for her secretly, to play their roles as merry adventurers seeking pleasures while gathering evidence against Isobail.

Gavin, meanwhile, was thinking about what she had just said. "Perhaps it is unwise for us to meet again until these dangers pass," he said softly. "I do not wish to endanger you. What if we are seen together? What

232

if you lead Isobail's men to mine? I am their leader, responsible for their survival. The peril of discovery increases each day for all of us. Until I can understand all of this matter and decide if and how we can help the Malverns, we should stay apart."

Alysa stared at him, stunned by his cutting words. "You do not wish to see me again?" she asked. "Were you displeased with our union yesterday?"

Gavin read the anguish he had given her, and it chewed on his heart. The difference in their stations, which had been gnawing at him, now led him to reply: "That is not my meaning, Thisbe. You are my heart's desire, as you say I am yours. But our desires might not be enough to span the differences between us. Each day I yearn to be with you, as more than a lover. You are a rare and special woman, but if we have no future together, it is selfish of me to steal all I can from you before departing. You are not free to leave this land without permission, permission from an evil woman you are working to defeat. And I cannot remain here very long. After we have shared so much together, what then, m'love? What if there is no hope for us? I do not want your love to turn to hate, and I cannot bear to see you hurt."

Tears pooled in Alysa's eyes. She understood his meaning all too well. They were drawn together, yet something was always between them. He had no way of knowing his feelings matched hers perfectly. "I, too, am selfish, my noble warrior. I understand that our paths might never become one or meet again. I do not care. Death could strike either of us at any moment, so what matters most is sharing what little time we have together. I know there are no promises between us. I will accept only that part of you which you can share, be it for one day or one week or one month. Is it not better to have me for a while than to never have me again?" she reasoned.

"With trouble everywhere, it is dangerous for us to meet, and even more dangerous to play with our emotions," he warned as his heart pounded heavily within his chest. Did he possess the will, the strength, the desire to refuse her? To resist her . . .

She said softly, "We cannot deceive each other when we both know where we stand, and we both accept the likelihood that this is a passing romance." She dared not ask: How can we know our feelings if we part now, so soon? She needed more time with him, and she would battle to obtain it. "Will we face any less danger by avoiding each other? No, we will challenge death each day, even if we remain apart. I believe the danger would be less if we worked together. How can you decide to help us if I do not pass along vital information and clues?"

"I will gather them on my own, without endangering you."

"How can you gather what occurs within the castle? Just yesterday many incidents took place there." She hurriedly related them. "Prince Alric is too ill to flee now, and Isobail acts as if she is already the ruler of this land! Isobail is like the disease she claims my . . . ruler has, and she will devour us all. She does not love her husband, and I fear for his life."

She breathed deeply and continued, for it seemed necessary to tell him almost everything. "Baltair now doubts that the prince is being poisoned. He fears that the Prince has consumed so much that he can never get well, even if it has been stopped even for a while, or for good. I watched Isobail and Alric together yesterday. Something is wrong there, Gavin, and always has been. At times I think she has some strange hold over him and he fears to challenge it. Yet he revealed great anger against her during the meeting of lords. I have never seen him behave like that before."

Gavin kept silent as she wandered about in the maze of her explanation.

Finally she said, "You were at Lord Daron's. Did she truly save Lord Orin's life? Or was it a cunning trick to delude him and others?"

"I believe it was a trick," he replied.

"Will she stop at nothing? She encouraged war against Logris, but Prince Alric won that argument for now. Somehow I believe she has more than the conquest of Damnonia in mind. Her visions of glory frighten me."

"What about Princess Alysa? Does she feel the same?"

"Isobail baits her each day she is home, but I doubt she thinks Alysa would battle her for the crown. Alysa knows everything I have told you, and my words to you are the same as hers. She will pay whatever price you ask for your help."

"Does this horse belong to Alysa?" he asked, eyeing the magnificent steed.

"Yes, it is hers. I can ride Calliope any time I desire. Why?"

"I just realized it is an expensive beast, and I was curious."

"Do you plan to make Calliope part of your price?" she inquired, dreading to hear his answer. She stroked the animal's neck lovingly as she said, "Alysa would be broken-hearted if you demanded him."

"If I asked for him, would she refuse or comply?"

Alysa swallowed hard and inhaled deeply. "You said the price for your help was me. Did you change your mind? Are money and jewels and glory not enough for you?"

"You must answer me, Thisbe. Would she make *any* sacrifice to save her father and her land?"

Alysa looked at him for a long moment, then replied, "Yes, she would. What is it that you truly want from her, Gavin?" Had this been a timely rescue or a trick?

Did he know who she was? Were their meetings more than accidents? No, she commanded herself, she must not allow her imagination to run wild.

Gavin sensed a change in her, one that matched her frosty expression and tone of voice. Gradually her implication settled in on him. He chuckled and shook his head. "I do not want Calliope or Alysa, my jealous Thisbe. I only needed to make certain she is serious. I have never met her, so I do not know if she is selfish, or spoiled, or simple-minded. I know I can trust you, but I must also be able to trust her. Would she die before betraying us?"

"Yes, I swear it. No one knows Alysa better than I do, and I know she can be trusted completely. It is the same with her; she trusts you, but she is fearful of trusting your men. Are they beyond treachery?"

"Upon my life and honor," he vowed. "We have remained here too long. We must get out of sight. Tell me what happened between you and those Jutes," he asked as they crossed the nearby meadow and entered a dense forest.

"I was right, they *were* Jutes," she said pensively. They dismounted and walked side by side, heading deeper into the woods. "Could that possibly mean Isobail's words are true? Could Vortigern be plotting against us, or allowing these bandits to hide and work from Logris?"

"I have met Vortigern. He is a foolish man, but not a stupid one. I believe the bandits are renegades from Hengist's clan. I doubt the Jute chieftain would want his men raiding here. That could entice Logris and Damnonia to band together to push them out of Britain. I would imagine that neither of them knows about the trouble here, or if they do, believe it has nothing to do with each other."

Shadows surrounded them as sunlight was blocked by towering trees. An aura of serenity danced upon the mild breeze which teased through the greenery around them, making little noise on the supple leaves. It was cool and refreshing here, and smells of nature teased at their nostrils. Only the singing of birds reached their ears. They dropped their reins to the ground and continued their stroll, hoping the tranquility of this place would spread to them.

When they halted and looked at each other Alysa asked, "Do you think it would help to send news of our trouble to Vortigern and Hengist?"

Gavin leaned against a tree before he replied. "No, Thisbe, that would reveal how vulnerable your land and ruler are. It is best to defeat the brigands here. Yet Sheriff Trahern makes little effort to do so. He seems to seek only enough action to fool the nobles and peasants. If we started foiling them, that would show it was possible, and should make the people suspicious. But if we do, we may get too much attention from the wrong people. Do you catch my meaning?"

Alysa locked her gaze to his, and stepped closer to him. Her fingers traced the shape of his sensual mouth and slipped over his strong chin to wander down his throat, halting at his heart. She felt its beat quicken, as did hers. She wanted to tell him she was his for the taking, but she knew her gesture told him for her. She saw him watch her, and she recognized an inner struggle exposed in his troubled eyes.

Gavin's hand captured hers, brought it back to his lips, and then his mouth pressed kisses to each fingertip. But his compelling eyes never released hers, and both knew what longings filled the other. Their eyes said far more than any words could, and they allowed them to speak to each other. Everything and everyone else seemed nonexistent at that moment. His hand eased into her hair and drew her head to his chest, then he placed his jaw atop it.

Alysa sensed his tormenting dilemma. He could not

deny that he wanted her, needed her, but . . . She closed her eyes tightly and prayed he would relent, for he was such a strong-willed man, and might adhere to his earlier words. She nestled against him and slipped her arms around his waist. She heard his heart pounding forcefully in her ear and felt the tautness in his body. She was afraid to speak, fearing the sound of her voice could break the romantic spell forming around them.

Time passed, and she wondered if he was summoning the strength to send her away. In panic, she tightened her embrace and waited.

Gavin recognized the reason for her tension, and his body responded to the way she was clinging almost desperately to him. He called her words to mind, and asked himself if she truly meant them. Even if she did, was it fair to her? One of her statements returned to haunt him. He had to respond to it. "You asked if I was displeased with our union yesterday. Nay, m'love; I have never experienced one of such beauty and pleasure. Perhaps that is what alarmed me, to discover such deep emotions within me. How can I ever desire another woman after taking you?"

She lifted her head, smiled, and told him, "I am yours for as long as you desire only me, Gavin. When that desire changes, I will let you go. But not yet. Please, not yet."

Thirteen

"Nay, m'love, not yet," he agreed hoarsely as his mouth drifted over her face and hair. "For as long as it is possible between us, I cannot resist you. I cannot be blamed, for you have bewitched me."

"As you have done to me," she retorted, pulling his mouth to hers, for she could wait no longer to taste his sweet submission.

Gavin's arms banded her securely and pressed her against his pleading body. His mouth sealed to hers and his tongue joyfully explored the delicious area. Had it only been one day since he had taken her? How so, when it seemed more like years?

They kissed and caressed until both their bodies were ablaze with fiery passion. Hands roamed freely and leisurely, as if they had forever to make love. The flames within them burned brighter and fiercer. Yet they continued to stimulate each other and themselves, not wanting to rush this precious stolen moment. They labored lovingly until their hungers craved to be fed, but still they tempted their appetites until they demanded immediate appeasement.

Gavin's adroit hands loosened and removed her garments, then lay her upon a bed of supple grass. His smoldering gaze wandered over her shapely figure, branding his messages of love and desire into her quivering flesh. He was glad she made no attempt to cover herself, but seemed to relish his admiring gaze. She was so sleek and beautiful, and he could wait no longer to feel her naked body touching his. He took off his boots, trousers, and loincloth, but not his short over-tunic. He reclined beside her and looked into her entreating eyes.

When his lips brushed over her nipples, she inhaled sharply and moaned her encouragement. His tongue circled one taut peak before taking it into his mouth to suckle on it, then he did the same to the other one. Blissful sensations rocked her body, and she pressed his head closer to her tingling breast. His hand drifted down her stomach and she parted her thighs in welcome, allowing him to travel into her furry domain. She writhed with delight as he tantalized the flaming bud of her womanhood. She had to touch him in a similar manner to feel his torrid shaft within her grasp. She boldly closed her lingers around it and massaged it gently, savoring its strength and heat and hunger.

His body was hard, yet yielding to her touch. Her fingers admired the heights and depths and curves they encountered as they journeyed over his enticing frame. He was magnificent, and he gave her such mind-staggering pleasure. How could she not want to yield to him time and time again? How could she not throw herself into his arms and tempt him beyond resistance? He was driving her wild with his actions, yet she entreated more and more.

Gavin's entire body ached for his throbbing manhood to enter her and he did so very gently. He had known his control would be tested the moment he slipped within her, but it was harder to master than he had imagined. It quivered perilously, and he went rigid as he silently begged it to resist for a while. His nerves were on edge from the tension of holding back when he wanted to make wildly passionate love to her. He tried to think of other things to help cool the torrid flesh, but nothing worked. She was too tempting and consuming. He risked a few strokes, but halted again as his willful manroot tried to plant its seeds in the moist and fertile area that surrounded it.

Alysa greedily feasted on his mouth and squirmed beneath him to take all of him. She locked her legs around his buttocks, driving him deeply and snugly within her. Her lips and tongue worked at his ear and over his throat. She sensed his tight control was unnecessary. "Love me, Gavin, love me now," she pleaded, fusing their mouths.

Gavin hoped he understood her urgent whispering correctly, for he began slowly to enter and withdraw, then gradually increased his pace until he was moving to the same beat of their hearts. Suddenly she cried out and clung to him, then matched his swift search for rapture. They rode love's stallion locked together until their victory left them weak and damp from their exertions. Still they held on to each other, waiting for total contentment to engulf them.

They lay snuggled together for a long time, and dozed in the peaceful aftermath of love's ecstasy. When Gavin opened his eyes he realized how late it was getting. He whistled for Trojan, and the steed responded. Gavin used water from his skin bag to wash, then quickly donned his garments. He sat down beside Alysa and teased hair over her nose, awakening her with his laughter as she tried to brush it away.

Her eyes opened and she smiled up at him. "It grows late," she murmured, then stretched and yawned.

"There is water in the bag to bathe with, m'love. When you are dressed, join me where Calliope awaits us. I will follow you at a safe distance until you reach the castle gate. No doubt Princess Alysa will question you about your late return. What will you tell her?"

Alysa grinned and remarked, "Why not the truth?" When he looked surprised, she said, "Well, most of it. She will tell no one about us." Suddenly she felt modest, and very naked, for he was fully clothed. She reached for her kirtle and covered herself.

He smiled, and warmed to her once more. "I will give you privacy, my fetching maiden, but do not make me wait too long, for our time together has vanished. Nothing would please me more than to spend the night here with you, making love to you many times. If you do not dress quickly and join me, I will be tempted to keep you here by agreement or by force."

She laughed merrily. "Our bloods have cooled, my lusty dragon, now we must cool our heads. Have you forgotten there are other matters to be consumed besides a helpless maiden?"

"Do you mean my fiery breath can have no more effect on you today?" he teased, dropping to his knees before her. His blond hair was mussed, and she finger combed it for him. His eyes sparkled with happiness and mischief. He seemed totally relaxed with her.

"It has singed me from head to foot, Sir Dragon. Is that not enough for you? If you do not remove your devouring eyes from me, I shall forget all else except you and your delightful threat. Then we will be in trouble, for the castle guards will be out seeking this lost maiden, and will not take kindly to your capture."

His keen senses took in her beauty and mood, and they returned his insatiable hunger for her. "I shall never have enough of you, m'love," he stated huskily, then left quickly.

Alysa watched his hasty retreat and guessed the reason for it. *As I shall never have enough of you, my love,* her heart replied. She hurriedly removed the evidence of her afternoon of lovemaking and pulled on her garments. She joined him, put her filthy cloak in her saddlebag, and mounted Calliope in silence.

They rode without talking until the castle was visible in the distance. "You best go no closer, Gavin. One of the men-at-arms may sight you and ask questions. I left a note for you in the tree, but I have told you all it said. Will . . . I see you tomorrow as planned?" she asked, fearing his answer.

Gavin wanted to yank her from the large dun and race away with her, but he could not. She had snared him good. He replied, "Be there at noon, or I shall come looking for you."

Alysa's radiant smile brightened her entire face. "Nothing can keep me away, Gavin, nothing. I promise to be more than careful when we meet."

He watched her until she safely reached the castle, then turned to head for his camp. He wished he could ask her about Squire Teague, whom Giselde and Piaras claimed she loved. He worried over their impression, as there had to be a logical reason behind it, but he could not explore that area without arousing her suspicions. She would think he had been asking questions about her, and he did not know how she would react to his curiosity. If she had loved Teague before meeting him, he mused, it could no longer be true. She had come to him a virgin, and she had called him her "heart's desire." She had yielded to him twice as a woman in love. That had to mean he was the only man in her heart and life. It had to. . . .

Alysa was not permitted to visit her father tonight, and had not seen him since his violent relapse. She depended on Leitis for reports on his sad state. But Alysa was too preoccupied to realize how subdued Leitis was today, or how the servant seemed convinced they had probably been wrong about the poisonings.

She was compelled to accept that fact because it seemed impossible for her father to receive any harmful herbs; yet he remained ill. Even Baltair, who was knowledgeable about herbs, had his doubts. He and Leitis were guarding Prince Alric closely, but could find no evidence to support such suspicions. That should relieve her, Alysa thought, but it did not.

At least there was one matter that delighted her; Kyra had avoided her almost completely for the last ten days, as if her stepsister had forgotten her offer of friendship. Perhaps, Alysa mused, Kyra has a secret love too. That would explain her frequent absences around the castle. If so, love might soften Isobail's daughter for the best.

The castle had been quiet since Isobail's return. Everyone had been taking meals in their rooms, leaving the Great Hall deserted. The servants and retainers had continued their tasks as if nothing unusual was taking place.

As for Alysa, when she was not riding or meeting with Gavin, she spent her lonely hours sewing, reading, grooming, and exercising in the outer ward. Since childhood she had enjoyed watching the workers and talking with them, and visiting the peasants and villages. While growing up she had been taught weaving, embroidery, cooking, social graces, and household administration. She had learned how to dance, flirt, converse, and sing. Yet such things seemed frivolous to her, and she wanted more than the boring existence of daughter and wife.

Until Isobail's marriage to her father, she had spent many hours with Baltair, studying and learning how to rule Damnonia one day. The seneschal was responsible for the keeping of accounts and the dispersing and collecting of food and supplies, fines, and taxes. It was Baltair's task to know all of the ins and outs of farming, to know what kinds of stock and fowl were available, and to know how to keep the prince's money cache full. It was the seneschal's duty to prepare any document the ruler might need. Running a castle and estate was a time-consuming task, but running an entire land was an enormous one, one which Baltair did for Alric with skill, and which Isobail had been undermining through favoritism and harder taxation policies.

It was after the evening repast when Princess Isobail summoned her. Alysa hated to confront her, but knew she must. At her stepmother's chamber Ceit opened the door and bade her enter and be seated. "You wished to see me, Princess Isobail?" she asked formally.

Isobail did not sit down; she leaned against a nearby table and looked down at her—intentionally, Alysa decided. Meanwhile she boldly watched her stepmother, her steady, neutral gaze concealing her apprehensions and dislike. Isobail's white-blond hair hung down straight, shiny, and beautiful; her sky-blue eyes exposed vanity and coldness tonight, as if she did not care what Alysa perceived.

For a time the two women studied each other. Then Isobail said, "As a mother and regent, I have given certain matters grave thought, Princess Alysa. I believe it is time for my two daughters to be wed. Kyra is approaching twenty-two and you are almost nineteen. When I return from Lord Orin's, I shall entertain suitors for you and Kyra. After my selections are made, the betrothals will be announced at a great feast. Although there is great trouble in our land, we must continue life as normally as possible. I leave for Sir Kelton's in the morning. During my journey I shall let it be known I am seeking to arrange marriages for my daughters. While I am gone, decide if there is a special man who catches your eye. If he is worthy of our land's princess, I will agree with your choice."

Alysa stared at the brazen woman. She could not believe what she had heard. For a time she was more angry than she was afraid. "You are not my mother or Damnonia's ruler, and you have no right to arrange my marriage," she stated defiantly.

"This command comes from your father, the Prince

of Damnonia. It is impossible for you to refuse your duty to him and to your land. You know you must obey him." Isobail's tone challenged her to refuse.

Alysa stood her ground. "Let my father speak this command to me, and let him choose my husband. It is not your place to do either."

"Your father—my husband—lies very ill. He is too weak to argue with a foolish child. He has commanded you to wed before winter. As regent, I will carry out his wishes."

Alysa angrily scoffed, "You cannot force me to marry a man of your choosing. Do you forget who I am? This land's future ruler!"

"After your father dies, Alysa, not before. While he lives, I am regent in his place. You will do as you are told. If you refuse, I will imprison you in your tower until you obey."

Many thoughts raced through Alysa's mind. If she were locked up—and she did not doubt that Isobail would carry out her threat—she could not see Giselde or Gavin or find ways to defeat this evil creature. She must behave as Isobail assumed she would. . . .

"Well, Alysa? What shall it be?" Isobail inquired. "Do you think I lie about Alric's orders? Or mishandle them?"

Alysa sighed heavily and shrugged in feigned resignation. "I have no reason to doubt your word, Princess Isobail. From what I hear, Father is lucky to have you step in for him. Everyone is praising your deeds, and all is running smoothly. I was simply unprepared for such news. If this is what Father wants, I must obey. He is very ill, so I must not distress him further. I suppose I have reached that age, but I have not given it any thought because of Father's illness and all the trouble. I will be allowed to study each suitor and make my own choice?"

"If you wish," Isobail remarked. "I will give you one month to become betrothed, and three months to wed."

"What of Kyra? She is the eldest and should wed first. She will be angry, perhaps embarrassed, if she is wed second."

"Upon my return, Kyra will be betrothed to Sir Calum. They will wed within the month. Keep this news a secret until I announce it."

"What does Kyra think about Sir Calum?" Alysa asked inquisitively.

"She and Sir Calum desire each other, so they will agree with my choice. Do not tell her until I speak with her. She will be surprised and overjoyed."

"I wish to see her happy," Alysa replied. "I am glad she approves of Sir Calum."

"I am pleased to hear that, Alysa, and I am pleased by your obedience. You will see, marriage will be good for both of you."

Giselde observed Gavin as the Prince of Cumbria spoke with his men in the morning. After they left, she would visit Trosdan in the hidden cave in the marsh. The Druid lived and worked like a hermit, spending all of his time on his outlawed religion. She wanted to see what the runes had to say about Gavin and Alysa.

Gavin squatted near the campfire and said, "We must split up again, my friends. Keegan will be gone for three or four days. Tragan and Dal, you two scout the area around Lord Orin's. Lann and Bevan, you take Sir Kelton's, and keep your eyes on Isobail. I doubt she will try to pull another trick this soon, but I could be wrong. Weylin will ride with me to Lord Fergus's. I want to look around that area; the bandits could fool everyone by attacking in the same place twice. Time is getting short. We have no choice but to try to join the brigands to unmask them. If we can encourage dissension among them, then we can use it to our advantage. If they split up into smaller bands, we can defeat them more easily, but first we have to make contact with their leader."

"You know what we will have to do if we join them."

Gavin grimaced. "I know, Lann, but we have no choice. Right now we should not be seen riding as a band. We could be mistaken for the brigands. Once we make contact, we will let them woo us to join them. If I have guessed right, we will be asked to prove ourselves. We can make it appear we are like them without harming anyone. Giselde has given me the names of some peasants who are trustworthy; they will help us make the raids look real."

"This is war, Lann," Dal added to Gavin's remarks. "We must fight it any way we can. We will try to prevent any deaths and destruction, but some will occur. It is sad, but such is the price for victory and peace."

"Gavin is right," Bevan agreed. "The only way to stop these raiders is by joining them and working from the inside."

Each man had his say before Gavin asked, "Are we together on this one?" The men looked at each other, and all nodded.

Gavin walked Giselde to her hut, then went to leave a note for Thisbe. He had seen her for the past two days and must not take so many risks with her safety, he thought. He had to get this trouble settled so he could clear things up with the maiden who had stolen his heart.

Alysa was ecstatic when noon arrived. She approached the meeting spot, but Gavin was nowhere in sight. She sat down to wait for him. In her state of mental turmoil, time passed quickly. When she realized how long she had been sitting there, she knew something was wrong.

Checking the tree hole, she found a note from him.

She read it and frowned in dismay. It said: "Clue found. Heading for K's. Returning in four or five days. Do nothing. Stay home where safe."

What clue? she wondered. Obviously he was heading for Sir Kelton's, the same place where Isobail was journeying. Four or five days would make his return on Monday or Tuesday. She needed to see him now!

Alysa paced the area as she pondered her new dilemma—an enforced marriage. While everyone had been packing Isobail's things and seeing her off early this morning, she had taken money and jewels from her father's and her own concealed chests: possessions that had never been revealed to the greedy Isobail. Alysa looked at the heavy pouch and clenched her teeth. It was dangerous to carry them back to the castle. She had no choice but to leave the valuables in the tree for Gavin to find on his return. Such a large payment would show the warriors Alysa was serious about hiring them, and it should hold their interest, and hopefully, their loyalty. She needed their help more than ever. She had only one month to defeat Isobail.

She was angry with him, and that mood perplexed her. She had asked for his help, and he was giving it, even before payment. He was off chasing down clues, and worried over her safety. What more could she expect? she scolded herself.

Maybe she was distressed because she needed his arms around her today, she thought, and because his note held no warmth. He was so passionate when they were together, but when they were separated, he was different; he could resist her pull on him. Before everything came apart, they needed more time together.

Alysa wrote only two sentences on the note to Gavin, and placed it in the pouch: "Princess Alysa urgently needs your help. Here is your payment."

Leaning against the tree, she fretted over her predicament. Isobail was eager to get rid of her, and soon.

Alysa feared she might not have to choose between her crown and her love; she could lose both. Was the woman so desperate to be rid of her that she would allow her to marry a common warrior? If so, would Gavin want to marry a deceitful, dethroned princess? Or marry at all?

Alysa began to pace once more, wondering what Gavin would do when he discovered the truth about her. She had to tell him soon, before he learned it from another. If he truly loved her, her identity should not matter to him. But her deceit might.

Princess Isobail reached Sir Kelton's at noon Sunday. The knight, a vassal of Lord Orin, was surprised by her arrival. Isobail reminded Kelton that this had been her home long ago with Lord Caedmon, and she wished to visit it for a day or two, if he did not mind.

Isobail was glad her son was out of the castle today, as it would give her time to study the servants and choose one to assist in Kelton's murder. Earnon had it planned perfectly. Once the helper was chosen, he or she would be given fish cakes to feed Kelton, cakes that Earnon stated were enchanted and would choke the man to death. Such a demise would appear a natural accident: strangling on fish bones.

Isobail had sent Ceit on to Lord Orin's to prepare things for her, and now she watched everyone as Kelton escorted her around the castle, from bottom floor to top. It did not take long to realize whom she could beguile to do her bidding.

"My serving woman was ill, Sir Kelton, so I sent her to Lord Orin's so she would not have to move twice. Do you mind if I select one of your servants to wait upon me during my visit?"

Sir Kelton quickly agreed, and Isobail glanced over

the group of serving women and pointed to a pretty female, saying, "She will do nicely."

All afternoon Isobail lavished attention on the impressionable girl. Before the evening meal, when Kelton planned a small feast, Isobail asked the girl to help her bathe and dress. From the way the girl watched her and touched her, Isobail knew she had selected wisely. . . .

Moran was happy but surprised to see his mother. Isobail embraced him with affection, as he was one of her few loves. He was a handsome man, virile and masculine. At twenty he could snare almost any woman with his charms and looks. She looked at his light brown hair and green eyes, and delighted in the fact that he did not favor his father, Baltair. She had great plans for her beloved son, one of which she would share with him tonight.

When the meal was over Isobail met with Moran. "I have good news, my son. For years you have desired Princess Alysa. Would you like to marry her and become the future ruler of this land?"

Moran's astonishment could not be concealed. He grinned and said, "Nothing would please me more, Mother. But Alysa does not care for me. How can I win her favor?"

"It is not necessary, my son, but it would help if she turned to you." She repeated her recent conversation with Alysa, and hinted, "Woo her swiftly and persistently. Who else is more worthy of her? If she does not choose you, I will command it. She fears me and she will obey."

Isobail read the lust in her son's eyes, lust for Alysa and power. She thrilled to that insight, knowing it would be easy to draw her son into her confidence soon. "Until Alric dies I will rule Damnonia. After me, you will rule as Alysa's husband." Yes, her son would make the perfect ruler for her in this land, as her throne would be elsewhere: Logris, her ancient land of Iceni. . . .

In his excitement, Moran lifted her from the floor and swung her around, then embraced her tightly. They shared laughter and hugs.

"Go to Malvern Castle while I am away. Begin to woo her. She is vulnerable and might respond quickly. I will ask Kelton's permission for your leave, but he could not refuse me anything. I will remain here a day or two to pretend to visit my old home, then I shall visit Lord Orin. I shall return home Saturday. If you have won her favor, I will announce your betrothal that day."

"But I am not a knight yet, Mother. What if others ask for her?"

"Soon Kelton will die and you will become owner of this castle," she divulged, to test him. "You and Alysa will live here until Alric dies."

Astonishment filled his eyes again, then a devilish smile took its place. "I will hold you to these promises, Mother, and you will never regret making them come true for me."

"You do not mind if I find a way to have Kelton die?"

"The sooner the better, for I wish to reclaim my birthright."

"Prepare yourself to leave for home at dawn," she said, pleased with her son. "Ensnare Alysa and all will be possible. Confide in no one, Moran," she warned.

"Only in you, Mother," he said, then hugged her tightly. "There are a few hours of daylight left. Ask Kelton if I can leave immediately."

Isobail complied, for it suited her other plans for the evening. Within twenty minutes Moran was racing toward Malvern Castle.

Later, as Isobail sipped a goblet of wine, she handed one to her servant girl. The young woman eagerly downed the heady wine quickly, overwhelmed by the kind treatment. The women shared another glass of the refreshing drink while the young woman combed the princess's waist-length hair. Isobail pressed a gold hairpin and silver coin on the simple girl. Isobail promised either to free the bond servant and reward her more heavily after this evil task was done, or she would bring the doting girl to Malvern Castle as her personal servant. The dense woman was overjoyed, and beguiled. Isobail knew her instructions would be followed.

Many things happened on Monday in distant reaches of Damnonia. Alysa checked for Gavin's return, and was disappointed to find him still gone. Prince Alric remained in a dazed state, as did Leitis. Kyra and Earnon stole hours together to love and to plot. Keegan returned to Gavin's camp to await his friends. Moran journeyed toward Malvern Castle. And far away, Gavin and Weylin connected with the brigands and met with their leader, Skane.

Tuesday morning Isobail left Sir Kelton's for Lord Orin's castle. Having accomplished her task, she was eager to reach the place where Trahern was to meet her. Soon the bewitched girl would follow her orders.

Fourteen

After checking their secret spot again to see if Gavin had returned, Alysa went back to the castle to find Moran waiting for her. She watched her stepbrother approach her with the cocky stroll she knew so well. She cringed inwardly at the sensual smile playing on his full lips and at the way his blazing eyes consumed her. There was no way to elude him, much to her disconcertment.

Moran frowned playfully and reproached her, "It is dangerous to go riding alone, Alysa." Sounding as if she were accountable to him, he asked, "Where have you been?" He assisted her as she dismounted, then handed the animal's reins to a stable boy.

Alysa reclaimed the reins, smiled at the boy, and dismissed him. She said to Moran, "I prefer to take care of Calliope myself." Ignoring her stepbrother, she led her horse into the stable to brush and feed him.

Moran followed, chastising her again, but this time softly, "You must not ride without an escort, Alysa, and this is not a task for a princess. Both are improper. Remember your position."

To silence him, Alysa casually remarked, "I was perfectly safe; I did not ride far. I enjoy riding alone and taking care of Calliope. What are you doing home?"

she inquired, suspecting that Isobail had sent him for a dreaded reason.

Moran grinned as he leaned against the stall, making it obvious he was going to remain there with her. "You do not look or sound happy to see me, little mouse. I traveled hard and fast to have time to visit you before Sir Kelton needs me. I have missed you, Alysa."

As she brushed Calliope's damp hide, Alysa did not remind Moran that she disliked his pet name for her. He had called her "little mouse" since childhood, first in spiteful taunting and later in undisguised affection. She was glad that her back was to him while she composed herself, and she hoped he did not notice her tension before she mastered it. In an even voice she asked, "Why did you not stay there and visit with your mother? I am sure she has many things to tell you and the others about this trouble plaguing our land. Every available man should be out hunting down these wicked brigands."

"A man cannot train or fight all of the time, little mouse, especially when there are other matters at hand." He stroked her arm intimately, then lifted a handful of dark brown locks to tease beneath his nose, inducing her to half turn and look at him. Smiling suggestively, Moran released her heavy tresses.

Alysa observed him momentarily as his fingers absently wandered through his light brown hair, causing his curls to settle most appealingly about his face. His eyes and nose were large, but not enough to detract from his handsome visage. She admitted that his exceptionally good looks and immense virility could lure most maidens into surrender, but not her. Although he was well-bred and charming, she had always found something repellent about Moran which spread warning shivers over her entire body. As for his body, his physique was muscular and tough, and colored pleasingly. Today he was dressed in a winter-green knee-length tunic, with wide wheat-colored bands at the neck, hem, and short sleeves. Beneath it he wore snug, matching trousers which were tucked into calf-high boots. His only weapon was a dagger in a jeweled sheath, suspended on a hip-hugging leather belt.

When Alysa returned to her rubdown of Calliope without reacting to his titillating behavior, Prince Moran asserted, "We have not had enough time during this past year, Alysa, and that has shown me how precious you are to me. Sometimes we are apart for months, and I miss being with you. I fear you continue to hold my childhood mischief against me, even though I have begged your forgiveness for a devilish boy who had no father to guide him.

"Those days and events are long past, and we are different. Over the years you have ensnared my heart and enflamed my body until I can think of nothing except making you mine forever. Yet when I come home, you still ignore me. Must you be so elusive? So cold and cruel to me? Surely you realize how I feel about you; I love you and want to marry you. May I court you, Alysa?"

Alysa's hand slowed its pace as he was speaking, and her heart pounded frantically. He was wasting no time during this unexpected visit. She had guessed accurately; Isobail had sent him home to make a bid for her! Keeping her back to him, she chided, "You said you were over your childhood mischief, Moran, then you tease me again."

His hands cupped her waist and he bent forward to whisper into her ear, "I am not jesting, Alysa. I want you to become my wife. Do not continue to thwart me. Let me enter your heart. Let me fill you with desire, as you have done for me."

Alysa's movements halted, but she did not turn. Her body felt rigid and cold. Her wits seemed to fail her.

She moistened her lips. "You must not speak this way, Moran; you are my brother. We shall forget you—"

Moran gently seized her shoulders and pulled her around to face him. "I am not your brother, Alysa. We are no blood kin. I am a man, and you are a woman. I desire you as such."

Alysa trembled with panic. She felt a hot flush crawl over her body. "But we were raised as brother and sister, and that is how I think of you," she argued.

"You mislead yourself, little mouse," Moran replied. "I lived in the outer bailey with my mother and sister until I was seven, then I became a page at Sir Kelton's. Since we moved into the castle six years ago, we have shared only a few short visits. You are no sister to me; you are a woman, a very desirable one. Let me prove to you I have become a man, a worthy suitor. Do not fear me or my love, for they are strong and true. Allow yourself to find joy with me, and I swear you will never regret accepting me."

Alysa studied his expression and knew he was serious. For the past two years she had hoped to prevent this scene, but it was too late. "You must choose another to love and woo, Moran, for I do not feel the same way about you."

"I cannot," he stated flatly. "I will pursue you until you yield. There is no man more worthy of you than I. Mother said it was time for you to wed, so I hurried home to court you. Do not reject me without giving me a chance to win you. For years I have dreamed of having you, but I was waiting until I became a knight to ask for your hand. Please open your heart to me, Alysa," he coaxed.

"You are not a knight yet," she reminded him, trying to think of a persuasive argument against his appeal. She dared not offend him and make an enemy of him. The problem was, if Isobail was not defeated, she could be forced to marry him. . . .

"Mother says Prince Alric will knight all eligible squires as soon as he is better. Mother says she needs all of the warriors she can find to rid our land of the brigands. Soon I will be a knight and a prince. Is that not enough for you to consider me? Do you want me to beg?"

"Please do not, Moran," she urged. "This is not the place to speak of such a private matter. Someone could hear us. Let me think on your words, for I did not expect them and I do not wish to hurt you. I have never thought of you in a romantic way. Since Isobail's marriage to Father, I have considered you my brother."

"My plea should not come as such a surprise, little mouse. Surely you have guessed my feelings for you by now. I have not hidden them. Every time I come home, I pursue you, but you turn aside. I am not ugly or crude or boring. What is it about me that offends you? Tell me, and I will change it."

"Please do not press me further, Moran. I need time to accept your mother's command and your stunning revelation. Marriage had not entered my mind until Isobail spoke to me about it a few days past. Choosing a husband is no minor decision and cannot be done rashly. You are being too forward and impatient today. Your sudden urgency confuses me."

Visibly jealous, he demanded, "Is there another knight courting you? I will challenge him or anyone for your hand. Mother's words are what spurred me into desperate action. I feared to wait any longer to approach you."

"Do not be silly," she said. "No man comes to call upon me. Surely Isobail told you so. I am young, Moran; I cannot imagine myself wed at this age."

"Others younger than you are married. You stand at the door to womanhood, little mouse. Let me open it and share that special moment with you. Your time is short, Alysa, too short to find a suitor more perfect for you than I am." His hand lifted to caress her hot cheek as he murmured intimately, huskily, "Let me teach you about passion, little mouse. I will give you more love and pleasure than any man could. I offer myself to you in heart and body; take me, love me, marry me."

Moran had attempted to entice her many times before, but never like this. Today he was alarmingly persistent, and also seductive. She heard an intensity in his voice that had not been present until now. If she had not known any better she would have believed he truly loved her and wanted her for herself, not for the crown through marriage to her. She felt trapped. She had to get away from him and bring a stop to his amorous siege.

Alysa tried to elude his grasp, but he embraced her and covered her mouth with his. She felt him tremble with hot desire, yet his kiss was tender and probing. She pushed him away and said, "Nay, Moran. You behave improperly. What if someone sees us and talks?"

Moran chuckled as he kissed her fiery cheeks. After capturing her face between his hands, he declared, "I want everyone to know I claim you for myself. Then no man would dare come to court you. I shall make certain I am your only choice, my beautiful Alysa. Waste no more time leading me a merry chase; marry me soon before I go mad with desire for you."

She scowled at him. "You are wicked and impulsive, Moran. Do not embarrass me before others. Release me and halt this devilish sport before we are flogged for misbehavior."

"It is a most important game to me, and I shall win it, Alysa, that I promise you. I shall leave you for now, else all of my control will vanish," he remarked with a roguish grin, then left the stable.

Alysa peeked outside and watched her stepbrother swagger to the south tower where his chamber was located, below hers. She swayed weakly against the stall

259

and sighed heavily. She realized it was going to be difficult, if not impossible, to discourage him. She felt Isobail's trap closing more tightly around her, and she feared it. With Moran around, she would have no peace or privacy. If she did not remain in her chamber, he would besiege her day and night, trying to wear down her resistance. How could she sneak off to meet Gavin? Or Giselde? She had to learn how long Moran intended to visit.

The evening meal was served in the Great Hall with six people present, and everyone sat at the same table: Alysa, Moran, Kyra, Baltair, Earnon, and Guinn. Moran had tried to get Prince Alric to join them, but the ruler was too ill. The servants moved about quietly and respectfully. The hounds had been locked out, at Moran's request. The candlelight and heady wine were conducive to romance, and the food was delicious: a meal and setting planned by Moran.

Moran and Kyra exchanged banter, while Earnon and Baltair sat quietly watching everyone, as each man knew that something was afoot. The court bard seemed particularly subdued tonight, and Kyra's attempts to draw him into the merry conversation failed. Within minutes it was obvious to all that Moran was eyeing Alysa with romantic interest.

His eyes glowed with desire and appreciation. "I have never seen you look more beautiful than you do tonight, little mouse," the squire complimented Alysa, who was wearing a soft and flowing gown of deep rose with matching slippers. Her brown hair tumbled enchantingly about her shoulders, and her eyes looked like two priceless sapphires set into a flawless surrounding. "How can I think of food when my starving senses have you to feast upon? Is she not the most ravishing creature alive, Guinn? How I envy you your days here with her."

If the distracted bard heard him, he did not reply. But Kyra teased, "Now I know what brought you rushing home, brother dear."

Moran looked at Alysa and smiled. "I have a challenge to meet, sister. I plan to persuade Alysa to marry me. With luck, we shall have a child before a new spring arrives."

Alysa choked on her wine and gaped at him. Moran chuckled and captured her hand. "My feelings are not a secret, little mouse. I will chase you eagerly, and I shall not let you rest until you yield. I implore your dear friends, help me persuade this lady to marry me."

Baltair was stunned by Moran's evident passion for a girl whom he did not know was his half sister. Surely Isobail was behind this sudden siege upon Alric's heir. The seneschal realized something had to be done to prevent such a forbidden union. Yet how could he halt it without exposing Alric's dark secret? And what if Isobail discovered that secret?

When Alysa ceased coughing, she retorted, "I have told you, Moran, I consider you my brother, not my suitor. Behave yourself."

Moran was not discouraged in the least. He grinned. "But as I told you, little mouse, you are not my sister and I plan to win you. Prepare yourself for my pursuit, for it will gain us a happy victory."

Kyra glanced from Moran to Alysa and back again. "Little brother, you surprise me. I did not know you were such a romantic, nor that you were in love with Alysa."

"I love her with all my heart," he declared boldly, grinning once more when Alysa flushed a bright red. "Help me, Kyra. Convince her no other man is worthy of her than a prince and a knight. Guinn, sing a fiery love song to melt her frozen heart."

Guinn frowned. He was not in the mood for such goings-on, but it was his duty to entertain them. He retrieved his lyre and obeyed Moran, much to Alysa's discomfiture.

Moran leaned close to her and repeated each line of the bard's song. His tone was sensuous, seductive, and embarrassing. Kyra could not suppress her amused giggles, causing Alysa to frown at her.

"Forgive me, Alysa," she entreated, "but this would make you my sister twice over, and that would please me. Listen to Moran; you can find no better choice for a husband. Soften your heart to him."

Moran smiled at Kyra, delighted with her support, but wondered why she was aiding his cause, as they had never gotten along. Obviously she would expect a favor in return. Yet Moran was alert to notice that Baltair's eyes had darkened and narrowed strangely. "Baltair, I beg you to take my plea to Prince Alric. Convince him of my love for his daughter. I must have her as my own or perish from denial."

Alysa warned, "Stop this foolishness, Moran. You are embarrassing me. Speak of other things."

"Nay, love, there is nothing more important or serious than my love and our impending marriage. Promise to let me court you, and I will try to control my ardor tonight."

"I will promise you nothing more than to think upon your words, if you will restrain yourself."

"Done, my beautiful temptation," he agreed merrily. "Remove your frown, Guinn, and tell us stories of olden times."

Once more Guinn reluctantly complied. All he could think about was Isobail, and having her only twice in weeks. The lovesick poet began to recite tales of heroes long dead and the legends about them.

Kyra sipped on her wine as her foot sneaked across the floor under the table and boldly wiggled between

Earnon's legs. Her toes teased his manhood until it was aching with need. They had planned to spend this night together, but Moran's arrival could interfere, since he shared the same floor of the south tower with Kyra. They had refrained from seeing each other during Isobail's stay at home, and Kyra had been in her womanly way for the past few days, preventing them from sharing passion. Earnon followed Kyra's action and tantalized her in like manner.

At last the awkward repast ended. Alysa bid everyone good night and hurried to her room to be alone. Moran left the castle to purchase the services of a buxom wench. Baltair hastened to inform Alric of Moran's intentions, but the prince was too groggy to communicate. Guinn lay across his bed trying to decide how to win Isobail's approval to travel with her, as he could not bear these lengthy separations. Kyra sneaked into Earnon's chamber to finalize their plots for Baltair and Sir Calum, and to spend hours cavorting wildly in and out of bed.

Within ten miles of Lord Orin's castle Isobail made camp for the night. After the evening meal she and Sheriff Trahern left the area for a peaceful walk. Before reaching the appointed meeting spot with her brigand leader, the princess donned a black hood and cape which totally concealed her identity.

She walked the distance to the clearing at Trahern's side. Skane, the bandit leader, stood and went forward to speak with them, leaving his men at their camp fire. Isobail made certain her voice did not carry beyond the small group, as no one except the brigand chief knew who she was. "You have done well," she told him. "Rest for a few days while I visit Lord Orin, then torment him with raids after I leave. The same is true of Lord

Fergus. But make certain your men do not attack those areas under my protection."

"My men are angry over the killing of their friend at Daron's. This task is becoming more and more dangerous. They want more money, and I want land," Skane demanded.

Fury consumed Isobail. "You agreed to his death, and it was necessary. Your men are fighters, and such a life is filled with danger. Do not become greedy and foolish, Skane. We have a bargain. I have paid you well, and I will reward you highly when all is done. Take what you need from those you attack, but do not make excessive demands on me," she warned, her voice cold.

"My men grow restless. They are tired of running and hiding in the wilds every day. If you want us to go on riding for you, give one of the land grants to me. We can make our quarters there."

"I cannot. When this matter is settled, I will give you enough money and jewels to buy land in Logris or Albany. It is dangerous to betray me, I warn you, Skane."

"It is dangerous to deny me rightful payment, Princess Isobail," he retorted. "There is a girl at the castle who would bring a large reward from Hengist. Give her to me to sell."

"What girl?"

"The Viking princess Alysa, granddaughter of Rurik and blood of Astrid, last of the royal Vikings. Hengist will pay highly for her. By marriage to her, he can claim the Viking throne and lands."

"I cannot give you Princess Alysa. She is to marry my son."

"Give me land or give me the girl, or your deeds will become as well known as mine are," he threatened.

Isobail realized she had to handle this man carefully. "I must have time to study such a bargain, Skane," she replied soothingly. "If Alysa refuses to marry Moran, then she is yours. If not, you will have your land when it is safe to hand it over to you. But do not blackmail me again, or my knights will chase you even into the dark region to slay you."

Skane chuckled loudly, calling his men's attention to the small group. Isobail glanced at them, and her eyes focused on a handsome warrior. She studied his face and body, and was glad no one could see her eyes as they glowed with curiosity. "Who is the stranger?" she asked gruffly. "He does not look as if he belongs with your group."

"He is from a foreign land. He heard of the trouble here and came to seek wealth and adventures. He decided it was worth more to join me than to hire out as a warrior for Prince Alric. He is strong and clever, but loyal to me. I hired him and his band to raid for me. He leaves at dawn to gather his men."

"Do you trust him?"

"I trust only my men, but he will prove himself to me, or die. I tested him in the ring last night, and he beat three of my best men. It does not matter who he is, for I will use him to draw attention from my loyal group, then slay him and keep his riches."

Gavin made certain he did not appear overly interested in the group meeting at the edge of the clearing, but his senses were on the alert. He knew who was concealed in black garb. Isobail should have known that no man would keep touching Trahern in such a familiar way, he thought, nor would one walk with such a feminine sway. Gavin was amused by the woman's oversights, for they told him she was not too clever to entrap and defeat. He felt her potent gaze on him as he laughed and talked with the brigands, intentionally calling her attention to himself, exhilarated by this perilous game of cat-and-mouse.

Isobail noticed how the brigands were responding to the new man, how they seemed to hang on his every word. The ruffians had accepted him easily, and she felt her lust for him rising. He had compelling eyes and tempting lips, with a body that was both. He was an earthy creature who surely knew a great deal about carnal pleasures and hungry women. She grinned wickedly.

Clearly she was losing control over Skane, who was a fool to make unreasonable demands of her, and he would pay with his life. Perhaps a new leader should take his place soon, she mused, eyeing Gavin intently. As the chief rejoined his men, Isobail related her thoughts about him to Trahern before they departed.

Gavin observed how Skane swaggered to the camp fire and took a seat, and how the flames exposed a victorious glow in the leader's eyes, one which Gavin suspected would be shortlived. The Cumbrian prince saw Isobail whisper something to Trahern before they left. He was depending on Weylin to relate their words, as his friend was hiding nearby during that meeting, although the bandits believed Weylin was in the woods taking care of private business.

Skane had boasted earlier of how he was going to "strike a richer bargain" with their employer when they met tonight, and Gavin could imagine what Isobail's reaction had been. Since joining this band on Sunday, Gavin had been studying the bandit chieftain carefully, noting the bandit's strengths and weaknesses, and those of his men. When he had won over enough of the band, he would make a challenge for the leadership. And win it, he decided confidently. Then he could tear it apart from the inside and confront the treacherous Isobail.

After arriving in this location for tonight's meeting, Gavin realized all of his men were in this same area. Tragan and Dal were somewhere nearby, and Lann and Bevan must have followed Isobail. That meant he could round up his men tomorrow, all except Keegan, who would join them upon their return to their own camp near Malvern Castle. With luck, Keegan should be waiting for them now.

Just then Skane called Gavin to his side. Withdrawing a crude map from his pocket, he said, "Gather your band tomorrow and carry out a special task for me at dusk on Thursday." The bandit pointed to a spot on the map that was between Lord Orin's and Prince Alric's castles. "Princess Isobail and her little group will be passing by. I want you to relieve her of her heavy chest of jewels and coins. Take it here, and hide it in these rocks for me," he ordered, pointing out another spot on the map, a few miles away.

Gavin scoffed, "You want us to prove ourselves by challenging the regent and her knights? You think us foolhardy? We could be slaughtered within minutes. Seven men against . . . how many?"

"The Princess is vain and foolish, my friend. She travels with only a few guards and many servants. They will give you no trouble. Just scare them and rob them, but no killing. Let her see how lucky she is to escape our power, then she will be afraid to sic her knightly dogs on us. Soon we will be able to take over this land. The lords and peasants will pay us to protect them and to leave them in peace."

"You want us to teach her a lesson, to stay home where women belong," Gavin bantered. "You are the leader, Skane. I will gather my men and prove we are worthy to ride with you. We will collect the chest without harming a single head, then we will ride behind you to conquer Damnonia."

"The man you saw visit me tonight will be with them. He is Princess Isobail's sheriff. Make sure he is not injured. He is one of us, but he does not know of this raid. I just planned it. It will give us a great reward, and it will throw off any suspicion of him."

"Never have I ridden with a man more bold," Gavin replied, flattering the chieftain. "I will learn much from you. I have heard this Isobail is very beautiful. What if my men want to enjoy her or her servants? They have been without women for many weeks. Tell me the rules of your raids."

"My men are free to ravish any female who captures their eyes, but this raid is different. Take no slaves to sell, and ravish no servant. Isobail is not to be touched. Soon I plan to take her for myself."

Late Wednesday afternoon Gavin approached the dying tree to see if there was a message hidden there from his love, yet he dreaded to find one. His hand reached inside the decaying hole, but touched nothing except rotting wood and trash. He grimaced, then recalling her recent attack, surmised she must think it was too dangerous to leave the castle for a time. Yet he realized that danger had never dissuaded her before, suggesting she might be vexed with him for not meeting her last Friday, as planned. Women were known to play silly games when misunderstandings occurred. Whatever the reason for no message, it aided his predicament. If she did not know he was back, she would not expect him to meet her, which was best for now. Gavin did not want to involve her in what he was doing, so he left no note for her. He would wait a few days before enticing her here, he decided, wait until he became a proven member of the band.

Gavin met with Giselde and the peasants whom she had chosen to help them make their raids appear real. With Keegan at his side, he promised the men that his band would return any stolen goods or replace them. He also promised that his band would not harm anyone, unless by accident. He knew that as long as he and his men were raiding alone, it would be easy to keep such promises. The problem would come when, and if, the other bandits wanted to combine their forces during attacks. He told the gathered peasants that if that happened, he would try to send advance warnings to the villages.

"If all goes well, my friends, we can end this matter soon. Encourage others to allow the bandits to have their way for now, but be careful who you trust. I suspect that Princess Isobail has spies everywhere. Do not approach us if we meet somewhere. We will pass all messages and plans through Giselde."

After the peasants departed, Gavin told Giselde he would visit her again in five days, and to leave any urgent messages for him beneath the rock at the pond. "We must avoid each other as much as possible," he said, "in case either of us is watched."

Giselde asked, "Will the same be true of . . . Thisbe?"

Gavin nodded. He waited until Keegan left the hut so they could speak privately. "Too much is happening, so I will not tell her I have returned. But the day will come when I have to settle matters with her."

"You love her deeply?" Giselde asked.

"Yes, Giselde, despite the differences in our stations, and I do not know what to do about it. She has become a part of me, and it torments me to think of losing her forever."

"Perhaps you will not, if it is meant to be," Giselde replied.

"I pray it is, as your words made me realize I must think of her before myself. I swear to all the gods above, I will give her up before submitting her to a life of suffering such as you and Catriona endured."

Giselde smiled at him, then surprised him with an affectionate hug. "It warms my heart to meet a man of such honor. Do not fear, Prince Gavin—the gods will smile brightly on you. Runes do not lie, and they say you will win the woman of your dreams."

* * *

On the rock-girt coast at Land's End, a satanic darkness covered the allegedly impregnable estate of Sir Kelton, a gloomy site that had once belonged to the Overlord of Damnonia: Caedmon and his young wife Lady Isobail. Tonight the sound of angry waves slapping fiercely against the slate headland was exceptionally loud, and the wind from the ocean was fierce. No moon or stars could be seen through the thick layer of clouds that vowed a violent storm.

Sir Kelton haltingly traveled the familiar path along the edge of the rock cliff to where Prince Moran was to meet him and deliver an urgent message from his mother. The burly knight had not known of the young squire's return, and he wondered what the secret message could be. A servant had crept into his private reading chamber to summon him, and she had made certain no one followed them. He was cautious in the dark, since the damp rocks were often slippery. This secrecy was strange, he thought, but he had to obey his regent's request.

When the servant delivered a stunning blow to Sir Kelton's head, he collapsed silently at her feet. She listened for any sound, heard nothing but the wind and waves, and calling on all of her strength, shoved the unconscious knight over the cliff. She turned away as the body thumped and bumped its way to the jagged rocks below. Knowing the fall would be fatal and appear an accident, she hurriedly returned to her room. Eager to please and aid her imminent mistress, the foolhardy girl had disobeyed Isobail's instructions by finding a quicker way to get rid of Sir Kelton. Hearing the storm unleash its fury, she knew it would wash away any trace of her presence.

Isobail had journeyed a full day's ride from Lord Orin's castle when Gavin and his six men ambushed her retinue. Although Gavin was dressed in dark brown leather tunics and wearing masks, she recognized the body of their leader, for she had dreamed of him for two nights. It was apparent that he led his own men since none of Skane's unkempt brigands were with him, and that her own entourage had no chance to fight or flee from the raiders. She was astonished and angered, but also impressed, by his daring. Obviously Skane had not told him when, where, or whom to raid or ignore.

When a mellow voice demanded her chest without a bloody fight for it, Princess Isobail ordered, "Keep your swords sheathed and your heads cool, my loyal retainers. I want no futile slayings of our cherished subjects over a few coins and jewels." Turning to the imposing leader she said, "Take the chest and be gone, barbarian! But you shall regret this day and this bold deed. I shall hunt you down and remove all your heads."

Gavin chuckled and remarked, "Would that I had time to claim the greatest treasure of all, Your Highness, for all other jewels pale when compared to you. It enflames my blood to imagine the blissful taming of such a fiery beauty. Perhaps another time I shall taste the sweetness of your lips and body."

"Silence, you insolent dog!" Sheriff Trahern shouted. "How dare you speak such shameless words about our ruler! Be gone before I disobey her and challenge you!"

"Calm yourself, Sheriff Trahern," Isobail said. "He only seeks to amuse himself. Do not endanger your life over silly words." And to the leader again: "I warn you now, brigand, leave this land or perish. I will not rest until all of you are defeated and Damnonia is safe and happy once more."

"Your mind is sharp, my beautiful princess. What man could refuse you anything? If you do not mind, we will borrow your sheriff to assure us of a safe retreat. If he holds his tongue and temper, he will return safely to your side. I would not want one as precious as you to go unguarded for more than a few minutes."

Isobail silenced Trahern's protest, saying, "Do as he asks, Sheriff. . . . But we warn you, brigand, do not harm him."

"If he obeys you, milady, you have my word no harm will touch him."

The brigands were miles away when Gavin told Trahern, "I did not plan this raid, and I think it unwise to make you appear weak before your princess. Skane said this robbery would throw suspicion off of you, but I doubt that is his true motive. I think perhaps he is beginning to make his own plans. I would watch him closely, Trahern, for he is greedy. Skane is not the man he pretended to be when he invited me and my men to join him."

"Then why did you carry out this raid for him?"

"To warn you of his deceit, and let you know you will soon be dealing with me," Gavin said frankly. "I want only those rewards I can hold in my hands. When they are full, we will move on to the next fruitful battle. Skane is a fool for not honoring a bargain, and more so for thinking he can use Gavin Hawk."

"Gavin Hawk," the sheriff said, as if familiarizing himself with the name. "When and how do you plan to assume leadership of Skane's band?"

Gavin chuckled heartily. "I must bide my time until I win them over to my side. Many of them are dissatisfied with his flawed command. I must prove that I am the best leader by demonstrating more honor, courage, loyalty, and cunning than Skane. No matter if we are bandits and adventurers, such traits must be practiced with those who follow us and those who hire us. This is our code. Skane does not act this way, and his behavior casts shame on his band."

"You may be the kind of leader we need, Gavin Hawk. When you are in command, you will work for us. But you must ask no questions about the one who gives us our orders."

Gavin laughed again. "It is my nature to be curious, Trahern, as it sometimes saves my life. I may ask you many questions in aid of our cause; answer only those you think reasonable, and I will accept your words. I will take my orders and payments only from you, unless you say otherwise. Return now before your eager knights come searching for you."

"There is one other matter to settle, Gavin Hawk. Never approach or insult Princess Isobail again. She will hold me responsible."

Aware of the love affair between Isobail and Trahern, Gavin chose his words carefully. "I did not mean to insult her. Jesting is my way to keep everyone calm and avoid trouble. Your ruler is pretty and shapely, but too old for my taste. I like my wenches with the bloom of youth still on their bodies and lacing their spirits. I think it would be smart if you convinced Skane to allow you to recover your ruler's jewels," Gavin suggested, knowing the chieftain would be furious.

"What I truly need is his head hanging on the castle gate to appease the people. When you take over, I shall expect it from you."

Gavin replied thoughtfully, "If his men have no objection, I will comply. Sometimes they remain loyal to old leaders even after they are replaced. Once we are rid of him, we should not encourage dissension among them."

"I look forward to dealing with a man of your intelligence and prowess. You are right, Skane is foolish and treacherous. He even stupidly refuses to conceal his face, as you do. His face and name are too well-known around the countryside. Meet me Tuesday night at the Boar's Inn in the village near Malvern Castle. We will enjoy a friendly talk and drink, and no one will be the wiser."

"I will be there," Gavin agreed.

He watched Trahern ride out of sight, then said to his men, "We have collected several victories today, my friends. We shall hide this chest where Skane desires, then we must change clothes and return to our camp. Tomorrow we have our first village raid. . . ."

Alysa paced her room with mounting tension. Since Moran's arrival two and half days ago, she had been unable to elude her stepbrother for more than a few minutes. He had stuck to her as tightly as a leech. They had shared meals, games, and conversations. They had gone riding together, read together, strolled together, and listened to Guinn's fascinating tales together. From her dark window she had watched the inner bailey since the evening meal, hoping he would leave the castle. Now it was too late, since the gates were locked from dusk to dawn, preventing her from slipping away to check on Gavin's return or visit Giselde. Even if she found the courage to use the escape route in the secret passage, it ended in the cold and swift river, and she would have no horse to cover the miles to the royal forest. Until Moran left for Kelton Castle or a diversion, escaping him for a few hours seemed hopeless.

Alysa wanted to trust Baltair to convey information to Giselde and Gavin, but she feared to confide in anyone completely. She could not bring herself to endanger her love or her friend, and felt as if she were suffocating in a frightening trap. She needed Gavin, but as of noon Tuesday, two days past, he had not returned. If he had by now, was he worried about her frantically worded note and lack of contact? What if he rushed here to rescue her? No, she had told him Princess Alysa needed him urgently. . . .

Alysa was repulsed by Moran's hot pursuit but did not know how to halt it. She closed her sea-blue eyes and murmured, "Gavin, my love, where are you? Return to me soon. I will go with you anywhere and will make no demands of you. When you return, I must tell you my true name and troubles. Please, understand me, forgive me, and love me. . . ."

If Moran had not arrived so unexpectedly, she could have followed Gavin and spent time with him. Or she could have visited Lord Fergus or one of the other lords who was still loyal to her father. Anything but fall into this trap! With Moran underfoot she could do nothing, except endure his courting.

She had spoken with Leitis earlier today. The trusted servant had sworn that Prince Alric was getting no herbs, but was not healing. Now Alysa believed her father was truly ill and might die. Leitis had also told her that Alric was so dazed by his sickness that he saw no one, and it would be futile for her to visit him. She had tried once, but ran from the depressing room in tears. She had asked for Gavin's help in defeating Isobail, but the problem was becoming so large and intimidating. At times all she wanted was to lose herself in Gavin's arms. Was this not a time when duty and honor demanded too much? If marriage to Moran was the only way to retain the crown, she did not want it! And if her father died and Gavin was lost, did the crown matter? No, but Damnonia and the Damnonians did. These were her people. She could not allow them to be destroyed!

Alysa realized that she had to see her father again, had to learn if he insisted she marry Moran. She had to make him listen to her and fight for his life. Gathering her cloak around her she bravely traveled the dark passage under the castle and pushed open the secret panel leading to Prince Alric's chamber. Someone grabbed her hand and yanked her into the smelly room as she stifled a scream.

Fifteen

"Princess Alysa!" Baltair said in astonishment. "When I heard noises, I feared a villain was sneaking into the room to slay my prince. How did you get here? I did not know of this hidden passage," he said, but did not sound miffed with Alric for keeping such a secret.

"It encircles the castle on the lowest level," she told him, "with openings in my chamber, Father's chamber, and the dungeon. It has an escape outlet at the river, but it must be several feet beneath the surface, since the water level has risen over the years. I have never checked it. Father made me swear never to reveal it to anyone. Only he and Mother and I knew about it. Those who built it were killed. I doubt it has been used until recently, when I exchanged Father's wine jugs. But now it seems as if the food and wine are not to blame for Father's illness, for he is not getting well."

Anguish dulled the seneschal's brown eyes. "He does not hear me or see me. His mind lives in another world, and I cannot reach it. I check each day to see if he has returned to us, but he has not." When Alysa mentioned her concern about Moran's marriage plan, Baltair captured her hands in his and vowed, "Do not worry, my child. Until Prince Alric revives, Isobail cannot force you to marry Moran, and I do not believe your father would allow you to wed your stepbrother. He is fond of Moran, but he does not want Isobail's son to marry you."

"Are you certain? Isobail claimed it was Father's command."

"I am certain my prince has not instructed Isobail to betroth you to anyone. Before his illness, he noticed Moran's interest in you, and it displeased him. Many times the prince has told me that you would choose your own husband and the right season to marry. He wishes love to guide you, not royal commands and your sense of duty to him or the Crown. Alric wants you to rule Damnonia, not Prince Moran, which he would try to do as your husband. When Alric awakens, he will stop Isobail's malicious plan. And until he does, I will battle them for you and my prince."

"Whatever would I do without you, Baltair," she murmured as she hugged him affectionately. "Moran has been so persistent, and I have shivered as a coward and weakling. If only I knew how to help Father."

"Please do not use the secret passageway for any reason. You might be caught again, and not by me. I am certain that Alric's messengers to King Bardwyn were slain, but I have sent out another. Soon help will arrive and this madness will cease. Be careful until then, Princess Alysa," he cautioned. "I will speak with Leitis and Piaras again, for they are helping me. Piaras chose the messenger and sent him on his way last week." Baltair had no way of knowing that Keegan was the messenger; Piaras did not know his identity when Giselde had vowed one was en route.

"What if my grandfather does not believe the message? What if he doubts Isobail is a threat to Damnonia?"

"The message relates Prince Alric's illness and inability to govern our land. Forgive me for saying such things about my prince and dearest friend, but only the truth can summon aid swiftly. With a ruler on his back so long, King Bardwyn will realize we are in danger of enemies within and without our borders. I am positive he will send someone to assume command until Alric heals or is replaced for the good of all. Our king will be told of the barbaric raiders who plague our lands, and will have no choice but to send aid. I love your father and owe my allegiance to him, but he would expect me to think of you and Damnonia before him during this dark period. If the messenger gets through, help should arrive within a week or two. At least an advance scout should reach me with Bardwyn's plans before Monday of the upcoming week."

Within a week, two at the most, it will all be over. . . . Alysa realized that she did not have long before her secret affair with Gavin must be settled one way or another. She wondered what she would do if her grandfather crowned her the ruler of Damnonia but refused her marriage to an adventurous warrior. What if Gavin did not want to wed a princess? Or wed at all? She had to tell him about herself soon, and see how he reacted to her deceit. Her timing depended on whether or not the messenger reached King Bardwyn.

Baltair glanced toward the rumpled bed, and tears glistened in his eyes. "I fear it might be too late to save my beloved liege from the bitter call of thwarted destiny. But if need be, I will die trying to save his child and our land. The stars chart our lives for us before we are born, Alysa, and we must follow their divine course or suffer for going our own selfish way. I beg you, Alysa, allow nothing and no one to sway you from your rightful path."

Alysa sensed a curious torment in Baltair, an obscure warning in his words. Evidently something terrible had happened in the old wizard's past that troubled him deeply, but she felt it was not her place to intrude. "How will I know what path I am to follow, Baltair? And how do I know who is to walk it with me?"

Oddly, he looked around as if checking to make sure no one was spying on them, then whispered, "There is an old Druid master living in the royal woods. If you can find him, he will read the sacred runes for you. Runes never lie. If you cannot find the Druid priest, follow your heart."

Alysa did not remind him that the Druid religion had been outlawed long ago. There was something in his tone and words which intrigued her. "Father followed his heart, but everyone thought him wrong, and he suffered greatly for doing so. Did he follow his rightful path, or choose his own?"

Baltair averted his eyes and sighed deeply. "Many times Prince Alric altered his predestined path, yet the gods still tried to guide him. When we alter our paths, we alter the paths of others. I believe that is what happened between your father and mother. If Alric had not entered your mother's life, she would have become a Viking queen. She was of the royal bloodline, and the Vikings wanted her returned to them. So they raided your ancestors' camps in Albany many times. They wanted Astrid, then Giselde, and finally Catriona. They wanted the women to marry Norse chieftains and restore the royal bloodline. Legend says the royal bloodline began with their god Odin, and the Vikings will lose their power if it is allowed to vanish completely. Your father has tried to keep news of your existence a secret, which is why he never allowed you to travel outside of Damnonia, even to visit Cambria and King Bardwyn. That is also why he greatly fears the Jutes in Vortigern's kingdom—they are of Viking birth and could learn of your existence. We must get rid of the renegade Jutes who raid our lands before they discover your secret. If the Vikings knew about you, Alysa, they would pursue you and attempt to make you their queen,

279

even by force. The Viking warrior who captured one of the royal Viking women would be made the ruler of all Vikings. You are the last of the royal bloodline, Alysa, so beware of strange warriors."

Alysa paled. After hearing those staggering words, she could not tell him about Gavin, and Giselde, whose prophecy about a green-eyed, light-haired enemy who posed as a friend now came to mind. *Jutes, Vikings, a queen by force, a strange warrior who might be after her to—* She shook her head, refusing to continue that line of thought. "I will be careful, Baltair, and you must too. Let me know the moment news arrives from my grandfather."

"Leave this depressing chamber before someone finds you here. Do not worry about your father; I will guard him."

Alysa embraced the old man and obeyed him. In her chamber she sat cross-legged on her large bed, consumed by pensive thoughts. When her life had seemed so bleak, a strange and irresistible warrior had invaded it and enchanted her. Despite their overwhelming attraction, Gavin was often contradictory: pulling her to him one time, but pushing her away another time.

Alysa frowned. "Who are you, Gavin?" she asked herself aloud. "Did you speak the truth about why you came to my land? What do you want from me? Or should I ask, what do you want from Princess Alysa? Please do not be my enemy. . . ."

The next morning before they could strike camp, a messenger galloped to Princess Isobail's tent and nearly slid off his horse like a limp rag. Both he and his mount were exhausted and winded, having ridden hard almost without rest from Land's End.

"I was heading . . . to Malvern Castle, Your Highness . . . to tell you of Sir Kelton's . . . death. Wednesday night in the storm. He slipped—fell off a . . . cliff. He is dead, Your Highness."

Isobail stared at the exhausted nineteen-year-old squire as he babbled about the knight's death. Controlling her eagerness to hear every detail, she told the youth to catch his breath before explaining his urgent mission. She ordered refreshments brought to him and sat him before her tent to eat and rest. As others gathered to hear the disastrous tale, the princess appeared patient, but she mentally rushed him.

Later the squire said, "When he did not come to bed, Lady Kadra looked for him in the castle. She aroused the servants and had everyone search inside and out. It was dark and stormy, and we did not find him until Thursday morning. His body was crushed by the fall. Lady Kadra said he often took long walks before bed. He must have slipped on the wet rocks and stumbled over the cliff's edge. We cannot reach his body until the waves calm or our boats will be crushed against the same rocks that killed him."

"Dear Kelton dead, and at a time when we need valiant knights!" Isobail wailed. "We have lost too many valuable retainers, and our land has been plundered by merciless brigands. When will this suffering end for us?" She pulled herself erect and vowed, "I will find a way to halt it!" To the weary messenger, she said, "Rest here, then return to Kelton Castle. Tell Lady Kadra I will come as quickly as possible. I must find someone to take Sir Kelton's place before enemies hear of his sad departure. I should reach Malvern Castle before noon tomorrow.

"Sheriff Trahern," she said. "I need you to take a message to Malvern Castle."

She gestured Trahern to follow her into her tent, then whispered, "Tell Earnon to get the Prince well enough to perform the knighting ceremony for Moran. Tell Earnon I want it carried out tomorrow, so my son can leave quickly. If that is too soon to clear Alric's head, we will do it Sunday." She smiled happily. "Once Moran has taken over there, we will have only Orin and Fergus to defeat. Perhaps after Phelan takes control of Fergus's estate, Orin will surrender peacefully and join us. He trusts me, but I cannot allow him to stand against me when I take over the throne. With this new victory in my hands, it will not be long before the final one, my love. You must also rid us of the serving girl at Kelton's. We cannot risk the loosening of her tongue."

"You have moved slowly and carefully, Isobail, so do not endanger your final victory with too much haste," Trahern cautioned. "Replacing all of the feudal lords with your followers in less than a year will look suspicious. We now control three of the five territories, and you control Malvern Castle. Take care before you get rid of Fergus and Orin."

"I cannot, Trahern. Skane is becoming more dangerous to my cause. I must finish with him before he—"

Trahern touched her lips and silenced her. He asked, "Have you forgotten about the new brigand? We are to meet with Skane near the castle Saturday night. We will let him think we are considering his demands. Meanwhile, Tuesday, I have arranged to meet with Gavin Hawk at the Boar's Inn. I will hire him to kill Skane and take command."

"Are you certain we can trust him, Trahern? He is not like them."

Trahern chuckled at her scowl. "I like what I see in him; he is a bandit, my love, but an honorable one. He will prove himself by getting rid of Skane and joining us. I believe he will be loyal to us."

Isobail shrugged and lifted her brows skeptically. She watched Trahern gather a few supplies and leave camp. Traveling swiftly, he should reach the castle before the evening meal. She would have gone with him, except such a ride would be strenuous, and she did not want to be exhausted for tomorrow's activities: her son's knighting; her meeting with Skane; confrontations with Alysa, Guinn, and Alric; and hopefully a stolen night with Trahern, though it was not the sheriff she thought about now.

Ceit joined her in the tent. The servant said suggestively, "I know that look, sweet mistress. What man do you ache for today? I know it cannot be eagerness to see Guinn. And Trahern does not bring such a glow to your eyes and cheeks. Who?"

"You know me well, dear Ceit," Isobail replied, laughing.

"Did you find a new lover while we were apart? Be careful of Guinn's and Trahern's jealousies. Neither wishes to share you."

Isobail nodded in agreement. "Men can be such irritations, dear Ceit. They seduce different women when the mood strikes them, but they want you to serve no one except them. Guinn is annoying, and I shall have to get rid of him soon. His use to me has worn thin, but he could be dangerous if rejected."

She glanced at Ceit and said, "I need you to drug Guinn's wine tomorrow night while I slip away with Trahern. We have a meeting with that offensive barbarian, then I want him to stay the night in my room. It could be weeks before I have a man again. If I could live without them, I would."

She laughed, leaned close to Ceit, and related her impressions of Gavin, as she had already told the trusted servant about her troubles with Skane. She left nothing untold about the handsome warrior, including his bold raid yesterday. "He is such a virile man, dear Ceit. I grow hot each time I think of him. Did you notice what a fine body he had? His voice—it caused me to tingle. I must have him, Ceit. But how?"

"You cannot have him unless you also get rid of Trahern. He would not stand for you to bed a common brigand."

"He cannot fight a battle he does not know exists. When he is far away one night, I will find a way to meet with my fine warrior. There is something about Gavin that makes me feel wild and restless. If he proves more valuable than Trahern, I will make him my new sheriff."

"And your new lover?" Ceit teased.

"From what I have seen of him, my only lover," Isobail responded.

Ceit had never seen her mistress so obsessed by a man, and she wondered if Isobail realized how taken she was with this Gavin Hawk. . . .

Alysa agreed to go riding again with her stepbrother, hoping for an opportunity to elude him and visit the tree and Giselde. They left the castle shortly after noon, with Squire Teague and ten guards trailing them. They rode for a time, chatting in an amiable way.

Finally Moran started to get romantic. "I have been wooing you for days, little mouse. Are you still set against me?"

Alysa had decided it was wise to deceive him for a while. That way, she and her father would be safe until King Bardwyn's men arrived. If all went as Baltair expected, their rescues should take place within a week or two. She smiled and lowered her lashes demurely. "You make it impossible for a woman to ignore you, Moran. I have never known this side of you before, and it affects me strangely. You have been most charming, and I like you this way.

"Does that mean you will marry me?"

Alysa's veiled gaze met his and she teased, "You are persistent, my handsome suitor, but you rush me. I have never been courted before, and I find it most enjoyable and exciting. The pleasures of life should not be hurried, my dear Moran. For so long, times have been bad in our land, and it is wonderful to relax and have fun for a change. If you continue with me as you have for days, I will give you your answer in a month," she vowed, smiling provocatively at him.

Later, feeling the timing was right to enlist support, Alysa motioned for Squire Teague to join them. "My friend Teague is also in love," she remarked casually. "After he is knighted, he wishes to marry my servant and dear friend Thisbe, daughter of Sir Piaras. I hate to lose Thisbe, but she is worthy of him and she will make Teague a good wife." Alysa turned her head toward the man riding at her left and winked at her friend, urging him to play along with this enticement for help with his marriage. "It would make me most happy, dear Moran, if you could persuade your mother to betroth them soon. As with you, Teague fears another suitor may come along and steal his love before he can claim her."

"I will agree, if you will promise to court only me."

Alysa smiled into his green eyes and responded, "I will allow no suitor to call on me at the castle, unless you cease your suit."

"I shall never cease until you are mine," Moran vowed.

"That pleases me," she lied. Turning to Teague and capturing his hand, she declared, "Perhaps my handsome suitor will stand with you at your dubbing and wedding."

Before Teague could answer, they rounded a bend in the road and came upon a robbery in progress. Alysa stared at the chieftain who was riding a golden charger with blond mane and tail; a bandit wearing a leather tunic and a mask. Nevertheless, she knew instantly who it was, and hid her shock from her companions.

Moran said to Teague, "Take her back to the castle

where she will be safe." To his men he shouted, "We must attack! Prepare yourselves!"

Gavin saw the group as his band, acting under Skane's orders, was relieving terrified merchants of their money bags. He spied his love riding between two men, and recognized the red-haired one as Squire Teague, the one holding her hand and smiling at her! Furious, Gavin was tempted to stand his ground and fight, but he quickly realized it would be selfish and rash. He shouted a retreat to his men, dropping the money bags. He would tell Skane of their foiled robbery, and the brigand leader should hear about it from other men-at-arms.

Alysa watched the brigands depart swiftly, with Moran and his men in hot pursuit. She could not understand why Gavin was involved in a robbery. He had been with six men, no doubt the band with whom she had seen him the day they had rescued her from the Jutes. Or had that only been a trick? She could not ignore the fact he was always around at convenient times, or when the brigands were close, or when Isobail was nearby. Surely Gavin had seen her with Prince Moran and Squire Teague. But why had he taken flight when he could contest Moran and his men?

Teague shook her shoulder. "We must return to the castle, Alysa," he urged. "There could be more of them in the area."

She had to check the tree, in hopes of finding a note that might explain Gavin's astonishing behavior. She galloped beside Teague until they were halfway through the royal forest, then stopped. "Come with me, Teague, there is something I must do." Leading him to the ravine, she said as she dismounted, "Remain here until I return."

"Where are you going?" he demanded.

"Ask me no questions, dear Teague, just trust me,"

she pleaded. "There is an old woman who lives here. I must make certain she is safe. I will not be long."

Teague sensed there was more to her actions than she admitted, but he trusted her enough not to press her. "Go, I will wait here. But hurry, before Moran gives up his chase and returns."

Alysa nodded, then vanished into the forest. First she checked the tree, and found no note. But the pouch of jewels and coins was gone. Why had he taken her payment, but left no word for her? If she had not seen him today, she would not have known he had returned! Alarmed, she yanked a handful of wild flowers from the ground and stuffed them into the hole, telling him she had been here.

Alysa rushed to Giselde's hut and found the old woman at home. "I cannot stay long, Granmannie, but there are things you must know." Quickly she told the old woman about her father's condition, Baltair's help, Isobail's demands, and Moran's pursuit. "There is a strange warrior in the area, Granmannie. Beware of him, as I fear I have trusted him unwisely. I hired him to help me unmask Isobail and protect me and Father, but I fear he has betrayed me."

Before Giselde could tell her granddaughter she was wrong, Alysa said, "I gave him many jewels and coins, but he kept them without helping me. He promises to meet me, then does not. Just now I saw him robbing merchants on the road. It seems I have no one to whom I can turn. Baltair told me to wait for Grandfather's soldiers, but if they do not arrive soon, Isobail will force me to marry her son. If I refuse, perhaps she will slay both Father and me!"

Giselde was bewildered and angered by what she heard, but tried to calm her frantic granddaughter. She had not heard of Moran's return and courting. Something was amiss, and she heeded to speak with Gavin before revealing matters to Alysa. Alysa must not be forced to marry her brother!

"Do not worry, my child. Baltair is right. Wait for King Bardwyn's men. I have also sent word to him, so he must know there is terrible trouble here."

"What if the messengers do not get through to him?"

"I will send another, and another if necessary. All of them cannot be slain. I am sure King Bardwyn is gathering his men to help us," she said, knowing Keegan had returned safely from the small camp whose messenger was to journey the last miles to reach Bardwyn.

"You are kind, Granmannie, and I have missed you. You have been away each time I have come to see you. I have been worried."

Giselde smiled and hugged the girl. "I have been worried, too, my precious child. I did not know about your visits, except for one. I feared you were angry, or following my order to stay away. I am glad to see for myself that you are safe. Surely you need more herbs for your father?"

"We have been giving him nothing for many days, Granmannie," Alysa confessed. "None of the herbs seemed to help." She related how Leitis was seeing to it that nothing pernicious reached Alric's lips. "I fear his illness is real, Granmannie, or he would be improved by now."

Giselde knew that was impossible, and she was confused. She decided to instruct Piaras to investigate. "Go now, but return Tuesday, and we will have a long talk then."

"I will, Granmannie," Alysa promised, deciding she would confess all about Gavin during that next visit.

"Are you sure you do not need more herbs?" Giselde asked, intending to send only healing herbs this time. She wanted Alric disabled, but it sounded as if he were dying. Perhaps she had judged him too harshly or falsely. Catriona could not have loved and trusted him

288

if he were so weak and evil. "Take them, then you can decide if you wish to try them. Perhaps the others were too mild. His condition is grave, and he might need stronger herbs to conquer it."

Alysa accepted the pouch and left. She returned to Teague's side and they hurried to the castle, reaching it only thirty minutes before Moran. As promised, Teague had asked no more questions, but had watched her carefully all the way home. As they parted in the stable, he warned, "Be very careful and clever, Alysa."

Later Alysa wondered if she should be delighted or saddened by the fact that Moran and his forces had not wounded or captured any of Gavin's men. Had Gavin's behavior been part of a crafty scheme to help her? she wondered. But if so, why had he not confided in her? Either something was amiss, or she had misjudged him terribly. Needing solitude, she rested in her room, knowing she would hear the entire tale at dinner, which she did, in colorful detail.

Moran sat at a wooden table in the Boar's Inn, sipping ale and congratulating himself on his progress with Alysa. A man bumped his chair, causing him to slosh his drink on his hand and the table. Before he could rise and demand an apology, the man gave one.

Gavin smiled genially and said, "Forgive my clumsiness, friend, but that serving wench tickled my loins and made me jump." He chuckled and jested, "The innkeeper must be working them too hard and long; seems they all want to get on their backs and rest. They appear so eager to be bedded, they are grabbing any man in sight. May I buy you a drink to replace the one I spilled?"

Moran laughed and invited the man to be seated. He motioned for a pretty serving wench to bring two drinks. As she leaned over to place Gavin's tankard before him, Moran boldly fondled and pinched one breast.

Aware of Moran's identity, the girl smiled in delight. Shamelessly, she asked, "Would ye be wanting me upstairs later? If I be not better between the covers than the silly lass ye purchased the other night, ye will owe me naught."

Moran winked at Gavin and commented, "You were right, my friend, and this wench's offer is too tempting to refuse. Give me a while to have a few drinks with my friend, then come drag me upstairs and prove your boastful claims."

After the girl left, Moran asked casually, "Where are you from, friend? I do not recall your face."

Gavin had seen the squire who had been riding with both his love and rival this afternoon enter the tavern, and hoped he could learn something from him. Claiming to be a warrior and adventurer from Strathclyde, far to the north, the Cumbrian prince spoke of make-believe journeys, then alleged he had been put ashore near the Damnonia-Logris border to work his way home. He claimed he did not care much for sea travel, but mostly wanted to seek a little excitement. Upon hearing of the goings-on in this land, he added, he had decided to look here for adventure and a few coins before riding north.

"Why do you not go to Malvern Castle and seek work there?" Moran asked. "I am sure Prince Alric and Princess Isobail can use a warrior such as you."

Gavin shook his head. "I prefer to work on my own. I like to come and go as I choose, and decide which assignments I will take and how long I will remain in one area. You are a squire, so you are used to following another's orders and timetables; I am not. Since I was a child, I have charted my own life. I roam freely and happily, and that has spoiled me for hiring out."

Moran was feeling merry by now. He chuckled and

confessed, "I am Moran, Princess Isobail's son. I was forced to become a page at seven, then a squire. When I am knighted, I will become the ruler of this land."

"I have never heard of a knight becoming a king," Gavin said.

"We do not have a king here; this is a princedom. I shall become ruler by marrying Princess Alysa," he disclosed. "She is beautiful and desirable, but a little gullible and lacking in keen wits. I have been wooing her for days, and she has weakened."

Gavin was astonished by the man's identity but his expression remained the same. His love had been riding with two squires, and one was Isobail's son! He asked nonchalantly, "If she is so valuable and beautiful, surely others are chasing her."

"No one would dare challenge me, friend. Alysa will marry me," he said confidently.

Gavin allowed a pleased expression to cross his face. "I am honored to share time and a drink with you, Prince Moran. I see this bonny princess does not rule your heart and life. That is wise, my noble friend. Never let a woman yoke you, any woman."

"Alysa is a woman who kindles a man's desires, but she might be too gentle to pleasure him sufficiently," Moran confided. "After we are wed, I will train her to feed me as best she can, then hire others to finish sating my appetite."

"I have found no woman who can sate a man on her own. You will have no trouble filling your castle with pleasing wenches who will be eager to serve you in every way. You are a lucky man, my friend."

"You are right again. Why should I pay for services that should be mine for free? What servant would refuse her ruler anything?" Moran grinned lewdly, then asked, "What is your name, friend? Perhaps I will invite you to share such treats for a few nights, if you are still around when I become ruler here. I would enjoy hearing more of your exhilarating adventures. A life is dull when it is controlled by others. Perhaps I can hire you to teach me how to roam wildly."

"If you do not tarry too long before needing my help, I will gladly give it. I have seen a fetching wench from the castle who whets my appetite. Perhaps as payment you could command her to . . . serve me while I am your guest and teacher. I asked a villager her name: it is Thisbe, daughter of a knight called Piaras."

Moran frowned. "You ask for a woman who is smitten by another squire, one named Teague, the son of Lord Orin. If I save her for you, Alysa will be displeased with me. She begged me to convince Mother to betroth Teague and Thisbe." Moran considered for a moment, then said, "Perhaps I can persuade my mother to deny their marriage request, but make Alysa believe I did all I could to help them."

"If this Thisbe and Squire Teague are truly taken with each other, a woman with a bleeding heart cannot be favorably enticed, so she would provide me with very little enjoyment."

"Then you must choose another from among my servants, for I hear they are much in love. Stay, and I will see that you are well rewarded with money and women." Moran enjoyed Gavin's easy-going personality, and since he had few friends, was easily snared by Gavin's entertaining company. The girl came to stand beside Moran, to lure him away to a back room. "How can I reach you?" he asked.

"I come in here every few nights or so. Just ask for Gavin Hawk, or leave a message for me with the innkeeper. Your offer sounds as tempting as hers," he said with a grin, nodding to the eager serving wench whose hands were wandering boldly over Moran's body.

Gavin took a long time returning to his camp in the royal forest. He needed to think, but he was baffled by seeing his love today and by hearing about her tonight.

She had not contacted him recently, and that worried him. It looked and sounded as if she had made her choice, and the winner was Squire Teague! How could she do this, now that he had decided to fight for her?

If she did not contact him within the next few days, he would find a way to reach her with a message. Tomorrow he would meet with Giselde and explain his problem, seeking her help. Another thing: he did not like how Prince Moran talked about Princess Alysa. Obviously Moran did not love Alysa, and only planned to use her. Even if Alysa was too naive, and even if she was charmed by Moran, she was Thisbe's friend and King Bardwyn's granddaughter; she deserved to be rescued by him, Gavin decided.

Due to a lame horse, Sheriff Trahern arrived at the castle near midnight. He went to Earnon's room to deliver Isobail's message. He was exhausted, so he would tell Earnon to pass the good news along to Moran. He had to knock many times before Earnon responded.

Isobail's sorcerer eyed Trahern oddly and asked, "What do you want?"

"I have an urgent message from Princess Isobail. Let me enter so we can speak privately." When Earnon hesitated, Trahern snapped, "I have ridden hard all day, and was forced by a lame horse to walk several miles. Waste no more of my time and energy. Move aside."

Earnon obeyed and motioned the peevish sheriff to a chair in his outer chamber. "What is wrong?" he asked.

Trahern related the news of Sir Kelton's death and how it affected Alric and Moran. "Can the prince be healed enough to hold the knighting ceremony tomorrow afternoon?"

Earnon considered the matter for a short time. "In the morning I can leave off the benumbing herbs and give him a potion to clear his head. At the last moment I can give him a stimulant to provide a burst of energy enough for him to look well and carry out a quick ceremony. But a stimulus does not last long and is dangerous to use on such a sick man."

"Would it be safer to wait another day?"

Earnon shook his head. "I would have to do the same thing. The only safe way to get Alric up and around is to take him off the stupefying herbs for a week or more. I doubt Isobail wants to wait that long."

"I am sure she does not. She wants Moran knighted and on his way to take over Kelton's territory before the lords suggest someone else. Take care of Alric, and tell Moran to prepare himself to be dubbed tomorrow. I need to eat and go to bed." Trahern left to seek a servant to bring him food and prepare a room for the night.

Kyra appeared from her hiding place in Earnon's sleeping chamber. He asked simply, "You heard?"

She nodded. "My mother will be home tomorrow. Soon she will order us to slay Baltair, and then hand me over to Calum as if I mean nothing to her. Do you agree with my idea to go along with her, then slay Calum and claim the castle for ourselves? How could she refuse us?"

"How can I allow Calum to touch you?" he said in torment.

"I will find many excuses to thwart him. I will get rid of him before he can bed me even once. Then we can have each other openly. If Mother tries to deny us, we will slay her too! Return to my arms, my love, for our time together is short."

Sixteen

It was early when Trahern handled what could have been a perilous oversight by Isobail: Baltair. He ordered an escort to pack supplies for a hasty trip, then summoned the seneschal and informed him, "I come with terrible news, Baltair. Sir Kelton met with an accident and he is dead. Princess Isobail is returning this afternoon from Lord Orin's, but she sent me ahead to give you a message. Our regent needs you to go to Sir Kelton's and govern until someone can be selected to fill his place. She is depending on you to keep everything in order and running smoothly."

Baltair, immediately suspecting foul play, concealed his shock. "What if I am needed here by Prince Alric?" he asked without inflection.

"The prince is too ill to need anyone, and you are the seneschal. You know how quickly things can fall into disrepair and ruin when no one is around to prevent it. You are needed there, Baltair. Why would you refuse such a simple request? In her name, I order it."

"It will take time to prepare for such a journey."

The sheriff said irritably, "All is packed except your personal belongings. Gather them quickly before Sir Kelton's servants scatter and possessions vanish. There are cattle to be fed, crops to be tended, and servants to be governed. The messenger said Lady Kadra is distraught and cannot handle such tasks. Kelton Castle has been without a master for several days, and there are bandits roaming the hills and moors. Princess Isobail wants you there as quickly as possible. The guards are waiting to escort you safely; you must hurry."

Baltair had no choice but to heed Trahern's command, and a servant was sent to help him pack. The worried seneschal was told that Prince Alric was sleeping and Princess Alysa bathing, so he could see and speak with neither before being rushed from the castle. Baltair sensed a clever scheme in the air but he could not discover what it was. As he was passing the gatehouse, he caught Piaras's eye, hoping the knight-trainer understood him and would continue to observe events in the castle.

From the inner ward Trahern smiled as he watched the group leave. Isobail would be pleased by his cleverness. Still fatigued, he returned to his bed for a few hours, since he had a busy day and night ahead of him.

Piaras observed the incident with intrigue. When time permitted late this afternoon, he would report these curious events to Giselde.

In the south tower on the first floor, Kyra sleepily answered the persistent summons on her door. "It is early, Moran. What do you want?"

Moran chuckled, pushed her aside, then entered her sitting room. He casually strolled around the room, fingering trinkets before dropping into a chair. He flung one leg over its arm and sank back comfortably, then gazed at the quizzical girl. "You surprise me, sister."

Called to wariness, Kyra closed the door. She came forward and asked in an even tone that matched his, "How so, little brother?"

"I need your help to win Alysa. I demand it," he added coldly.

"Did you come here to play games?"

"I have no time for games. I saw you leave Earnon's chamber last night, too late and too mussed for an innocent visit. I do not know why you crave an old man's touch and body, but that is your affair. I am sure Mother does not know her advisor is bedding her daughter and I doubt you two want her to learn such an amusing secret. Do as I say, Kyra, or I shall expose you."

"We love and desire each other, Moran, things you know nothing about, but Mother would never betroth us. She needs me to wed Sir Calum. I will obey her, but only after I have taken my fill of Earnon. I will help you win Alysa, but not because you demand it. Nothing would please me more than to see her under your sadistic control, or at your mercy. You will not open your mouth to Mother about us, or I will tell Alysa where you go and what you do when you leave the castle. Afterwards, I doubt she would marry you for any reason."

Moran laughed heartily. "It is good to see your backbone has hardened, sister. I feared you would allow Mother to keep it soft forever. We have a bargain. While I am away, work on Alysa for me."

"You are leaving today?" she asked, curious.

"Ah, yes, you have not heard the good news," he teased, then enlightened her. "Soon I will have Sir Kelton's castle and Alysa, as you will have Sir Calum's. Whatever your fascination with the old man, use him up quickly before you leave. Calum is not a fool, so do not risk secret meetings with your old lover. Do you think you can handle Sir Calum? I hear his appetite is large and varied."

"More so than yours, little brother?" she taunted.

"Which do you prefer, yes or no?" he asked amidst chuckles.

"If Calum is as skilled as I hear you are, then I hope it is yes."

Moran studied Kyra's expression and grinned. "We

are more alike than I realized, sister. Perhaps we should become allies."

Alric was propped upon many pillows in his bed. He felt better this morning; no, he felt strange and wonderful. His body was tingly and warm, and no gripans tormented him. There was no sour taste in his mouth, his eyes were not heavy, and his body did not feel sluggish and limp. It was as if he could feel his blood racing wildly, blissfully, through his body to heal it. He was alive and happy, almost ecstatic and carefree. He wanted to jump out of bed and dance around the room, but dared not try such a foolish thing. He almost giggled, for he felt like a young lad again.

Trahern had just left his room, delivering a mixture of good and bad news. His friend and vassal was dead, but Prince Moran would take Sir Kelton's place. What an honor and joy to knight your own son, even if no one knew that secret! Alric decided it was only right for Moran to receive Kelton Castle, for all believed he was Lord Caedmon's son, and that grant had belonged to Caedmon and Isobail Ahern. It was the best and only way to reward his son, since his daughter would get the crown and Malvern Castle. On this special day Alric wished he could tell Moran the truth about his heritage, but knew he could not, not without exposing his dark deed against Isobail while she was the wife of another man. He had guarded that secret for years, and for more reasons than he could recall clearly at this moment, he must continue to do so.

This was going to be a wonderful day. He would show everyone he was still their ruler—a good ruler, a strong ruler, an undying ruler. He would be careful not to overtire himself. He would avoid all food and drink, keeping them from racing treacherously through his body and sending him back to bed. His beautiful wife was coming home today, and he was eager to see her. Sometimes he and Isobail had disagreements, but that did not matter today. His emotions were soaring, and he could forgive her anything. He would order her to spend tonight in his bed, as his manroot was strong and hot this morning, and it itched madly to be cooled by the moist and stimulating walls of her receptive womanhood. Nothing, he decided headily, could go wrong for him today.

From her window Alysa furtively observed Isobail's arrival and her exuberant welcome by her son. The two laughed, embraced, and chatted as they entered the Great Tower arm in arm, practically ignoring everyone around them. Alysa had received the news about Sir Kelton's death and Moran's imminent knighting. She hated to leave her chamber, but she could not avoid the ceremony. She did not want to confront Moran, suspecting he would pressure her for an answer to his proposal on this "momentous day." What, she fretted, would he do if Isobail brazenly announced their betrothal after the dubbing?

Things were going awry. Alysa had been frantic after learning of Baltair's hasty departure. She had wanted to visit her father, but Thisbe and Leitis had told her that people kept going in and out of his chamber, which prevented her from sneaking inside via the secret passage. She had been told she could visit Alric only with Trahern or Earnon present, to make certain she did not upset the prince today, when he had such a taxing schedule before him.

No one seemed to think her father's sudden recovery unusual, not even dear Leitis. She heard that he was feeling wonderful and was looking forward to the ceremony; yet despite his improvement, he had not asked to see her. She had wanted to go riding, but Sheriff

Trahern had ordered the gates locked to prevent any intrusions today. Everything was going crazy, and she did not know what to do.

She needed to question Gavin, and she had to explain her predicament to him. She needed Giselde for advice and information, and to ask her if there was a reason to suspect Gavin of treachery, because of what Baltair had told her about the Vikings. She needed so much!

Within an hour she must stand with her family to witness her stepbrother's dubbing. Sir Kelton was gone, Lord Friseal was gone, and Lord Daron was gone; in their places were Moran, Trahern, and Calum: all members of her stepmother's force. Only two left, but Lord Fergus was under siege and Lord Orin was charmed by Isobail. If help did not arrive in a few more days, as Baltair promised, she would have to take drastic steps. . . .

Having taken it with her to Malvern Castle after Caedmon's death, Isobail sent Moran the sword that had been in the Ahern family for three generations. Moran placed it upon the altar for consecration, as was the custom. There was no time to carry out the entire ceremony of feasting, which included spending the night in a chapel for the *Vigil At Arms*—hours of praying and fasting and purifying of soul and body, and the confessing of his sins to a priest. Moran did what time allowed: he bathed, donned white garments, clipped his hair short, and awaited the *accolade*.

Alysa watched her father enter the Great Hall, mount the dais, and take his place in the throne chair beside Isobail. Sheriff Trahern had escorted Alric, but not assisted him. Alysa could not believe the difference in her father since sneaking into his room Thursday night.

Leitis had told her Alric was receiving no herbs of any kind, and Alysa had not given the trusted servant the new herbs from Giselde, so his recovery was astounding. She had to admit, he did look vigorous today. He was smiling and nodding to those around him, but it was not the old Alric on the throne. His eyes looked too bright and shiny, his cheeks glowing with too much excitement. He was dressed in his finest garments, as was everyone. All knights present were gathered nearby, and in jocular moods. The village priest had arrived to bless Moran's sword and say a prayer before and after the ceremony.

Alysa felt in a daze as she watched Sir Phelan, Captain of the Guard, press the hilt of Caedmon's sword to Moran's lips, then buckle it around her stepbrother's waist. Sir Piaras had been given the honor of "the girding on" of Moran's golden spurs. Moran approached Prince Alric and knelt. In a clear and strong voice, Moran recited the Vows of Chivalry. Using the Malvern sword, her father firmly tapped Moran on both shoulders and then atop his head, completing the *accolade*. Alysa was intrigued and dismayed by the look on her father's face: fierce pride, fatherly pride, and inexplicable happiness.

Minstrels began to play merry music, and the festivities got under way. The tables were covered rapidly and abundantly with food and drink, and even the servants were allowed to feast and dance on this day. Isobail reigned over the afternoon like a majestic queen, and Kyra danced with nearly every man present. Alysa tried to converse with her father, but he was too distracted. She knew he was not intoxicated, for he spoke clearly, and in fact refused all refreshments. She did not know why she was so frightened by his behavior—laughing, joking, having fun—but she was.

Alysa danced with a few knights and squires, and nibbled lightly on the tasty feast. To keep her head clear, she drank no wine. She tried to appear happy and calm,

301

but wondered if she were succeeding, as she felt neither. The first dance had been shared with Moran, then he had been caught up with colorful tales and advice from the other knights. Each time she glanced at him, he seemed to be enjoying himself immensely. For once she could not tell what part of Moran's conduct was false and what part was honest. Suddenly he was at her side, grinning suspiciously.

When Isobail arose and asked for everyone's attention for an announcement, Alysa feared she would faint from dread. Moran placed his hand at her waist, drew her close, and smiled into her frantic eyes. Alysa waited tensely for her world to spin away wildly.

Smiling, Isobail called Squire Teague and Thisbe forward. Alysa's gaze widened as she witnessed the unexpected scene. Isobail joined the lovers' hands and Prince Alric betrothed them, promising to knight Teague within the month so they could marry before autumn. Teague hugged Thisbe, and nearly everyone present cheered their approval.

Moran leaned close to Alysa and whispered, "As I promised, little mouse, I asked Mother to betroth them as my gift for today. I wanted to ask for your hand, but I knew you were not ready, and I did not want to frighten you away from me. Does that please you, and warm your heart toward me?" he teased.

Alysa met Moran's smoldering gaze and said, "That pleases me very much, Moran. You have acted kindly and unselfishly by sharing your special day with others, the deed of a true knight. I am glad you did not coerce me today; such behavior reveals you can be patient even when you desire something greatly. I am warmed by the changes in you during the last year. It is like . . . like meeting you for the first time. Before you must leave, will you join me for a dance and a goblet of wine?"

"That pleases me very much, little mouse," he said,

echoing her earlier words before taking her hand and leading her to the dancing area.

The two-hour ceremony and feast passed swiftly. Then it was time for Moran to leave. He spoke privately with his mother who told him not to worry about Alysa, as if he would after hearing Alysa's pleasing words. Isobail vowed that no man would come to court Alysa and she would be given to Moran within the month.

"If I give her to you today, my handsome son, it might appear improper to others. Sir Kelton dies, you are knighted, you take his place—our old home—and you get Damnonia's heir all at once. It could look as though we are taking advantage of Sir Kelton's death. Wait a while to claim her. First get settled in your new home."

"You are right, Mother. I will wait to have her, but make certain you save her for me. In fact, I think I have won her over to me. Like you, I can be most charming and persuasive."

Isobail was called aside to speak with a messenger from Sir Calum, who had taken over Lord Daron's castle near the Logris border. She was furious to learn that the brigands had raided that area three times lately, even though she had given orders that they were not to attack lands her men controlled. Sir Calum demanded that Isobail stop the raids and insisted that she send Kyra to him within two weeks. Isobail told the messenger to return quickly to Calum, advising him that both matters would be handled promptly.

Meanwhile, Alric began to feel terrible. He was becoming weak and his head was pounding. Isobail knew the stimulant was wearing off but she had been unable to slip more to him.

She whispered, "I am not surprised that you are beginning to feel badly, my beloved husband, for you have had nothing to eat or drink." She urged him to return to his room and bed, warning him he could take ill again. "Please go and rest, my husband, and perhaps you can return to the feast again later. If not, I will join you in your chamber. I have not seen you look this way for so long, Alric, and it delights me to watch you become as you were long ago, the man who stole my heart and enflamed my passion. Today you look so handsome and virile—you are in command again. I am so proud of how you handled yourself and the ceremony, but you are pushing yourself too hard on your first day out of bed. Remember what happened the last time you recovered, but overdid? Make this healing last. Please save your remaining strength to share with me in your bed tonight."

There was enough of the stimulant in his bloodstream to arouse him. Alric glanced at her and smiled weakly in gratitude. "This has been a good day, a happy day. But you are right, it is time to end my part in it. Will you escort me away so the others will not guess the truth? And return to my bed and arms later?"

"I will do anything you ask, my beloved husband," she replied, knowing he would be unconscious within the hour, even if Earnon and Trahern had to force the potion down his throat. She handed him the silver goblet from which she indicated she had been drinking, though in fact she'd held it in readiness for him. "Here, take my wine and refresh yourself. I have only half a cup left, but I will fetch you more if you desire it."

Moran persisted until Alysa walked with him in the garden. "I must leave, little mouse, and I shall miss you terribly. I do not know when I can return. Will you promise to keep your heart open to me?"

"I will not receive any suitors until I decide if you and I are fated to wed. Do not worry; your mother will guard me as closely as she protects the royal jewels," she teased.

Moran seized her gently and pulled her into his arms.

She tried to push him away as she cautioned, "Someone might see us, Sir Ahern. Have you forgotten, we have been here without appropriate attention while your mother was away. We do not want the servants spreading wild tales about us."

Moran laughed and hugged her possessively. "I do not care who knows how I feel about you, Alysa, and I can hardly restrain my craving for you. The thought of being parted from you at this time is maddening. How I wish I could sweep you into my arms and carry you home with me. But there is much to be done before I can marry you and take you there. I pray it takes no more than a few months. If only you could visit me while I am getting settled, but that would be more improper than stealing kisses in this garden."

Moran captured her face and sealed his lips to hers. He kissed her hungrily and moaned with urgent desire. To him, she was more than a ravishing woman—she represented everything he wanted. He was determined to win her and all that accompanied her. He murmured against her ear, "Do you know how much I want you, little mouse? I am trembling like a virginal lad, and my head is spinning wildly. I think I would perish if I failed to win you. Please, Alysa, become mine soon."

Alysa rested her face against his chest. She could hear his heart pounding forcefully and his irregular breathing. She felt the tension and tremors in his body. His hands were stroking her back and his lips were brushing the top of her head. He was not lying and pretending; he was highly aroused by her!

Moran lifted her chin and looked into her eyes, which were clouded by confusion, surprise, and a little panic. His glowed with hot desire and possessiveness, and believing she was an innocent, he assumed her reaction stemmed from virginal fears and modesty. "Do not be afraid, little mouse. When the time is right, I will teach you all you must know. I would never harm you."

Moments before, Alysa had sighted Isobail watching them from Alric's window. Perhaps she could fool the woman into believing she was enchanted with Moran, and fool him too. If Moran and Isobail were misled, they might not have her watched so closely. When Moran's mouth came down on hers again, Alysa slipped her arms around his waist, responded timidly then lowered her head demurely.

She was glad when Moran led her back inside to say his farewells to everyone. Shortly afterwards she watched him mount, smile at her, then ride away with his heavy escort. She knew Isobail was still observing her, so she dreamily stared after the retreating prince, sighed lightly, and headed for her room.

In her chamber Alysa hurriedly stripped to her kirtle and had Thisbe prepare her a bath. While she waited, she poured water from her ewer into a basin and washed her mouth, inside and outside. She had to scrub herself from head to toe, for she felt soiled after Moran's kisses and caresses.

As Thisbe assisted her, the servant reproached, "You should not allow Sir Ahern to woo you just to help me and Teague. My love told me how you tricked Moran into getting us betrothed. I am so grateful, Alysa, and so happy. But it is dangerous to fool Moran."

Alysa smiled and patted Thisbe's hand. "It is done now, and nothing can prevent your marriage. Someone should be happy during this horrid time." Revealing all she dared to her trusted companion, she added, "If help does not come soon, as Baltair promised, I do not know what we shall do. I must tell Gavin the truth about who I am before he hears about your betrothal to Squire Teague, or he could misunderstand and vanish forever. I have to see him and my old teacher tomorrow." Changing the subject quickly, she remarked, "I wonder how Father is feeling. Perhaps I should visit him."

"You cannot," Thisbe replied. "I heard Isobail ordering a bath sent to Prince Alric's chambers, for herself. She also ordered wine and a light meal for both of them. She plans to spend the night with him."

Alysa gaped at her servant. "Are you certain you heard right?"

"There is no mistake, Alysa. Did you not see them snuggled together in the Great Hall? It looked to me as if they are planning to do more than sleep together" Thisbe said modestly.

Alysa frowned, realizing she, too, had perceived the intimate aura surrounding them. She had not wanted to admit that Isobail was sinking her seductive talons into her father again. "At least Moran is gone!" she snapped irritably. "Now I understand the difference between lust and desire, and love and sex," she said without thinking.

"Do you love Gavin and want him?"

Anguish filled Alysa's eyes and voice. "If he is all I believe he is, then I shall fight to win him. I have to see him, Thisbe. He must tell me what he is doing and why. If only he had not tried to keep his return a secret from me . . ."

The servant suggested, "Perhaps there is a good reason, Alysa. Do not doubt him or your love until you hear his explanation."

"As long as there is hope, I will cling to it."

Piaras went to report to Giselde, and the old woman was staggered by the new facts. The moment Piaras left, she hurried to the rock by the pond and left a message for Gavin to come to her swiftly. Things were worse. Someone was playing with Alric's life, because she knew her herbs would not have healed him so quickly or caused such a reaction. As for Alysa, at least she was safe from Moran for a while. Giselde vowed to do anything to halt such a forbidden union, even slay Moran. . . .

Isobail and Trahern were let out the south gate in the outer bailey by one of their trusted men, who would remain on duty until their return. Dressed in dark colors and riding dark steeds, the night cloaked them quickly. As they rode, Isobail told Trahern that Alric was under Earnon's spell again and it was safe for him to sneak to her chamber tonight. As planned, Ceit had drugged Guinn so the bard would sleep soundly all night. But, of course, Isobail did not tell one lover about the other.

During their meeting with Skane, the brigand leader claimed that the raid on Isobail's retinue was a mistake by his new man, Gavin Hawk. He laughed and said not to be angry with the eager bandit, as his raid served to remove suspicion from Trahern and possibly from her.

Isobail and Trahern knew he was lying, and it galled them. When Isobail demanded to know why the brigands were raiding Calum's land, Skane shrugged. Then Isobail ordered him to stay away from Land's End, where her son was now ruling.

"You leave us few areas to feed on," Skane complained sullenly.

"It should appear as if I am responsible for making the lands under my control safe again," Isobail replied, "as I told you before. I cannot let you raid foolhardily. This land will soon be mine, and I do not want it in ruins. I have paid you well in coins and jewels. What you take from others is an added reward."

"I need more, Isobail. I have many men to feed and supply. If they grow restless, I will be unable to hold them together."

"If you are the leader you claim to be, you can hold your men. Tell me, Skane, are you losing your power and control while mine grow stronger each day? My men trust me and obey me. They do not grow restless or make extra demands. If you cannot obey me, our bargain is over. Consider my words, then meet with me again Tuesday night."

On the way back to the castle, Isobail said, "The meeting planned for Tuesday night will keep Gavin Hawk in the area. Meet with him as you have planned. If he agrees to take over for us, he is to meet with Skane and kill him." She wished Gavin had been present tonight, then warned herself not to ache for him so feverishly, as she must not betray her desire to Trahern. Then she praised the sheriff to disarm him, saying, "When Baltair returns, I shall have him removed. That was clever of you to handle him. I will reward you in my bed tonight."

Alysa could not sleep. She threw the cover aside, walked to the window and noticed a rider gingerly prodding a horse along the narrow space between the castle and the precipitous bank to the river wall. As the rider glanced up, the dark hood slipped, revealing white-blond hair. The woman quickly covered her head, but Alysa had recognized Isobail. She went to another window, stared at the south gate, and saw a guard furtively make his way back to his quarters. Alysa had not seen Trahern pass by moments before, scouting ahead to be sure Isobail would not be seen. While watching the traitorous guard, she missed seeing Isobail and Trahern slip across the inner ward. She wondered where her stepmother had been alone, and whom she had met. . . .

Gavin waited until dark before heading for Giselde's hut, and had meanwhile concealed himself at the edge of the forest to observe the castle. There had been many comings and goings at the castle today, but none had been his Thisbe, and he needed to see her and explain about the raid and his lack of contact. He had seen Isobail return, and Prince Moran leave with a heavy guard.

Just before heading to Giselde's, he had spied two riders sneaking from the castle and followed them. He managed to get close enough to overhear Isobail's words to Trahern. All was going better than Gavin had expected. He had tied Isobail to the brigands, and it was time to expose her to King Bardwyn. Tomorrow he would send Keegan with another message. Tonight he would check the tree for one. Certain he was not followed, Gavin rode to the tree, even though he doubted his love could have sneaked here since he checked it before the raid.

At first Gavin was confused by the bunch of dying wildflowers he found in the tree hole. Then he realized it must have been the only way his love could let him know she had been here. But when? he asked himself testing the stems to see how long ago the flowers had been plucked. He reasoned she had stopped here while Moran was chasing him. But she had been with Teague!

Gavin paced and fretted unnaturally. Why did everyone think those two were in love? How could she love Teague then yield to him? She had to be terribly confused after seeing him yesterday. He berated himself for not having a scrap of paper or writing instrument so he could leave a message for her. Thinking quickly, he found a rock and used his knife to etch on the smoother surface, "Trust me, my love."

He placed the rock inside the hole. He instantly reached to retrieve it to add the day and time, but it was gone. His hand roamed the dark and damp area to find that the hole had decayed further and was filling up with rotting trash. As he tried to recover it, his fingers touched and withdrew a leather pouch. He opened it, and was astonished by its contents. From the message, he learned she had placed it there before his return. She had found it missing, but no message from him, he thought, and then after seeing him during the raid yesterday . . .

For safekeeping, Gavin stuffed the leather pouch back into the hole, since he did not want Skane finding it on him. After placing several rocks atop it, he covered the newly decayed area with more concealing trash. Afterwards, he placed the rock with his message on the firm setting. What must she be thinking and feeling? he wondered. Hopefully she would return soon and find his urgent words.

Gavin was in for a bigger surprise at Giselde's hut. The old woman related all she had learned since seeing him last, except the news of Thisbe's betrothal. Gavin told her all he had seen and done, including his meeting with Moran, and the old woman clenched her teeth in anger.

"I do not mean to vex you, Giselde, but I had to know about Thisbe. Yet the more I hear, the more confused I become," he admitted. "How can she trust me when she must believe that I deceive her?" he murmured, then related being seen by her during the raid and his more recent discovery of the jewels and note she had left him.

Giselde, having been told these same details by Alysa just yesterday, had prepared for this moment of truth. "When Piaras visited me today," she said, "he told me of the betrothal of his daughter to Squire Teague."

"It cannot be!" The Cumbrian prince stormed to the hearth and leaned against it, staring into the small fire. "How could she yield to me if she loves him?"

That was what Giselde had to know—the depth of their commitment. "Come, Prince Gavin Crisdean," she called to him. "Look at these and tell me which is your

Thisbe." Giselde had sketched the figures of two women, then used juice from plants to color their eyes and heads.

Gavin sullenly approached the table and glanced at both, his eyes settling on the haunting image of Alysa. His finger traced the line of her jaw, as it had in reality. He stared into the blue eyes which could not see him, looked at the pink lips which could not kiss him, and the soft smile upon them. The picture was so realistic that he could almost feel her warmth and hear her laughter. He remembered what it was like to hold her, to make love to her. She was such a joy to be with, day or night. "You are very good, Giselde," he said. "You have captured her perfectly. Is she not exquisite? Yet, she possesses more than physical beauty."

"This explains everything, yet nothing," Giselde remarked mysteriously. "This is Thisbe, daughter of Piaras and love of Squire Teague," she said, pointing to the other girl's image. "This girl," she murmured with affection, "is Princess Alysa Malvern, my granddaughter."

"You must be mistaken!" Gavin gasped, then knew she was not, for it explained much.

"This girl is not in love with Teague," Giselde said. "This girl is in love with a mysterious warrior named Gavin Hawk."

She could tell that Gavin was too excited to speak. She murmured, "You are both nobles, Prince Gavin. She is not out of your reach, nor you out of hers, as you both feared."

"She told you about us? Why did you say nothing?" he demanded.

The old woman spoke quickly, "Nay, she has not spoken of such things. Why I do not know. She has never kept secrets from me before. I guessed the truth that time you described her and spoke of her horse. Only Alysa rides Calliope, and Thisbe does not ride at all.

And as you can see, Thisbe is not overly pretty, as you described her to me, and has brown eyes. You spoke of your love's beautiful blue eyes. The more you spoke about your love, the more I was certain it was Alysa."

"Yet you kept silent to me. Why?"

"Because I feared for both of you. I feared you would tell her our plan and allow her to help us. I do not want her endangered, and there are things I cannot reveal to her at the present. I would have to tell her terrible things about her father. There are many reasons she must not know about you and me at this time. Yet one day, Prince Gavin, you can tell her the truth and claim her."

"How can she love me? She thinks I am nothing, beneath her! She has lied to me, deceived me."

"No doubt for some of the same reasons that you have lied to her and deceived her," Giselde retorted. "How could you love her when you thought she was a servant beneath you? You would have chosen your duty over her, as she felt she must do. Yea, she thinks you are out of her reach, but because of the role you are playing. Even if that were not so, you have no doubt told her you cannot marry her."

Gavin considered those painful words, and recalled several talks between him and . . . Alysa. "You are right. We were both trapped by a love we thought was impossible."

"If I know Alysa, she is troubled by her guile, and she will confess it soon. Even then you must not reveal yourself to her. If you love her, Prince Gavin, then protect her until this terror is conquered. We are too near our victory; please hold your tongue a while longer."

"If you did not feel you could trust me completely, you would not have ended my torment by telling me who she is. Now I understand why she is so special; Alysa Malvern is a rare creature."

Suddenly Gavin realized that Moran had been talking

about his love last night. Fury consumed him. "I will slay Moran if he touches her!"

"Piaras told me of the ceremony this afternoon," Giselde replied. "But now Moran has left for Land's End, so Alysa is safe from him for a time."

Gavin met Giselde's gentle gaze and pleaded, "If she comes to you and tells you of a wandering warrior, please speak of me favorably. Help me hold her love and trust until I can reveal myself."

"Your hearts and bodies are already joined, and one day your lives will be too. But only if you do nothing to endanger either of you."

Moving aside some jewels, coins, and other valuables, Giselde showed Gavin the secret compartment in a chest. She retrieved the amethyst ring and told Gavin, "If anything happens to me, take this ring to Alysa and tell her about me. If you hold your silence until King Bardwyn arrives, she will wear it when she marries you. I wore it with Rurik, Catriona wore it with Alric, and Alysa will wear it with you. The runes told me this the day you arrived, before you met Alysa. When you spoke of your love for Thisbe, I was confused, for the runes never lie. But the runes warn of destruction and death if you claim her as Prince Crisdean before Evil is defeated. I warn you, Gavin, believe such things or she will suffer."

Seventeen

While carefully scanning her surroundings, Alysa slipped through the woods. She was relieved that she had convinced Princess Isobail to let her go riding, but Isobail had insisted on an escort of seven men. Anticipating such a requirement, Alysa had asked Squire Teague to select a group he could trust. When they came near her destination, she claimed to be ill from too much feasting and excitement yesterday, and said she needed privacy. The men had dismounted to await her return.

Alysa stood at the tree several moments before reaching inside the hole. Baffled, she withdrew the large rock. The scratchings seized her eye, and she read them eagerly, noticing the date and time.

Last night, after he found my flowers, and after he knew I saw him at the raid, and after he might have heard of Thisbe's betrothal, she thought.

"Trust me!" she said aloud. "Is that all you have to say to me?" What about his actions? Alysa thought. And his secrecy? What about the jewels and money? Her groping fingers did not find the pouch. What did this mean? Did Isobail meet with Gavin last night? Were the two of them plotting against her? "Of course!" she shrieked as an idea came to mind.

How clever her wicked stepmother was! Moran's courting her was a disguise to disarm her to cast suspicion away from Isobail and Moran when she disappeared! Isobail did not want the real heir to remain! Alysa laughed almost wildly. "I wonder if you know how taken your son is with me," she said to herself. "I wonder if he will allow you to send me into barbaric captivity, when he can have me and the throne if he defies you. . . ."

The time carved into the rock caught her attention again. Yes, it was after she had witnessed Isobail's return to the castle. But that didn't mean she had met with Gavin, Alysa reasoned, recalling how tender Gavin had been with her. She reflected on their talks, their visits, their lovemakings, envisioned his expressions and mused on his personality. How could such a man be a deadly criminal? A treacherous deceiver? He was an admittedly carefree adventurer, a hired mercenary, a devilish rogue, an unconquerable lover. Yet she could not be so wrong about him; she could not be!

Alysa hurried to Giselde's hut and was ecstatic to find the woman home. "I do not have much time, Granmannie, so I must speak swiftly. I know you will think me shameless and wicked, but I must tell you the all of it for you to understand and advise me."

Alysa placed the rock on the table as she revealed everything about Gavin, Moran, and her actions. She left no thought, feeling, deed, or word unspoken. Winded after her quickly spoken revelation, she remarked sadly, "After Baltair told me about the Vikings wanting to restore the royal bloodline, I feared Gavin might be a Viking warrior who was after me. Why did you not stress this danger to me?"

Giselde stroked Alysa's arm and replied, "It was long ago, and I believe they do not know about you or have forgotten about you. If the Jutes were aware of you, they would have come after you by now. I have heard tales of this golden-haired warrior you speak of. His raids are strange, like clever tricks to fool the brigands. I think he is trying to help you by pretending to be one of them. Perhaps he feared if you knew about his return, you might be in danger, and that is why he avoided you."

"But you warned me of a sunny-haired man with green eyes, and Gavin has both," Alysa argued. "All of your warnings fit him."

"I have had more dreams since then, my child. The warning was about Moran, but his hair changed over the years, as did his heart. Moran is evil, Alysa; never surrender to him. The runes tell me Sir Kelton's death was not an accident, and others are in peril."

Giselde had decided that there were things Alysa could not be told now and things she should never be told. The old woman had to watch her words carefully, and guard against slips. "In my recent dreams I saw a warrior at your side, one who can help you, one you can win if you heed my warnings."

"You really believe I can trust Gavin?" Alysa asked.

"You can, but you must step aside for now or death and destruction will result. You must not interfere with or hinder or question him. The forces of Good say to trust him, and you must not intrude. To do so will endanger both of you."

"Why did you say I could win him? We are too mismatched."

Giselde said, "If your love is true, he can be yours."

"But how, Granmannie? He is a warrior and I am a princess."

"The forces of Good will find a way to make him worthy of you. Return to the castle and remain there until King Bardwyn arrives. What of your father? Are the new herbs strong enough to help him?"

"I gave them to Leitis this morning. She will begin using them today. Father seemed to be doing so well,

317

but he collapsed after the knighting ceremony. With so much happening at the castle Friday and Saturday, I did not have a chance to give them to her privately. I must go now, or they will come looking for me. Thank you for helping me, Granmannie. I love you. I will see you again soon."

Giselde embraced her tightly. "I love you, too, my little Alysa. When this evil is conquered, perhaps I can return to the castle and become your teacher again, if you wish it so."

Alysa hugged Giselde and replied joyfully, "Oh, yes, Granmannie, I wish it so."

"Place these roses in your hiding spot, and the warrior will understand you love him."

Alysa took the flowers and departed. She quickly ran to the tree, placed them inside the hole, and returned to where the men were waiting nervously. "I am sorry I took so long, Squire Teague, but I feel wonderful now. Shall we race back to the castle?" she laughingly teased the men, who merrily accepted the challenge.

Princess Isobail answered Alysa's knock at her father's chamber door. "May I see Father this morning, Isobail? I picked these flowers for him while I was out riding. I worry so about him."

"I am sorry, Alysa, but he can see no one," Isobail replied. "I will place the flowers near his bed and tell him they are from you if he awakens. You may peek inside, if you wish."

Knowing her stepmother would not have made such an offer unless Alric was sleeping and looking terrible, Alysa shook her head. "I hate to see him like this. Can we do nothing to help him?"

Isobail sighed heavily before answering. "I have summoned every healer I know, Alysa, and Earnon has tried every potion and herb he has in his collection. Nothing has cured my Alric, or even helped him. I have tried all remedies and followed every suggestion I have received, however foolish it sounded. If you can find another healer or know of another restorative to try, send for him or use it today. I am desperate to have my husband well again, to have him as he used to be. Please, try anyone or anything you believe will work."

At those words, Alysa knew her father's condition was hopeless, at least for now. Once her grandfather arrived, the king would find someone to heal his son. "I know of nothing and no one you have not tried, Isobail. His life is in the hands of the gods. We are helpless."

"You must not spend all your energy worrying over Alric. Your father would not want you to be so depressed and listless. You are young, vital, and beautiful. Have you given a suitor any thought?"

Alysa was thrilled by the unexpected blush that colored her cheeks brightly. "I—We—Your son asked . . . to court me," she stammered effectively, hoping to appear smitten by Moran. "I told him I would make no decision until . . . he could return and woo me. While you were gone, we spent most of our time together. He has changed much since childhood. He is no longer the mischievous boy who pulled my hair and teased me unmercifully. Does this displease you? Should I not . . . consider Prince Moran? I told him it might not be proper, but he is so . . ." She lowered her eyes and blushed again. "He said we were not truly kin."

"Is there no one else who catches your eye?"

Alysa smiled dreamily. "Who could compete with Moran? I mean . . . Moran asked me to see no one else while I was considering him. If you think it best to compare him with others, summon anyone proper to address me."

Isobail smiled and teased, "But, you do not wish to be courted by others, do you, Alysa?"

"I do not want to sound vain, but I can think of no

319

other man who is a perfect choice for me. Everything seemed to go so smoothly between us. Moran is handsome, charming, and smart . . . and romantic." She cleverly hurried on after the last word, "And our ranks are matched. When he approached me, I was surprised. I had thought of him as my brother, a naughty one at times," she added, appearing to smile at some private joke. "But he is a man now, a very—" Alysa stopped abruptly, as if she'd been about to reveal too much of her feelings. She praised herself for her convincing performance, and delighted in her newly acquired power to blush on demand.

"This news is most unexpected, Alysa, but you and Moran are right. Who could be more perfectly matched than Princess Alysa and Prince Moran? I will give you two lovers time to discover each other and to enjoy this newfound attraction. I'll summon him home as soon as it is wise, but I fear that cannot be for several weeks."

"Moran explained his duty to me before he left, and I understand. Perhaps Father will recover before Moran's return. It would distress him not to be the one to approve of this match and announce it." She inquired hesitantly, "Could you ask Earnon to study his books again and see if there is some cure he has overlooked? We have never gotten along, but would it help if I implored him to try again?"

"I will speak with him for you. He is skilled in such matters, but sometimes nothing and no one can cure an illness. I am glad you have accepted your duty, Alysa, and I am glad you are leaning toward my son."

Alysa laughed and said, "I doubt Moran would let me refuse his quest. He can be most persuasive. When he reasoned with me, it all seemed so logical that I wondered why I had not grasped it before. He is a rare person. He charms everyone he meets."

Isobail gazed at Alysa's innocent face and believed she was sincere. She asked herself if true love was responsible for the change in Alysa or if Moran had used some bewitching power on her that he did not know he possessed. Feeling victorious, she smiled and replied, "Yea, Moran is quite charming. Now, Alysa, I am extremely tired. I think I shall take a hot bath, a goblet of heady wine, and a long nap with your father."

"Do you wish me to summon Ceit for you?" Alysa offered politely.

"That would be most kind, Alysa. Thank you."

Alysa left the room and located Isobail's servant. She sweetly passed along Isobail's orders and returned to her private chamber, then paced to relieve her tension and anger. Her father was still cut off from her by Isobail's presence, but she had won a great victory today. If she was not mistaken, she had duped her stepmother completely.

Gavin completed another raid and turned the bounty over to Skane. Later he and his men would secretly retake the goods and return them, as promised. Aching for news from his love, he went to the tree. He could hardly contain his joy when he found the two roses snuggled together in the damp hole. He closed his eyes and smelled them, then continued his journey to Giselde's. He found her waiting for him, grinning playfully.

"She left the roses for you?" the woman asked.

Gavin chuckled happily and nodded. "I have never seen any this color."

"That is because they are magical flowers, enchanted ones."

"Such things are foolish, Giselde, only tricks."

The old woman frowned. "Tricks? How naive you are, Prince Gavin. Do you believe in nothing except what you can see and do yourself? Do you say the incantations lie? You walk on dangerous ground. Your ridicule will drive Alysa away."

"I did not mean to insult you, Giselde," he apologized. "I do not claim to know everything; only a fool does. But it is hard for me to accept superstition and magic. I have been taught to depend on my instincts and my wits."

They sat down at the table. Giselde handed him an unusual red flower and said, "Tell me what its smell reminds you of, Prince Gavin."

To humor the old woman, Gavin obeyed, and passed out instantly. Giselde reached across the small table and caught his head before it crashed to the hard wood. "Sleep a while, little prince," she murmured. She unfastened his leather collar and opened the harnesslike contrivance to his waist. She studied the royal tattoo, then used one liquid to remove it and another to stain the pale area to match Gavin's tanned flesh. She refastened his collar and straightened the bands and straps connected to it and his belt. Carefully she painted the same blue design in her palm. "Lift the flower and awaken to answer my question," she commanded, and Gavin obeyed without realizing he had been dazed for a time.

"Nay, Prince Gavin, it is the smell of doubt," she said. She quickly placed her hand against the wide leather strip over his heart. "I shall remove your dangerous disbelief by removing the symbol for it." She chanted incoherently, then held her palm before his face.

Gavin stared at the tattoo there, then yanked his collar loose to gape at his bare chest, finding only tanned flesh. "This is impossible! Nothing can remove such a mark. What trick is this?"

"It is no trick!" Giselde crushed the red flower in her grasp, then washed her hand in a basin of water. "You must forgive me for acting so rashly," she said, "but when you scorned such powers, I had to prove you wrong and to open your eyes." And also, she thought, it would hide Gavin's true identity were he to be captured and disrobed.

Gavin touched his chest and realized the tattoo was truly gone. He looked at Giselde with intrigue and awe. "I have never believed in such things before. How are they possible?"

"I only use my skills and knowledge for Good. But others do not; others use theirs for Evil. I warned you of such forces, but you doubted me and their existence. Sir Kelton was slain by Evil, and others will be too. Alysa is protected against it by what is called a *fith-fath* spell. With it, she cannot be slain, but she can be harmed. As a powerful spell can be used only once, I could not place one over you. That is why I gave you the amulet, which you are not wearing. There is an evil curse on Prince Alric; that is why he cannot heal, no matter what anyone does for him. I did not tell you this before because you are a doubter. You would have thought me mad and not taken me seriously. Wear the amulet, Gavin, or you will find yourself in terrible danger."

Gavin said, "Do not worry about the tattoo. Perhaps it is good that you removed it. This way no one can see it by accident. When I return home, it can be replaced. Whether I believe as you do or not, I will wear the amulet," he relented.

"Many things come to me in dreams, Prince Gavin. I saw Alysa far away and in great danger. I saw you in a dark place, but you were not trapped there. I saw you save the life of the man you once viewed as your rival. I saw many fires and much suffering. I saw you and Alysa fleeing the evil of Isobail together; you branded as a wolfshead and she as a traitor. I saw the death of Prince Alric, and my own."

"They are but dreams, Giselde; do not fear them."

Giselde looked into his worried eyes and argued,

323

"Nay, Hawk of Cumbria, they are warnings. As each one takes place, you will come to trust me more and more. You will beg me to use my powers to aid you; by then other powers will be stronger than mine. Our victory will depend on you, and you will question your instincts, prowess, wits, and skills."

A strange feeling raced over his flesh, and he did not debate her again. "I sent Keegan with another message. If King Bardwyn and his people can accept my charges against Isobail without physical proof, they should arrive soon and end this conflict. Then I will claim Alysa for my wife."

"He will believe you when the messages reach him, but all I told you must happen before he arrives. You will see, and believe."

After leaving Giselde's hut, Gavin called Alysa's image to mind. She was not lost to him, and never would be. She knew he loved her and they would be together somehow.

It was after the evening repast when Leitis found a moment to speak privately with Alysa. The head servant hated to impart such dire news, but knew she must. "The herbs you gave me for your father are bad, Alysa—evil, harmful ones," she said. She did not realize the two pouches Alysa had given her contained different herbs, so she had used some from Giselde's first bag.

"What do you mean?" Alysa asked incredulously.

"I have given your father nothing but nourishing food for a long time. When you asked me to give Prince Alric the healing herbs, I was afraid to do so without trying them on others first. I did, Alysa. Each one took violently ill within a short time. I burned them afterwards. Beware of the person who tricked you with them," Leitis warned.

Alarmed, Alysa protested, "That cannot be, Leitis. I

trust the one who gave them to me, trust her with my life."

"There is no mistake, Alysa. I tested them on several people to make certain I was not wrong before coming to you. All are sick like the prince. I swear it on my life and honor," she vowed.

The distraught princess knew the woman was telling the truth, and what it meant. "Calm yourself, dear Leitis," Alysa said. "I believe you. You were right to destroy them. Do as before and give him nothing but good and nourishing food. Tell no one about this trouble. I am sure it is a mistake."

The moment she was alone, Alysa sank to her bed and cried. She could not forget how eager Giselde had been for her father to get the herbs. On each visit, the woman had asked her about them and Alric's condition, almost insisting the herbs be used. Alysa's troubled mind filled with suspicions. She did not believe that Giselde was partnered with Isobail, but she suspected the old woman wanted her father dead. Perhaps Granmannie held Prince Alric responsible for Catriona's death and for her—Her what? Alysa mused. Banishment? Terrified flight? Perhaps Giselde wanted Alric dead and Alysa to become ruler so Granmannie could return to the life she had once enjoyed here in this castle.

Alysa knew there was no way she could leave the castle walls again today, especially this late in the day. She must not condemn the woman who was so special to her without delving thoroughly into this alarming matter. First, there was the irresistible, mysterious Gavin who tormented her; now, there was her cherished Granmannie. Was this evil invading everyone? Would it eventually consume her too?

So many dead. So many doubts and fears. So much treachery and deceit. The past was clouded. The present was shadowed. The future looked bleak and dark. If only Baltair would return . . .

The next morning Isobail summoned Earnon to her chamber. Imperially she gestured him to her side and complained about the defiant bandit chieftain.

"There is but one way to prevent all dissension and defiance," the learned man advised, wanting to appear to cooperate. "It is a special ritual which grants you total power. The 'principal man of your blood must die.' He must be sacrificed on *Lugnassad.*"

"Are you mad? Kill my own son, my only son! *Lugnassad* is a Druid belief, a ceremony of the dead on the first of August. What do you know of such forbidden rites?" she demanded.

"I know that only through that ritual can you become all powerful," Earnon vowed, knowing the date was over a month away and Isobail would never kill Moran. "You can understand why I have never mentioned it before. If it is done properly, nothing could ever harm you and no one could disobey you. You would control everyone's will."

Earnon could not believe Isobail's next question, and it panicked him. "What do you mean by 'done properly'?"

The alchemist thought quickly and replied, "His heart must be carved from his body while he still lives, then you must consume it while it is still warm and beating. Which only lasts a few minutes."

She scoffed, "No one could do such a horrid thing!"

"That is why there has never been an all powerful ruler."

Isobail quickly changed the subject. "What of Baltair? I want him dead this week, the moment he returns and I have sent for him. I'll rely on you to handle it."

Earnon knew he would lose Kyra to Calum after Baltair was dead. He had no choice. He must comply, then wait to be reunited with his love soon, as they had planned. "This week is perfect. I was to tell you when you returned, but things distracted us."

"Yes," she murmured, "perfect . . ."

Near the stables Alysa listened to the men's disheartening tales about the new band of raiders terrorizing the area, led by a masked man on a golden charger with blond mane and tail. She could not believe they were talking about Gavin. Why would he go so far to dupe the real brigands? But Giselde had told her she could trust Gavin! Things were not going right. She had to see Gavin and Giselde.

The gates were locked and guarded today. Under Isobail's strict orders, no one was to leave the castle without her permission. Nothing Alysa said convinced Isobail to allow her to go riding, and Alysa realized she could not press Isobail without arousing her suspicions. When her stepmother suggested "tomorrow," Alysa could only smile and agree.

Eighteen

Kyra's betrothal to Sir Calum was announced Tuesday morning and the banns sent to all large villages to be posted. Kyra played her part well, convincing everyone she was in love with Calum and eager to marry him. As plotted, many overheard the girl begging her mother to allow them to wed within the next week or two. Finally Princess Isobail relented and sent for Sir Calum, who could arrive by Saturday for the wedding to be held on Sunday.

Work began immediately on Kyra's special dress and other additions to her wardrobe. Servants were set to cleaning the castle from top to bottom and the wards from end to end. Plans were made for meals and the wedding feast. Invitations to guests were sent by messengers, and arrangements for their accommodations were discussed. Nearly everyone in and around the castle was involved with the impending event.

Alysa hoped she could get away during the commotion; not just away from the castle for a ride, but away to her grandfather for help. She believed she had allowed her imagination to run wild too long. Now she *must* act, wisely and bravely. She had to stop depending on others to solve her problems, especially when she did not know whom to trust anymore. There was too much mystery surrounding Gavin, and Giselde had often seemed unsympathetic to her father's plight. At times she even had the impression that the two were partnered in some curious way, and that added to her distrust.

She recalled, for instance, too many inexplicable clues: Giselde had warned her not to help, hinder, endanger, or question Gavin, and to remain at home. Was there some reason why Granmannie wanted to keep her away from her love? Worse, Alysa felt so confused about people's loyalties that she wondered if she had exposed Gavin to danger by enlightening Giselde about him.

Distraught, she secretly packed a change of clothes and a few supplies. From the kitchen and pantry she sneaked a water pouch, which could be filled along the road later, fruit, cheese, and a bag of bannocks—flat cakes made of barley and oats. She stuffed everything into a bag, including a sharp dagger, then slipped to the stable to hide them in Calliope's saddle pouches. Everything was ready.

The moment for her escape came late that afternoon. From her window she saw carts preparing to leave for the village to collect supplies for the castle and the wedding. She hurried out and asked Isobail if she could accompany the servants and guards. Preoccupied, Isobail promptly relented. Alysa rushed to the stable, saddled her beloved horse, and left.

In the village the soldiers entered a local pub while the servants gathered provisions. Everyone thought Alysa was visiting friends while they carried out their tasks, so she easily slipped away without being seen. She galloped northeast, planning to reach the coast and ride along the shoreline through Logris and into Cambria. Once inside her grandfather's border, she would find someone to take her to him.

An hour later Alysa was surrounded by a large band of unkempt bandits. No path or time for escape was left open to her. Petrified, she stared at their leader who was approaching her from the wide circle of attentive men with hungry faces. She was reminded of the legend of Bran, who found himself surrounded by drooling wolves, but he unsheathed his enchanted sword and slew them. She eyed the leering, intimidating bandit who called himself Skane.

"I know who you are, my pretty wench," Alysa's captor teased in a way that alarmed her further. When he lifted a heavy lock of hair she slapped his hand and glared at him, causing him to chuckle loudly.

He yelled to his followers, who held back at a distance to observe the entertaining confrontation, "A woman with real spirit and courage! She will make a good wife and slave for our friend Hengist, a tasty morsel to tame and enjoy!" He made noises in his throat which implied lustful hunger, then licked his lips suggestively. Leaning toward Alysa, he murmured, "Hengist will pay a fortune to purchase the last Viking queen."

Leaning so close, Alysa smelled his foul breath and odorous body. She suppressed the urge to vomit by swallowing rapidly, since she wanted to reveal no weakness before this dangerous man. Baltair had been right, she thought: the Vikings were a real threat to her. His next words stunned and distressed her.

"Our leader will not be happy with me for stealing you, little flower; she has picked you to become the wife of her unlucky son. She warned me to leave you alone, but how can I refuse when you fall into my lap? Besides, you will vanish before she learns I am to blame." To his men he shouted, "Where is Gavin Hawk? This is his task."

His task? Again a veil of mystery shrouded the handsome warrior. Alysa hoped her astonishment did not show, because it would look suspicious for her to respond to Gavin Hawk's name. Her love was supposed to work with the brigands and unmask them, but she

330

had not expected to hear his name in this manner. Again she wondered if she could trust him.

When the men shrugged ignorance, Skane said, "I cannot wait to find him. I must send her to Hengist myself." The leader chose three men to deliver Alysa to the Jute chieftain who lived in a stronghold that had been carved from Logris's belly. He ordered, "Tell Hengist to get the money together and we will come for our reward soon. If he refuses to pay heavily for her but keeps her, tell him I will reveal her captor and location to the rulers of Damnonia, Cambria, and Logris. He will not want to provoke them."

Frantic, Alysa screamed at him, "I have heard that Hengist already has a wife! Why not ransom me to my father? Or to King Vortigern?"

Skane laughed and replied, "Vikings take more than one wife if it suits them, and you will more than suit him. One look at you, pretty wench, and no doubt Hengist will toss out all other women in his bed. As for your father, he could never match the Jute's reward for you, if he could even crawl out of bed to offer one."

"But what of King Vortigern?"

"Vortigern has made enough mistakes without getting entangled with the sale of Damnonia's heir," Skane retorted, his words telling Alysa that the King of Logris was not involved with the brigands. "Nay, pretty wench, you are a feast made for Hengist's table and lips."

The band howled and laughed, agreeing with their vulgar leader. Skane shouted, "Boast of this deed to no one, then we can keep the whole reward to split amongst ourselves."

Despite the fading light, Alysa noticed a few quickly concealed looks that implied tightly leashed dissention. Obviously this was not the entire band, and their leader was suggesting disloyalty to the others. She was relieved when Skane ordered his three men to keep her safe and not "touch a single hair on her bonny head." He crudely declared that if she were not "pure of body on delivery," Hengist might reject her and come after them.

In the rapidly approaching twilight, Alysa, bound and gagged, was led away by three men while Skane and his remaining band rode off to drink, whore, and revel in the nearby villages.

By this time Alysa had been missed and a search was on for her. Word had been sent to the castle, and Isobail had nearly panicked. She had ordered every available man to look for the princess.

Isobail did not know Alysa had run away from the castle with clothes and supplies, and she suspected that Skane was behind Alysa's disappearance. Isobail would speak to him about it at their scheduled meeting that night. She and Moran had Alysa ensnared, so she was not going to give up the girl easily.

Gavin invited Sheriff Trahern to join him at his table in the tavern. A familiar face in the region by now, no one—except the women—paid much attention to the adventurer who claimed to be merely passing through. No one seemed to realize that Damnonia, almost encircled by water, was not a land to be "passed through" casually.

Trahern whispered, "There is big trouble, Hawk. We need to speak privately. Wait a few minutes, then join me at the edge of the village." The sheriff finished his drink, thanked Gavin for standing the round, and departed.

Gavin lingered a while, then followed. He met Trahern and they rode a short distance away. "We believe Skane has betrayed us, and we need your help," Trahern explained, then told Gavin about the afternoon's events and the chieftains prior words about Alysa. "We want you to find her and return her. Then kill him."

Within an hour Gavin located one of the disgruntled brigands and enticed the drinking man to disclose the incident and Alysa's whereabouts. At his camp, as Gavin prepared to go after her, he told his men to stay away from the brigands so they would not suspect he was missing. Then he rushed to Giselde and revealed the bad news, explaining that he was heading to rescue Alysa.

"Wait!" the old woman shouted.

"What is it, Giselde? Time is precious."

"Before you find her and speak with her, there are other things you must know." She revealed everything to the shocked man, including the truth about Moran's parentage. "This is why I must keep silent, and you must too."

"You warned me of Alysa's capture, and that has come to pass," Gavin said. "The more I learn about you and Isobail, the more I believe she might have murdered your daughter. Do not worry, my dear Giselde, I will never tell Alysa about Moran."

"Then tell her nothing now, Gavin, or she will suspect you lie or keep things from her," she warned. "She is clever and persuasive."

Gavin promised, "When I find her, which I will, I will tell her only that I love her."

After hours of riding, the three brigands escorting Alysa stopped to rest and water their horses. Then the hard journey began once more, with no further rest until dawn. They slept only a few hours before the journey was under way again.

As the day slipped beyond noon, Alysa realized how

much distance was being placed between her and her home, her father, and Gavin. She had been allowed little privacy, and she despised these men more and more with each mile traveled. There had been no way to reason with them, to evoke treachery against their leader, leave a trail, or escape. She questioned her fate, the powers of Good, and her strength to endure whatever lay before her until she could slip away.

In the royal forest near Malvern Castle Princess Kyra Ahern made her way to "the witch's hut." She had learned enough from Earnon to know which herbs she needed for her purposes, but she dared not steal them from her lover. She was delighted when she found the old woman was not at home. She quickly collected the things she wanted and placed them inside a leather pouch.

Before Kyra could leave, Giselde returned with a basket of plants, saw her and asked in her feigned tongue, "What be ye doin' 'ere?"

"I needed certain herbs, old woman. You were not home and I was in a hurry, so I gathered them. Here," she said, offering Giselde a jeweled bracelet, "this should be enough payment."

Giselde eyed the collection and realized the girl had learned much, no doubt from Earnon. Having heard about Kyra's betrothal, she wondered why the girl needed such dangerous items. "Hae ye become ae witch?" Giselde inquired, pointing to the pouch.

"I have been studying under a powerful sorcerer," Kyra admitted.

"Why do ye not ask him for supplies?"

"Ask no questions, old witch, just take the payment," Kyra shouted.

"Nay!" Giselde shouted back. "Tis not enough, an' they be bad! Why need ye them?" she demanded.

"Out of my way, old woman!" Kyra warned, narrowing her eyes. "Do you want me to sic my mother's dogs on you?"

"Do so after ye tell 'er why ye want me dead!"

Kyra frowned. "You have been paid, witch. Out of my way."

"Ye canna leave 'ere wif me special potions an' herbs! They be mine! Tell me why ye need them! If ye reason be good—"

"It is private, stupid beast!" Kyra screamed, and glanced about for a weapon. She seized a heavy clay pot, and before the old woman could react, smashed it forcefully over Giselde's head. The old woman was knocked to the floor, and blood oozed from a deep gash. Kyra noticed no breathing, and was satisfied that the old woman was dead. Smiling, she gathered more herbs. While ransacking the hut, she noticed Giselde's locked chest. Yanking the key from the woman's neck, Kyra opened it and searched it. Finding the jewels that she and others had used as payment to the old woman, the avaricious girl stole them and left.

Alysa stared into the camp fire. On this second night alone with the brigands, she was cold and afraid. The men were drinking heavily, joking crudely and glancing at her in a frightening manner. If only they would untie her . . .

She was startled when another man entered camp: Gavin Hawk! She listened to him explain that Skane had sent him to make certain the girl reached her destination safely, and heard him joke about how tempting she was. He glanced at Alysa and grinned, passing his tongue over his lips suggestively. She did not know if she wanted to scream, cry, or faint.

The men were lulled by Gavin's behavior into settling back, drinking, and talking. Suddenly Gavin attacked, punching the man sitting on the log next to him, whirling and kicking another in the gut, then flinging his blade into the chest of the third man with a gracefully sweeping motion. The man he had punched sat up, ready to fight, but Gavin forcefully elbowed him in the nose. Then drawing his sword, he plunged it into the man he had struck in the midriff.

Alysa watched Gavin check each man for life, finding none. She could not believe how quickly and expertly he had slain all three. He crossed to her and cut her free. She removed her gag and stared at him in confusion, remaining still.

"I wish I could have signaled you not to be afraid, but they might have seen me. I had to pretend until I had them fooled, and until they drank enough to even the odds," he teased. "Come, m'love, before others arrive," he coaxed, offering his hand. "If they discover they have captured Thisbe instead of Princess Alysa, they will be angry with both of us. When I heard of this deed last night, I came after you as quickly as possible. Did they harm you?" he asked, wishing he did not have to deceive her.

"I am fine, Gavin," she replied. "How did you find me?"

"Since my return I have been riding with them to unmask their leader and to obtain evidence against Isobail. Many of the bandits are disenchanted with Skane and impressed with me, so I was told of your capture. I followed you as quickly as possible."

"Why?" she asked.

"Because I love you, silly woman," he retorted. "And I plan to make you mine when this trouble is over. It seems your snare for me is too tempting to resist. There are differences between us that must be resolved, but later."

Alysa stared into his eyes, unaware that he knew her identity. She said, "The brigand leader said you were

336

the one who was supposed to abduct me and deliver me to Hengist."

"Either he lied or his words confused you. I swear to you I knew nothing of this deed until last night, when Sheriff Trahern met with me. He suspected Skane was responsible for your disappearance. He hired me to find you and return you. Afterwards, I am to slay Skane and take his place. It seems their brigand leader is causing them too much trouble. In fact, I was supposed to slay him last night, but he was too busy abducting you to rendezvous with Trahern and I think Isobail too . . . and I was too concerned about you to bother with him anyway."

"He said his leader would be unhappy with him for stealing me," Alysa said, still not fully trusting Gavin, and determined to preserve the fiction that she was Thisbe, not Alysa. "He would keep it a secret from *her*, said he. She wants Alric's daughter to marry her son, Moran, so the bandit was ordered to leave Alysa alone. Some of Skane's men do not trust him," she remarked, and explained the dissension she had observed.

"That is how I am worming my way into their confidence. Once I take over, I can defeat them a few at a time and disband them. Remember I have only six men, so I must be cautious."

"You were right about King Vortigern. He is not involved. I am uncertain about Skane's connection to Hengist, but I doubt the Jute chieftain is behind our trouble. Isobail is the leader, I am sure of it. Skane never called Isobail by name, but he kept dropping hints I could not miss. I saw her sneaking back into the castle Saturday night, in disguise. She must have met with someone."

"I did not want you to know I had returned," Gavin admitted, "since I feared your streak of courage might hinder my task. I wanted you to remain safe in the castle while I gathered proof and foiled the bandits.

After you saw my raid, I had to see you and explain my secrecy so you would not doubt me, but it was not possible.

"Nevertheless, I succeeded in sending a message to King Bardwyn, warning him of the treachery in Damnonia. We must be patient until the king can travel here with his men. Soon Alysa and Alric will be safe from them."

Gavin smiled as he told her, "When I found the roses in the tree, I knew you loved me and trusted me. Come, we must leave quickly and find a place to hide. Soldiers are searching everywhere for you. Soon I will take you back to the castle, where you will be safe until I complete my task for your mistress. I expect no payment from Alysa, m'love, as you are all I want, and I do this for you." Knowing it would seem strange if his band earned no living while here, he added, "But my men must have money to live on. I did not find the jewels you placed in the tree for many days after my return; they had fallen into a rotting hole. When next you leave a message or seek one from me, if the hole seems empty check the decayed area to the rear of our hiding spot. I worried over what you must be thinking when you found the pouch gone, but no message from me. When I saw you out riding, I wondered why you had left no word for me, then I found the pouch had fallen deeper into the tree. My heart rejoiced at unmasking nature's trick."

Gavin noticed how she was observing him, and realized he was destroying the doubts she had about him. While he had this advantage, he explained how and why he was raiding—falsely and cunningly.

Still scrutinizing him, she asked, "Do you know why Skane wanted to kidnap Alysa and sell her to Hengist?"

"Trahern said they considered Alysa the last Viking queen," Gavin replied. "He said that would make her a valuable temptation to any Norse warrior who wanted to force marriage on her and become the ruler of his people. Hopefully I can slay Skane and his men before news of Alysa's bloodline spreads to others. If I fail, it could place her in more danger."

"Would you steal and wed such a woman to become a king? Or hire out to capture one to sell to another man to do so?"

"I do not believe in slavery of any kind, m'love. And I would never wish to become a Viking ruler, or help any man take command of them. It is better to have them scattered into groups, which weakens their power and prevents them from looting our island."

Gavin's words sank in, and suddenly Alysa laughed and hugged him. He gazed at her strangely and asked, "Are you sure you are fine?"

"Yes, my love, I am more than fine," she replied.

Gavin lifted one brow and inquired, "Is there something more?"

"Later my love. We must flee this place of death."

Hours later Gavin found the large cave Giselde had mentioned to him on several occasions. He left Alysa with the horses while he inspected it with a torch. Located in a ravine it the base of an earth and rock cliff, it was a perfect hiding place. The cave was sturdy and deep, snaking into the land beneath an overhang of dirt and greenery, making it nearly impossible to spot. Pleased, he returned. He lifted Alysa and carried her inside, placing her on a large boulder while he built a fire to chase away the chill and darkness. "Trojan, take care of Calliope," he ordered softly, and the golden steed obeyed, leading the dark animal to water and grass.

After Alysa and Gavin had eaten in near silence and were cuddled between his two blankets near a romantic fire, Alysa confessed in a strained tone, "There is something I must tell you, Gavin. The bandits did not make a mistake with their capture—I am Princess Alysa Malvern, not my servant Thisbe. I lied to you, but with good reason. Please forgive me for deceiving you, but I thought it was necessary."

Gavin propped upon his elbow and gazed down at her. "What did you say?" he asked, staggered by her total trust in him.

Alysa explained everything to him, and prayed he would understand and forgive her. "I love you, Gavin Hawk, and I have fallen under your spell. Since we met I have been torn between wanting you and obeying my duty. My father needs me, my people need me, and I must follow my fate. But I must have you at my side or my life will be empty. With all my heart, I believe it is possible for you to find a way to be accepted in my land and life, if you agree. What more can I say?" she asked tearfully.

Gavin gazed into her deep blue eyes and considered being as truthful with her as she had been with him. But he decided he must keep the secret of his identity a while longer. "There is nothing more you need to say, Princess Alysa. Fate has thrown us together and joined our hearts; surely it will join our lives one day. I love you, and I will prove I am worthy of you."

Tears of joy blinded Alysa as she embraced him tightly. "There is no need, my love; for no man could be more worthy of me than you are. If my people say you are not, then they are not worthy to have us as their rulers. More than the Crown, you are my destiny."

"As you are mine," he responded tenderly. Gavin's arms encircled her and held her snugly against him. He felt as if his heart would burst through his chest if it did not slow down from its excited pace. Alysa was here in his arms, safe and warm. Of her own will, she was his. She was not an unattainable servant; she was a princess whose rank matched his, and a woman who wanted him. His lips drifted over her hair and face, seeking hers.

340

Alysa's hands slipped beneath his tunic and caressed the flesh that covered his hard back. She yielded her mouth to his, reveling in the honeyed rapture that flowed sensuously through her veins. She closed her eyes and allowed the wildly sweet sensations to assail her as his lips kissed every inch and feature of her face. His hot breath stimulated each area to fiery life, and her skin tingled even after his lips moved onward. Gavin nuzzled her left ear, then her neck, bringing tremors to her yearning body. Alysa felt her passion building to an uncontrollable and feverish pitch.

Gavin's hands roamed her body tentatively, as if he were hesitant to touch her. Her hands gently clasped his head and meshed their mouths hungrily. She heard a groan of desire escape his lips as they nibbled at hers. No matter how many times he kissed her, her mouth seemed to plead for another and another. There was no place on her flesh which did not crave to be touched and stroked. It had been so long, and she wanted him desperately, swiftly, urgently, and forever.

Alysa leaned away slightly and tried to remove his upper garment. Gavin shifted to assist her bold action. His green eyes widened in surprise when she pulled off her own over-tunic and kirtle, baring her body to his gaze and touch. "I am yours, Gavin. Do not hesitate to touch me or take me. Even if I am a princess, I am your woman first. I love you and want you, more so tonight than ever before. Do not restrain yourself. Love me freely and wildly."

Gavin's igneous gaze roved her face and body with intense desire that could not be masked. In the light of the camp fire she saw beads of moisture appear and glisten on his brow, upper lip, and in the enticing depression beneath his lower one. Her tongue mischievously licked it away, then danced over his mouth.

Gavin groaned once more and pressed Alysa to her back, searing kisses over her throat and chest before

341

fastening his mouth to a supple breast. He teased his lips and teeth over both, stimulating them to eager life. At his action, the taut peaks became harder and her breasts firmer. He fondled them and kissed them for several minutes as Alysa's fingers played in his tawny hair and her head arched with pleasure.

Gavin found another bud and tantalized it until it grew fiery and hard and burst into beautiful bloom. He felt her fumbling with his battle apron, and realized she did not know how to unfasten it. While kissing her greedily, he removed it and his loincloth, leaving nothing between them.

Their ravenous bodies met and clung together, feasting madly and creating stunningly blissful temptations. Creamy flesh titillated golden flesh, and golden flesh did the same to creamy flesh. Emotion-dampened skins caressed each other and caused passion's flames to burn brighter and hotter than the fire nearby.

Each lover's hands and lips journeyed over the other's body. They kissed, caressed, and examined this magic between them, this irresistible force that had drawn them together and bound them tightly. As if they had forever to linger making love, all inhibitions and modesty were cast aside. Together they explored and enjoyed this greatest and rarest adventure of all: love.

Gavin was glad the royal tattoo was missing, as he relished being able to feel lips traveling over his muscled chest. Never had he experienced anything so rapturous and enlivening as surrendering himself to this unique woman and claiming her at the same time.

When he could take no more of her staggering torture upon his senses, he captured her exquisite face between his hands, gazed deeply into her passion-glazed eyes, and vowed hoarsely, "I love you, Alysa Malvern, I love you with all my being." As she smiled happily into his eyes, he joined their bodies, to labor lovingly, persistently, intoxicatingly, until mutual victory was theirs.

They nestled together between the blankets which, thankfully, he had brought with him, kissing lightly as they gradually relaxed. The fire was nearly out, and the damp air was getting chilly. Gavin reached across her to toss a few more small branches on the fire. The fresh wood crackled, popped, and caught fire slowly. Gavin lay down on his side and curled against her, locking her within his protective embrace.

As she wiggled to make sure no space was left between their naked flesh, he chuckled and teased, "Lie still, m'love, or you shall get no rest tonight. You can have me again at dawn, and noon, and dusk. We shall remain here during the day, then travel to the castle at night."

Those plans sounded wonderful to Alysa. She sighed peacefully and teased, "If I must wait for you to rest, my weary dragon, then I must."

Gavin nibbled seductively at her nape and bare shoulder. "I was restraining myself because of your fatigue, m'love. If you have none, turn to me and take me again," he coaxed.

Alysa rolled to her back and fused her gaze to his. "Fatigue or not, my meetings with you are too scant not to be used fully."

That was all the encouragement either needed. . . . After which he held her serenely until they were asleep.

At Malvern Castle Thursday morning more treachery was afoot. Baltair returned from Land's End, where Ahern Castle stood against the bleak coastal setting where Moran had been sired and now ruled.

As the seneschal passed through the Great Hall, Kyra rushed to him and said, "I must see you privately, Baltair. Wicked things have happened during your absence. Mother is—We cannot speak here. If we are caught, we will be slain. Treason abounds, Baltair, and you must

343

save the prince. Hurry to my chamber where we can talk. We must find a way to thwart Mother's evil." She rushed away from the intrigued man, who responded rapidly to her summons.

Kyra let Baltair into her room then locked the door. She paced nervously, dramatically. She had to carry out the murder of Isobail's enemy as she and Earnon had planned, not as her mother insidiously desired. By helping her mother get rid of Baltair, it should make the woman beholden to her, especially since Isobail seemed to hate Alric's seneschal so deeply. When Baltair asked her to explain her fears, she sat down at the table where he was waiting, and poured them tea, with a strawlike herb inserted in Baltair's, supposedly for flavoring. In fact, the special herb would interact with the potion in the tea, activating it. Kyra pretended to drink hers while she calmed herself. "I am so afraid, Baltair," she murmured as he drained his cup.

"Why so, Princess Kyra?"

"I believe Mother is trying to kill Prince Alric and take over this land. Sir Calum is her hireling, and she has given me to him as his reward. She has always hated me, and this is her way of punishing me. Have you never heard of Calum's cruelty to women in bed?"

Kyra babbled on as she waited for the maddening drug to take effect, as Earnon had said it would. When Baltair's head began to fall this way and that and his brown eyes took on a glazed look, Kyra retrieved the strawlike herb and tossed it into his face. As Earnon had taught her she chanted, "Wisp-of-Straw, blind him to all things but me. Wisp-of-Straw, make his blood boil for me. Wisp-of-Straw, make his manhood ache for me. Wisp-of-Straw, control him for me."

Quickly Kyra pulled off part of his garments and tossed them around the room. She rumpled the bed and flung covers here and there. She ripped her garments and mussed her hair. After she unlocked the

344

door she went to the window and screamed several times. Then, as instructed by her lover, Kyra approached the dazed seneschal and said, "By the Wisp-of-Straw I command you to ravish me wildly. Let no man or threat halt you."

Driven mad and lustful by the powerful herbs, Baltair seized Kyra, dragged her to the bed, and began to rip wildly at her already torn garments. Kyra commanded, "By Wisp-of-Straw, the more I scream, the more you shall desire me. You must kill anyone who tries to stop you from possessing me. By Wisp-of-Straw, ravish me now or die trying, Baltair."

Kyra screamed and screamed, arousing Baltair to the height of madness. Then she feared the guards would arrive too late, as his strength and desire were too strong to battle. When they finally burst into the room, Baltair had imprisoned her beneath him and was trying to drive his exposed manhood into her sprawled body. Several inquisitive servants peeked inside the noisy chamber and could not believe what they witnessed.

The guards' commands to halt his brutal attack had no effect on the crazed Baltair. He ordered them to leave, vowing he must have Kyra. When the men pulled him off her he battled them to get back to Kyra. "She is mine, not Calum's! Get out! I must take her!"

Baltair snatched a dagger from one of the guards and shouted, "I will slay you all if you do not leave so I can possess her. Mine!" he shouted. "She is mine, or she is no one's! I will kill her first!"

When Baltair tried to slay Kyra, one of the guards drew his sword and slew the madman. Kyra stared at the bloody corpse and sobbed, grasping her torn garments about her bruised body.

One of the guards comforted her "Do not weep, m'lady. You are safe now."

"What will everyone say?" Kyra sobbed. "I swear I did not entice him. He came to my chamber and pleaded with me to wed him, not Calum. When I told him I loved Calum, he went mad."

"We saw m'lady, and we will avow to it. No one can blame you," the man said. Although astounded by the gentle Baltair's crazed behavior, the other guards agreed that she was guiltless.

Kyra looked at them and smiled through her tears. "You are so kind, sirs," she said as fresh tears flowed.

As planned, Isobail rushed into the chamber and demanded, "What is wrong here?"

Kyra glanced at her mother and began to sob, allowing the guards and servants to relate the grim tale. Isobail went to her daughter embraced her and commanded, "Take his body and burn it. Perhaps his death will end the curse that hovers over my husband and land. Spread the word that his name shall not be spoken again and his life is to be forgotten. Destroy his possessions and seal his chamber, for we must not allow his evil to attack others. Anyone who disobeys my order will he banished."

After ordering everyone from the room, Isobail eyed Kyra's disheveled state and asked, "Did he harm you? Were the guards too late?"

Kyra sobbed and continued to dissemble, thinking to use the event with Baltair to cover her affair with Earnon. "I fear they were too late, Mother. Whatever shall I tell Calum? The potion was so strong that I could not fend him off before he drove himself within me. I struggled and managed to roll free before the guards arrived, so they do not know Baltair entered me. He did not complete his task, but I am no longer pure. Calum will know after we wed. What if he is angry and refuses me as his wife? Help me, Mother, for I obeyed you and now Baltair is dead."

"Do not worry. Calum will understand when you tell him. Wait until your wedding night, then confess this deed and beg his forgiveness."

"What if he does not understand or forgive me?" Kyra asked.

"I will speak with Calum and explain. If he balks, I will command him to keep silent and accept you. You are beautiful and clever; use your wiles on him. Remember all he can give you."

Nineteen

Late Thursday afternoon Gavin returned to the cave after completing a lengthy task. He was greeted by a relieved and joyful Alysa, who embraced him and covered his face with kisses. He had gone back to the campsite where he had rescued her to bury the brigands' bodies and possessions and to free their horses.

"If no one finds them for a long time, m'love, it will aid our cause. Our little tale should protect you, please Isobail, confuse and infuriate Skane, and fool everybody."

"You are so clever, Gavin," she said. "I was such a fool to try to run. . . ." She hesitated, lowered her eyes. She confessed that she had been escaping to King Bardwyn, candidly explaining why.

"You have doubted me badly, m'love," Gavin told her. "I only seek to unmask the brigands and your stepmother. I have told you my raids are false. What more do you expect of me? Is there some reason why you continue to have such suspicions?"

"I am sorry I mistrusted you, Gavin, but I was confused, and I am so afraid for my father. You were a stranger, and things were so terrible here. Please do not be angry with me," she beseeched him.

"Calm yourself, m'love; I understand everything

now." He cuddled her head against his chest and stroked her hair. "All that matters to me is your safety, and that of your father and your land."

"I know Father's illness is unnatural, Gavin, and I do not know how to battle its source. Either it is a wicked spell or his evil wife knows some way of getting the poison into him that I cannot uncover. I tried to give him healing herbs, but they do not work. Oh, I only wish I knew why they did not work. Granmannie, I know, does not like Father, and because of that I have wondered about the herbs she gave me. . . ."

"Perhaps she gave you the wrong pouch," Gavin replied. "Or, if her eyes are old and bad, perhaps she gathered the wrong herbs. I can see you love her deeply and this matter pains you. Why do you not wait until she explains before you judge her guilty?"

"You are right, Gavin," she agreed. Her hands roamed his hard torso as she said, "There is something else that troubles me. You must use another horse during your raids, my love, for Trojan is easily recognized. I have heard him described several times, and knew at once who his master was. He is a rare steed, so he can point a dangerous finger at you."

"What a reckless mistake," he chided himself "I mask my face to conceal my identity, then ride a one-of-a-kind stallion! When I was trying to snare their attention, I wanted others to see and report who I was. But you are right—it is dangerous to be recognized now."

Gavin lifted her chin and looked into her worried eyes. "I have chosen myself a keen-witted, sharp-eyed woman to love and wed. I adore your mettle, m'love, but do not try to ride alone to your king again. The distance is too great and perilous. I swear to you, I have sent messages to King Bardwyn about Damnonia's troubles. You told me others had done so too. Your king cannot ignore so many summonses."

"I will obey you, my wandering warrior," she promised, hugging him.

"No matter what command I give?" he asked, nibbling on her ear.

She looked into his eyes and watched as passion flickered, then blazed within them. There was something so special, so appealing about his grass-green eyes. Not just their color and shape, but their range and depth of expression. He had a way of slightly lowering his handsome head and gazing from beneath his upper lids and brows that caused her flesh to tingle and her heart to race. His nose was so pleasingly shaped that it enticed her to kiss it, as did his sensual mouth. There, too, he had a way of holding his lips that demanded kisses. There were so many compelling features and traits about him that her soul soared with love.

"If you do not command me to make love to you, I shall order you to take me home this moment," she whispered.

"How could an enthralled adventurer not obey his ravishing captor when she is a beautiful and powerful princess? I am yours to own and command for life, m'love." The message in her intensely blue eyes was clear: take me.

Slowly and tantalizingly Gavin undressed Alysa. He lifted her long curls and placed them behind her, baring her entire body to his smoldering gaze. Then he sent his adoring eyes to wander leisurely over her sleek flesh and lovely face. She did not protest her nudity and his boldness, or try to shield herself from his enflaming touch. His fingers moved over her lips and she kissed them until they drifted down her slender neck, between firm breasts, and circled each in turn. Each of Gavin's strong hands gently cupped a breast and began to caress it. His thumbs sensuously stroked the taut nipples and caused them to grow larger and harder. She watched him bend forward to playfully tease the aching

350

peaks with his lips and tongue. Alysa closed her eyes and allowed her head to drift backward as she absorbed the splendid sensations.

Gavin eagerly spread kisses over her shoulders, chest, and midriff. His hands roamed past her slim waist, over rounded hips, and into her feminine region. He whet her appetite for him until she was ravenous with hunger. His hands guided his lips on an exploration of her body, leaving her limp and quivering.

Alysa could wait no longer to have him. She followed his lead, boldly and shamelessly undressing him and exploring him. Her hands and lips traveled his golden frame until he was shuddering with need and restraint.

He quickly lifted her and carried her to their make-shift bed. He loved her until their mutual cravings were sated, an intense experience that was reality-shattering and emotionally binding. While he was still breathing hard from his loving exertions, he gazed into her eyes and murmured, "I would perish if I could not have you forever."

"That is what Prince Moran said," she unwittingly said.

Fury flooded Gavin's eyes and he coldly vowed, "I would slay him before I allowed him to touch you with one finger! No matter what threat they use, Alysa, flee the castle if he comes near you."

There was something about his tone that intrigued her. Sometimes he sounded and acted just like Gran-mannie! How strange, she mused, that she should think that. . . .

After Alysa related her dislike for her stepbrother, Gavin calmed down and felt sheepish about his outburst. "I belong to you, Gavin, and no one shall ever take me from you. I swear."

"I am twenty-seven, Alysa. Until now I have loved no woman nor wanted to marry. You ensnared me and be-

351

witched me, so you are responsible for my life and happiness."

"The same is true of you, my love," she retorted, kissing his cleft chin. Then they rolled upon the blanket, tickling and teasing each other as they shared mirthful laughter and heady kisses.

After dark Gavin and Alysa left the romantic cave and rode toward Malvern Castle. Gavin stayed on full alert to avoid running into anyone. An hour before reaching the castle, he bound and gagged Alysa securely, then blindfolded her. "I am sorry, m'love, but the bonds need time to make marks on this exquisite body. From here on I must not speak. I shall take you near the castle, then Calliope will do the rest. I love you, Alysa, and soon we will be together again."

Gavin followed their plan, stopping within sight of the stone battlement and urging the dark horse onward. Calliope trotted to the castle entrance and whinnied several times, then stamped his foot impatiently. Two guards unlocked the gate and led the horse inside. One cut Alysa's bonds free from the pommel and helped her dismount before removing her gag and blindfold.

"Home?" she murmured, then pretended to faint. The guards carried her inside the Great Hall and lay her on a table. Quickly Leitis was aroused to tend Alysa, and as she did so, Isobail was summoned. Alysa's stepmother arrived and observed Leitis affectionately examining the young girl and spouting her outrage at the abrasions upon Alysa's wrists and face.

Alysa tried to calm the frantic head servant as the woman placed ointment on her scraped wrists and used a cool cloth to soothe the redness around Alysa's eyes and mouth.

"Fetch Princess Alysa some warm milk with honey," Leitis shouted to a serving wench standing near the door. "How dare those ruffians kidnap my sweet princess! They must be hunted down and slain! Beasts!"

she sneered, then mumbled, "They knock this child unconscious, then injure her like this. Devils!"

"Please, dear Leitis, I am home now and barely harmed."

"But you were unconscious and bound," a guard protested angrily.

"They should be hanged for what I saw done to you! A daring crime indeed!" the other guard added.

Alysa smiled gratefully at them and teased, "Never have two faces looked better to these eyes than yours did when you removed that dirty blindfold. I do not know why he—"

Isobail stepped forward and halted Alysa's words with a command: "Leave us. I wish to speak with Princess Alysa alone." She sat down beside Alysa and smiled. "I will tend my second daughter myself."

Leitis did not like being forced to leave, but she obeyed. Everyone else did, too, and the room seemed very large and quiet.

"Are you all right, Alysa?" Isobail inquired.

"I think so. It happened so quickly and strangely."

"Tell me everything," Isobail ordered softly, patting her arm.

"I was in the village strolling around, and everything went black. When I awoke, I was the prisoner of a terrible villain and his men. They bound and gagged me, so I could not speak or move. I was terrified. The big, ugly man ordered three others to sell me to the Jute Hengist."

Alysa's eyes widened as she said, "Do you know what they dared to do? They tied me to Calliope and hauled me away like a slave! We rode for hours in the dark. When we halted to rest, they gave me little to eat and little privacy, then bound me to a tree!"

"What happened later? You have been missing for two days."

"That is the strange part," Alysa mused. "A warrior—

I think he was a warrior from his garments and size—entered the camp and killed the three bandits. I could not see his face, for he was masked. He told me not to be afraid, that he was taking me home. He said I had been redeemed by Princess Isobail for a great many coins and jewels. He said he had learned I was stolen and where I was being taken, so he bargained with Sheriff Trahern for my rescue."

Alysa pretended not to notice how Isobail reacted to that astonishing news, as Gavin had made up the ransom story to pretend to deceive Alysa and to cover Isobail's part in this deception. She went on, "He kept me bound, gagged, and blindfolded until I reached the castle. He said if I told anyone he rescued me and sold me to you, he would capture me again and beat me. I was ordered to tell you and the sheriff the same thing. We are to claim those three bandits ransomed me and fled into the night. Is that not strange?"

"We must do as he said, Alysa. He knows who we are and where to find us, but we have not seen his face. I am sure he does not want that fierce bandit leader to hear of his deed and chase him with a blood lust. If we keep his secret, perhaps we can hire him again to help us thwart those bandits. I cannot tell you how glad I am this warrior earned the reward I gave to Trahern to pay for your rescue," she said, knowing there had been no ransom paid to Gavin. "You never saw his face?" When Alysa shook her head, Isobail asked, "Would you recognize his body or his horse?"

Alysa pondered for a moment, then shook her head. "I did not see his horse, and he was clothed in a tunic and breeches like most fighters. And when he talked to me, he whispered so I could not catch his voice." She added slyly, "I overheard a few of the bandits' words. They said I was being sold to the Jute chieftain. The big, ugly one hinted that I was worth a fortune to Hengist. There must have been more bandits elsewhere because he talked about not splitting my reward with them. I could tell some did not like this idea. I heard a bandit call him Skane. Do you think my rescuer is one of the bandits, perhaps a malcontent one? But as my champion, if only for hire, he certainly did not have to be so mean to me!"

"How so?" Isobail asked, intrigued.

"At first he did not bind me securely, and I got free. When I tried to yank off the gag and the blindfold, he was angry. He tied my wrists so tightly, they ached. Look at them," she stated, holding out the chafed flesh. "I could hardly breathe after he tightened the gag, and I was frightened at being unable to see. I hope you catch him and punish him! Moran will be furious at this dark deed."

Alysa asked hurriedly, "Have you sent word to him about my abduction? He will be frantic."

Isobail responded, "I have tried to keep it quiet to protect your honor. There was nothing Moran could do that was not being done by my soldiers, so I did not worry him. He is to arrive for Kyra's wedding Sunday. We will tell him everything then."

Alysa sighed and declared, "That is a relief, else he would worry himself ill over me. I am glad Kyra's wedding plans have not been halted by this wicked act. What should I say to the others? You said to follow the bandits words, and I am afraid to disobey him. He could walk up beside me and I would not know to scream and run."

"Since we have no clues to unmask him, we must do as he says."

Alysa apologized, "I am sorry you had to give him your jewels and coins to pay for my return. Perhaps you shall get them back if ever he is captured; I hope so. Does Father know about this?"

"He has been too ill to tell him. Soon you will be my daughter twice over, so do not worry about the bandit's reward," Isobail said soothingly. "Perhaps he will approach us again, and we could find him useful."

For the first time Alysa embraced Isobail and said, "Thank you for saving my life and honor, my generous stepmother. I shall not forget this deed. It will bind us together as friends and family."

"Go to your chamber and sleep, Alysa. This ordeal has been rough on you. We will speak more tomorrow. Follow my lead around others."

Isobail returned to Trahern's side in her bed. She laughed and remarked, "The Hawk is smarter than we imagined, my love. He convinced the little fool she was ransomed by me, and he never even let her glimpse his face. He scared her into keeping her mouth shut and into letting Skane's men take the blame for her return. When you meet next with Gavin, tell him to get rid of Skane immediately."

Gavin went to see Giselde and relate Alysa's rescue, and found distressing evidence of a fight and robbery. He noticed the broken jar with dried blood on it, and the suspiciously dark spots on the hard earth floor. His sharp eyes scanned the plundered abode, and when he saw the unlocked, open chest, worry consumed him. Gavin had seen many coins and jewels there another day, but found none tonight. Anxiously he pried open the secret compartment and sighed in relief to find Giselde's wedding ring still hidden there. The clues added up badly, especially Giselde's absence. Knowing something had happened to the old woman, he put the precious ring in a small leather pouch that hung from his belt, then went to look outside.

Since it was too dark to see anything, Gavin returned to his camp without finding her. He told his men about the rescue, and the girl's identity. He related his grim suspicions about Giselde's disappearance: bandits or Isobail. "At first light we must scour the entire area for her. Any news from Skane or Keegan?" he inquired, and was answered no about both.

Gavin was gravely concerned. There was no way to get word to Alysa. Alysa . . . If Giselde had been unmasked, that meant his love could be in peril. No, he decided, something else had happened to Alysa's grandmother, and he would discover what.

On Friday Alysa slept until past noon. She hoped by the time she appeared, everyone's questions about her ordeal would be answered. By now there was no doubt in her mind that Isobail was a traitor, and she could prove it when King Bardwyn arrived. She prayed that her grandfather would hurry, as things got worse each day. She summoned her handmaiden to her side.

During her bath Thisbe related the stunning news about Baltair's death and Princess Isobail's commands concerning it and him. She listened as her friend revealed the shocking account of the seneschal's alleged attack on Kyra. Alysa could not believe what she was hearing. She had known Baltair since her birth and had spent many hours with him over the years. Baltair was a good and kind man; he would never attack any woman! "It cannot be, Thisbe," she argued. "He was such a gentle man. Why would Kyra lie about him and get him slain?"

Thisbe told her what the guards and servants had said, but Alysa knew something evil had occurred in that room. *Baltair gone . . . His name and existence stricken from their land forever . . .* What, she fretted, were Isobail and Kyra plotting these days? Yet in view of Isobail's clever edicts, she could ask no questions about the shocking incident. She wept for her old friend, vowing to restore Baltair's honor when this evil was conquered.

Later Alysa headed for the stable, but was halted by Isobail, who asked, "Are you going riding again?"

"Nay," Alysa replied quickly "I was going to check on Calliope. I wanted to make certain he is all right after that terrible incident."

Unconcerned and duped, Isobail returned to her business. She despised the idea of having to deal with Alric for the next few days, but in order to delude the people it was necessary to let him make an appearance.

In the stable Alysa stroked Calliope's neck and fretted over the news of her friend's death. She had been wise enough to let Gavin keep her pouches to make certain her real actions—that of running away from the castle—remained a secret. When Piaras entered Calliope's stall to check on her, she smiled. Hoping she could trust him, she asked, "Can you get a message to the old woman in the woods for me, Piaras? We are friends, and I do not want her to worry about me. But you must promise to tell no one—no one—about the message."

Piaras confided, "The old woman has vanished, Princess Alysa. She knew of the trouble here and was trying to help us by getting a message to King Bardwyn. When I went to see her Wednesday afternoon, I found a terrible sight." He related the grim evidence he had found in Giselde's hut. "I checked again Thursday and this morning, but she was still not there. She is a good woman. I fear for her life."

Alysa wondered if Isobail had unmasked Baltair and . Giselde and gotten rid of both of them. She feared that help might not be on the way after all. Suppose the messenger had not gotten through . . . Suppose Isobail also knew about Gavin . . . He could be in great danger! Yet with the gates locked to her, she could not get away to warn him. The important thing was to protect her father by playing along with these villains until she could slip away unnoticed.

Later she talked with Kyra, telling her stepsister she

was sorry for her trouble, meanwhile hoping to extract clues from her. Kyra offered none, saying she was glad "the ferocious beast" was dead, and reminding Alysa that Baltair was a dead subject because of Isobail's edict.

Alysa was allowed to see her father for a short time. His head seemed to be clearing slightly, and Alysa guessed why: Isobail must somehow be helping him recover to allow Prince Alric to appear at Kyra's wedding and allay the peoples fears about his condition. She dared tell her father nothing, as his life could be in peril if he knew what was happening and tried to do something about it. Yet she wondered why he said nothing about his friend Baltair's alleged behavior and death.

The day's meetings left her forlorn. If the message had reached King Bardwyn, she thought, as Baltair believed and hoped, the king should have arrived by now. . . .

Saturday morning all Alysa could think about was the trap closing swiftly around her and her father. She knew Moran was on his way, and she feared Isobail would try to betroth them. Guests were arriving steadily for the wedding tomorrow, including Sir Calum, so the gates remained locked and guarded to prevent anyone without reason or invitation to enter Malvern Castle.

News had spread swiftly about the bandits' alleged ransom of her—the only good news to be heard, along with that of her father's gradual recovery, which she knew would be short-lived. Even so, she watched him greet his lords and retainers, glad to see a little happiness and health in his life. Yet, again today, his eyes seemed too bright and his mood too gay. . . .

Alysa eagerly waited for bedtime, hoping to sneak a visit with her father, only to learn that Isobail was spending the night with him. Her choice was made; stay in her room and pray.

Very late that night four things took place of which Alysa was ignorant: Guinn became more discontent and dangerous, Moran arrived and entered the chamber beneath hers, Keegan returned to Gavin's camp with bad news, and Isobail spent an hour making love to a beguiled and drugged Prince Alric.

Sunday morning Alysa was summoned to join Moran for the early meal. She dreaded it, but complied, surprised to find the entire family and all guests present, except for Earnon. Since there was much to do and time was nearing for the wedding ceremony, everyone hurried.

Again Moran was romantic, allowing his intention to be noticed by everyone, and her fears of coerced marriage increased. When they were alone, he tried to embrace her, but she pulled away from him.

"What is wrong, little mouse?" he inquired peevishly. "We have not seen each other for days. Why are you so cold this time?"

Alysa thought quickly and replied, "You have not been true to me, Moran, even when you were home. How can I take you seriously?"

Moran's face became red with guilt and fury. "What has Kyra told you?" he demanded, a harsh expression lining his face.

"Nothing. I heard talk from servants and in the village," she replied, and realized she had guessed accurately.

"Talk is talk, Alysa, put no faith in it," he commanded.

"If it is not true, why are you so angry?" she retorted.

Moran tried to conceal his annoyance. "Surely you realize that men have needs before taking a wife, but they mean nothing."

"If they mean nothing, why must they be fulfilled?" she asked.

"You are such an innocent, Alysa. If not, you would understand, and forgive such a normal weakness of the flesh."

"I understand it. Have you forgotten I was taken captive by men with just such weaknesses?"

"Did they harm you?" he asked coldly, seizing her shoulders roughly.

"You are hurting me, Moran! Stop it." she shouted.

He loosened his hold but did not release her. "Answer me."

"No, but they would have if I had not been rescued when I was. They were getting drunk and staring at me in a frightening way."

"Then we must be grateful that Mother bought your release."

"I am grateful, but that does not excuse your behavior. You vow you love me, then run off to . . . You know what I mean."

Thisbe arrived to tell Alysa she had to hurry to dress for the wedding. Moran frowned at the servant's untimely intrusion, and said, "We will discuss this later."

"Yes, later," she concurred, and left him.

Alysa admitted that Kyra's wedding was lovely, and most appeared to have a good time, including her father. Guinn entertained at the feast, but appeared darkly subdued. Alysa could not help but notice how the bard kept watching Isobail furtively, hungrily. As soon as time and opportunity allowed, she left the Great Hall, hurried to her chamber, and hid from Moran,

361

claiming she was still overwrought from her recent misfortune with the bandits.

In Kyra's chamber early that evening the young bride burst into tears and confessed her tale to her new husband. At first Calum was furious to learn that she was not a virginal bride, but then he calmed down. "I should have told you before the ceremony, but I was so ashamed and frightened," the girl lied, weeping convincingly.

"Do not distress yourself, woman," Calum soothed, for his desire for her was enormous. "Come, I will be gentle with you."

Kyra knew she had to submit to Calum tonight and other nights, although she had told Earnon she would find an excuse not to do so. She could not allow Calum to become suspicious of her. Earnon had tried to find a way to prevent Isobail from giving her in marriage to Calum, but he had failed, so he yielded for now. They both agreed that in time they would be together again.

To avoid seeing her with Calum, Earnon had remained in his chamber as much as possible since the hasty marriage preparations began. Kyra was not particularly unhappy about this, as she was eager to experience passion with another man. And, after all, her husband was handsome. She smiled and yielded to Calum's embrace, covering his face with kisses. "Tell me what I am to do."

"Do nothing except undress and lie upon the bed. Tonight I will pleasure you. Later, I will teach you all you must know."

Isobail was duping Alric in a similar manner in the prince's chamber. As she tantalized him with her skills, she confessed, "I have been slipping a newly discovered herb into your food, my lusty husband. See how beautifully it works. You are getting well. Soon it will be as it was between us long ago."

With passion and drug-glazed eyes, Alric smiled as he watched her naked figure perform. "This has been a marvelous day, my precious wife. The feasting was fine, but two nights with you can compare with nothing else."

"Only two nights with me?" she teased. "Nay, my love, we will have many nights together. Your stamina has returned, and we must fulfill your every desire. It has been a busy and tiring day, relax while I tempt you beyond control," she purred as she worked upon him. Isobail closed her eyes and pretended it was Gavin Hawk who lay beneath her hands and lips, and then her hips, driving him to writhing pleasure and bliss. When Alric was sleeping soundly, she glared at her husband and vowed, *That was the last time you will ever touch me, foul beast. . . .*

Gavin and his men made plans. Keegan had rested, gathered supplies, then left the camp with Bevan for Cambria to speak with King Bardwyn. Upon his return from his last mission, Keegan had told Gavin that their messengers' camp had been deserted and the men could not be found. Suspecting treachery, Gavin ordered Keegan to deliver the news to the king personally—they could no longer rely on other messengers to carry the report to the king. To prevent more trouble, Gavin instructed Bevan to accompany him, each man leading an extra horse to make the journey pass swiftly. Still unable to locate Giselde, Gavin was deeply worried about the old woman. He was also concerned about Princess Alysa and Prince Alric. He asked the king to come quickly, but knew that if this was the first message to get through to the king, the preparation and trip to Damnonia would require at least seventeen days.

As he had agreed, Gavin met again with the sheriff, but told Trahern he could not locate Skane and slay him. Gavin suggested that the brigand leader had somehow learned that he was in danger of revolt and gone into hiding. Gavin promised to find the man, kill him, and take over the band. He was pleased to learn that Alysa had played her part well and was safe at the castle.

The Cumbrian Prince was surprised when Trahern asked him to meet with the mastermind behind the rebellion on Wednesday night. He did not need more evidence against Isobail, but he knew he must continue his dangerous ruse until help arrived.

Monday morning the guests departed Malvern Castle, as did the newly married couple. Within an hour Isobail went to Alric's chamber and handed him a specially prepared drink, telling him it was an aphrodisiac. But recalling the previous reports and suspicions he had had about the food and wine he had been served, Alric declined the offering.

Isobail had reached the end of her patience, and no longer feeling the need for pretense with Alric, returned with Trahern and Earnon. The two men imprisoned Alric's wrists while Isobail forced the liquid into his mouth, clamping his nose until he was forced to swallow the draught.

He glared at her, outraged. She laughed and said, "There is no more need for caution, dear prince. You are a weakling, and soon you will have little value to me. Then, with great pleasure I will slay you. I alone shall rule this land, and soon others will follow. Trahern will sit beside me."

Trahern's worshipful eyes followed Isobail as she spoke and he restrained Prince Alric from shouting for help until the herbal brew took effect. After which, Isobail commanded Earnon, "Make sure his head does not clear again before I end his miserable existence." Earnon nodded and vowed to comply.

Alysa allowed Moran to convince her to go riding with him that afternoon, hoping Gavin would see them and snatch her. But he did not. When they returned to the castle, which was shrouded in gloom and darkness, she learned of her father's relapse. She was beside herself with worry, but learning that Alric was carefully guarded, there was nothing she could do except escape to her private chamber and hold Moran at bay.

At dusk Isobail and Trahern went riding and invited Guinn to accompany them. Out of sight of the castle they dismounted and strolled in a lovely wooded glen. "Look there, Guinn," Isobail called, pointing deep into the small and secluded valley. When Guinn turned, Isobail stabbed him fiercely, killing him at once. Trahern was shocked and bewildered by her action, until Isobail quickly explained. "He has been spying on me, and learned about us. He threatened to tell Alric everything if I refused to become his lover. Can you imagine such a brazen threat, Trahern? I did not know what else to do."

"How will we explain his death?" the stupefied sheriff asked. He was becoming concerned about the number of people Isobail had murdered in her quest for the rulership, and the obvious pleasure she appeared to derive from the brutal slayings. It was not safe for a ruler to have so much blood on her hands. Yet he was beguiled by her open declaration about them to Alric and Earnon.

"We will say we were attacked by brigands and they

killed him. Do you not remember how we were forced to flee for our lives?" she said, watching him closely to insure his compliance. After a few moments of hesitation, he nodded. "Come, we must move into the open, where Skane can see us."

"I am here," the brigand leader informed her, stepping from behind a group of dense bushes and joining them.

"You heard all?" she inquired, her tone expressing her annoyance. When he nodded, she shrugged and said, "It was necessary. As you know, Skane, I despise threats and blackmail. You must take the blame for his death."

"What is my payment?"

"Payment!" she shouted. "You demand payment after what you just took from me! You become too greedy and bold, my hireling."

"What do you mean?" he demanded. In the village earlier he had heard the crazy tale of Alysa's kidnapping and ransoming by three bandits, but the tale had not been accurate, so he had dismissed it as rumor. Since Alysa's capture, he had been lazing around in a camp with his men while they awaited this meeting for new orders. He supposed Gavin was raiding northwest as they had discussed, as he had not seen the Hawk and his small band for days.

From Alysa's explanation, Isobail leveled her charges against him. "Last week, Skane, on the very night you were to have met with me, you were abducting Princess Alysa Malvern. You intended to sell her to Hengist, but your men disobeyed you. Within two days they brought her home after receiving ransom. I warned you to leave her alone. She is to marry my son."

"I gave no such orders!" Skane shouted.

"The bandit leader told Alysa as much, and she told me. Where are my jewels?" she demanded, for she had indeed discovered that some of her jewels were missing from the castle, though she had no idea who had taken them.

"I do not have them, and I did not abduct the girl," Skane argued, her unexpected charge.

"Alysa described you perfectly, Skane. Do you take me for a fool? I paid them at one gate and they released her at another." She spouted off the false charge, and watched Skane's cold fury mount.

Baffled, the brigand leader wondered if his three men had betrayed him by selling the young princess to Isobail instead of to Hengist. Or did the girl escape them and only claim as much? No, he decided, Alysa could not ransom herself. This matter was perplexing and infuriating. Was Princess Alysa afraid, he wondered, to expose him to this woman, since it would expose her daring flight? Had she persuaded his three men to take her home for a hefty reward? Did the little beauty expect silence for silence? Whatever her motives, Princess Alysa knew too much now and could be a threat to all of them.

Skane decided that even if Isobail was angry with him, it should be Isobail who dealt with the girl. "All right, I will tell you the truth of the matter. I did capture the wench. She was riding northeast, to Bardwyn I guessed. She was carrying food and extra clothes. I figured you would want her captured so she would not be a danger to your scheme, but I did not order her to be ransomed. I told my men to take her to Logris and sell her to Hengist. No doubt she enticed my men to betray me and ransom her. I will track down the traitors and kill them myself, after they confess the truth to us!"

Isobail did not argue with Skane's tale, but she was convinced that Alysa was too meek to have actually run away, much less sought out Bardwyn. "Do that, and see that my jewels are returned," she said. "I told you the girl is promised to my son, and she is eager to marry him. If you thought she was running away, you were mistaken. See that she is not endangered again. If you are losing control over your men, I can easily replace you. Find and return my jewels, Skane, or I will do just that."

The brigand watched her ride away, and his eyes narrowed. There was something about this matter that did not sit right in his gut. Plus, he did not like the way Isobail was treating him. Perhaps it was time to make his own plans, starting with his own disloyal men. . . .

Tuesday morning Skane and his band rode hard and caught up with Kyra and Calum and robbed them, taking the jewels Kyra had stolen from Giselde, which the bandit assumed were Princess Kyra Ahern's. The moment the raiders were out of sight, Calum sent a trusty messenger to Isobail to tell her what had happened. But when Kyra begged her new husband to return to Malvern Castle, he refused.

Alysa went riding with Moran again, but was not able to elude him and find a few minutes of privacy. It was difficult to mask her impatience with his words of love and passion. She found herself snapping at Moran peevishly, thinking only of Gavin and wondering how she could get word to him.

For over an hour after their return home, Moran persisted with his wooing. Finally he went to see his mother and related the change in Alysa. Isobail listened, but was distracted by the news about Calum's robbery.

"Be patient with her, my son. Perhaps you frightened her with your excessive eagerness. She had a terrible experience with those bandits. Give her time to relax. If she does not, I will fix things. We have become friends, and she trusts me. She will obey me."

Gavin had been taken by the Druid priest to Trosdan's cave in a distant glen in the royal forest to meet with Giselde. The livid scar on her forehead as she lay abed attested to her serious injury.

"We need no more proof against Isobail," Gavin told her. "Alysa's kidnapping seals her guilt. Skane told her about Isobail's involvement with the marauding brigands. It is good to have a witness against Damnonia's regent besides myself. But there is nothing more to do except await King Bardwyn's arrival. Until then I must continue to play this role to protect Alysa and Alric. Your granddaughter wonders why your herbs did not work with Alric, Giselde. She tried to run to Bardwyn herself, to help her father, and that is how she was captured," Gavin informed the distressed woman. "Could Alric's illness be the result of a spell?" he asked, implying his budding belief in magic and in her powers.

Giselde smiled and replied, "Yea, it is possible, Prince Crisdean. But I do not know how to break it without knowing what kind it is."

"What about Moran, Giselde? How shall we deal with him when the king arrives? I cannot deceive Alysa once this matter is settled."

"Let love guide your tongue, Gavin. What more can you do?"

After the two exchanged information, Gavin told Giselde to remain in the cave with her friend, as things were dangerous everywhere. Reluctantly Giselde agreed, then told Gavin how it was possible to reach Alysa even while she was in the castle: the secret passageway.

Twenty

Wednesday morning was stormy, so everyone was forced to remain inside the castle. At such times irregular chores were carried out by the servants. Today Leitis turned the eating tables in the Great Hall on their sides so she could scrub and oil their legs. On her knees behind one, Earnon and Isobail did not notice the woman's presence as they passed through the hall.

Isobail had asked Earnon to explain his enchantment on Leitis, and he had done so, ending with how the spell could be broken. "Only the word Non Rae can end it," he informed her within Leitis's earshot.

The head servant rubbed her head as several curious pains knifed through her skull, then vanished. Humming merrily and daydreaming about Piaras, Leitis returned to her task at hand.

That night Gavin pretended to be shocked when Princess Isobail appeared at the prearranged meeting place in the forest. Gavin was glad Trahern had remained at a distance with the horses since he wanted Isobail to speak freely and openly with him. Gavin looked admiringly at her face and figure. "How could I ever forget such a ravishing creature? It seems we have met before, my beautiful lady," he murmured seductively, "though perhaps you do not remember, since I was masked. I hope you forgive me if I angered you that day. Skane was a fool to order me to rob your group; you could have been injured."

"You do not mind working for a woman?" Isobail inquired in a husky tone, her bold gaze matching his own.

"Not when she is as exquisite and intelligent as you. I have thought of you often since that day on the road," he said, his eyes of liquid fire searing her flesh and nearly burning away her wits and control. When he smiled provocatively, temptingly, enticingly—white teeth amidst a tanned face drew Isobail's eyes to his sensual lips. He knew he was standing in such a way as to call her attention to his well-developed and well-toned physique. He watched her expression glow with rising desire and she licked her lips thirstily, awaiting the taste of nectar from his. From the way her ravenous eyes were examining and devouring him from head to foot, she clearly wanted him and wished they were alone.

Isobail stepped closer to him and replied softly, "And I have thought of you often, since that night in Skane's camp. The afternoon you robbed me, although you were masked, I knew who was beneath it. I have been seeking you for days. There are many things to discuss."

"It was best to conceal myself and my men for a while, to convince Skane we were raiding near Lord Orin's as he commanded. If I had known you . . . *needed* or *wanted* me, I would have raced to you."

Isobail was snared by his intimate insinuation, along with his good looks and build. A wanton smile curled her lips and she moved even closer to him. "I am more than pleased with you, Gavin Hawk. You are an exceptional man. I was delighted by your recovery of Alysa and by your crafty act. The ransom tale was a clever ruse but I wish I had known about it to avoid looking surprised when she related it. But what of my other jewels, the ones you stole from me on the trail?"

"As you know, m'lady," Gavin replied, glad his ruse had pleased her, "it had nothing to do with me. Skane has them. When I slay him, I will try to recover them for you."

"Very well," Isobail replied. "But how did you manage to locate her?"

His honeyed voice replied, "One of his men told me; that is how I found her for you. She was a real nuisance, tried to escape twice."

"I was wondering why we could not locate you before tonight," Isobail said. "I thought you told Trahern you were looking for Skane but could not find him." She fingered with his leather garb. "You just said you have been in hiding to avoid Skane. I am confused. . . ."

"At night, sweetness," he replied casually, "I search for Skane when I can move around without being seen. During the daylight I keep hidden until time for me to return to where he said to meet him. Saturday night," he answered before she could ask when. "I promise you, by Sunday morning I will be the only leader who is working for you. Perhaps there are other matters I could take care of for you?" he asked, trailing the backs of his fingers over her flushed cheek. He saw her respond instantly and eagerly to his touch. "Soon my days will be filled with work for you, but my nights will be free and barren."

Isobail glanced toward Trahern, and realized he could not see or hear them. Her fingers snaked up his hard chest to his lips as she responded quietly, "For now, my devilish rogue, mine are neither free nor barren."

Gavin's hand slipped behind her head and slowly drew her mouth toward his, halting only a few inches away. His green eyes bored into hers as he echoed, "For now, sweetness? Or forever?"

"Only for as long as it takes to safely replace him

with you," she whispered against his mouth before hungrily slashing hers across his. Never, she realized, had she been so tempted by a man! From the first moment she had seen him, she had been obsessed. When she was queen and Trahern was gone, Gavin must become her love slave.

Isobail was allowed only one blazing, mind-dazing kiss before lightning charged across the cloudy sky and thunder followed it, announcing the arrival of another storm, one of many small and violent ones to torment the land that day. She knew Trahern would be summoning her to depart, so she reluctantly freed herself from Gavin. She felt weak and trembling, and passion raced feverishly within her body. "Keep this between us alone, Gavin Hawk, and you shall have me soon. I will give you pleasures no other woman can."

"Just as I shall give you something no other man has. You must go before Trahern sees us and causes trouble," he warned when she reached for him for a parting kiss and caress. He did not think he could bear for this malevolent and satanic woman to touch him again. Gavin vowed silently that he definitely would give her something unique: defeat and possibly death!

"How do you know what is between Trahern and me?" she asked oddly.

Gavin grinned. "From the way Trahern looks at you and touches you, even when he is unaware of his actions and expressions. It is obvious to me there is more than wishful desire pulling at your devoted sheriff. Who can blame him, sweetness? I envy him every moment he spends with you, especially alone. I doubt Trahern will give you up to me or to anyone without a death struggle."

"Could you beat him in one?" she asked half playfully, half seriously.

"I am certain of it. If you say the word, I will do anything for you, Isobail. When I said I had thought about you often since seeing you, that was not true. Actually, I have dreamed of you, and craved you, and plotted how to get you. If you had been the one kidnapped by Skane's men, I would not have returned you home for weeks for any reward or because of any threat. Perhaps I would never have released you if I could have gotten away with enslaving you, or if I could have enchanted you beyond your will."

Gavin's tone and expression altered while he reasoned aloud. "You are a ruler, Isobail, and I am only a warrior, an adventurer. I am not foolish enough to think I could win you away from such a life, or join it. But for as long and as often as I can have you, I want you."

"Give me a little time to study this complicated matter and to work it out favorably for us," she asked, then glanced at the lightning that filled the sky again. "Get rid of Skane before Sunday, and I will send Trahern to Lord Orin's and other places to weigh my subjects' loyalty. While he is gone, I will find a way for us to get together many times, if you wish."

Gavin's heart nearly stopped in panic. King Bardwyn and his men could not arrive for two more weeks! Gavin knew he did not have enough men to challenge and to battle Isobail, her followers, and her brigands. He had tempted her too successfully, too recklessly. What could he do now?

"You do not answer me, Gavin," she asked curiously. "Why?"

Trapped, he teased her, saying, "I did not know you asked a question, sweetness. What could keep me away from you if you summoned me?"

Isobail smiled and replied, "I hope nothing, for I want you fiercely."

"I also want you fiercely," he responded. *I want your defeat fiercely,* his mind corrected him. He observed Isobail and Trahern's departure, then leaned against the rock behind him to figure out an escape to this offensive predicament. He was willing to do many things to snare Isobail and protect his love, but bedding that bitch was too much for anyone to ask of him!

The storms did not subside until noon on Friday, but Alysa refused to go riding with Moran or play games with him downstairs. She claimed she was feeling badly, evoking a visit from Isobail at Moran's request.

Isobail visited her in her chamber. "My son tells me you are ill, Alysa," she said. "What troubles you? He says you have been chilly to him since his return. He is hurt and confused. Is there a problem between you two? Can I help solve it?"

Alysa looked at her stepmother pitifully and replied, "I cannot tell him what is wrong; it is too private. The trouble with those bandits brought on my monthly earlier, and I have felt awful for days. I was so queasy Sunday that I could hardly enjoy Kyra's wedding. My head and belly have ached, and I feel as if I want to scream or cry every few minutes. Nothing helps except to lie down and remain still." Part of what she was saying was true; her monthly had begun late Saturday, but had ended yesterday, if Isobail boldly checked out her excuse.

Isobail smiled, deciding Alysa's moodiness and distance from Moran were explained reasonably and truthfully. "I understand. Remain in bed a few days, and I will handle my anxious son for you."

"Thank you, Isobail. It is simply impossible to respond to his romantic overtures when I feel so terrible and gloomy. This weather has not helped me either. You know I have never liked powerful storms. If only the sun would appear tomorrow," she murmured.

Isobail patted her arm and tucked the cover around

her. "Would you like Thisbe to bring you some warm milk with honey?"

"That would be nice," Alysa agreed, but did not smile or brighten.

Isobail suggested, "Shall I get Earnon to put something in it to ease the pain and help you sleep? He often does this for me."

"That sounds wonderful; thank you. Please assuage Moran's worries and tell him I am truly ill so he will understand my silly behavior." Alysa decided, when Thisbe arrived with the medicinal drink, she would order a hot bath to soothe her nerves and relax her taut body.

"Of course," Isobail told her gently, then left. She went to see Earnon first, who headed to the kitchen with a special herb for Alysa's discomfort and rest. Then she went to see Moran. She told him exactly what was wrong with Alysa and explained such matters.

Moran laughed in delight. "I am glad it is nothing more than naughty nature. I was beginning to worry."

"I told you not to. The girl is smitten with you. How could she not be enchanted by my only son?" she teased. "Leave her be for a few days, then pursue her hotly once more. She will yield, I promise you, for a woman is most receptive and lustful when 'naughty nature' finishes with her."

The storm had caused the river to rise and flow swiftly, too swiftly for Gavin to find the underwater entrance to the secret passage before tonight. He had paced for two days awaiting this moment.

After dark he entered the water and made his way to the spot Giselde described to him. It took three dives before he found the hole which was half clogged with limbs and other debris. He pushed them aside and swam upward until he surfaced. Locating the stairs with

376

probing toes, he ascended cautiously because they were slick and hazardous. The worst part was the total darkness surrounding him. Never before had he realized how black darkness could be! Barefoot, and attired only in a soaked loincloth, he was miserably chilled.

The odors of rot and mildew that reached his nose were repulsive, but he ignored them. Finally reaching the top of the steps, he searched for the torch and flintstone Giselde said would be in an alcove. He could find neither, so he tried to carry out his intentions in the blackness. Placing a hand against the slimy wall on either side of him, he gingerly traveled onward. When his right hand felt nothing, he assumed he was at the turn near the gatehouse and southwest wall. He continued.

He senses were on full alert, but he heard and felt nothing except a cobweb brushing his head and shoulders here and there, and slime oozing between his toes and around his feet. He presumed this area was too dark, cold, wet, and black for rats and bugs, or at least he hoped so. This time and place reminded him of another one of Giselde's premonitions: he was in a dark place, but not trapped there, which made two of the eight accurate so far. The first—Alysa away and in great peril—had come to pass although he had rescued Alysa.

For a time his mind was distracted in the inky blackness. He wondered if the other premonitions would come true. Was Teague the rival he would save? When? How? What fires and whose suffering loomed in the near future? Alysa, branded a traitor, and he a wolfshead? Prince Alric and Giselde dead? All of this before the king's arrival? Could he defend those he loved until Bardwyn's rescue? Once more Giselde's words echoed through his troubled mind: "Our victory will depend on you, and you will question your instincts, prowess, wits, and skills"; another warning that had come to pass.

While he groped his way forward, Gavin reflected on how, he had returned the old woman's wedding ring to her after he found it still hidden in the secret compartment in the ransacked chest in her hut. He pondered how to recover the other jewels Kyra had stolen from the old woman.

His journey seemed endless until he suddenly banged his toes against a rock and nearly howled in pain. Repulsed by contact with the slime, he nonetheless clutched his foot in his hands, massaged his aching toes, and mastered his nausea. When the throbbing ceased, he felt around, discovering spiral stairs. He had to be at the base of Alysa's tower. Carefully he climbed upward until he reached a landing. He noticed he could feel and smell fresh air, but the night allowed no light to aid him while he fumbled for the latch and found it.

Praying this was Alysa's chamber and she was alone, Gavin shoved the door open and peered inside. Only a candle was burning near a bed. He slipped into the room and checked the person sleeping there: Princess Alysa Malvern. He smiled, then noticed how filthy he was. Spying the tub, he headed for it. Before rinsing himself with the tepid water, he thought about the door and went to lock it, but it was already bolted.

He quickly bathed and dried off, then washed his dirty tracks from the floor. He approached the bed and sat down near her waist. As he stroked her hair, her lids fluttered and her eyes opened.

Alysa blinked several times, then stared at the incredible sight. Gavin was smiling down at her and caressing her cheek. "If this is a dream, do not arouse me," she pleaded. Her hands reached for him and contacted chilly flesh. "You are cold, my love. Lie under here with me," she said, lifting the edge of the coverlet. Her actions and words were instinctive, for she was still groggy.

Gavin eased his nude body between the covers and snuggled with her, warming almost immediately. "I have been worried about you and aching to see you, m'love. How have you been?"

Now, awakened completely, she replied, "Miserable and lonely without you." She cuddled against him. "A week is too long to go without seeing and touching you."

"One day is too long," he replied huskily. "Tell me everything."

Alysa did, even modestly relating her visit from Isobail this evening. "What has taken place with you, my love?" she asked after she had finished. "I have worried so about you since Piaras told me of Giselde. She is still missing?"

Gavin began an episode he dreaded, but knew must take place. "I know, m'love, but she is fine." As Alysa stared at him, he disclosed Kyra's attack and theft, and Giselde's survival and escape.

Consternation filled Alysa's blue eyes. "I knew Kyra was wicked, but not this bad. She married Sunday and left Malvern Castle, I hope forever. What would my stepsister want with dangerous herbs? I wonder if Kyra was fetching them for her evil mother or for Earnon. Perhaps those plants or berries are the ones that keep Father abed or drove Baltair mad. My friend is dead, you know, it was a terrible thing. But tell me, how did you find Giselde?"

Gavin answered, "After I left you here, I went to visit her. I worried over the signs of trouble in her hut, and I searched for her for days and did not find her. I am sure Kyra believes she killed Giselde. Indeed, the old woman would have died if the Druid priest had not found her soon after the attack and tended her in his cave. Trosdan came to my camp Tuesday and took me to her. Wait," he entreated when she started to ask questions. "There is more you must know. Remember when you made your confessions in the brigand camp and in the cave?" he said, and she nodded, her dark sapphire eyes wide and full of rising panic. "There are some confessions I must make tonight, and you must hear me out and understand, and forgive me."

Alysa's alarm increased. "What is it, Gavin?" she asked reluctantly, fearing this unknown, this nerve-racking mystery, and his strange mood.

"There have been many secrets between us since we met, m'love. We had the same fearful torments, but it is time to vanquish them." He inhaled deeply and quietly before saying, "I am not unreachable for you, Alysa, nor unworthy of you. I am not an adventurer or a mercenary or a bandit of any kind, and never have been. I am not Gavin Hawk, nor in your land by chance or for hire."

He gazed into her eyes, which were focused intently on his face. He knew from her respiration that her heart was pounding forcefully in distress. Her bewildered expression seemed to ask: What are you? Who are you? As if she could not speak, she remained silent and watchful.

He continued, "I am Prince Gavin Crisdean, son of King Briac Crisdean of Cumbria. King Bardwyn sent me here to study the trouble in Damnonia and to unmask its villains. I was ordered to reveal my identity and mission to no one. Partly with your help, I gathered proof against your stepmother and the brigands, and I sent word to King Bardwyn to summon his help. Your grandfather should arrive with his men in twelve to fifteen days and defeat Princess Isobail and her henchmen."

Alysa's look said she was stunned by this revelation. Gavin quickly went on. "At first I could not tell you anything about me or my actions because of the same reasons why you could not confide in me. Later I had to keep silent to protect you. When I learned how brave you were, I feared you would never sit still while I handled everything. I knew you would insist on helping me unmask Isobail, and I could not allow you to endanger yourself or this crucial mission. Giselde is the one who initially sent for help from your grandfather; she wanted to protect you during this mess because she loves you very much. Giselde and I have been working together since my arrival. King Bardwyn sent me to uncover the truth before he and his troops rode into this country. He could not invade without proof of Giselde's charges. I was instructed to get that proof, and to tell you nothing until your king arrived. But Giselde told me about the secret passageway to you from outside the castle, and I can hold silent to you no longer, Alysa, for I love you. I know you love me and trust me, so I cannot mislead you. I beg you, m'love, do nothing except be patient and careful until these dangerous days are over."

Alysa's eyes wandered over his face. Giselde and Gavin had worked together since before she met him, and she had discussed each with the other. Dismayed by his incredible confession, she spoke hoarsely, "You and Granmannie have been lying to me all this time. You doubted my wits, as if I possess none. If you two really love me, why did both of you deceive me? Why was I never included in your plans? Why was I left to worry and fear when the truth could prevent them?"

Gavin tried to recall each of her rapid questions so he could answer them. "I duped you no more than you duped me, m'love. I thought you were a servant, while I was a prince, one day a king; that is why I kept telling you a future between us was impossible. Yet I came to love you and want you more than my own life, and I was determined to find a way to keep you. You felt the same; as a princess and future ruler, you viewed love and marriage to a warrior impossible. We both worried over an irresistible attraction which we feared could go nowhere—but it can, m'love. Are you not happy that we are matched perfectly and can marry when this trouble is settled?"

Alysa was happy over that fact, but she was still too angry to admit it. "But you said nothing after you learned the truth about me. Why did you and Giselde keep me ignorant for so long?"

"Until recently Giselde did not know about my secret meetings with you. When I did confess them to her, I said I was in love with Thisbe, as I truly believed you were the daughter of Piaras. Knowing who I was, Giselde tried to discourage such an impossible match, and she fretted over my possible slips to a servant who lived in Isobail's castle and over my distraction from my mission. One day at her hut I was talking about you and worrying over how I could keep you or part from you. That clever woman suspected the girl I was seeing was not your handmaiden. She asked questions until she was certain it was you I was seeing, then she kept quiet about her amazing discovery for a time. Giselde grasped the depth of our relationship and did not want to confront you about it. She also thought you should be the one to enlighten me, not her. The same was true with you where I was concerned. Finally that sweet woman had to tell me that my Thisbe was actually Princess Alysa Malvern so I could save you from Moran's pursuit. She confessed it to me the day Moran was knighted, the same day I found the pouch you left for me. Giselde realized we were perfect for each other and hated to see me mess things up for us."

Alysa remained quiet, allowing him time to explain everything in his own time and way.

"When I heard the truth," he continued, "I assumed you were fooling me for the same reasons I was fooling you. I wanted to go to you and straighten out everything, but I did not want to draw you into more peril by letting you help me. I swear to you, m'love, I did not and do not doubt your wits; I only wanted to keep you safe. After you confessed all to me in the cave, I knew I owed you the same to prevent any misunderstandings. I can no longer bear to keep such secrets from you. I never want you to mistrust me again, or to allow you to fear you would have to sacrifice all you are and possess to have me."

Gavin sat up and pulled her with him. Gently grasping her forearms and staring into her troubled eyes, he pleaded, "Do not turn away from me, Alysa, I love you and need you. I want you to become my wife. If I have hurt you or angered you, I am sorry. I truly did what I felt was best for all concerned."

Alysa could not deny that Gavin had the best interests of everyone at heart and had borne a heavy burden of responsibility. Clearly he loved her and was deeply troubled over causing a rift between them. They were perfectly matched, and soon the trouble here would end. A reality filled her: there was nothing to prevent her from having him!

Alysa smiled as her hand gently stroked the worry lines on his handsome face, and she told him, "You do not need these, my love. My shock is gone and my wits have cleared. I understand and believe you. A prince, the future King of Cumbria . . ." she murmured, her awe returning. "I should have known you were too unique to be what you claimed," she teased, hugging him.

"And you," he responded merrily, "a princess, future ruler of this land, and future queen of Cambria. And of Cumbria," he added. "If we remain here to rule after we marry, how can I train to become king of my land? Once I am King of Cumbria and you are Queen of Cambria, where shall we live and rule? Their names are similar and they exist peacefully, side by side, but can we unite them into one land? There are ranks, locations, and dilemmas for us to settle later."

"Yes, my love, much later," the happy girl agreed. Their gazes fused and they smiled at each other.

Gavin clasped her to him and whispered into her ear, "How I have loved you so intensely since our first meeting, and I have missed you madly since we left our passion-filled cave. . . ."

"It was good we shared that special time together before we confront this battle ahead," she replied. "From now on, Gavin Crisdean, we must share everything. I am glad Gavin is your real name, for it suits you well. 'Hawk of the peaceful valley' . . . Yes, it is perfect for you."

Calling to mind the meaning of Alysa and Crisdean, he replied, "As perfect as 'Noble of the peaceful valley' after we wed. That day cannot come swiftly enough for me. I want everyone to know that Prince Gavin has captured the greatest prize of any land, the most exquisite treasure in existence."

"It is I who have the highest prize: you." Alysa pressed him to his back and lay half atop him. She spread kisses over his chest and nibbled up his throat to his inviting mouth. Nose to nose, she grinned and murmured, "I love you more than anything in life, more than my life itself." She sealed their lips.

They made love for hours, leisurely, tranquilly, swiftly, urgently. They shared soft laughter and countless kisses. They talked and embraced, then they planned and loved. It was as if a beautiful dream surrounded and protected them.

It was nearly three in the morning when Gavin told Alysa, "I must go to see your father, m'love. If he is alert enough, I will tell him what is happening and what is going to happen soon. It should put his mind at ease to learn his father is on the way with help."

"You are thoughtful, my love. I only pray he can be awakened. I will go with you," she said eagerly.

"No, you must remain here. Someone might come to

384

check on you," he said, gently refusing her company. "Your door is locked; if there is trouble, it would look suspicious if you do not answer a summons to it. If you leave it unlocked and someone arrives, it would look strange to find you missing, and we could be sighted returning. I will see you again before I leave," he promised, hoping to appease her.

"What if someone sees you inside the castle?" she asked frantically.

"I'll use the secret passage again. It would be safer and wiser for you to remain here. In case of trouble, I can escape easier alone. Please," he urged.

Alysa realized she could accompany him if she insisted, but she decided against it. Besides, it was doubtful Gavin could arouse her father, considering Alric's recent relapse. Too, she refused to endanger her love's life. She smiled and yielded. "I will wait here for your return. Will you tell Father about us?"

A broad smile brightened Gavin's features. "Yea, m'love, if he is reachable. Do you know how much I love you and how lucky I know I am to win you?" he said proudly and happily.

"Yes, for the same is true for me."

Green eyes locked with blue ones, and love flowed between them like a peaceful river. Each confirmed the powerful bond between them, and was thrilled that it was shared. Each realized it was more than a physical attraction, much more. Each knew it would last forever.

"If I tarry much longer, it will be too late to visit your father," he said mirthfully. He finger-combed her brown hair as he gazed longingly and possessively at her, as though he could not absorb enough of her beauty.

"The day will come soon, my wandering warrior, when you no longer have to leave my side." She laughed and stroked his jaw. "I forget, you are not a wandering warrior. Besides being a prince and future king, are you a knight? A lusty dragon? A rogue?"

"I must confess to being all of them, m'love, and I shall be a greedy and demanding husband," he added, a playful grin tugging at his lips and glimmering in his eyes.

His eyes . . . She gazed into them. "You have the most striking and bewitching eyes of any man alive," she murmured dreamily.

"As have your, my blue-eyed goddess. When I look into them, I am lost to all but you. Surely they have enchanted me."

"We are fated, you and I. Granmannie told me so."

"She is an amazing woman. I can see why you love her. She has powers I never knew existed, and find hard to believe. Yet she has proven herself to me." Gavin told Alysa about most of the premonitions, and which ones had come true. He told her other things the woman had revealed to him, and about the removal of his royal tattoo.

"I have never doubted her powers, Gavin," she replied. "I have seen them work too many times in the past. I missed her terribly after she vanished years ago." Alysa quickly explained her past to him. "You must hurry, my love," she warned him, aware of the passing night.

The entire time Gavin was gone, Alysa paced and worried about his safety. When he finally returned, she embraced him in relief.

"I aroused him enough to speak with him, Alysa. He knows he is being drugged, but somehow he has been overcoming the potion's force for the last few days. When anyone enters the room, he pretends he is unconscious or very groggy to fool them. But he is very weak because he eats or drinks very little. He said to warn you not to use the passage to visit him because he is watched closely and you might get caught, then both of you would be in grave danger."

Gavin did not tell his love what the prince had told him about the scene in his room with Earnon, Trahern, and Isobail; he knew how that news would distress her. It added more evidence against Isobail, but caused Gavin to be deeply concerned about the man's safety. If Alric's ploy was discovered . . . Gavin did not want to think about that possibility. Hopefully King Bardwyn would arrive soon and end this madness. Gavin also did not tell Alysa about Moran's true identity, a fact that the prince divulged but had begged him to keep secret.

"I must leave now while I still have the cover of night to shield my escape. I will return in three nights to let you know what is happening everywhere. Be on guard at all times, but do nothing to provoke them against you," he cautioned.

They embraced and kissed before Gavin left, then Alysa watched him disappear down the spiral steps. When all light from his torch was gone, she closed the panel and unbolted her chamber door. She returned to bed and snuggled into the spot where earlier he had lain.

Just before sunset on Saturday, Prince Crisdean met with Skane. When the bandit assumed Gavin was challenging him for his rank, a bitter fight ensued. The two argued, then fought with swords, then with bare hands, then with knives. Being warriors, both were strong and skilled, and knowing this struggle was to the death, both fought savagely. They circled, slashed, and struck, yet, neither was injured seriously. Then Skane began to weaken. Finally Gavin was able to subdue his adversary, throwing Skane to the ground and slaying him.

Later Gavin met Trahern and turned Skane's body over to him, and shortly afterwards he entered the brigands' camp and declared himself their new chieftain. The men were pleased, and easily accepted Gavin and his orders, which were to split into small bands and raid in different parts of Damnonia. What Gavin had in mind, however, was to use his men and trusted peasants to attack and kill the raiders a few at a time. Meanwhile Piaras would keep his eyes and ears open at the castle so he could pass along information about the castle's soldiers' whereabouts. Gavin knew he could plan raids that would throw the bandits into the soldiers' paths, thus making use of them to destroy the outlaws.

A stroke of luck placed Giselde's stolen jewels in his possession; when Gavin went through Skane's belongings. Later he could return them to Giselde, as he had done earlier with her wedding ring. Tonight everything seemed to be going perfectly for him and his side, and he dreamed of victory and Alysa.

Sunday afternoon things did not go well for Prince Alric. Feeling better, he tried to sneak a walk in his room. Isobail's guard saw him and reported to the princess. Earnon solved the mystery of Alric's recovery when he hypnotized Leitis and questioned her. Discovering he had unwittingly broken the spell, he promptly put her under another one, again ordering her to administer tainted food and wine.

Isobail, the guard, and Earnon then forced another herbal potion into the struggling prince. Afterwards, the guard returned to his duty. Before Alric was subdued by the drug's power, Isobail scoffed, "Thought you could escape me, you worm! You have seen your last light of day. When next your eyes open, you will be with your barbarian wife. I will slay you with pleasure, like I killed her long ago. I no longer need you to help me obtain my desires. I will rule this land and others as my ancestor Queen Boadicea did."

In a highly emotional state, Isobail raved, revealing all she had done and all she planned to do. "I even have that weakling daughter of yours in my power. She is to marry my son within the month, then Moran will control her for me."

Horrified, Alric fought to recover his wits. His slurred mumblings about "sin" and "heir" and "son" and "justice" went past Isobail and Earnon. Alric wept bitterly until blackness encased him.

Near the Logris border on Monday, Princess Kyra ended her brief marriage to Sir Calum by taking her husband's life. Unable to wait any longer to get rid of him, she used the herbs she had stolen from Giselde and brewed them in her husband's wine. Calum appeared to have a coughing fit, and strangled before several witnesses.

Kyra wailed and grieved artfully, then told the castle guard to bury Sir Calum before escorting her to Malvern Castle. In her room alone, she rejoiced, eager to reclaim Earnon and to bring him here where she could learn more from him, learn all he knew. There was no way her mother could deny them Lord Daron's castle and land grant, she thought, not after all she and Earnon had done to help Isobail. If her mother refused, then she would die too. . . .

Twenty-one

Monday night Gavin sneaked through the secret passageway and visited Alysa and Alric again. His time with Alysa was spent loving and talking. He told her how he was foiling the bandits and duping Isobail. Alysa was delighted to hear that he had found some trustworthy peasants to help dispel the raiders. From village to village news of an imminent battle spread, and people prepared to join the King upon his arrival. Gavin had sent word to Lord Fergus, but he was reluctant to trust Lord Orin at this point.

Gavin's second visit with Alric did not go well at all. Clearly the prince had been heavily drugged. Gavin prayed that the man had not revealed anything about him and Alysa to Isobail, or about Moran. "Only another week, two at most," he reminded Alysa when she wept over her father's sorry condition.

"What if he does not survive that long, Gavin?" she asked, her blue eyes red and wet with tears. "Isobail is getting bold."

"If I could sneak him out of the castle, m'love, I would do so. He is too weak and ill to make it through the passageway and down the river, even with more help. Such an attempt could kill him faster than Isobail can. And you know we cannot get him through the gates and away before one of the guards on the battlement sighted us and sent out an alarm. We would all be captured and slain. We have no choice, m'love; we must wait for your grandfather."

All of Tuesday Moran persistently trailed and wooed a nonreceptive Alysa. He would not even allow her peace and privacy in her chamber. When she could endure his irritating gropings no longer, she told him, "I do not love you and cannot marry you, Moran. I have tried to make a relationship between us work, but it cannot. The more you press me, the more I want to withdraw from you. Please do not distress me further by continuing this futile pursuit."

"You are . . . rejecting me?" he stammered in outrage. His scowl melted into a look of fury which reddened his face. His green eyes became wild and cold. He glared at her, then turned and left without another word.

Alysa knew he would not let her off this easily. She wondered what he would do next. She had not meant to spurn him so soon or so frostily, but he had pushed her to a breaking point. Surely Isobail would know within minutes that she had rejected Moran.

Alysa quickly summoned Thisbe and related her action to the frightened servant. "If anything happens to me, alert your father at once and he will help me. Watch over me, dear friend, for I am in terrible trouble this time."

While Alysa paced her room, Thisbe sought out not her father, but her betrothed, and informed him of Alysa's possible dilemma. Squire Teague told his love, "If any danger befalls Princess Alysa, come to me swiftly. We will find a way to help her escape."

* * *

That evening Moran came to Alysa's chamber, carrying a jug of the castle's best wine. He looked at her apologetically and asked, "Will your forgive me, little mouse? You are not to blame if you cannot love me as I do you. I will return home to Ahern Castle and give you time to recover from those bandits' cruelty. I am sure that is what has distressed you. I realize I have been too eager, and I have frightened you away. All I ask is that you rest easy and think kindly of me. If your answer is still no in a month or two, I will cease to court you. Come, let us share a parting drink as friends," he coaxed, and filled two goblets.

Alysa understood her danger. If she declined to drink, he would try to force the drugged wine into her. If she accepted the goblet, she was doomed. She had to escape, now.

She pretended to sip the wine, then walked to the window and gazed at the starry sky. To make certain Moran did not join her there, she asked him to hand her the cape on her bed. As he complied, she dumped the wine out her window but appeared to be drinking it when Moran approached her.

"Shall we go for a walk? It is so lovely outside tonight."

"I prefer to remain here, little mouse."

Alysa walked to a chair and took a seat, placing the empty goblet on the nearby table. "Will you be leaving at first light to make full use of tomorrow?" she inquired, sounding nothing more than polite.

The devilishly grinning Moran leaned against the window, watched her intently, and did not reply. His behavior told Alysa that he expected the drug to act quickly. If she could get him out of the room, she would lock her door. "I am tired, Moran. I will rise early to see you off in the morning. Will you excuse me so I can retire for the night?"

"No, Alysa, I will not excuse you, nor release you,

tonight or ever. After we spend a few hours in your bed, you will have no choice but to marry me tomorrow," he said calmly; too calmly.

"What are you saying?" she demanded, glaring at him.

Moran rapidly covered the distance separating them. Clasping the arms of her chair, he imprisoned her in it. He bent forward until he was nearly nose to nose with her. "I am saying you will become mine tonight, all mine. Do you feel strange, Alysa? Perhaps a little weak and hungry—hungry for me? Come to bed and I shall feed you."

Alysa gaped at the crude man who suddenly looked ugly and vile to her. "Nay, I feel fine, my wicked stepbrother."

"Not for long," he vowed, then snatched her into his arms, carried her to the bed, and tossed her upon it.

Alysa scrambled off the other side and yelled at him, "Get away from me, you vulgar beast! I detest you. I will never marry you or surrender to you, with or without your seductive potions!"

The truth that she had eluded the drug dawned on Moran, and it infuriated him to be outsmarted. "With or without magic potions," he sneered, "by the devils below us, I will have you!"

"Come near me and I will slay you, vile dog."

Moran laughed sardonically. "We shall see, little mouse, we shall see." His menacing look intimidated her, as he knew it would.

Alysa wished Gavin would appear and battle this enemy, but he was not to return to her side for two days. She feared that even if she screamed for help, no one would rescue her. Still, she had to try, as Moran was strong and determined to ravish her. She ran to the window and got out one cry for help before Moran yanked her away from it. They struggled wildly as he ripped at her clothes, casting entangled shadows on the wall from her lamplights. His hands were rough and painful as tried to subdue her, meanwhile laughing and taunting her, and her terror mounted. Then her reason returned, and as Piaras had taught her long ago, Alysa entangled his leg and flung him to the stone floor. She seized the wine jug and slammed it against his head, knocking him unconscious. Almost immediately the door opened and she jerked around to see who had entered.

Thisbe and Teague surged forward and gaped at the fallen knight with a bloody temple. Teague checked him and told her, "I heard you scream and I saw Moran in the window. He will come to his senses soon, Alysa. You must flee. Come, I will help you get away."

Alysa sneaked out the door and into the outer ward. She hurried to the south gate behind her tower, she concealed herself under the torchlit portcullis, and waited for Teague to fetch Calliope. To make it appear he was only walking the horse, Teague did not saddle him, as instructed by Alysa, who could ride bareback skillfully.

Teague had left Thisbe in the stable saddling two horses for them. As Thisbe had confided all she knew to her betrothed and things appeared to be getting worse, they planned to get away with Alysa. Since the princess's safety came first, Squire Teague walked Calliope around the inner wall near the steep embankment to the river, Moran shouted an alarm from Alysa's window, "Seize Princess Alysa! Do not let her leave the castle!"

Without delay or second thought, Teague ran the horse to Alric's daughter. "Go quickly, Princess. They will be upon us in a few moments. I will guard your back."

"Nay, Teague," she protested. "I cannot leave you and Thisbe to face Moran and Isobail."

394

"If Prince Alric dies at their hands, you are our ruler. You must stay alive to defeat them. Do not argue! Go!"

Alysa hated to desert him in such danger, but she obeyed. She mounted Calliope as Teague raised the small gate. To make certain no one galloped after her, Teague used his sword to cut the ropes. The gate crashed down and locked in place. Knowing the futility of battling the four guards coming at him, Teague lay his sword on the ground and lifted his hands in surrender. He knew a dead man could not find a way to escape.

As ordered if an alarm was sounded, Thisbe concealed herself until she could slip to her room. She could not bear the uncertainty of her love's fate, but had to remain free to help him later.

News spread quickly of Alysa's flight. Moran alleged she had fled because she was sick and confused, and had not been herself "since those barbaric brigands abducted her." He claimed she had ranted wildly about hunting them down and killing them this very night. Moran asserted his fears that she would fall prey to them again. He gathered his mother's faithful men and raced off after Alysa, who had a good head start. Teague was captured "for allowing the disoriented princess to trick him into aiding her to imperil her life." He was taken to the dungeon and imprisoned there, to await Moran's return and torture.

Alysa molded herself against Calliope's back and held securely to his mane. Sensing his mistress's urgency, the horse raced as swiftly as possible toward the concealing woods. Alysa knew her foes could not trail her easily in the dark, but she made deceptive tracks to mislead them at first light. To hide her true direction, she used two streams, blended Calliope's tracks into other sets of hoof prints on the dirt road, and doubled back a few times. When she thought it safe to proceed, she rode to the tree where she and Gavin had left messages for each other. Surely her love would come here when he heard of her escape. She paced for nearly an hour before sitting down and leaning against the special tree. She rested her forehead on her raised knees, closed her moist eyes, and prayed.

Wednesday morning Gavin gingerly approached Trahern, as he had seen the sheriff galloping here and there with a red sash tied to his arm: the signal for an urgent meeting. "You summoned me?" Gavin inquired, nodding to the blood-colored cloth.

"Yes," Trahern stated, clearly relieved to see him. "I was afraid you were not in this area today. We have more trouble with Alric's daughter."

Gavin struggled to remain calm. "What kind of trouble this time?" he asked, trying to sound annoyed with her.

"Moran got a little too . . . friendly last night, and she ran away. We have to get her back to the castle before she runs her mouth and causes problems for us. If you see her, catch her and hold her for me. You will receive a big reward this time."

"How did she get away from Isobail's son and out of the castle?"

"The little enchantress clobbered Moran with a wine jug and sneaked outside. She had help from a friend getting away. Squire Teague let her out the back gate, then chopped the lift rope to impede our chase. We have him in the dungeon. I am sure the prince has plans for him when he gets back to the castle; Moran has been searching for Alysa all night. As far as I know, she has not been found. Damn clever wench, if you ask me."

"Any idea which way she headed?" Gavin asked. He prayed his tone revealed a nonchalance he did not feel.

"I told you she is a clever girl; we found her tracks everywhere. I think she set up false trails to fool us. She could be anywhere by now. Find her, Gavin, or Isobail will flog us both."

Gavin chuckled slyly. "I promise you I will have her within my grasp before she can convince anyone of her tales. When I have her back, I will hang a red cloth on that last tree in the meadow before reaching the castle. Check it every morning and night for my signal. After you see it, meet me near the edge of the forest at the next dawn or dusk to retrieve her. She will be safe, if she behaves."

"Make sure she is not harmed, if you grasp my meaning."

Gavin scowled effectively. "If I wanted the little enchantress, as you called her, I would have taken her the last time I had her. Who could notice a silly young girl with a stepmother like Isobail around? The princess is what I call a real woman, a matchless beauty. When she moves or talks or smiles or speaks, I get all hot. Why not make my reward a night with her?" he suggested, hoping his feigned interest in Isobail would enflame Trahern.

Trahern's face glowed with anger as he eyed the virile outlaw who stood before him. "Keep away from Isobail, Hawk."

Gavin lifted his brows in faked enlightenment and grinned. "You lucky devil, Trahern. She belongs to you! I should have guessed from the way you treat her. Surely you realize she is a woman of fiery blood and great passion, the kind of woman a man finds hard to keep and sate. She is mighty tempting. If I were you, Trahern, I would stick close and hold her tightly."

"I plan to do both, Hawk, and you remember it."

"You give the orders," Gavin remarked genially.

* * *

Alysa hugged Gavin tightly and cried softly in his comforting embrace. She had told him she was uninjured, just frightened. She lifted her tear-streaked face and murmured, "Dear Teague must be in such danger, my love. We must help him escape. I cannot imagine what they will do to him. The secret passage has an entry to the dungeon. I am sure they will imprison him there. We must free him, Gavin."

"Not today, m'love. They will be guarding him closely this soon. No doubt they are questioning him about you. We cannot risk capture. I promise to rescue him," he swore, and recalled Giselde's premonitions about him saving the man he had once viewed as his rival.

"I wonder if Thisbe is in peril, too, and her father Piaras," Alysa said. "They are in danger because of me, Gavin. I must help all of them."

"I saw Sir Piaras before I came here to look for your. He was heading to Lord Orin's to relate his son's trouble. I asked him to explain everything to Lord Orin and demand the man's loyalty and help."

"At least he is safe, but what of Teague and Thisbe?" she pressed.

"Come, I must take you to safety at Trosdan's cave. Then we will decide what to do about your friends. Giselde is there; she can advise and comfort you."

"I need no one tonight except you," she said.

Gavin briefly tightened his embrace and placed kisses on her forehead and hair. "The same is true of me, love. I have never been so scared as when I heard of your bold escape. I know it could be perilous to remain here for the night, but I believe we know the forest better than anyone." Lifting her chin and looking into her eyes, he said, "I promise you, Alysa, nothing will happen to you or your friends."

"As long as I have you, I will fear nothing and no one." She pulled his mouth down to hers and sealed their lips.

They kissed and caressed until Gavin used his saddle blanket to make them a bed upon the dewy ground. They undressed and fused their bodies eagerly and urgently, then Gavin held her securely in his arms while she slept as peacefully as possible.

In the large and torch-lit dungeon of Malvern Castle, Moran circled the suspended body of Teague, clad only in a loincloth, deciding which torment he would use first to extract the information he needed—the hiding place of Princess Alysa. Upon his return, he had questioned the Squire for over an hour, but Teague kept silent. Moran's fury mounted steadily to an eruptive level. He lifted a whip and seemingly fondled it before violently lashing Teague across his back, chest, and legs. The twenty-year-old redhead groaned and shook his head. He would not speak.

Moran laughed satanically. He read fear in Teague's blue eyes, fear which the captive could not hide completely. "I will arrest your father, charge your entire family of treachery against the Crown, destroy you all!" He shrieked the words with each lash of the whip and Teague screamed in pain, but revealed nothing.

Moran threw aside the whip and approached a round hearth which held glowing coals. He lifted a metal pole whose tip was fiery red. Wisps of smoke rose from its point as the Prince came to stand before the squire. "You are being brave and foolish for naught," Moran warned, touching the hot poker to Teague's vulnerable belly. Teague smelled the odor of his own burning flesh and moaned. Then, when he looked across the dungeon floor and saw Isobail approaching, smiling the same sadistic smile as her son, he knew he was lost.

It was nearing dawn when an exhausted and pain-riddled Teague could endure no more torture from Isobail and her son. He had been tormented for long hours, and in great agony, finally revealed the location of Giselde's hut. Even amidst his pain he did not call the old woman by name, he only called her "the old witch in the royal forest." He mumbled that Alysa had met the old woman while playing there as a child and liked to visit her, helplessly disclosing that Alysa might have gone there to hide from Moran.

Thinking they had won a victory, Moran and Isobail exchanged pleased smiles. They lowered Teague to a blanket on the stone floor in the dungeon and covered him with another one, but did not untie him.

As they left the guarded underground room, Isobail whispered to Moran, "I will awaken Trahern and send him to find this old witch. If Alysa is not with her, we will bring the old woman here and entice information from her lips. We will let Teague rest all day, then enjoy ourselves with him again tonight. I am sure he knows more than he has revealed."

After an intensive search, Trahern located the hut, but could not find Alysa or the woman who lived there. He searched the cluttered abode and the area around it, then burned the dwelling to the ground. He reported to Isobail, who was not pleased with his failure to find either woman. She demanded he look for Alysa until she was found.

That day held another annoyance for the weary Isobail, who had not gone to bed until Trahern's return from the forest: Kyra arrived and related her grim news of Sir Calum's death. "Some force is working against me, but I shall defeat it!" Isobail raved in fatigue and vexation. After pondering this new situation, she announced, "I will place Sir Phelan in charge there."

Kyra argued boldly, "Nay, Mother, it is my castle and land. You promised it to me for slaying Baltair. I came to tell you of this matter in person, for I did not know whom to trust with a message. I will work with you and control that area for you. It is mine by right."

"Do not be greedy, sister," Moran said, having been aroused from his light slumber by Kyra's noisy arrival. "Mother knows what is best. Why not marry Phelan, then you can still have Daron's holdings?"

"That groping pig? Never, little brother! Leave the room, as this matter is between Mother and me," the girl ordered coldly, furious because Isobail had allowed him to join their private conversation. It gradually became obvious that Moran was now in her mother's confidence, that the two were working hand in hand and trying to exclude her.

Isobail turned to Moran and revealed the details of her plot to usurp Damnonia and then conquer Logris. Kyra was not surprised, but at first Moran looked shocked. Then greed and pleasure flooded his features. "I am proud of you, Mother. I will be loyal to you in all matters. Command me and I will obey."

"Kyra, do you feel the same?" Isobail challenged her daughter.

Kyra had a powerful urge to physically attack her mother, but quelled it. "I will help you any way I can, Mother, but that area is mine. Moran has Kelton's holdings. Why can I not have Daron's?"

In an unpleasantly condescending manner, Isobail replied, "You are a young woman, so men will not obey you. Surely you realize that a princess by marriage only has no real power? Besides, there has not been enough time since your marriage to win the people's confidence. I require a strong and loyal knight on the Logris border. You can marry Phelan or remain here."

"Nay!" Kyra replied with visible hostility. "I wish to marry Earnon and share Daron Castle with him. We can hold that area for you. No one would dare disobey your close advisor."

"Earnon? You and Earnon?" Isobail said skeptically, insultingly.

Moran quickly interjected, "They have been lovers for a long time, Mother. Kyra coerced me into silence about them. After I was knighted and left the castle, I decided to sever her grip on me by telling you everything when I returned home. But with Kyra gone and with things so hectic here, I truly forgot about it."

Kyra called Moran vulgar names until Isobail silenced her with a demand to know how her son was being compelled into secrecy. Kyra glared at both of them and insisted on telling her side of this matter.

"Later!" Isobail warned sharply. "Moran, explain this deceit."

Moran claimed he had discovered the affair by accident, then confronted Kyra with it. His sister had constrained him to silence by threatening to expose his sensual nature and behavior to Alysa. "I could not allow Kyra to destroy my progress with Alysa, so I agreed. But I only planned to keep silent until Alysa was mine and it would not matter what Kyra told her. Then, after I left for Ahern Castle, I realized you could keep Kyra silent for me because you also wanted this marriage between me and Alric's daughter."

Not wishing to make a deadly enemy of his sister, Moran cleverly said, "Kyra and I have never gotten along well, but she is my sister and I do love her. I think she truly loves Earnon and should marry him one day. Until that time; perhaps she could keep him as her lover. But first she needs to help you win your greatest victory, by marrying Phelan or anyone necessary. I will do the same, Mother, anything you command of me.

402

As heir to all you obtain, I will work hard to make your kingdom large and powerful."

Kyra wondered why Moran was now trying to help her. There had to be a motive. For now, she decided, she would accept his assistance.

Isobail's face had gone scarlet with rage as she comprehended how Kyra and Earnon had duped her. "Baltair never touched you, liar; you only said that he had in order to conceal your treachery, and Earnon's!" The moment Isobail made that accusation, she realized that Earnon had probably told Kyra everything. "You and Earnon worked together and deceived me! I shall never forgive either of you. You killed Calum, did you not?" she accused.

"Ask anyone there; he choked to death," Kyra shouted back.

"With your help, you little witch—yours and Earnon's! Damn you, Kyra, I needed Calum there and Phelan at Lord Fergus's! Your greed could spoil everything. You shall be punished, girl."

Earnon was summoned, and Isobail glared at him and charged, "You betrayed me with Kyra, you fool! I no longer need you. Leave my castle this day or I shall carve out your heart."

Earnon glanced at Kyra just before the girl shouted wildly, "Place a curse on her, my love! Destroy her this minute! She has used and betrayed us. Slay her and I will take her place."

Isobail walked to within inches of Earnon and challenged him, saying, "Yes, my powerful sorcerer, place a curse on me. Go before I slay you with these eager hands."

"You will be sorry to lose me," Earnon said, his voice low and even. "The day will come when you will beg me to return and help you, as forces are mounting against you this very moment. Give me Kyra and

403

Daron's Castle and I will forget your insults and remain loyal to you."

Isobail's eyes narrowed and chilled. "You are a fool, Earnon. You sacrificed all I could give you for that," she sneered, pointing to Kyra. "I could forgive you for most things, but not for teaching her how to slay Sir Calum or for being more loyal to her than to me. You know I needed Calum there for the next few months. If you wanted Kyra so badly, you should have told me. I would have given her to you until Calum claimed her, then I could have arranged secret meetings for you two. Take her with you, for I have no further use for her. I shall announce your banishments today, so never come here again." Isobail glanced at the sulking girl and laughed.

Trosdan had tossed his sacred runes upon a rock and read them. Their message was clear and inspiring. He sat upright and stared into nothingness as a vision filled his mind. He smiled and gathered several items, knowing what was required to slay a weakened sorcerer. . . .

When Gavin found Giselde's hut burned, he realized Teague must have been tortured to the point of revealing Giselde's location to Isobail. He realized he had no choice but to ask Alysa how much Thisbe and Teague knew about recent events, to decide what Isobail might have learned or could learn from the vulnerable squire. Somehow, he had to free Teague and Thisbe before they were of no use to Isobail.

When Gavin returned to the cave, Giselde smiled sadly and remarked, "I know, Gavin, the hut was burned. When I slept, I also saw fires in the castle dungeon, and much suffering. I will tell your how to save Teague and Thisbe, but it is already too late to prevent

404

them from telling all they know to Isobail and Moran. You will be unmasked today as Alysa's lover and Isobail will declare you an outlaw, a wolfshead. She will pursue you and Alysa with a vengeance, as I warned you. But she does not know your true identity and mission here in this land. Soon she will brand Alysa a traitor. . . ."

Gavin gazed at Alysa's grandmother and lightly touched her cheek; he knew that she had also prophesied the deaths of Prince Alric and herself. "You must speak with Alysa before fate strikes, Giselde. The truth should come from your lips, not mine or King Bardwyn's, after . . ."

Giselde smiled and hugged Gavin affectionately. She knew he was suffering from his burden of knowledge and responsibility "I will tell her everything, Gavin, but not until the night before our final battle. There are reasons why destiny must work this way, in its own time."

Gavin left the old woman's side to inform his men of the plans. He must order everyone to remain hidden until Bardwyn's arrival—surely within a week or less, he decided optimistically.

At midnight in the Malvern Castle dungeon Giselde's premonition was taking place. Thisbe was dragged from her bed and taken to the shadowy chamber so that Isobail and Moran could coerce the truth from the lovers. Desperate to protect his love from shame and the tormenting savagery he had recently suffered, Teague spoke up when he saw Thisbe shivering and weeping in the dungeon's gloom.

"Cut us free, and do not harm Thisbe. Then, I will answer all your questions," Teague insisted, dreading to trust them, but desperate to save Thisbe.

Knowing the dungeon door was locked and guarded, and Teague was too weak to battle them successfully,

Isobail calmly complied. "Now, tell me where Alysa would go and who is likely to help her."

Praying this information could not harm Alysa, Teague haltingly related the facts about Alysa, Giselde, and Gavin to them. When Teague and Thisbe had responded to every query from Isobail and Moran, Teague said, "Release us, for there is nothing more to tell."

Isobail shrieked angrily, "You only weakened because you believe Gavin Hawk can save her from us! You were silent until now to give them time to escape! Unless—" She halted to ponder the infuriating situation. "Unless Princess Alysa Malvern thinks she can arouse the people against me. Yes, they are probably still nearby, working to thwart me. I shall have them captured, flayed, and slain. I will torture and kill Gavin Hawk myself!"

At her behavior and her naming the warrior, Moran asked astutely, "You know this adventurer?"

"Yea, my son, I thought he was my brigand leader. This explains why so many bandits have been killed lately. Obviously Gavin and his loyal band are trapping and slaying them. So, he would rather have Alysa than . . . work for me." Recalling Alysa's abduction, Isobail guessed what had taken place between Alysa and Gavin Hawk. It heightened her fury and madness to suspect that Alysa had possessed him. She concluded that Gavin was trying to win Alysa, defeat Isobail, then get everything by marrying a grateful princess. She remembered how Gavin had deceitfully enticed her the other night, made a fool of her. "How dare he trick me! He must be killed. Perhaps I can set a trap for him, since he does not know he is unmasked."

"What about these two?" Moran asked, assuming they would not be freed. "Shall I slay them?"

Isobail eyed the two lovers who were clinging together and watching her pitifully. "Come, we have much work to do. We will deal with them shortly. Prepare to die, fools."

Twenty-two

Unable to sleep after hearing Thisbe speak of "Alysa's old teacher" as the "witch in the woods," Isobail had paced her chamber until mid-morning. It had come back to her that in a moment of weakness long ago, Alric had confessed the identity of Alysa's guardian and servant: Catriona's mother. To learn the Viking half-caste was still close at hand and in contact with Alysa alarmed Isobail. She speculated that somehow Alysa had found the old woman living in the woods, but doubted that Alysa had guessed the truth about their relationship, for it was a closely guarded secret.

A few hours after she finally fell asleep, Isobail was awakened by Trahern with grim news. She followed him into the inner yard and gaped at the two bodies on a cart. A brass rod had been driven into Earnon's heart and his hands had been set aflame, then doused quickly: the ritual for slaying a sorcerer. Isobail eyed her deceased child with intrigue, and fear. Never had Kyra looked more like her than she did at this moment. It was like looking at her own lifeless body!

"I found them in the forest, near the hut we burned," Trahern said. "I was checking it again to see if the old witch and Alysa had returned to it. They have not been dead long. I cannot say how Kyra was killed. I have never seen wounds like these before. She was beautiful, Isobail. Why did you hate her so much?" he asked abruptly, glancing at the quiet woman.

One of Trahern's words had seized her attention: witch. She tossed the cover over the bodies and said, "Bury them immediately. And find Alysa and Gavin for me! Have him declared an outlaw, and her a traitor. Spread the word Alysa has been poisoning her father to steal the Crown. Tell everyone she and her wolfshead killed my advisor and daughter. Offer a large reward for them. But make certain Gavin Hawk is not killed. Bring him to me alive. I plan to torment him until he begs for death."

"You still want the old woman?" Trahern asked, worried over the wildness that glazed Isobail's eyes.

"Yes, bring her to me," she ordered coldly. At last she knew who was working against her. Perhaps Giselde had bewitched Gavin into working for her and into yielding to Alysa. Perhaps that handsome rogue was not to blame for his actions of late. If only Earnon were still alive . . .

Isobail stormed around her chamber as Earnon's last words filled her ears. She should not have sent him away, to be slain by that powerful woman. She had to calm down and think clearly, or all was lost. She rushed to the stable and caught Trahern before he left.

"Offer a reward for the old witch too. Say it is she who is helping that traitor and wolfshead. Find her and bring her to me, Trahern. Only her blood can prevent our defeat."

"The peasants fear her, Isobail. No one will capture her."

"Tell them a reward will be paid for revealing her hiding place, then we will seize her. I am not afraid of Giselde."

"Giselde? Is that not the name of Catriona's old servant?"

"One and the same," Isobail said with a sneer. "She knows about herbs and potions, but she lacks the power to harm us."

"Do you think everyone will believe our charges against Alysa?"

"There is no way anyone can prove them false, and I doubt anyone would dare challenge us after we slay the brigand leader."

Alysa was glad she had worn boots into the secret passage to protect her feet from the thick mire. She was wearing pants, and the torch she carried prevented rats from running up her legs, since this section and the one adjoining it were food storage areas and animal shelters and were likely to be infested with the rodents. There seemed to be more air shafts and light in this section, which pleased Alysa, for it made it an unlikely home for bats. As Gavin walked before her and Weylin behind, they sent the furry creatures to squealing and scampering. With company the passage was not frightening, but their mission was. Finally they reached the hidden panel to the dungeon.

Torches were placed in holders and swords were drawn. The concealed ingress groaned and squeaked when Gavin shoved against it. Unused since its construction, the panel resisted opening. Weylin lent his shoulder to the task, and it slowly yielded. The tension mounted.

The three rescuers stayed in the passage for a time, waiting to see if soldiers charged them. When all remained quiet, Gavin peeked into the dim chamber. He saw two people lying on the floor: the redheaded Squire Teague, and a brown-haired girl. He suspected the two imprisoned lovers could be drugged or dead, since the captives had not reacted to their noisy arrival; or perhaps this was a trap. Just above a whisper, Gavin insisted that he enter alone to check over the situation. Alysa seized and held his arm as she shook her head.

Gavin embraced her before easing her into the other knight's firm grasp. "Weylin, be ready to close the panel and flee if trouble strikes. I will fend them off until you two have time to escape. Protect her for me."

Alysa protested, "Nay, my love, do not enter alone." She tried to get free, but could not. "If this is a trap, we will not close the panel and leave you," she informed him sternly. "We have swords and can use them. Let us come with you as guards."

Gavin smiled encouragingly at her and caressed her cheek. "Have you forgotten you promised to obey my every command?"

Alysa recalled her vow of obedience to prevent endangering any of them. She nodded, and ceased her struggles. "Please be careful. I love you," she murmured.

"As I love you, Alysa," he replied tenderly.

Gingerly he stepped into the dungeon and looked to both sides. All was still, except for the flaming torch near the steps. He walked slowly toward the prone bodies, alert to every sound. His keen eyes darted here and there, watching for any sign of danger from the numerous shadows. He knelt beside the captives and called their names as he shook each one.

As if his voice and touch broke a spell over them, Teague and Thisbe awakened and looked at the man leaning over them. They sat up and looked around in confusion.

"We must escape quickly before a guard comes to check on you," Gavin said urgently. He helped them to their feet and led them to the passageway. As Alysa, Teague, and Thisbe exchanged hugs and words, Gavin cleared away the evidence of his entry and departure. He and Weylin closed the panel securely.

Since this section of the passageway was drier and

airier, Gavin said they would remain until dusk before trying to slip away in the river. Following Giselde's plan, the rescue had gone perfectly. Sitting on blankets they had taken from Alysa's chamber, the five exchanged information while the hungry Thisbe and Teague devoured the fruit and cheese Gavin provided. To relax and to quench their thirst, all shared the wine in Gavin's leather skin.

When Teague had recovered somewhat, he implored, "You must help me get a warning to my father."

Gavin assuaged his fears saying, "Sir Piaras has taken a warning to your father."

"After you risked your life to rescue us, Princess Alysa, how can you forgive us for betraying you?" Thisbe asked, then wept.

Alysa comforted her, and entreated, "Do not cry, dear Thisbe. I would have done the same to save Gavin."

They continued to talk in the near darkness, providing information and comfort to each other. Gavin mused over the accuracy of Giselde's premonitions again and, without thinking, asked Alysa, "Do you have the same powers as it was said your mother had, and Giselde?" He was relieved he had not slipped and called the old woman her grandmother.

Alysa pondered his question and shrugged. "I do not think so. If it comes from Viking blood, it must be weak in me. Nay, that cannot be, for Granmannie is Albanian. Though once I did think my mother came to me, and told me my father would join her soon. But as far as I know, I have no magical powers or dreams of foreboding."

"Aye, but you do have magical powers," Gavin teased to lighten everyone's mood. "You bewitched me, did you not?"

"Nay Prince Crisdean, you enchanted me," she retorted.

Thisbe snuggled against Teague, Alysa cuddled with

411

Gavin, and Weylin decided it was time to find himself a special woman.

When Isobail and Moran approached the entrance to the dungeon, the guard was asleep and the door was open. The man was aroused, and the chamber found empty. Swiftly the alarm was sounded, but the prisoners could not be found within the battlement. Isobail ordered soldiers to search for them at first light, as dusk had fallen.

Returning to the dungeon, she shouted at the confused guard, "Fool! You let them escape from under your nose while you slept!" She seized a poleax from the wall and madly attacked the man while several of the soldiers who had accompanied her looked on in horror at her fury.

Trosdan's cave was a merry place when Gavin and his party returned, wet but safe. They sat near a roaring fire to warm themselves as they shared their tales with the others. Upon hearing the news of fire and pillaging around the land, Gavin glanced at Giselde. All but two of the eight prophecies had come true. He absently rubbed his tanned chest and wondered how such powers could exist, and how he could defeat them to save Alysa's father and grandmother.

If only he had the skills and wits to fight magic, then . . . When he realized his line of thought, he again recalled Giselde saying, "You will question your instincts, prowess, wits, and skills," and, "As each one takes place, you will come to trust me more and more."

When the others were asleep, the Cumbrian prince approached Trosdan and said, "I need your help, wise man."

Without speaking, Trosdan shook the bag of runes

412

and tossed them on the ground. "I can tell you how to prevent one death, but not both," he informed Gavin, who wondered how the white-haired man with gentle blue eyes read the question in his troubled mind.

Trosdan smiled and replied, "Because the runes tell me all things."

"But I did not ask my questions aloud," Gavin stated in wonder.

"There is no need for words when my runes can reveal a heart and mind to me. This is what will take place before and after Bardwyn arrives in five days, and how to save one near to her by blood," the Druid master began, then revealed terrible and wonderful things.

On Saturday Isobail's men were searching everywhere for the lovers and rebels, but could find no trace of them. The evil princess became wild and furious at her defeats, which worried her son.

Trahern located the remaining brigands and hired a new leader from among them, the crude bandit who had led the first attack on Alysa on the road. The bandits knew by now that Gavin and his men had duped them and tried to destroy them. By nightfall, soldiers and bandits alike were seeking Isobail's foes.

Gavin, Alysa, and their friends remained in the large cave, hoping their enemies would believe they had left the area after rescuing Teague and Thisbe. Amongst Gavin's men guards were posted and rotated, but time passed slowly for everyone.

When this new trouble began, Isobail had tried to break Earnon's hypnotic spell over Leitis so she could arouse Alric to question him. She quickly learned that

Earnon's second enchantment carried a different breaking word. Finally she decided that it was best to keep Alric under heavy medication, and to increase his dosage in order to kill him. Isobail knew what Earnon had been giving Alric, but she did not know by how much to increase it to bring about the prince's natural-looking demise within a week. On Sunday she began to pour an extra daily potion down his throat.

Orin was delivered to Isobail on Monday, and she sent out the word that the feudal lord would be executed if his traitorous son did not surrender. Dressed as a peasant, Lann, one of Gavin's six men, had visited the local village pub to pick up information. Upon his report, all knew that Isobail was plotting, to torture the truth about them from Teague, who paced the cave and worried.

Gavin said, "I will let you decide what to do."

Teague glanced at Thisbe before replying, "Isobail cannot be trusted to keep her word. Even if I surrendered, my father would be slain. I know I could endure my own torture and hold silent, but I could not endure his agony and hold my tongue," he stated sadly but honestly.

Gavin slapped him on the back proudly and fondly. "To give you time to learn about her threat, she set Saturday to execute Orin. I am certain King Bardwyn will arrive no later than Wednesday and we will attack at dawn on Friday. Before the siege, we will sneak into the secret passage and rescue your father and Prince Alric, then open the gates for the King's men."

Indeed, Keegan returned from his journey on Tuesday to say the King of Cambria and his large band would arrive by morning. Keegan had ridden ahead to report that the King and his troops were covering these last miles carefully to avoid alerting Isobail and her forces to their approach.

Alysa and Gavin snuggled together near a small fire to the back of the cave. Each was aware that the next three days would bring about a resolution to Damnonia's miseries, if all went favorably. But each could not help but wonder what to do if Isobail got wind of their plans or if she learned of the secret passage from Alric.

Alysa trembled at the unknown, and Gavin cuddled her closer to him for comfort. He stroked her arm and back soothingly, and his mouth brushed against her hair. Alysa's lips pressed kisses to his bare chest and her fingers lightly grazed his powerful shoulders. Surprisingly there was no draft or chilly dampness in the enormous cave.

Alysa and Gavin were warm and safe and together, tonight and beyond. Their small fire gave off just enough light and heat to encase them in a romantic setting, despite their companions presence not far away. It seemed that everyone was asleep except the guard outside. The few noises that reached their ears were muffled. They were nestled together and very much in love, but no raging hunger to unite their bodies tormented them. Instead, this was a time for sharing emotions, strengths, encouragement, and solace. It was a tender moment when only soft kisses and caresses could be shared, when a gentle passion had to control them.

Alysa shifted her head to look into Gavin's face. Their eyes melted together as warm honey and fused for a long time. Neither spoke for a while, then they did nothing more than murmur exchanges of love. His lips drifted over her face until they lightly touched her lips. Each nibbled and played without kissing the other. Then his mouth locked with hers and they enjoyed a lengthy kiss which caused them to flame and tremble. They parted and looked at each other, smiled knowingly in caution, and cuddled to sleep. A special tranquility washed over them and bound them snugly.

Alysa paced anxiously while Gavin and Weylin were gone to meet King Bardwyn. The Cambrian forces were to be divided into several large bands and shown where to camp while plans were made for the assault on Malvern Castle tomorrow if Princess Isobail refused to surrender. To help conceal their identities, the knights and warriors had been told to wear simple garments and to hide their shields and the King's markings.

Alysa knew Gavin would probably be gone for hours, and she worried about him being recognized and captured. She was also apprehensive about meeting her grandfather for the first time, and wondered how she felt about him for ignoring her existence for almost nineteen years.

Giselde approached her and said mysteriously, "Come, my little Alysa, for there are things I must tell you before they arrive."

The woman looked very old and tired today, and Alysa asked if she were ill. Giselde smiled sadly and replied, "Nay, child, it is the burden of what I must tell you that weighs heavily and painfully upon me."

Giselde led her to the back of the cave, where Trosdan lived, studied, and worked. She told Alysa to sit on a pile of feather-stuffed pillows, then she dragged a wooden chair over and sat, gazing down into Alysa's upturned and quizzical face.

"I beg you, Alysa, do not interrupt until I finish," Giselde pleaded, "for this story is hard to reveal. No matter what I tell you, hold your questions for later. You must hear everything before this tormenting tale is clear. It is not a good or pretty truth, little one, but it is long overdue. Please understand and forgive me for holding silent all these years, and forgive your parents for their mistakes and silence."

As Giselde appeared ready to weep, Alysa asked in panic, "What is it, Granmannie? Your clues are frightening and confusing."

"Promise me you will let me finish before speaking again."

Alysa stared at the woman and knew something awful was about to be told to her. She saw how it was torturing Giselde, and noticed how the old woman was pressing her gnarled fingers to her heart, as if it ached terribly. "I will listen and be quiet," Alysa complied worriedly.

Giselde began by repeating Alysa's ancestral history to her, up to the point where Catriona miscarried and returned to Albany. "I was not Catriona's serving woman, and that is not why I came to Damnonia with her. I am Giselde, child of Connal and Astrid, wife to Rurik, mother to Catriona. Your grandmother, my little Alysa." When Alysa gaped at the woman and started to query that shocking claim, Giselde protested, "Nay, not yet, my child. First I must tell you why this was kept from you."

Giselde related the Viking attack from which Prince Briac Crisdean of Cumbria rescued her and Catriona. The woman revealed how Briac had once loved Catriona but could not marry her. Giselde told of their long stay with Briac and his father, King Crisdean. She told of how she met secretly with King Bardwyn to discuss Alric and Catriona, and explained to Alysa how and why King Bardwyn had trusted her in this matter of Isobail's treachery. Giselde paused a while to rest and wet her mouth, and was pleased that Alysa remained still and silent.

Giselde continued her tale to Catriona's death and her flight into hiding. "This is the worst part," Giselde hinted before sharing the news of Catriona's murder by Isobail.

"She killed my mother?" Alysa whispered with horror.

"Yes, my little Alysa, but there is more. I know this is the worst pain you have known in your life, but hear all of it before we talk," Giselde urged. When Alysa mastered her anguish and anger, the woman exposed the darkest moment of Alric's life: the episode at Lord Caedmon's that made Moran her half brother.

"Nay, nay!" Alysa refuted in alarm. "It cannot be! You are wrong, Granmannie! Why do you speak such lies about Father?"

"If I could spare you this pain, I would die before revealing such things. But I believe it possible that Isobail might extract this information from your father in his weakened state, and expose this truth at the right moment in order to use Moran to seize the Crown. It would be more cruel for you to find out that way than by my telling you about it now."

Giselde slowly continued with her revelations, leaving out very little. "Because of who I am and what I know—because my very presence, if known, would have endangered you—I had to leave the castle long ago and hide in the forest. It is also why I held silent until now. When I told Gavin everything, he—"

"Gavin knows all of this, and he kept silent too?" Alysa asked.

"I told him pieces here and there, but I had to expose Moran to him so he could halt you from marrying your half brother. Gavin begged me to tell you everything, and I said the right moment was today. He did not wish to wait, as he felt he was deceiving you. Yet he believed such words should come from me, not him, for he did not know the all of it. When he met with Alric, your father confessed the truth of Moran's birth, and Alric

418

begged Gavin to keep his dark secret from you and everyone. Gavin is a man of honor and obeyed."

Alysa asked more questions, until she was certain she had heard it all. She jumped up and walked around the confines of the rock chamber, halting with her back to Giselde. She went over and over this tale in her mind, trying to understand it and to forgive those involved in such deeds and secrecy. As she had suspected, Giselde and Gavin had been partnered in many things. Yet it always came back to a love for her that ruled their actions. So much seemed to fit now. . . .

Alysa turned and looked at Giselde, who was watching her closely. Her grandmother . . . Alysa walked forward and knelt before her. She smiled into Giselde's face and pressed the gnarled hands to her cheeks and lips. "I love you, Granmannie, and I am glad you are my grandmother. You will return to the castle when this is over?"

Tears left the woman's faded blue eyes and rolled down her wrinkled cheeks. "How I have longed to tell you the truth about me so I could share your life. I so feared losing you as I lost Catriona. Soon Evil will know defeat and all will be good once more. Do you forgive me?"

"Yes, Grandmother, I understand everything and do not blame you. Even Father was misled, and he has paid terribly for his weaknesses."

"Gavin is here for you, my precious child. Love him with all your heart and cling to him forever; he is your destiny."

Alysa beamed with happiness. "I am glad your words are true, Granmannie." Alysa laughed and corrected, "Grandmother."

The two embraced and talked a while longer until excited voices reached them and told of Gavin's return and the arrival of Bardwyn.

Alysa looked at Giselde and asked, "What if he does not like me?"

Her grandmother smiled and teased, stroking her granddaughter's hair, "How can he not love you?"

Alysa and Giselde headed for the cave entrance and halted there while the men dismounted. Alysa studied the man of seventy who was eyeing her with sharp green eyes that belied his age. But his snowy hair did not. Alysa was amazed by King Bardwyn's sturdy body and agility, and she was awed by his air of dignity and power. It was obvious that Bardwyn commanded himself and others easily and wisely.

Alysa started to bend her knee to the King of Cambria and Damnonia as he reached her, but Bardwyn caught her hand and prevented it. She said nervously, "I am honored to meet you, my liege."

Bardwyn chuckled and teased, "Can you not call me Grandfather?"

A blushing Alysa glanced at the laughing Giselde before she looked into King Bardwyn's gentle eyes and said, "I am more than pleased to meet you at last, Grandfather, and I am so glad you have come to help us." Her joy increased when the elderly man embraced her fondly.

"Come, let us sit and talk before we must speak of wicked matters." He took Alysa's hand and led her inside the cave. "I was a foolish man to make an oath that kept us apart for years. I pray you will forgive my stubbornness."

"My grandmother explained all to me this morning," Alysa told him, glancing at Giselde and smiling with love.

Gavin joined them, having finished his task with the men and horses. He sat down beside Alysa and they exchanged telltale looks. His keen gaze probed hers to see how she was feeling after her talk with Giselde; he smiled when her eyes told him she was fine. Despite the presence of others, Gavin clasped her hand in his.

King Bardwyn chuckled and remarked, "I see you have carried out several missions here, Prince Gavin. Am I right in assuming you have captured my granddaughter's heart?"

"When this trouble is settled, I shall ask for her hand in marriage. I love her and must have her."

King Bardwyn looked at Alysa and asked, "Do you feel the same, Granddaughter? Do you wish me to bind your lives this very day?"

"Yes, Grandfather, I love him and want him."

"This is good," Bardwyn announced merrily. "I shall have my priest marry you tonight. If you two agree . . ."

Gavin and Alysa were astonished by Bardwyn's suggestion. It meant they could spend tonight together. Both said, "Yes," at the same time, then all laughed.

Bardwyn called in one of his guards and told him to alert the priest who traveled with them about a marriage between Prince Gavin Crisdean and Princess Alysa Malvern at dusk. Afterwards, Bardwyn commanded gently, "Tell me of the treachery that abounds in my son's land."

Between Gavin, Alysa, and Giselde, the startling facts came forth. The many deaths and secret meetings were discussed, as was Alysa's abduction. Gavin revealed all he had seen, heard, and done. Alysa did the same, distressing the King over his son's treatment and danger. None of them doubted that Isobail was controlling Alric's illness. Afterwards, plans for the battle were made.

"The two men who were to bring messages to me finally arrived, two days before Sir Keegan reached me. I was already preparing to ride for Damnonia. They had been robbed and beaten by common bandits. One had a broken leg and could not be left alone, so they traveled slowly but steadily, finally reaching me with their grim news."

"We wondered what had happened to them, sire," Gavin said.

When Trosdan approached, Bardwyn looked at the elderly man with the snowy beard and reverent air. He knew who the man was from his garments and possessions—a flowing white robe, a large golden neck collar indicating high rank, sandals, a wand of yew with tiny bells, and a circlet of sacred oak leaves. Clearly the man with lucid blue eyes was a Druid high priest, a member of a religious sect that had been outlawed long ago. Bardwyn recalled how Druids were known as teachers, guardians of the law and history, healers, magicians, astrologers, and figures of power and mystery.

Gavin related Trosdan's skills, and King Bardwyn did not appear skeptical or scornful. Gavin went on to relate Giselde's talents to Bardwyn, whose smile indicated the King already knew about them. "I was doubtful at first, but she proved herself to me," Gavin said, telling how Giselde had removed his tattoo as proof.

It was past dusk by the time they concluded the lengthy meeting. The priest was waiting outside to marry Gavin and Alysa. Bardwyn said, "This is only a brief ceremony to bind you two. Later we will have a big wedding with many guests and hours of feasting. I must confess why I want you two wed tonight: once the battle is over, I shall declare Alysa as Damnonia's ruler. It will be easier for the lords and peasants and soldiers to accept her quickly if there is a strong man, a royal prince, at her side. Can you remain here with her, Gavin?"

Gavin and Alysa understood his motive and accepted it. Within moments they were man and wife, and they spent the night in a crowded cave. Alysa gazed at the ring on her finger which revealed her as the daughter of Rurik and Giselde, as the last Viking Queen. She reflected on the two women who had worn it before her and prayed she was worthy of it.

Before dawn broke, Gavin and Alysa and four of Gavin's men were to ride to the castle and slip into the secret passage. They were to stay there during the day; then they were to rescue Orin and Alric, hide them in the passage, wait for King Bardwyn's forces to get into position during the night, and open the gates for a surprise attack at dawn the next day.

Alysa whispered provocatively to Gavin, "If we sneak into my chamber in the castle and lock the door, we could spend all day there alone. Surely there is no reason for anyone to come there tomorrow."

Gavin hugged her and grinned. "What a clever woman you are, m'love. This will help me endure the next hours without being able to touch my wife. To distract myself, I shall help pass along the plans to the other camps. Rest, for we have a busy night, and day, ahead." Before Gavin left camp, he took three men and scaled the cliff above the cave. As instructed by Trosdan, they removed several rocks, which would have fallen and created a landslide that would have slain Giselde, thwarting her premonition of her own death.

It was an hour before the sun arose when Alysa and Gavin sneaked into her chamber at Malvern Castle to fetch the extra covers for his chilled friends, after Gavin had checked out the room for safety and locked the door. After a talk with Gavin earlier, Weylin suggested they split into two groups so everyone could get out of their wet clothes and warm up for a while. Although the men were not fooled by this ploy, Weylin led Dal, Tragan, and Lann to the better section near the dungeon to make camp for the day and night. They stripped off soaked garments and lay them aside, for they had brought along their battle garments which had been wrapped tightly in cured leather to keep them dry along with some food.

In case they had to leave this chamber quickly, Alysa and Gavin hurriedly washed away their dirty trail to and from the secret panel. She spied the tub of unused water which had been prepared for her last week and had not been removed since her escape—unused because of Moran's intrusion and attack and her hasty flight. Without delay, they stripped and bathed. Alysa encircled her wet head with a cloth to thwart a chill. After cleaning away their grime, they hurried to the inviting bed and nestled beneath the covers warming their quivering flesh. Gavin whispered in her ear, "I wish I could build a fire to dry your hair m'love, but it would be rash."

"I know," she replied, squirming closer to his enticing frame.

Gavin's last words to the men filled her mind. He had entreated them to remember who they were, why they were here, and what their victory or defeat would mean to so many people. With love and pride, she sighed peacefully and looked into his eyes. "Surely this is all a dream. How else could I be wed to you, but lying here before such an awesome battle and thinking of nothing except how much I want you?"

Both were keenly aware they had not made love for a week, and their passions were blazing fiercely. They were married, and yet nothing seemed different between them, unless it was the intense joy that came from knowing such a fact existed.

They began to share kisses and caresses, leisurely ones. But soon their hunger for each other gnawed at them, causing their lips and hands to work feverishly and greedily. Later they could make love slowly and tantalizingly, but for now they had to feed their fierce cravings. They came together blissfully and labored until their minds spun with sheer rapture. Ecstasy seized them, soared with them, rewarded them, and placed them on a bed of serenity to rest.

Each time they came together it was better, richer,

more binding. Yes, both decided contentedly, they were perfectly matched.

They whispered for a time, talking about Giselde and Bardwyn, and her "father's son." They dozed for a while, and made love again. It was nearly dusk when Gavin suggested they dress and join the others, not wanting to take too many risks by remaining there. Besides, soon they would be unable to see in the darkness, and dared not light candles or torches which could be sighted from the battlement. Alysa agreed with him, amazed by how calmly and blissfully they had used her chamber to consummate their wedding vows.

Alysa took warm peasant garb from her chest and donned it for the chilly night ahead, then brushed her lengthy brown hair. Gavin strapped a battle apron of darkest leather over a dark linen loincloth. Alysa could not help but admire his shapely legs and hips, and sigh dreamily at the sleek muscles that rippled in his torso as he moved. In his pack he had knee-high sandals and leather armbands to wear during the battle. She eyed his bare chest and was glad Giselde had insisted on replacing the blue tattoo over his heart, which identified him as a royal prince from Cumbria. She could imagine Isobail's reaction upon seeing it tomorrow. His tawny hair had dried, curling this way and that to frame his handsome face. Dark stubble grew most appealingly on his strong jawline. In the closing shadows his eyes looked remarkably green, like priceless gems. Her pulse began to throb erratically, and burning desire flamed within her.

Alysa could not believe how urgently she wanted him after spending the day in bed with him! She told herself to change her line of thought. Gavin's weapons had been stored on the landing outside her chamber to be reclaimed before dawn. The plan was to rescue Orin and Alric, then leave Orin and Alysa to guard and tend the prince while Gavin's men split up and used the three egresses to approach and open the two battlement gates: the large west gate and the smaller south gate.

Once the room looked as it had before their arrival, Gavin unlocked her chamber door. Quickly Alysa and Gavin slipped into the passage landing and closed the panel securely. Gavin lit the torch and they made their way past Alric's landing to join the others.

The six talked in whispers and laughed softly as they awaited their duties. From their behavior Alysa could tell the men were close friends who had worked together many times, the kind of friends who would die for each other and shared empathy with each other. She had noticed this same tight friendship and rapport with Keegan and Bevan, who would be arriving with her grandfather at daybreak. Alysa liked Gavin's friends and told them so. The men smiled and thanked her, and vowed she was perfect for the prince. Gavin grinned and concurred.

The moment they had anticipated eventually arrived, and the six exchanged looks that said, Be careful. Alysa closed her eyes and said a quick prayer for their success and survival.

With weapons drawn, Gavin and Weylin entered the dimly lit dungeon while the others remained in the opening to stand guard, ready to fight and flee. The shadowy chamber was quiet and empty. Alysa motioned for Gavin to come to her, which he did.

She whispered, "There is a room on the far side which could be used as a keep." She pointed to it and to the key on a peg nearby. From daring childhood games, she knew this area well.

Gavin gingerly approached the door and placed his ear against the wood. He heard nothing. He unlocked the door and slowly opened it, to find not only Lord Orin captive there, but also Sir Piaras. He roused them, delighted to find no marks of beatings on the two men, who were amazed to see him. "Follow me to safety. King

Bardwyn has arrived and will attack Isobail at dawn. To avoid discovery, we had to wait until it was nearly time to attack before rescuing you.''

Once everyone was in the secret passage, Gavin sneaked up the steps to see if the dungeon door was locked and guarded. He was delighted to find it was neither, which would make it useful later. Alysa hugged him tightly after he returned. The hidden panel was closed, and the prisoners shared their tale of capture.

Gavin quickly related the rescues of their children and the imminent battle plans to both Teague's and Thisbe's fathers, then guided everyone toward Alric's landing. Again they carefully opened the secret panel, to find the prince alone and sleeping deeply. Without wasting precious time by trying to arouse Alric and explain, Gavin lifted the limp body and carried it to the landing, placing the frail ruler on covers lain there by Dal and Lann. Weylin and Tragan rapidly checked the floor, erased any telltale clues that might signal their presence, then closed the panel.

Alysa covered her father to prevent a chill in the damp passageway. Tears filled her eyes, for her father was so heavily drugged he was barely conscious. She met Gavin's comforting gaze and drew solace from it. The others looked on in sympathy, knowing the prince was nearing death.

Piaras said, "Let me go with you and help. Most knights and guards and men-at-arms do not know I was taken captive with Lord Orin. I can get past them easily and lead you to the gates."

"I must go, too, Prince Gavin," Orin added. "Isobail made a fool of me, and I must be allowed to regain my honor by helping to defeat her."

Before Gavin could insist that someone had to stay with Alysa, she shook her head and said, "Nay, my husband, I will be fine alone. No one knows of the secret

427

passage. We will be safe. If Father awakens, there are things we must say to each other before it is too late."

Gavin grasped her meaning and complied. A torch was left burning above Alysa and Alric as the others left in separate directions.

After a while no sound reached Alysa's ears. She removed dampness from her father's brow and lay his head in her lap. She could not halt the tears that flowed from her eyes. "Oh, Father," she sobbed in anguish, "have we come too late?"

Alric's eyes fluttered and opened, but they were red and puffy. He had trouble focusing on her. "Alysa?" he murmured weakly.

"Yes, Father, I am here. You are safe now. I have you in the secret passage, and King Bardwyn's forces are attacking Isobail this very moment. Soon she will torment you no more."

"There is . . . little time, A-lysa. I . . . must tell . . . you," he began, struggling to shape the words.

Alysa touched his lips gently and said, "Do not try to speak now, Father. Wait until you are better."

"Nay, my precious child, the truth . . . must be told quick-ly," he argued, mustering all of his strength.

"There is no need to exhaust yourself, Father. My grandmother, Giselde, has told me everything, as did Grandfather, King Bardwyn." She uttered the names to make certain he understood her.

"But they do not k-now my side. Hear . . . me, Alysa, please." With great difficulty and discomfort, Alric related the truth as he knew it. "Forgive me, my child," he pleaded.

"I understand everything and forgive you, Father. I love you. I know that Isobail is to blame for your condition now. Grandfather will defeat her today." Realizing that her father could lose consciousness any moment, Alysa quickly related her love for and marriage

428

to Prince Gavin Crisdean. She held up her left hand for him to view the wedding ring.

Alric's eyes brightened more than Alysa believed possible. He caught her hand and pressed the ring to his lips. "Catriona, where is my precious Catriona?" he asked groggily. "There you are, my love," he answered, gazing past Alysa. Alysa turned, but saw nothing behind her. She watched her father's head shift away from her as he smiled happily and said, "I knew you would return to me. You are more beautiful than ever. Yea, I will come with you."

Alric looked at Alysa and beseeched, "Do not grieve for me, my child. At last I shall have peace and strength again. Be happy with Gavin. I am coming, Catriona."

Isobail had given Alric too much poison too swiftly, and he died in his daughter's arms. A scream of anguish left Alysa's lips. She sobbed until she believed she heard her mother say, *Suffer not, little one, for we are together again and happy. Let us go peacefully as you seek your destiny at Gavin's side.*

Alysa knew her mother was right. It was time to let go. Her father had suffered greatly for such a long time, and she doubted he could have recovered fully. Their fates had been fulfilled.

Alysa covered Alric's body, prayed silently, then said in a whisper "I love you, Mother, Father. Be free and happy together. I have Gavin; I will be happy."

Gavin! He was out there battling foes to save her land and people. She had to go and help him.

Gavin stared at the place of the battlement where Isobail had been standing moments ago. He was bewildered by what he had witnessed. Isobail had been coming at him with a sword and with madness in her eyes, which were sealed to his royal tattoo. He had feared he was going to be forced to slay a woman. But suddenly she had fallen against the battlement wall and then over the side to her death, her hands moving as if two people were grasping them and battling her. . . .

Prince Moran raced to his mother's body, then looked up at Gavin with hatred. He glanced around for the nearest path to the battlement and Gavin, and ran toward it.

Weylin confronted and fought Isobail's crazed son. Gavin watched with relief as Weylin defeated and killed the man, glad he did not have to fight Alric's son and Alysa's half brother to the death.

Gavin rushed to the gatehouse tower and looked out over the outer and inner wards. He saw Trahern and Phelan lying dead with their swords beside them. He saw Ceit, Isobail's personal servant and friend, dead by her own hand with a dagger. The fighting had ceased, as all who had sided with Isobail during her mad grab for power were either dead or captured. Many who had been misled, or coerced, into following the wicked princess pleaded for mercy and forgiveness.

All knelt as King Bardwyn and his guards rode into the inner bailey and dismounted. The King studied the situation and issued his commands, quelling any lingering turmoil. Gavin saw Squire Teague and Thisbe embracing their fathers and each other. He quickly searched the area for his six men, and sighted all of them alive. Then he saw Alysa on the Great Tower steps, looking for him. He waved, and caught her attention. As if there was no one else present, she began to run toward the gatehouse. Gavin hurried down the spiral steps and into the yard, lifting her in his arms and embracing her.

"I love you, Gavin Hawk," she declared, hugging him tightly.

"It is over m'love," he whispered in her ear.

"Nay, prince of my heart, it is only beginning," she refuted.

Twenty-three

Two weeks had passed since the battle to defeat Isobail. The brigands had been captured and slain, or sent fleeing into Logris. Peace ruled Damnonia once more, as did Prince and Princess Crisdean.

King Bardwyn was to depart tomorrow, and he was taking Giselde with him. Giselde knew that Gavin had saved her life by preventing a fatal accident. Teague had been knighted by King Bardwyn, and he and Thisbe had wed two days ago. After Lord Orin's departure for his castle, Teague and Thisbe had left for Lord Daron's old castle to become the feudal residents there for Alysa and Gavin. Piaras was to remain at Malvern Castle in charge of the knights and guards. He and Leitis had wed, too, after Giselde had suspected that Leitis was inspelled and managed to free her from it. Finally Alysa understood why Giselde's herbs had seemingly had no effect on her father's illness. After discussing it with Gavin and her grandmother, all three of them decided not to tell Leitis about her innocent part in Prince Alric's poisoning.

Sheriff Trahern's holdings had been placed in Weylin's control, and Land's End had been assigned to Sir Keegan, who was eager for his wife to arrive from Cumbria. Once more Damnonia was serene.

Alysa was looking forward to the impending visit of King Briac Crisdean and Queen Brenna. Her grandfather and grandmother would be gone at first light, but she did not mind. She was looking forward to a few days of quiet with her husband. As if reading her mind, Gavin clasped her hand and led her to their private chamber.

Alysa removed the golden collar around his neck, then the purple cloak which was secured about his manly shoulders with a broach of intertwined gold and silver. She lifted the golden circlet from his tawny head and placed it on the table. Then loosened the fretted silk tunic and matching warrior's apron and tossed them aside. Within minutes his bare frame was exposed to her admiring gaze.

Alysa removed her garments and crown, then sensuously snuggled her naked body against her husband's. "I cannot wait until we are alone for days on end," she murmured, placing kisses on his chest and neck.

Gavin grasped her head between his hands and lifted it to fuse their gazes. "Nor can I, m'love. It is strange—the more I feast on you, the hungrier I become for more of you. I fear I shall never be sated."

Alysa laughed merrily and retorted, "I surely hope not. Wild is my love for you, Hawk of Cumbria, and it shall never be tamed. I would challenge all dangers to keep you at my side. Love me," she urged, leading him to their bed.

Lying atop her, the Prince of Cumbria and Damnonia murmured huskily, "You are mine forever; Giselde told me so, and this tells me so," Gavin said, pressing the special ring to his lips. Gavin's eyes engulfed his wife, knowing he was looking into the beautiful and passion-flushed face of the Last Viking Queen.